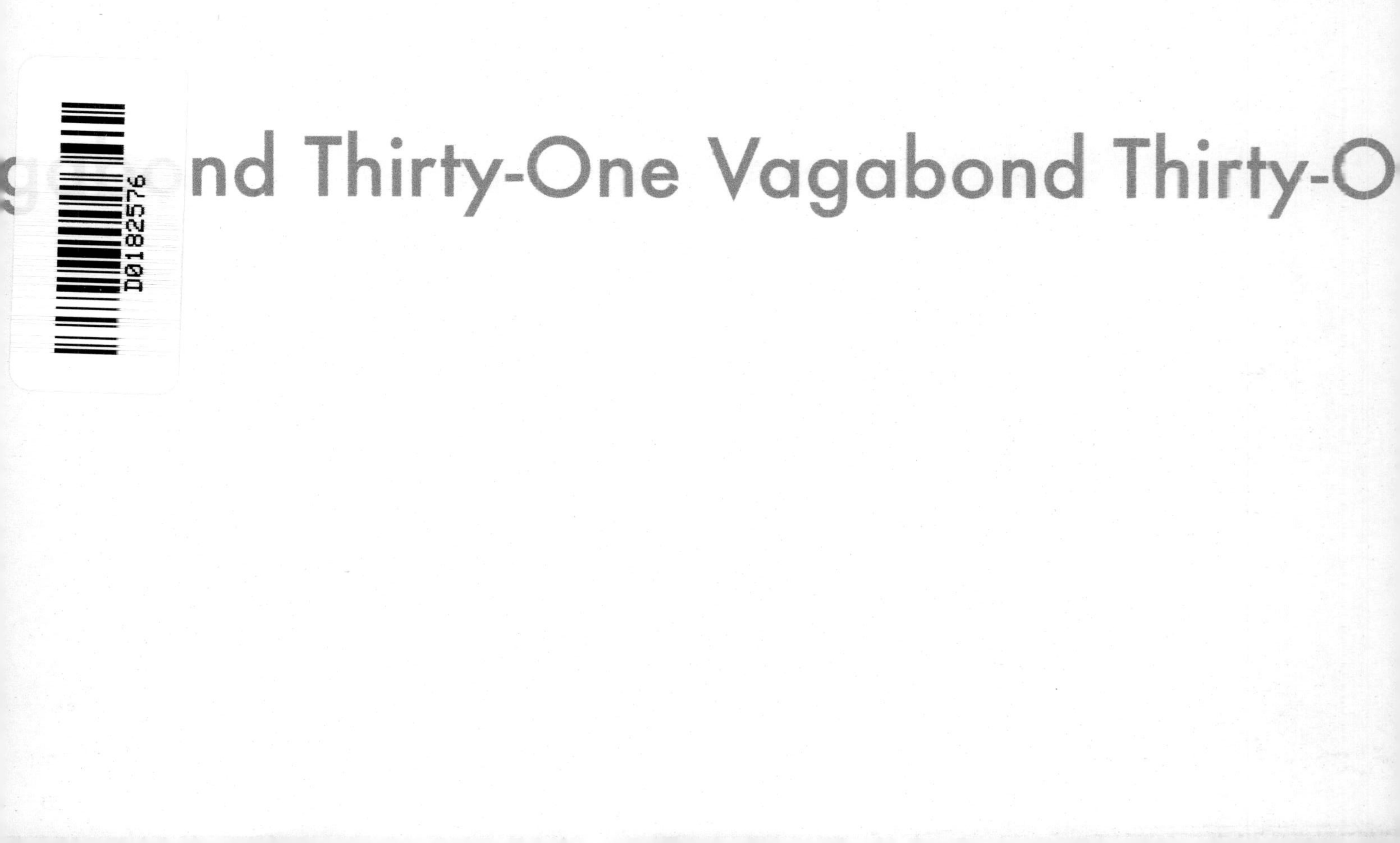
nd Thirty-One Vagabond Thirty-O

Blessed Assurance

by
Stewart Ennis

Vagabond Voices
Glasgow

First published in November 2019 by
Vagabond Voices Publishing Ltd.,
Glasgow,
Scotland.

ISBN 978-1-908251-92-3

Printed and bound in Poland

Cover design by Mark Mechan

Typeset by Park Reads, parkreads.co.uk

The publisher acknowledges subsidy towards this publication from Creative Scotland

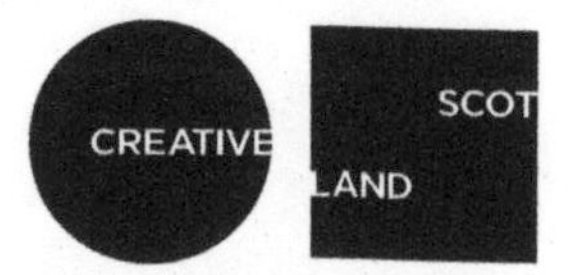

For further information on Vagabond Voices, see the website, www.vagabondvoices.co.uk

To my daughter Flora,
for the days and miles spent telling stories,
and to all my family, blood and otherwise

Contents

Blessed Assurance

"…of God himself can no man thinke…"

– Anon, *The Cloude of Unknowyng* (fourteenth century)

"The believer will fight another believer over a shade of difference; the doubter fights only with himself."

– Graham Greene, *Monsignor Quixote*

A MAP OF KILHAUGH
BY
JOSEPH KIRKLAND
The Hall
The Lele
The Seppie

CHAPTER ONE

Joseph Kirkland's First Dream: Episode One

This is my story, this is my song
praising my Saviour all the day long

Blessed Assurance was not the hymn Joseph would have chosen, but that's not how dreams work. This was one of the vivid dreams, so lacking in ambiguity it might have been lifted from the pages of his Children's Illustrated King James Bible. Take the sky for example, a deep dark pink *dream* sky with Bible-black clouds. Or those hailstones the size of marbles, rattling down the flutes of Kilhaugh Gospel Hall's corrugated iron roof like a military snare drum, dislodging a million flakes of old red rust – an eschatological snowfall from the Book of Revelations. Our boy, *The Dreamer Joseph Kirkland*, believed that this portentous weather had been laid on just for him, by *Him*, that this was all part of it, that everything was part of it. And it was. Even the eczema on his wrists and ankles, which was itching like fury now. He pushed up the sleeves of his big grown-ups' Baptismal gown and scratched – *mmm sooo good* – till his nails were choked with red-black scab. The clatter of those hailstones should have been deafening, but nothing on God's good earth could drown out Auntie Ishbel pumping her harmonium in full on Hallelujah, as everyone sang His praises. And how they sang His praises; as though their souls depended on it. And they did.

Blessed Assurance, Jesus is Mine!
Oh, what a Foretaste of Glory Divine!
Heir of Salvation, Purchase of God,
Born of His Spirit, Washed in His Blood.

Joseph Kirkland walked tentatively, slower than a funeral march. But then Joseph Kirkland did everything tentatively. He even dreamed tentatively. He sensed an unusually big gathering but it was hard to tell with these specs, one lens patched, the other steamed up.

"Joseph has been SAVED," shouted Mister Agnew from the platform.

"Joseph Kirkland has been SAVED!" shouted another, and they clapped their hands and cried "Hallelujah!" No, no, no. This wasn't right. Shouting? Clapping? Hallelujahs? No, no, no. This wasn't right at all. These folk experienced ecstasy, of course they did, when the Saviour filled their hearts with joy, but they would never express it so ... *flamboyantly*. "JOSEPH KIRKLAND has been SAVED!" they cried out in one voice.

Stone-cold fear crawled up Joseph's spine and he did what he always did when screaming didn't work and there was no high window to jump out of; he pressed his calf against the blistering radiator till he felt something akin to pain. It had the required effect. He woke up.

CHAPTER TWO

Intermission

He had not been Saved.

Sorry.

That all too familiar leaden pall of cold, clammy dread wrapped itself around him and he felt the usual combination of relief, guilt at feeling relief, and fear. He bit his lip, dug his nails into his forearm, did all those things he must do to make absolutely certain he was not still asleep, that the recurring nightmare he assumed had ended, had in fact ended; not just taken some unexpected and terrifying twist. Because honestly you never knew sometimes.

There was a street lamp on the lane outside his bedroom window. Every night it shone through the gap in the curtains, hitting the window frame at the perfect angle to cast a cross – long, black, skewed, but still a cross, still *The Cross* – onto the bedroom ceiling.

In the shadow of the cross let me hide.

It was the last thing he wanted right now, dark lines from hymns or Scripture.

Sorry.

Sorry, sorry, sorry. These days – since he'd reached *that age*, the age of *no more excuses* and *knowing the consequences* – he seemed to spend half his life saying *sorry* to God – or Jesus. *Sorry* for being bad. *Sorry* for thinking bad thoughts. *Sorry* for trying to avoid Him – or *Them* – by thinking other things, frivolous earthly things. *Sorry* for doing frivolous earthly things, like reading comics procured by Archie Truman or playing commandoes with Archie Truman. *Sorry* for taking an interest in Archie Truman's colourful accounts of the films he'd seen at the Regal Picture Palace in Templeton. *Sorry* for most things involving his hush-hush friendship with Archie Truman – one of the *Glasgow Overspill*, as Gran menacingly referred to the folk who'd moved into Kilhaugh's new housing scheme. *Sorry* for all those other things – too many to mention – that took him even further away from God or Jesus. Not that it was ever possible to avoid Him... Them? That was another thing. He should just ask Uncle Andrew or Mister Agnew – *Should I be praying to God or Jesus or both?* – get it sorted out once and for all. But he was eleven for goodness sake, going on twelve; this was something he should've asked long ago.

Joseph's bedroom was as sparsely furnished as the Hall and similarly free of anything that might be called décor. There was a heavy bedstead, a wooden chair, a chest of drawers and a small desktop bookcase, all the colour of dark marmalade. The street lamp that produced the *Shadow of the Cross* also illuminated his library; a grown-up Bible, a beloved *Children's Illustrated Bible – you're too big for that now* – a collection of Oliphant's *Heroes of the Cross* missionary biographies, and three framed samplers that Gran had embroidered, a gift for each of his last three birthdays; his 11th,

"**Be sure**
your **sin** will
find you out"

Numbers 32:23

his 10th,

"For **God** so **loved** the **world**,
that **He** gave **His** only begotten **Son**,
that whosever **believeth** in **Him**
should **not perish**, but have **everlasting life**."

John 3:16

and his 9th,

"For the **wages** of **sin** is **death**;
but the **gift** of **God** is **eternal life**
through **Jesus Christ** our **Lord**."

Romans 6:23

And it shined its light upon a gaudy poster which at first glance looked like a cover of one of those American *Good Housekeeping* magazines that often found their way into the Episcopalian jumble sale and Doctor Baranski's waiting room. The poster was indeed American but not from *Good Housekeeping*. An illustration of *The Pre-Tribulational Rapture*, it featured a despondent beige-suited husband at the moment of discovering that the gingham-clothed kitchen table had not been laid for his tea. If only the silly man had been less bothered with his tea, *Look out the window! Oh for goodness sake. Quick!* Then he'd have seen his pretty fair-haired, barefoot wife in her yellow cotton, flower print dress and white apron, ascending body and soul into a sheep-clouded blue sky. And writ large against that sky:

Then We Which Are Alive And Remain
Shall Be Caught Up Together With Them In The Clouds,
To Meet The Lord In The Air:
And So Shall We Ever Be With The Lord

1 Thessalonians 4:17

In Gran's eyes this was, *Glorious, Miraculous, Proof if proof were needed.* For Joseph it was deeply troubling. How would the poor husband feel when he realised his wife had gone forever? No, *more* than forever. Gran did nothing to reassure him, "If the husband has been Saved," she'd say, always at bedtime, "he might go with her. But if the Lord calls him *home* and he's not *ready*...well... he'll be going somewhere quite different, that young man, somewhere quite different." And as she switched off the light and closed the bedroom door, "That's something for you to think about, eh?"

She was blissful and beautiful, the young wife in the yellow cotton flower print dress. And kind. You could just tell. But surely she must be scared. How could she not be? Okay she'd be with God and Jesus... but even so. Not even a wee bit scared? Floating up to Heaven? On her own? In her bare feet? But at least the Pre-Tribulational Rapture poster was colourful, like the book jackets of his *Heroes of the Cross*, like his *Children's Illustrated Bible*, like the tartan barley-sugar tin of Scripture texts, and the pictures on the front – *sorry*, the back, *it's about the Scripture, not the picture* – of the texts themselves. At least there was colour.

Oh no. Please.

He'd wet the bed. Again.

The big light hurt his eyes but it also burnt off the shadows and took the spotlight off the scripture samplers and so on, giving it all equal weight. Joseph put on his dressing gown and rolled the sodden pyjamas and sheets into a ball. There were blood spots on the top sheet. This is what happened sometimes, things from nightmares seeping in. The broken skin on the underside of his wrists was sticky, pink and shiny like the wee polythene bags of giblets from the inside of Mister Underwood's chickens. It stung when he touched it, but how could he not?

He tiptoed along the lobby avoiding the squeaky bits of floor. His task was simple; get the soiled things into the dirty linen basket in the kitchen, get clean sheets, don't wake Gran up...

"Joseph!" So it wasn't as late as he'd thought, "What are you up to out there?"

He could do a Grandpa. Decide to not hear her. Go back to bed. Pretend to be asleep.

"Three sets of sheets," she said with her big exasperated sigh, her big shake of the head, her big roll of the eyes, her folded arms, her pursed lips. The whole routine.

Joseph missed a lot of it. He was looking at the display cabinet. Anyway, Gran didn't like him looking her in the eye when she was giving him a row. Joseph looked people in the eye for far too long. *I've told you umpteen times it makes people feel uncomfortable*. Or not at all. The cabinet contained Gran's modest collection of fancy – not *too* fancy – china, Apostle spoons, assorted ceramic whigmaleeries from Scottish seaside towns, etcetera. And here was a new thing. A plate with a picture of Hong Kong. And next to it a framed photo of cousin Sam – Uncle Andrew and Auntie Ishbel's eldest – proud in his hero-white Royal Navy uniform. Apart from a few more scripture samplers and a mantelpiece clock, there was nothing else to tempt the eye. No rich brocaded fabrics. No paintings. No patterned wallpaper. No lurid colour. The walls were a solid mushroom. The curtains a solid green. The carpet a solid brown. The three-piece suite a solid oxblood. *You'll find little mention of the "colour" of things in the scriptures. Why? I'll tell you why. Because the Word is enough, it doesn't need dressing up or colouring in*. The harmonium, with its fantoosh fretwork might be on the fancy side but it was functional, and when it wasn't being played it had a drab grey dust cover thrown over it, in case it – or anyone else – got ideas. There were no other distractions. Except for Peter the yellow budgerigar.

"*Cooo*," said Grandpa, in a wet throaty warble.

"Three sets!" said Gran, again, looking over at Grandpa, who was sitting by the window in his pyjamas, toothless, cooing to the budgie perched on the end of his thumb. "In one week! And there's me thinking, *oh maybe I can take that rubber sheet off now*."

"*Cooo*," said Grandpa, seemingly oblivious to Joseph and to whatever Gran was saying. "*Cooo* wee Peter," His hands shook so much these days, but never when he held Peter.

"*Cooo*, bonnie wee birdie. Pretty wee Peter. Ma pretty wee boy. *Cooo*."

Gran carried on, seemingly oblivious to Grandpa's oblivion. "I don't know," she said, shaking her head, sighing, at Grandpa, Joseph, Peter, anyone, the photograph of Sam, no one, herself – *Him*...*Them*. She did a lot of that, the head-shaking, the hand-wringing, the sighing.

"Bonnie wee yella birdie," said Grandpa, "*Cooo*. Who's a hungry wee birdie?"

A bulging catheter bag hung from a frame on the floor beside him. Gran looked away as he fiddled with the rubber tube that led into the front of his pyjama trousers. He broke a tiny bit of millet off a stalk jammed in the side of the cage and put it in his mouth. In the blink of an eye Peter had snatched the morsel from between Grandpa's puckered lips,

"Oh my, ho ho, yon was fast but, eh? Feart I might bite your head off wee boy?" And then again to Gran, but louder as though she was the one who was deaf , "Ho ho! Did ye see that mum?"

"It's *frightened*, not 'feart' – and that's disgusting that so it is. Letting it eat from your mouth like that. It is so. You could at least put your teeth in."

"Clever wee birdie, so you are." A tiny yellow feather clung to the side of his mouth,

"You'll catch something, so you will," said Gran, "Mark my words. Then that'll be you. That'll be the next thing."

"Fly away Peter," he said with a big cheery gummy baby smile and the ghost of a glint in his milky blue eyes as he threw the budgie up in the air like Noah sending forth his dove.

"Some other thing for muggins here to contend with."

The budgie flapped once around the room, tried and failed to land on the mantelpiece clock, then flew into its cage and onto its swing. Grandpa gave a high chirruping trill, just like a budgie and Joseph worked his mouth and tongue, *How does he do that?*, feeling for the place that enabled Grandpa to make such a sound.

"That's all ye need, eh wee birdie?" said Grandpa. Peter swung back and forth, "A wee bit millet, a wee bit flap about, a wee bit swing and that's you. Happy as Larry. Ho ho. There's a man I'd like to be pals wi ... *Larry*! There's naebody as happy as Larry, eh mum?"

"Oh for goodness sake, dad. And it's *nobody*, not *naebody*."

Gran and Grandpa never used each other's Christian names, *Sarah* and *Samuel*. He called her *mum*. She called him *dad*. That's how it was.

As Grandpa fiddled with his hearing aids it crossed Joseph's mind, *Are his ears even bigger tonight? And his nose?* Or did it just seem that way because in every other department there was less of him every day. He'd taken to shouting, *Lugs, neb and a bony bahoochie! That's yer auld Grandpa*, or *I'm like yon Cheshire cat, mum. Soon there'll be nothing left but a big glaikit grin*. Or his latest thing, *I'm fading away mum*, like a slowed down record, *help me, help me*, waving like a drowning man being carried off by the tide.

She didn't like all this mocking of death. She didn't like this quoting of literature. And she really didn't like this new *fading-away* business. Because he was. Fading away.

"Are my ears deceiving me," he wheezed, "or did I hear some kind sowl say *tea*?" He looked side to side, up and down, for the person or creature that might've done so.

"It's *soul* not *sowl*!" She tutted and sighed. "Tea? At this time of night?"

"Heel," said Grandpa, slapping his thigh and whistling at his catheter bag like it was a well-trained terrier. He picked it up and shuffled over to the big chair beside the electric fire with its plastic coal and flickering fan-assisted glow: "Not heving tae geng tae the levvy, does hev its edventeges," he said in mock Scotch posh to the imaginary television camera located somewhere above the pelmet, and bent over to switch on the third bar of the fire. Even that short sequence of movements had taken it out of him.

"Oh that's right," said Gran, "Three bars! Just waste

electricity, why don't you. Is it for this I spend half my life on my knees, scrubbing posh folk's toilets? If you'd wear your dressing gown you wouldn't need three bars. And we wouldn't have to see that –" she averted her eyes from the unmentionable catheter tube – "paraphernalia. It's not nice, so it's not." She turned her attention back to Joseph, still perched on the edge of the settee, "You should be wearing your spectacles by the way," then to the damp bundle in her hands, and remembered what it was she was supposed to be annoyed about, "As if I don't have enough to put up with." And away she went, sighing and mumbling and tutting all the way into the kitchen.

Grandpa seemed to see Joseph properly for the first time and did one of his comic double takes, all wide-eyed and drop-jawed. He stared at the clock, half past ten, well past Joseph's bedtime, and added his funny head-scratching, Laurel-and-Hardy confused look. His whole wonderful, irresistible shtick. He winked, and jerked his head towards the birdcage where Peter was busily rubbing his beak on a cuttlefish bone.

"Clever wee birds, budgies, eh?" Joseph smiled. Grandpa's antics were the one thing that could always be relied on to crack a smile on Joseph Kirkland's poker face. "Eeny meeny miny moe," he said, picking a briar from the pipe rack on the hearth. He fumbled about his person for something that wasn't there. Stuck his hand down the side of the chair. Whatever it was wasn't there either. Here was an excuse – not that he needed an excuse – to burst into song, "Come out, come out, wherever you are…"

Joseph handed Grandpa his leather tobacco pouch. It had been on the back of the chair all along. Grandpa wagged his finger at it, *tut tut tutting*, like Gran. "Naughty wee thing. I cannot let you out my sight for one minute." He opened the pouch, eyes darting this way, that way, like it was filled with who knows what secrets, that had to be hidden from who knows who – Gran – then stuck his big beak of a nose inside and inhaled, "Aaah, *Bisto!*" He stuck the pouch under Joseph's nose. This was his grandson's cue,

"Aaaah, *Bisto!*" whispered Joseph, breathing in the aromatic blend of ready rub and flake he'd helped Grandpa mix. Joseph lit a taper off the top bar, something he'd never do if Gran was in the room. *Do you want to electrocute yourself?* Grandpa held it to his pipe, sucking and puffing louder and harder than necessary, a pantomime puff, and extinguished the burning taper on his tongue. It sizzled. He smacked his lips, gave his nose a conspiratorial tap and, with a flourish of his long bony fingers, flicked both the off switches on his hearing aids and sank into his chair, content as a baby with a bottle. Thick yellow pee trickled down the catheter tube. His half-shut eyes rolled and flickered and away he went, deep down into his thoughts or his thoughtlessness or wherever it was he went these days. And that was it. Curtain down. End of show.

Gran came back in, clutching two mugs and a saucer with a couple of digestive biscuits. "Ach, you and your weeds," she said, wrinkling her nose, "There's your tea." But Grandpa was miles away and Gran stood for a moment, lost. "I've no clean pyjamas so you can just…" Her tongue rummaged around for an acceptable alternative to *nude*, *naked* or *nothing on*, "… sleep as you are. And I've no sheets either. You'll need to fling down a bath towel." She was not happy with this solution. Or with Joseph. But even so she thrust a mug into his hand, "Hot milk and honey." She frowned, "It'll help get you back to sleep. And you might as well take a digestive since they're there. He mouthed a *thank you*. "Aye, well…" and detecting a softening in herself, she readjusted her stony-faced armour.

Grandpa's head was flung back, his mouth wide open like a basking shark grazing for plankton. She put his tea on the mantelpiece just in case, and performed what was now a nightly ritual, the clamping of the catheter tube and the removal of the bulging bag. Grandpa snored a loud snore, like he'd just been deflated and Gran sighed a big sigh like she'd also been deflated. Joseph was still standing in the doorway nibbling like a mouse on his biscuit, "Och away and sit down if you're going to eat that. No crumbs on that carpet mind. Then bed. Have you said your prayers?" He nodded. "Aye well, you can say them again, it'll do you no harm."

She went away to empty the bag. Her lips were moving again, searching for a combination of common words and scripture that would finally move Joseph to do the thing he must do, now he was at *that age*. Something other than her daily mantra; *Have you been Saved? Have you asked the Lord Jesus Christ into Your Heart?* But she was done in.

Joseph finished his biscuit and was about to go when Grandpa's pipe fell from his hand, spilling a dod of smouldering tobacco onto the *Templeton & Kilhaugh Gazette* that lay on the carpet. Joseph felt compelled to stay and watch. To see if it would take.

The blankets were rough against his skin. Might not that be a good thing? Like those monks his teacher Miss O'Donnell spoke of, who wore horsehair shirts as an act of … an act of *what was that* again? But it was a Catholic thing. Maybe it was as well he couldn't remember.

Several times he slipped over the edge into sleep and each time something snatched him back into wakefulness. A whisper. A falling. A shadow or shape seen through the corner of a half-closed eye. Through the lid of a closed eye even.

I'm not going to think about the Devil… I'm not going to think about the Devil. And the more he tried not to think about the Devil, the more he thought about the Devil. And the more he tried not to think about the thing that had to be said, the thing he was avoiding saying; *God and Jesus I want you to come into my heart* … the more he thought about the Devil.

Sorry.

He put the big light back on. His eyes were that sore. He

was that tired. No wonder, with all these sleepless nights. The bed-wetting. The recurring nightmares. All the rest. He got up and looked out the window at the moonlit December night. The stars were out in force.

The Plough. It was the only constellation Joseph could name. Grandpa knew them all. Or so he said. "Aye, I could tell you all the names. Orion's Belt. O'Brian's Braces. When I could see them. The only Milky Ways and Galaxies I can see these days are the chocolate ones at the back of Moretti's ice cream van. Ho ho."

There was no one down on the back lane. Sometimes, late on a Friday or Saturday night, you'd see folk on their way home from Faulkner's Public House, noisy with songs, jokes and *language*. Uncle Mathew too once, with a drunk girl who sang loudly. A pop song as well. Right outside Gran's:

> *The only one who could ever reach me, was the son of a preacher man…*

Gran and Grandpa's room was at the other side but even so. Uncle Mathew tried to haul the girl down the lane out of range, but she was that drunk and floppy it was impossible to get her to go in any particular direction. The girl was young, much younger than Uncle Mathew. Joseph had seen her around in her Templeton Secondary uniform. Uncle Mathew was as nervous as he was angry. He kept looking up at Gran's house and hissing at the girl, *God sake, will you just shut it*, looking and hissing. She thought it was all hilarious, a proper grown-up man scared of his mum. She stagger-danced around him, clutching her half-bottle, singing away, laughing and dancing, not a care in the world:

> *The only boy who could ever teach me, was the son of a preacher man…*

Uncle Mathew looked like he was going to hit her. He

slapped his hand over her mouth. She did not like that at all and tried to pull it off. But he ignored her and made another attempt at dragging her away. That's when he saw Joseph's face at the back window and gave him a *I'm warning you* look. There was no need. Joseph knew better than to report anything Uncle Mathew said or did. Two years ago he'd shamed himself after overhearing Uncle Mathew nattering to his policeman pal, Duncan Carmichael,

"Are you *shaggin'* anybody?" he'd said.

Joseph was a million miles away from boys his age. An innocent abroad in the village he was born in. It was the first time he could recall hearing this word. There had been no dirty laugh accompanying it to suggest it might be *language*. And so later that afternoon, when Gran, Auntie Ishbel, Mrs Agnew, Mrs Sangster and a couple of ladies from the Hall were in the living room having tea and biscuits after the women's prayer meeting, Joseph didn't think twice about walking in quite the thing and asking,

"What does *shagging* mean?"

No one uttered a word. No one looked at each other. The air was congealed with embarrassment. Diluting it with light-hearted laughter was not a possibility. In that mortifying silence Joseph intuitively knew what must be done. He must leave immediately. He must he never speak of this incident. He must convince himself, as they would convince themselves, that the incident had never taken place. That the word had not been spoken. Now if Joseph didn't understand a word or wasn't quite sure about something – which was most things – he kept it to himself.

Here was something new though. A big dog had appeared and sat itself down beneath the lamp post. Some kind of shaggy mongrel thing with a bit of collie? A bit of Alsatian around its muzzle? Black or brown? It was hard to tell in the dark, under the moonlight and the yellow lamplight.

It wasn't one he'd seen before. It looked up at the window, head tilted to one side. Was it looking at Joseph? Maybe it was thinking the same thing, *is that boy looking at me?* Lots of children at school had dogs. He'd see them following their young masters and mistresses to school, sitting outside the shops, slapping their tails on the ground anxiously waiting for them to come out, missing their masters and mistresses so much. And when they reappeared the devoted dogs would pant and bark and run around in circles, so excited, like their masters and mistresses had been away for weeks and they'd gaze at them… adoringly.

"That must be so nice that."

There was a man there now, in the shadows, close to the wall. He was wearing a bunnet so Joseph couldn't see his eyes or his face properly. He was heavily bearded, he could see that much, and had a tweed jacket on and big boots. A workie? Or a farmer. The man clicked his fingers just the once and the dog pressed itself against his legs. So it was the man's dog. Well trained. A working dog. For hunting. Sheep maybe. Or just plain loyal and loving. A *do anything for you* dog. A *lay down and die for you* dog. A *loyal companion*. He made a roll-up, one-handed, like a cowboy, lit it and blew a smoke ring up into the lamplight beam like in that film…? Archie would mind the name of it. He belonged to the night this man. He carried on down the lane. No, he *moseyed on down*, roll-up stuck in the corner of his mouth like the black-clad gunslinger Kit Mossman in the Zachary T. Mayfield books, that Grandpa read in secret and kept hidden away under his side of the mattress. The dog looked up, sniffed the air, like it was adding *Bespectacled Boy at Back Lane Bedroom Window* to its canine directory – or map – of interesting scents, and padded off after its master.

He was drifting away. At last. Just let go. Just give in. *Oh please…* Almost there. But then the Devil whispered in his ear and… Bang! He was back, fumbling for the light and wiping cold sweat from his neck and sternum. If only he could lure that black dog into his room, get it to sleep on the end of his bed, one ear cocked, one eye open. A dog like that would keep the scary things at bay. Then Joseph would sleep. No problem.

Up again. Sitting in the toilet now. He didn't need to, but it was bright in there. There were no Bible things and he liked the coolness of the linoleum under his bare feet. A shiny black beetle was trying to crawl up the inside of the bath but it kept slipping back down. Up and down, up and down, up and down. It would not give up. How had it got in? Up the plug hole? Should he flush it away? What if it had fallen in? What if it wasn't the kind of creature that could swim? But then if he left it there, struggling…

From the lobby Joseph could hear Gran praying her urgent fearful prayers. She'd be on her knees, which wasn't easy these days, and Grandpa in no fit state to lend a hand,

"Lord, forgive me. I know I'm not an educated woman."

Just as Joseph was forever saying *sorry* to God and Jesus for the error of his ways, so Gran was forever apologising for her lack of schooling. She didn't talk much about her childhood but her wee sister, Great Auntie Abi – *enough of the "great"* – had told Joseph that right after their father died, their mother had immediately taken not well. "Ach, mother was aye *fragile* at the best of times. Then when father passed away, well… your Gran was the eldest, so she had to take it all on. She was barely twelve year old. But that's how it was then. There was none of this, *Oh how will I cope?* You just coped. I was only a toddler. Your Uncle Edward just a year older. Aye, me and my big sister might no see eye to eye on some things. Most things. But she did good by us. And she never complained. Not back then," she laughed, "Made up for it since mind. Don't you dare tell her I said that."

"I know I can't mind the scriptures as well as I should," said Gran, "but please Lord, tell me what to do. What to say. So that when the Day of Judgement comes you shall not find him wanting."

"I will. I promise." It was inaudible, Joseph Kirkland's promise, the promise of someone not wanting their promise to be heard, by Gran or by God.

Another hymn popped into his head"

Don't turn the dear Saviour away / Oh think of that great judgement day

One that Gran was fond of singing at him these days:

Oh think of your fate, when the Judge says "too late"/ Don't turn the dear Saviour away.

The fact of the matter is Joseph Kirkland was afraid. Afraid of *not* being Saved. Afraid of *being* Saved. Afraid of the transformation that would surely occur the moment he uttered those words, *Jesus! God! I want you to come into my heart!*

"It will be glorious!" says Gran.

"Glorious!" says Mister Agnew.

"Glorious!" says Uncle Andrew.

"Oh it will be glorious!" says everybody who's ever been Saved.

But *what? What* would be glorious? What would this "it" feel like? Would he still *be* Joseph Kirkland? When his cousin Jenny was Saved three years ago, she changed. It was hard to say how. But she was different. Noticeably so. More hesitant. More serious. It was hard to put a finger on it, but there was no doubt that she was absolutely not the same happy-go-lucky Jenny she'd been before. She had been altered.

Gran was crying again, getting herself into a right old state. And frightened. Terrified. And rightly so because Hell was not just some metaphor for something, anything. Hell was real. Solid. Tooth and bone. Flesh and blood. Fire and brimstone. *Eternal Damnation.* Actual *Burning Embodied Souls* in the actual *Fires of Hell. Weeping and Wailing* and *Gnashing their Teeth.* Getting poked and prodded, gouged and goaded by a larger-than-life pitchfork- wielding goat-horned Satan. *For All Eternity.* Not a fortnight or so of discomfort or despair. Not even *Forever.* For *More than Forever.* And one of those tortured souls might well be her own beloved grandson. And he really was beloved, despite her tutting and her sighing and her head shaking. So of course she was terrified. How could she not be terrified?

"Please *please,* guide me Lord."

It was too much, too painful, to see her like this. And it was Joseph's fault. It was in his gift to do something about it. A few simple words. That's all it would take.

He rattled mechanically through his *Gentle Jesus:*

"*Gentle Jesus meek and mild look upon this little child, pity my simplicity, suffer me to come to thee, fain I would to thee be brought, dearest Lord, forbid it not in thy Kingdom of thy Grace, give this little child a place.* God bless Gran, God bless Grandpa, God bless Uncle Andrew and Auntie Ishbel, Auntie Abi, God bless Uncle Hector, God bless ... God bless..." He couldn't remember who he'd God Blessed and who he hadn't so he skipped to the end, "God bless those that I don't like and God bless those that don't like me. Amen."

And he was asleep.

And like the weekly serial at the *Saturday Morning Pictures,* Joseph's dream continued exactly from where it had left off.

CHAPTER THREE

Joseph Kirkland's First Dream: Episode Two

"Joseph Kirkland has been Saved," drawled the ruddy-faced wee man with the mutton chops. Mister Agnew was even more animated than in *Episode One*. His arm trembled beneath the great slab of Bible he was struggling to hold one-handed above his head like an American penitent at a Billy Graham evangelical Crusade. "JOSEPH KIRKLAND HAS BEEN SAVED!"

The crowd murmured its approval. *Crowd?* In the Hall? He wiped the condensation from his spectacle lens. Yes, all the benches were filled; everyone who was anyone in Joseph's life, its centre or periphery, had turned out to bear witness. Uncle Andrew of course, and Auntie Ishbel, his cousin Jenny and her big brother Sam in uniform were there. Auntie Abi, Uncle Hector and Uncle Mathew, who never went to the Hall any more, were there. Miss O'Donnell and the next-door neighbour Mrs Merryweather were there. As were old mamma Moretti, the recently deceased old man Moretti, and they were all Roman Catholics. And of course Archie Truman, who'd probably never been in a place of worship in his life, was there, along with his sister wee Maggie, and in case there was any doubt that this was a dream, Archie was clutching the latest edition of *The Believer*. Even that bearded man from the lane was there, who Joseph knew nothing about, yet here he was claiming a place in Joseph's dream. He still couldn't see the man's face properly, it was still in shadow, but it was him all right, and the black dog too, lying under the bench at the back, beside the door, as if they hadn't yet decided whether they were going to stay or go.

Blessed Assurance Jesus is Mine / Oh what a foretaste of Glory Divine

The singing increased in volume and passion, Auntie Ishbel improvised a series of impossibly loud and dissonant horror-film chords on the harmonium and Uncle Andrew hauled open an impossibly large horror-film trapdoor that led deep down into a horror-film cavernous rock- hewn pool, where Mister Agnew awaited him, black rubber waders over his cavalry twill suit. He reached out his arms to guide Joseph down the steps but the baptismal gown was so long Joseph's foot got caught in the hem and he stumbled into the pool. The water went right up to his chin. The shock of the fall and the iciness of the water made him gasp,

Heir of Salvation, Purchase of God / Born of His Spirit, washed in His Blood.

Joseph shivered. His teeth chattered. This hymn didn't help, it was that dark and Old Testament. Why would Blind Fanny Crosby, who lived her entire life in darkness for goodness sake, want to write such gloomy hymns as *Blessed Assurance* and *Rescue the Perishing*? Why couldn't they sing a bright and buoyant cheery children's chorus; *Jesus Wants Me for a Sunbeam, Jesus Loves Me This I Know, My Cup's Full and Running Over, Give Me Oil in My Lamp Keep Me Burning, This Little Light of Mine, I'm H.A.P.P.Y.*

Mister Agnew cupped Joseph's face in both his hands,

"When THE LORD calls him home THIS BOY will NOT be FOUND WANTING!" His voice reverberated all around the cavern, "When his time comes – and that time may be TONIGHT or it may be TOMORROW but you may BE CERTAIN his time WILL come – HE WILL be READY! For it is WRITTEN in the BOOK of…"

Joseph didn't find out what was written or in which book, because Mister Agnew had pulled him under the water so violently he'd no time to take his specs off or draw breath. Mister Agnew's voice was distorted now, a drowning voice. Was Mister Agnew drowning? Somebody was. Joseph eyes bulged. His lungs felt like they were going to explode.

Is this it then? Is this me getting Saved?

"Big deep breaths," said Mister Agnew, "don't fight it," except it wasn't Mister Agnew anymore, it was the anaesthetist from Templeton Eye Infirmary, "Good boy," said the anaesthetist, "that's it, just breathe and count backwards from ten. And... ten... nine..."

I don't want this. I don't want it.

"Just breathe," said the fair-haired pretty young barefooted woman in the yellow cotton flower print dress, the one from the Pre-Tribulational Rapture poster. Her hair was perfect, and wasn't that odd her being underwater and all?

This is my story, this is my song
Praising my Saviour all the day long
Perfect submission, all is at rest
I in my Saviour am happy and blest

"Breathe Joseph," she said, quite calm, "A big deep breath." She was Scottish, not American as he'd imagined, and she was laughing, like it was just a game they were playing, and it felt like that now, playful. "Look at you, my wee man," she said, "my wee soldier. You'll be all brand new, so you will. Come on. Wee soldier. You'll be fine, so you will."

And he would have, just because she said so, but that was never how this dream went.

The trapdoor slammed shut. And then there was blackness. There was no leg-scalding radiator, no high window nightmare escape to leap from. Joseph inhaled the ice-cold water deep into his lungs. And there was emptiness. And then ...

CHAPTER FOUR

He That Believeth Not Shall Be Damned

"Thank you Lord for our nice breakfast," said Joseph.

"Sausages are the boys, eh?" Grandpa gazed admiringly at the two grilled links on Joseph's plate. He was awful wheezy this morning, his breathing more laboured, his skin more jaundiced; not far off the colour of his catheter bag. Gran shushed him like a librarian but Grandpa was impervious, "The old bangeroos eh? The old laughin links, ho ho. The old surprise bags, eh mum?"

"For goodness sake." She waved her hand in front of his face, overarticulating ev-er-y syll-ab-le, "Jo-seph – is – in – the – mid-dle – of – giv-ing – thanks."

There were two crustless toast triangles on Grandpa's plate, and an egg cup filled with half a dozen tablets of various shapes, sizes and colours. He ignored the tablets and played with the toast triangles, shifting them this way and that as though trying to solve some complex geometric puzzle.

Gran often asked Joseph to *give thanks* and he always felt uncomfortable. This morning he felt more awkward than usual, more insincere, like he was doing a not very convincing impersonation of Uncle Andrew or his cousin Jenny.

"And also, Lord…" he searched for something profound, "we pray for all the folk who are starving in the world, in places like … Africa and… India and…" He tried to think of other places where folk might be starving, and failing that went on to cover other international issues, "and for folk in East Germany and … Russia and … other countries where folk aren't allowed to give thanks. So … thank you Lord for …" He opened his eyes to remind himself what he was giving thanks for, "…these lovely sausages and toast and tea that you … and Gran …" for surely she should be credited for her part, "put here … for us … to eat. Amen."

"Amen," said Gran hesitantly, not sure what to make of his effort. She tapped the side of Grandpa's egg cup, "Mind – you – don't – for-get – those – tab-lets."

"Sausages are the boys though, eh? *Surprise bags* right enough, eh mum? Ho ho!" Joseph loved how Grandpa actually said *ho ho* and *ha ha* when he laughed, without it sounding fake. "Mind? Dearie me. Eh? Ho ho."

"Dad!"

"You never knew what was in them," he was shouting again, "Eh mum? So you didn't?"

She was shouting too now, trying to let him know he was shouting.

"Dad!"

"In the war. Could've been anything in those sausages, so it could. Could've been mice! Plenty of mice around, eh? Ho ho! Wi' all those cats killed. And the doo men wi' their pigeons too, mind that? Och, yon was a crying shame that but, eh?" He allowed himself a moment's *in memoriam* sadness for the doo men and their pigeons, slaughtered for the war effort. "Mind you. Mouse meat! Eh? Ho ho." He placed one hand on his heart and gestured grandly towards the remaining sausage on Joseph's plate, "Wee cowrin tim'rous sausage."

Gran stirred her tea, tutting at him for even *mis*quoting Robert Burns at table. Grandpa had told that story, made that joke, umpteen times, but Joseph liked it when Grandpa reminisced about the war, or the time when Gran and Grandpa were ages with himself; an extraordinary notion. He'd liked to have been pals with Grandpa when he was wee. Gran? Maybe not so much.

Sorry.

Gran, though she'd never admit it, liked them too, the old stories, the funny stories, and even with all her tut tut tutting and her interruptions, she had to let him finish.

"And by the way," she said, "I made that toast special for you. Nice and soft and buttery. There's more butter than bread in that toast."

Grandpa held the toast up to one of his many imaginary television cameras,

"Toast, the breakfast of choice for retired gentlemen. And meh word, doesn't this toast just melt in yer mooth."

Gran covered up her wee grin with an exasperated sigh, and sighed again when he tore off the tiniest piece of toast and chewed on it forever.

"For goodness sake, will you just swallow it." Chewing was hard enough these days, swallowing was almost beyond him. "Daft old man." Grandpa cupped his ear, so she'd say it again, louder, "I said you're a *daft – old – man*."

"Begging your pardon? What did you say?"

"I said…"

Grandpa winked at Joseph.

"Oh, so the two of you are in cahoots now?" she said, "Didderum and Dodderum, that's what I should call the pair of you. Fine, that's just fine."

"Maybe another wee splesh of the old Derjeeling mum? Eh? To wesh doon the auld toastie boys. Eh do believe thet tea might just do the trick?"

"The only tricks round here are the tricks you're up to. Same tricks you're teaching him. Think I'm as daft as you're deaf? Aye, deaf when it suits you that is." She shook her head but another wee hint of a smile had begun to creep around her mouth. "I don't know."

Grandpa's playfulness was infectious. It took her out of herself. Made her feel almost at peace with this world. And she loved him for that. And she got terribly annoyed with him for that. And with herself.

The second she was out the room, Grandpa emptied his toast onto Joseph's plate.

"The Queen of play pieces that." The camera rolled and he was off again, "I say chaps! Do my eyes deceive me or does that young fellow have the Royal cold toast play piece?"

Joseph wrapped the toast in two sheets of old Gazette and shoved it in the pocket of his school shorts just as Gran came back. She saw Grandpa's plate was empty but said nothing. Grandpa picked up the newspaper from his lap, already open at the racing section, slid his specs down the end of his nose and puckered his lips, for another turn,

"Thenk eh'll jast ketch ap with the latest nyoos," he said, in his mock Scotch posh that he deliberately kept letting slip. He removed a pencil stub from behind his ear and circled a few racehorses, kidding on he was reading the news, "Meh goodness," he said, "they say thehr's a mehn lehndit oan the moon. Well he'll be awricht fur his cheese sehnd-whiches."

Gran never made any direct reference to Grandpa's weekly trip to the bookies, or to his dominoes at the British Legion, and anyway, he hadn't been for months, not since he'd taken not well. She stirred her tea, and stirred and stirred, thinking and stirringtThat's the only news worth reading," she said, as she always said, looking up, as she always looked up, at the big family Bible on top of the harmonium. More stirring. "Let me see your wrists." Joseph pushed up his sleeves. "Och for goodness sake, you and your scratching, look at the state of you." She shook her head, "I'll get more ointment up at the chemist." More stirring, so much stirring, "As if I don't have enough to do." She picked up a piece of her own toast, looked at it and put it back down. Her appetite had gone the same way as Grandpa's. Not that she had much of an appetite at the best of times. Most Hall folk were as thin as rakes. As though fat were a sin. As if *eating* was a sin. *Descended from the House of Jack Sprat*, according to Grandpa. Taking too much pleasure from eating was definitely a sin. Folk from the Hall did not *dine*, they *ate* and when they gave thanks for their *daily bread*, it was not because their daily bread had *an excellent nutty crust* or a *wonderfully light and airy texture* or *an unexpected depth of flavour*, but because it was necessary to sustain life, to keep them here on this insignificant planet just long enough to learn to love Him, to spread His word, so that others might love Him, so that those others might in turn spread His word. And so on and so on and on... till the Day of Judgement.

Gran took a deep breath. Joseph held his. He dreaded what was coming. Grandpa too. The song-n-dance man had picked up his catheter bag and was quietly singing,

"*Pardon me boy…*" while doing a slow softshoe shuffle over to the budgie cage, "*… is that the Chatanooga choo choo?*"

"Well?" said Gran. Joseph looked at Grandpa.

"*Yes yes… track twenty-nine…*"

"Forget about him and his antics."

"*…boy you can gimme a shine.*"

"You know fine well what I'm going to say but I'll say it anyway. Are you *ready*?"

Joseph got as far as opening his mouth.

"Ach, you can save your breath. Oh I know exactly what you're going to say, *I will be Gran, I'm going to Gran, tomorrow Gran, the next day Gran*. And what if there isn't a tomorrow? Or a next day? Mm? I mean with the world the way it is … all this palaver right now with … atomic bombs and… not that I know much about it …what if He decides to call you in the middle of night? Or on the way to school? Or right now. Right here." She tapped the table. "At this breakfast table? And you're *not ready*? You're found *wanting*? What then?"

"Wee yella budgie," Peter sat all of a tremble on the end of Grandpa's finger. "Who thinks he's a wee yella canary then? *I taut I taw a poody tat, I did, I did, I did…* "

"What'll you say to Him then?"

Peter took a toast crumb from between Grandpa's lips.

"Clever wee birdie."

Gran's face registered her usual revulsion, but she bit her lip.

"*Lord I was going to*? Is that what you'll say? Mmm?" And she also burst into song, "*Almost persuaded, now to believe.*" It was a trick she had in common with Grandpa, the ability to seamlessly segue from speech to song and back again, "*Almost persuaded Christ to receive…*"

"Fly away Peter." Grandpa threw the budgie into the air. It flapped around the room, "Fly away Paul." He looked at the finger on his other hand, then at Joseph with his clown surprise, "No Paul?"

Gran ploughed on. She was not going to let Grandpa upstage her:

> "*Seems now some soul to say,*
> *Go, Spirit, go Thy way*
> *Some more convenient day*
> *On Thee I'll call.*"

She stopped, sat up straight, clasped her hands, ready to segue back into scripture, "*He that Believeth and is Baptised Shall be Saved; but he that Believeth Not Shall Be Damned*; Mark sixteen, verse sixteen." She took a sip of tea. Her mouth was dry. It often was. And no wonder. Who wouldn't be parched with all that singing and scripture quoting. And fear.

Joseph spoke, cannily, cautiously; he was only trying out the words, a rehearsal, not yet intended for a full public performance,

"I … did."

"Did what?"

"I …asked Him…"

"?"

Joseph dithered for a second or two, only now realising he was centre stage and it was too late to retreat into the wings (Gran would never have used such figures of speech; theatre, like all entertainment, was one of the many Gateways to Hell).

"I asked God… Jesus…."

Gran carefully put down her cup, not daring to take her eyes off him in case he or the moment shattered. Or disappeared. Joseph didn't play the part particularly well. It was gawky, all twitching fits and starts, but Gran was the best kind of audience, willing – no, *desperate* – to suspend her disbelief.

"…to come into my heart…"

She was rubbing away at her knees. No wonder. She'd spent who knows how many hours on those knees, cleaning floors. And praying. For this moment. When she spoke, her voice was soft without its usual sermonising edge, acutely aware perhaps that the grandson had something of the small frightened woodland creature about him. He might scurry off into the undergrowth, if she was too abrupt,

"Son, are you telling me that you've been Saved?" Joseph nodded. Oh what he would've given to be able to scurry off into the undergrowth right now. "That's what you're telling me?"

He nodded again. Nodding was something he did a lot of. One of his *things*. Grandpa had his winking, his nose tapping, his songs and his telly adverts. Gran had her head shaking, her hand wringing, her sighing and her scripture quoting. Joseph had his vacant stare and his nodding (and his burning, but that was secret). Under normal circumstances, she'd have remarked upon it — *You and your nodding, that head will fall off one of these days, with all that nodding* – but these were not normal circumstances. This was a dream – *her* dream – come true. A prayer – *her* prayer – answered.

"Dad!" She so wanted Grandpa to be a part of this glorious moment, "Dad!"

But Grandpa was in the middle of a Mills Brothers calypso number:

> "*Yellow bird yellow bird, up high in banana tree…*"
> "Oh for goodness sake, will you … dad!"
> "*Yellow bird yellow bird, you sit all alone like me…*"

That daft old man and all his budgie nonsense would not ruin this moment. She wrapped her bony wee self around her grandson and sobbed. Oh the relief of it all, the relief, her tears running off Joseph's otter-slick Brylcreemed hair.

"Och Joseph. Och son. You've no idea. Honestly… Joseph… son…" But the Good News had to be spread, "I'll away and phone your Uncle Andrew and your Auntie Ishbel. And Mister Agnew of course, he'll need to know." Her voice trailed off into the lobby, "And the Sangsters. Uncle Andrew can tell them. And your Auntie Abi and your Uncle Hector. I know they don't go anymore but… hello? Oh Ishbel, pet, oh pet, wait till I tell you…"

She needn't have worried about spreading the Good News. Mrs Merryweather, the "poor misguided catholic" from next door would see to that. She worked up at the Telephone Exchange and was no doubt listening in at this very moment. *Watch what you say on that telephone*, Gran would say, *unless you want that old gossipmonger from next door to know your business*. But this morning Gran did not give two hoots about that old gossipmonger. Indeed she wanted that old gossipmonger to tell Kilhaugh and the world, because Kilhaugh and the world would be all the better for hearing it; *Joseph Kirkland has been Saved!*

Oh Joseph, Joseph, Joseph.

He pushed the door to. He could not thole it. Gran crying tears of terror at the possibility of a very real Damnation was awful enough, but crying tears of joy at a sham Salvation? And it *was* a sham Salvation. Oh, Joseph tried to convince himself that what he'd told Gran was not in fact a lie, merely the truth in advance. After all, wasn't he genuinely *intending* to be Saved? Of course. No two ways about it. And soon he would be. Very soon.

Tonight. I'll be Saved tonight. I will. I really will.

And then the truth will have caught up with the lie and rendered the lie null and void. It'll be as though there had been no lie in the first place. Hip hip hurray!

Gran was wet-eyed and tingling with euphoria from tip to toe of her arthritic body. But in control. She belonged after all, to Kilhaugh Gospel Hall, a picture postcard of Scottish sobriety and restraint. Yes, she was a great admirer of the charismatic American evangelist Billy Graham. But the kind of abandonment on display at some of that man's Evangelical Crusades was not for her or hers. To simply sing His praises was more than enough for her and her newly Saved grandson. She sat down at the harmonium; the boy deserved a treat.

"You choose," she said, nostrils flared with jubilation, pointing at a well-thumbed copy of *The Good Shepherd Pamphlet of Popular Hymns & Choruses*. This was Gran's treat, and good practice for eternity.

What will Heaven be like? Joseph once asked her.

That's beyond the powers of our imagination, she'd replied, but imagined anyway. *It'll be glorious. Sitting at the Lord's feet, singing His praises all day long. For all eternity.*

He never asked again.

Joseph considered a serious hymn, to show he was a serious boy, but the first one he thought of was the last one he wanted, *Oh Come, Oh Come Emmanuel,* the only Christmas carol he knew that referenced *Satan's Tyranny* and the *Depths of Hell*. No. And anyway, Gran had such a queer and almost festive-free relationship with Christmas, it was best not to go there.

"*Jesus Wants Me For A Sunbeam.*"

Gran pumped the harmonium's threadbare carpeted pedals.

Jesus wants me for a sunbeam
To shine for Him each day
In every way try to please Him
At home, at school, at play…

Joseph sang in his usual low mumble just above the level of human audibility. But Gran's high theremin tremolo was plenty voice for both of them. It could cut through anything.

A *sunbeam, a sunbeam…*

Even Grandpa's deafness. He was fiddling like mad with his big flesh-pink plastic hearing aids, trying to turn them down or turn them off…

Jesus wants me for a sunbeam

… until he realised, they were already switched off.

A sunbeam, a sunbeam… I'll be a sunbeam for Him…

The phone rang,
"That'll be Mister Agnew," she was all wee-girl excited, "about your Baptism."
My Baptism. Joseph's breakfast curdled in his stomach.
Grandpa's lungs emitted a low whistling sound as he stroked Peter's head. He was unaware, or so it seemed, of the *Glorious* goings-on all around him. Joseph envied Grandpa's deafness. He'd inherited his lazy eye, maybe he'd get his deafness too. Recently Miss O'Donnell had been wondering if Joseph might already be going deaf and had sent him to the school hearing lady on one of her once in a blue moon visits.
"Deafness isn't your problem young man," said the hearing lady, "it's daydreaming."
Oh to be deaf, dumb and blind right now. Or daydreaming. Oh to be utterly insensible to everyone and everything right now. Grandpa was singing again, one of his *heathen music hall songs*, shaking his Swan Vestas like a maraca,

While you've a Lucifer to light your fag, smile boy, that's the style!
What's the use of worrying, it never was worthwhile, so…

Joseph sniffed the sulphurous sandpaper on the side of the matchbox, tasted its tang with the tip of his tongue, struck a match and held it over the pipe. Grandpa sucked and puffed half a dozen times to get it going, then tilted his head towards yet another imaginary television camera – they were everywhere,
"A wee bit a' beccy," he said with a wink, a lopsided grin and a smooth suave burr, "It's the perfect way, to stert your day!" and blew a plume of smoke out the side of his mouth.

Joseph loved his pretend telly adverts. Gran hated anything to do with telly. *That box. It's just one more Gateway to Hell.* Unless of course *He* was making some special use of it, such as a live broadcast of one of Billy Graham's *All Scotland Evangelical Crusades*.

Joseph tried a smile for Grandpa's sake. Such a phoney smile, but Grandpa didn't notice, or chose not to, or maybe Joseph Kirkland had already turned into a top-notch liar. Grandpa lost himself in pipe smoke. Joseph lit another match and stuck it in his mouth, holding it between his teeth, minding what Grandpa said about exhaling all the air, *so the match doesn't flare up and burn the roof of your mouth*. Joseph tried and failed *not* to exhale.

"Open that windae, eh son?"

Joseph tugged open one of the curtains and pulled up the sash window a couple of inches. The cold blast was sudden, shocking.

"Oh my, that'll blaw the cobwebs away, eh? Be a pal and get us a chair son. And put my tea on the windowsill, eh?" When Joseph had attended to all his needs Grandpa sat himself down facing the window, "Ho ho. The VIP treatment, eh?" leant back and rubbed his hands together, "Right then, when's the big picture start?"

Grandpa's blithe banter was no match for Joseph's dread, a feeling that intensified to near apocalyptic proportions when he looked outside. A dense and dirty grey fog had descended, rendering the front path almost invisible. Even the street light was no more than a hazy glow.

"Oh my, yon's a right auld rouk, eh?" Agnew's Paper Works had completely disappeared and it was just across the road. "A real pea-souper, eh?" He added a cheeky wink, "Fact it's more like yer Gran's porridge than pea soup, eh son? Ho ho."

That wasn't the worst of it. The fog was drifting into the living room, clinging like candyfloss to whatever it came in contact with. It had already formed a thick miasma all around Grandpa,

"You daft old man!" shouted Gran, waving her hand through this poisonous halo, trying to disperse it, "Are you trying to kill yourself?"

"Don't shoot, ah'm a comin' out," he said, surrendering his pipe.

"And you," she said to Joseph, "with that chest of yours. Honestly, I can't let the pair of you out my sight for one minute without you getting up to some flumgummerie."

She could've and would've continued at length but for Joseph's *Good News*. So she let it go, though it took an effort. All this for her newly Saved grandson. This was the last thing Joseph wanted. Given the choice of guilt or Gran's fury, he'd've taken the fury any day. She pulled her cardigan tight around herself and slammed shut the window. It was only when she yanked the other curtain wide open that she saw the full extent of this unco fog.

"Oh, will you look at that!" She pressed her face against the glass, "I've never seen the likes. It's a wonder Ishbel never mentioned it." She footered with the hem of her apron, as if there was a secret something sewn inside, "There was nothing about fog on the wireless," she added, transferring her footering onto the hem of the curtain, like it was one continuous piece of material. "*Clear blue skies* and *crisp winter sunshine*, was their so-called prediction."

Gran put up with the wireless like she put up with the newspapers, *Fine, if you must, but between the hours of midnight on Saturday and midnight on Sunday they'll have no place in this house*. The morning Weather Forecast was the only time that Gran personally turned on the wireless. *Entertainment* programmes were in the same category as the television, the pictures, novels, jukeboxes, the theatre, pubs, bookies, dinner dances and other worldly distractions – *Gateways to Hell – flickering lights and fool's gold – glitz and glamour created by Satan to tempt and tantalize and take you further from God.* The fact that the weatherman kept getting it wrong only confirmed it; God made His own decisions about the weather like He did with everything else in this world and it was a sin for man to even try to second-guess Him.

"Look at them with their weather balloons and their satellites and all the rest of their clever scientific accoutrements; still trying to build their Towers of Babel, so they are. *Nothing is restrained from them, which they have imagined to do.* Genesis eleven. It's all there, *Let us down, and there confound their language, that they may not understand one another's speech.* And now look at us. All this carry-on with the East Germans and the Russians and ... all the rest of them ... and is it any wonder?"

Grandpa made his way back to bed. Gran held up the empty egg cup: "Did – you – take – those – tab-lets?"

"Worry not Doctor Kirkland. Doon the old thrapple they all have gone." Cue for a song.

"*Red and yellow and blue and green, purple and orange and pink...*" he looked up at one of his telly cameras, "...and the ones that make ye wee wee wee... all the way home!" and with a sway of his hips and a wobble of his head, he shuffled off in something approximating a shimmy. She made disapproving noises, but seeing him like that, a wee spring in his step, the stuff of life still burning, or at least smouldering, how could she not feel a little joy?

"Right, school," she said, as stern as she could muster, "I'll get you a play piece."

Here was an opportunity to display some *honesty* and *integrity*. He showed her the toast,

"Grandpa said he couldn't eat it." Gran opened her mouth, but Joseph was on a roll with his *honesty* and *integrity*. "He does it a lot. With his toast. And his sausages and..."

She held her grandson's face tight and gave him that *Who are on earth are you?* look, that *Where on earth did you come from?* look. Joseph gave a wee shudder, her hands were that cold these days, like Grandpa's.

"The size of you," she said, "I'll need to stand on a chair soon." She was all teary again. "What am I like? I'm getting as daft as dad." She took a hanky from her cardigan sleeve, blew her nose, tried to get herself together, "I've spoken to Mister Agnew and Uncle Andrew and … och son, everybody's that happy, so they are. It's the most wonderful thing, so it is." Joseph would've nodded if his head hadn't still been clamped between her hands.

"Mister Agnew's going to speak to you after Sunday school about the Baptism. I thought maybe a fortnight on Sunday but no, he's thinking next Saturday."

A week tomorrow? No. Please… It's okay. It'll be fine. I'll be ready. I will be ready.

She held up a sheet of paper with *Six Things To Remember* written across the top.

"Things Mister Agnew said you should be thinking about in the meantime. You get your school things and I'll read it out," Joseph went into the lobby for his duffle coat, Gran hard on his heels, holding the note at arm's length,

"One: *Habits; things you do that you shouldn't be doing.* Mmm, well, no shortage of things there, I don't wonder. Two: *Thoughts; things you're thinking that you shouldn't be thinking.* Yes, well – I dare say you'll know more about that than I do. Three: *Motives; why are you doing the things you're doing and saying the things you're saying?* And mind, it's not me who'll be watching. You can hide from us, but you can't hide from Him. And don't forget your mittens and your balaclava and whatnot, you've seen what it's like out there."

He got into such a fankle trying to get his balaclava over his specs that she snatched them off him in exasperation and shoved them into her apron.

"Four: *Companions; be careful of the company you keep. 'Blessed is the man that walketh not in the counsel of the unGodly.'* Psalm one, verse one." She raised an eyebrow. She didn't need to say his name; Archie Truman was the unGodly companion she had in mind.

"*Five …*" a big rolled-up sheet of paper sticking out his school bag had caught her eye.

"It's homework ...for Miss O'Donnell."

"Oh yes. And what homework has your Miss *O'Donnell* given you now?"

Gran always referred to Miss O'Donnell as *your* Miss *O'Donnell* or *this* Miss *O'Donnell,* and always emphasised the Irishness of her name and *Saint Rita's* as her place of worship. Like the Morettis and Mrs Merryweather, Miss *O'Donnell* was a *poor misguided* Catholic and so Gran was suspicious of her, of Joseph's fondness for her, and of anything she taught. Only a week ago Gran had discovered that this Miss *O'Donnell* had asked Joseph to learn a verse of *Tam o' Shanter*, for a school Burns Supper. Not the only vaguely sensible bit – which Gran seemed to be surprisingly familiar with – where Tam's wrath-nursing wife Kate warns him about the dangers of alcohol. No, it was the verse about warlocks and witches – dancing *in a church*! She'd no option but to write a note to his Miss O'Donnell.

While I disapprove of Robert Burns at the best of times, I'm not an unreasonable woman. If Joseph must take part, could he not at least say the Selkirk Grace? which she also disapproved of, it being written in Scots, *a rude language*. But at least it was a prayer.

"She asked us to draw a map."

"Oh did she, indeed?" Gran folded her arms like a procurator fiscal, "A map of *what*, may I ask?"

"The village."

"Kilhaugh?"

"She said we've just to put in special things... important things."

"Important things?" She laughed, a short disdainful laugh, "In Kilhaugh? Aye, well, that'll not take long. There's the Hall and there's here. And maybe the doctors and the police station. And the school maybe, though I sometimes wonder. Why, what are you thinking of putting in this map of yours?" Joseph shrugged. "Well I can tell you what you *won't* be putting in Miss *O'Donnell's* map. You won't be putting that café in your map, and you won't be putting *Faulkner's Public House* in there either, and I don't see why you'd want to put in *Kilhaugh Episcopalian*, as you're never in there except for their jumble sale once a year, which is tomorrow by the way, so mind go and see if there's any winter things that might do you, especially any quality coats and suchlike handed in from up the hill. Anyway, you decide for yourself what needs to go into this map of yours, I'm not doing your homework for you. Just mind what I said though. What number are we at?"

"Five."

"*Reflect upon the suffering of Christ.* What *He* suffered for *me* and *you.*" She handed him his specs, "And mind wear them. Or that skelly eye of yours will never straighten itself out. Although, if you ask me, it's already too late."

He went in to say cheerio to Grandpa. He looked sound asleep but when Joseph kissed him, he began speaking, slowly, eyes closed, as if in a trance,

"And if you mind your p's and q's,
your three times threes, your two times twos,
your musts and must nots, don'ts and do's,
your pardons, pleases and no thank yous. Then ..."

They said the last line together, "You won't go far wrong."

Grandpa opened one eye and wheezed a *ho ho ho*. Gran tutted a tut tut tut.

"*Six. The Books of the Bible song*, which you've to do off by heart at *Sunbeams* next Friday. He says it'll *focus your mind.* Anyway you'll already know it from Sunday School."

He didn't know it, not really. He just echoed his cousin Jenny and the others.

Please don't ask me.

She didn't have to. She just stood there, waiting till he began his hesitant tuneless murmur, "*Gen-e-sis, Ex-o-dus... Lev-it-icus and Num-bers, Deuter-onomy, Joshua ... Judges. Ruth, and Sam-u-el, Sam-u-el, Kings, Kings... Kings, Kings ...* em ...*Kings, Kings...*"

"Is that it? Aye, well, maybe if that Miss O'Donnell of

yours wasn't filling your head with Robert Burns and maps of Kilhaugh… away and get your Bible."

He'd held his Bible a thousand times but this morning it felt heavy and awkward. Gran took it from him and slipped Mister Agnew's list of *Things to Remember* under the fold-out Map of the Holy Land at the back.

"Now *there's* a map that'll mind you of things that need minding. You keep that Bible in your duffle coat pocket and do your Books whenever you've a minute. And straight to school. No wandering."

Joseph the Deceiver opened the door onto an unrecognizable morning. He pawed at the thick grey fog with his mitten, as though it was possible to scoop it up in lumps. When he got to the end of the path he turned round to wave cheerio to Gran, as he always did, but the house and everything and everybody had already faded away to nothing.

CHAPTER FIVE

The Great Freezing Fog of Unknowing

"Gen-e-sis, Ex-o-dus, Lev-it-icus and Num-bers, Deuter-onomy, Joshua, Judges, Ruth and Sam-u-el, Sam-u-el, Kings, Kings… Kings, Kings…Kings…?" What came after *Kings?*

Kilhaugh was barely there. It was just a chalk drawing of a village, wiped over with a blackboard duster, leaving nothing but a ghostly grey-white trace. Joseph's steamed-up spectacle lens didn't help. The cold rasping fog immediately got to work – *mind that chest of yours* – and his eyelashes went through an endless cycle of frosting and thawing, sending wee ice melt tears running down his cheeks. He wrapped his scarf tight around his nose and mouth, pulled his hood over his balaclava, went into a mild claustrophobic panic and pulled it all off again. He hated wearing all these bulky knitted layers, that suffocating feeling of being inside when he was outside.

In many ways this was perfect weather for *Joseph the Wanderer*. In this fog he might happily wander through the village, his world, invisible to everyone, even to God.

Sorry.

Joseph Kirkland of all people could never be invisible of course, not in Kilhaugh. Folk would recognise him immediately, by his patched-up specs or by his gait, stiff and awkward as a tin man – *Heh speccy / Heh Clarence the cross-eyed lion/ Heh four-eyes / Heh Cyclops / Heh Frankenstein! / Heh Tin Man! / Heh Holy Joe! / Heh weirdo! / Forget to take the coat hanger out yer duffle coat?* – or by all the other things that singled him as a person of interest; *That Kirkland Boy / Elspeth Kirkland's Boy / Holy Joe / One of that Gospel Lot / The Jesus Freak / Yon's a Strange Boy and No Mistake.* Whenever Joseph walked into Rattray's the Newsagent, Hoskins the Bakers,

Underwoods or anywhere else, conversations stuttered to a halt, replaced by raised eye-brows, nods and fragments of murmured gossip, *Trouble at home / Poor wee soul / Shush / Don't tell me you don't know / Oh wait till I tell you / Well now…*

He began again, "*Gen-e-sis, Ex-o-dus, Lev-it-icus and Numbers…*" his lips rubbing against the inside of his balaclava, damp now with hot breath, "*…Deuter-onomy, Joshua, Judges, Ruth and Sam -u-el, Sam-u-el,*" the whispered words rang unexpectedly loud within the confines of his head, "*Kings, Kings… Kings, Kings… Kings, Kings…?*"

From the direction of Agnew's Paper Mill came the sound of dirty laughter and *language*. Joseph couldn't see the men, so they couldn't see him, but still he slunk deep into the fog, close to the wall, like the bearded man in the lane, just in case. Archie Truman's dad was the loudest among them:

It's a fuckin' joke, so it is. Pair a shite bags the baith a them. Kirkland's the worst. Yes Mister Ehgenew, no Mister Ehgenew three fuckin bags full Mister Ehgenew. Mister fuckin' Agnew? Mister fuckin' agony mair like / Heh, keep it doon Jimmy / Creepin' fuckin' Jesus, so he is / Fuckin' God squad. Thick as fuckin' thieves as well. Ye cannae get a fuckin' look in / The fuckin' mafia so they are / Holier than fuckin' thou as well. Takin' time aff fur their fuckin' early mornin' prayers. But wan eh us saunters in wan minute late n it's ther's yer jotters boys / Ah'm away inside, this fog's fuckin' killin me / Ah've knocked aff hunners a reams eh his fuckin' bible paper / Whit dae ye use it fur Truman? Roll-ups? Wipin' yer fat erse ? / Too fuckin' right! / (Laughter)

The *Munday Memorial Bridge* vibrated, but just a little, so he stamped down harder. Usually you could hear its steel cables twang and the rush of the Lele running below. He leaned over the railing. Nothing. And when he got to the middle, he couldn't see either end of this bridge in the clouds. This fog had soaked up everything, sound, smell, everything. He was hot now and his eczema was itching again. He pulled off his mitts, rolled down his socks and held a wrist then an ankle against the frosted metal railing. It made his eyes roll it was so good, sore too, but a good sore. *Kings, Kings… Kings, Kings…?* He checked his Bible; *Chronicles, Chronicles*. Of course, two *Kings*, two *Samuels*, two *Chronicles*, then *Ezra, Nehemiah, Esther.*

He kept getting them in the wrong order and was going over and over them, *Esther, Ezra, Nehemiah … no, Esther, Ezra, Nehemiah… no, Esther, Ezra…* when a great shaggy black flurry of excited dog came bounding out the grey and knocked the Bible out his hand. Right away it was up on its hind legs, paws on Joseph's chest, its big spam tongue hanging out, panting, breathing its hot meaty dog breath in Joseph's face and the next thing it was looking down at the Bible with those bright amber eyes, wagging its tail like mad, looking at the Bible, then at Joseph, then the Bible, saying, *Come on! pick it up and throw it* and then sensing that this particular game of fetch was never going to happen, it ran twice round Joseph and disappeared back into the fog, only to reappear a second later with a big sinewy bone hanging from its jaws, which it dropped in a pool of slabbers right on top of the Bible. Joseph picked it up and wiped the slabbers on his duffle coat, so now the dog was dancing, thinking *the game is on again* and had got crouched ready for a throw – of the bone – or the Bible.

Joseph wasn't scared, not at all. He liked dogs. They took to him. He had a way with them. Sometimes he'd lure a dog from out of some big up-the-hill garden with meat scraps or biscuits. He'd try to get the dog to stay close, to be devoted to him. And some of them would, for a while. They'd do *sit, paw, fetch, roll over* even, let him rub their ears, go for a walk with him, but then they'd wander off home, or their owners would come looking for them. Or guilt would get the better of him and Joseph would take them back himself. Their owners would be in tears sometimes, they were that relieved, that grateful. They'd even give Joseph money, a reward for finding their beloved dog, and the dog would go daft at seeing its beloved master or mistress. So everyone was happy. Everyone got something good.

But this dog was too rough and raw, too wild in the eye for an up-the-hill dog which were mostly well-groomed posh pedigree thises and thats. And there was no collar on it. Even the big dogs and mongrels down-the-hill had collars and were pampered in their own way. Not this dog. It just sat there, looking at him expectantly. Joseph rubbed its head, under its chin, its chest, its velvety ears. The dog nuzzled into him, it was taking comfort from this. So was Joseph. It nudged the bone with its nose, *Let's play*. How could he deny the dog? When he picked up the slabbery bone the dog almost turned summersaults, it was that excited. Joseph was as far away now from *Nehemiah, Ezra and Esther* – or whatever it was – as you could get. But it wasn't safe to throw a big bone in this fog. Folk might appear from any direction and you wouldn't know so he dropped the bone and kicked it, just a wee bit, beyond the edge of the mist, but before the dog even had a chance to go after it the bone came skiting right back. And before Joseph had time to think how odd this was, a big bearded face appeared. Not a peely-wally village lard-fed face, or a cadaverous House of Jack Sprat, Kilhaugh Gospel Hall face, but a deep-lined, weather-browned face, as leathery as Grandpa's tobacco pouch with hair as black as the black dog's, as black as Joseph's hair, and dark brown eyes, as dark as Joseph's eyes. It wasn't a frightening face, unreadable maybe, definitely, but not frightening. Joseph let out a squeal all the same – it was just the surprise – and breathed in sharply through his nose. The man smelled strongly of worldly, earthy things, and petrol. And then as suddenly as they'd appeared, the black-bearded man and the black dog were gone. It was the man from the lane and that was his dog. So he hadn't dreamt it. That was good to know, because sometimes...

Up on the main street there were more voices, more fleeting glimpses of wrapped-up disembodied faces drifting in and out the fog, fumbling their way to school, work, the shops, who knows where. They crept towards one another like the newly blinded in Archie Truman's beloved *The Day of the Triffids*, or firemen in a smoke-filled house, arms outstretched, feet testing the ground in front lest there be an icy puddle or dog dirt or some dangerous obstacle or no ground at all, just a hole, or not even a hole, nothing. Each was unsure if the fog-shrouded figure in front of them was friend, foe, stranger or ghost and each case of mistaken identity was met with laughter; nervous, genuine or fake.

Hello John? / Ha ha, no it's Jim Nisbett. Alasdair? / No it's Henry Thompson / Irene? / Beg your pardon / Ha ha quite all right/ Nice day for Bible John / Don't say that, he still hasn't been caught / It's like the war so it is / Ha, ha / The last one or the next one? / The next one will be the last one / Ha ha / I opened the curtains, nothing. Next thing, there it was / Descended upon us / My words exactly, / Descended upon us.

Was that Scripture? Again Joseph tried to think of other things, such as his map and what would go in it? But *He is Everywhere. Always and Everywhere* and Joseph found himself right beside the Hall's newly varnished notice board.

KILHAUGH GOSPEL HALL

"For where two or three are gathered together in my name, there am I in the midst of them."

(Mathew 16:20)

LORDS DAY
11.00 am Breaking of Bread
12 noon Sunday School

3.00 pm Ministry
7.00 pm Gospel Meeting
8.00 pm Bible Reading

MONDAY
7.30 am Working Men's Prayer Meeting
6.15 pm Choruses, Quizzes and Bible Stories
8.00 pm Prayer Meeting

TUESDAY
7.00 pm Bible Reading
8.00 pm Men's Prayer Meeting

WEDNESDAY
7.30 am Working Men's Bible Meeting
8.00 pm Bible Reading

THURSDAY
11.00 am Women's Prayer Meeting
7.00 pm Prayer Meeting

FRIDAY
9.15 am Young Mothers' Prayer & Bible Meeting
6.00 pm Sunbeams Club
7.30 pm Bible Teaching

SATURDAY
9.00 am Prayer Meeting
7.30 pm Bible Reading

Their numbers were few but their hours were long. *Time spent studying scripture means less time getting caught up in profane and vain babblings*. Joseph already went to Sunday School, Choruses, Quizzes and Bible Stories on Mondays, Sunbeams on Fridays. Should he also go to a *Bible Teaching* and a *Prayer Meeting*? They were supposed to be for grown-ups but if he asked? Might not that be a good thing? If he immersed himself then might not God or Jesus think, *Credit where credit's due, at least the boy is trying.*

Sorry.

It wasn't right to try to make God and Jesus think something. Or possible.

There were two faces, with bodies this time. Mister and Mrs Sangster, who took it upon themselves to put the heating on and the tea things out for *Young Mothers* before Mister Sangster went to his proper work as daytime caretaker up at the Robert Munday Home for Orphans and Unfortunates. This was late for him.

"If Bertie can't cover for me I don't have much choice," said Mister Sangster, "and I'm not driving anywhere in this." He spotted Joseph: "Oh, hello son, you taking the long way to school?"

"I'm practising my Books of the Bible." *That's the truth.*

Mister and Mrs Sangster nodded and smiled at one another, impressed. *Well of course. What else would a newly Saved Joseph Kirkland be doing?*

"Let's take a gander at you," said Mrs Sangster.

A gander at what? And would they see it wasn't there? He clutched his Bible close to his heart, an attempt to form a picture that might confirm what they'd no doubt heard.

Motives; why are you doing the things you're doing and saying the things you're saying?

"Your Uncle Andrew's just after telling us," said Mister Sangster.

"Wonderful news Joseph," said Mrs Sangster, "wonderful news."

"Well, I'd better get going, if I'm hoofing it," said a cheery Mister Sangster.

"If you're not back by teatime, we'll send out a search party," said a cheery Mrs Sangster.

"Aye well, make sure you do, in this fog there's no telling where I might end up."

"Cheerio son, if we don't see you before we'll see you next Saturday."

A week. He had a week to catch up with this lie and turn it around.

I will be Saved. "I will."

The Books of the Bible was a good start, and he mustn't forget Mister Agnew's list. He opened the back of his Bible. *Oh no.* The list was gone. It must've fallen out during that carry-on with the dog. This was not a good start. *Be careful of the company you keep!* Did that include dogs? Possibly. God was well known for His cryptic signs. Always tempting and testing folk so He was. The Bible was full of it: Abraham, Jonah, Job, Simon Peter, Daniel, loads of others. Even Jesus Himself was tested: *Examine me, O Lord, and prove me; try my reins and my heart.* Gran often put that into her prayers. She wanted to be tested. She knew she'd pass with flying colours. She knew she would *not* be found wanting. *The Liar Joseph Kirkland* on the other hand…

It was the first time he'd been in the Hall on his own. A stranger might imagine it to be a cold damp place but it was already sweltering. The industrial cast iron-radiator pipes that skirted it ran scalding hot whatever the weather. And to outsiders the decades-old dark brown painted woodwork, scoured floors and chalky walls unadorned by crosses, crucifixes or other Christian signs, might seem a picture of drab uncompromising austerity. But in here they had the Good Book, and within its covers, the Good News. Everything else was superfluous. Like Gran's living room, the Hall's only concession to ornamentation was the harmonium. Crafted by W.C. Burden & Co of Granby Street, Leicester, this highly polished Gothic beast was grander than Gran's and built to last a lifetime and beyond, its sole purpose being to grind the seeds of doubt and move the brethren of Kilhaugh Gospel Hall to sing God's praises.

Even a Baptist would have found the place small but Kilhaugh was a small village and Hall folk, though fervent proselytisers, were realistic. It would be unusual to find more than twelve saved souls at the Meeting. Even fewer at Sunday School. Spanning the Hall were six rows of long pitch pine benches, (no one called them *pews*). They'd been there since the place was built *to the Glory of God* in December 1946, thanks to funds raised from many years of tithing, and a lot of hands-on help from German Mennonite and Baptist medics, who at the time were still incarcerated in Kilhaugh's small P.O.W camp. The front bench had a well-worn lustre achieved by time and the tweeded backsides of labouring brothers, itinerant preachers, wandering evangelists, and by two generations of restless, shuffling Sunday School children. The bench at the back had a less pronounced sheen attained by guilty latecomers sidling in, and – less so – by years of hatted and headscarved women who sat still and silent, while men – for it was only men – preached the Word, bore Witness and gave Testimony. The dullish benches in the middle were rarely used, except at funerals and even then only if the deceased was well kent and well regarded outside the Hall. But as Hall folk had a habit of keeping themselves to themselves, these benches tended to remain empty.

Joseph shivered despite the heat, and looked over his shoulder at who knows what. *The Devil, that's what*. This was the Hall, *the Lord's House*, for goodness sake, a good, familiar place, a second home to the Kirklands. A boy should not be fearful in this place. Unless he had good reason to be fearful.

A bare bulb hung over the raised platform above the baptismal pool. The trapdoor was as heavy as he'd imagined and inside was as dark and cavernous. He couldn't see or hear anything; no ripple or gentle lapping, no glint of light on water. No water. Nothing, just cold treacly blackness. Like in his dream. And like in his dream an icy terror grabbed the back of his neck and ran him down the aisle that fast he was almost at the front door by the time the trapdoor slammed shut.

Mister Agnew's list was on the step, under a stone to stop it blowing away. Not that it would have, there wasn't as much as a breath of a breeze. He walked-ran, a run pretending to be a walk, because running would show *them* just how afraid he was.

It was nine o'clock but the school doors were still locked. The playground was teeming with wee screaming, chattering, winter-coated figures darting in and out the fog: clockwork toy children, all wound up for the day, especially the primary ones.

"This is great, so it is," said one wee voice as it brushed past Joseph.

"Look! Look! I'm smoking," said another running in the opposite direction, holding a sweetie cigarette to its lips pretending to be some film star, while another one dragged on a rolled-up bus ticket, pretending to be its own mum or dad.

A group of young headscarved women stood in a huddle beside the gate, smoking for real, fag in one hand, toddlers, babies, message bags, prams and all the other accoutrements of womanhood, wifehood and motherhood in the other.

"This is hellish."

"Has the bell still not rung?"

"Did ye no hear? The Templeton tunnel's closed."

"We'll no be seein' the headmaster then."

"Aye, and we'll no be seein' sliced bread either. It all comes in frae Templeton."

Another mother joined them, "Good morning ladies!" It was Mrs Chaddock from up the hill, her moon-faced five-year-old Ivan clinging to her hand.

"Good morning, Mrs Chaddock," said the mothers in Sunday voices reserved for their *betters*. Their cigarettes looked awkward now but where could they hide them.

"I've just heard the trains are off," said Mrs Chaddock, "So that rules out Mister Ironside, Miss Colquhoun, Miss O'Donnell and Miss Grieve."

"Do you think the school will open?" said one of the mothers.

"Even if it does, will there be any..."

Old Mister Scrivener the janitor had started ringing his big handbell,

"Right everybody, listen up!" he shouted, "Mister Brunstane's just aff the phone. There'll be nae school the day!" And offering no further information went back inside.

"Well, I think the charming Mister Scrivener has answered your question, Mrs Baird," said Mrs Chaddock, and the ladies laughed. Genuine laughter. They didn't blame Mrs Chaddock for their discomfort.

Mrs Chaddock was *Hall*. When she saw Joseph, she smiled and gave him a wee wave. So she'd heard the good news too. Joseph held his Bible close to his heart, like he'd done with the Sangsters, in that fraudulently pious, *Look at me, look at how Saved I am* pose. Mrs Chaddock whispered something in Ivan's ear. His mouth opened in a wee "o". What had she said? *See? That's what a boy who's been saved looks like.* Was that it? What she should have said was, *See – that's what a liar looks like, Ivan. You don't ever want to end up like him.* A lie upon a lie upon a lie upon. Enough now. He needed to do something about this. Mister Agnew's list,

One: Habits, things you do that you shouldn't be doing.

Two: "Thoughts", things you're thinking that you shouldn't be thinking.

Three: Motives, why are you doing the things you're doing – like a boy holding his Bible in a way that makes folk think he's Saved when actually he's far from being Saved.

Four: "Companions", be careful of the company you keep...

"Joseph!"

It was the voice of the one person whose company he definitely ought *not* to be keeping. "Joseph. It's me!"

The one voice he desperately wanted to hear right now.

And in that moment, the fearsome Old Testament God, the God that Joseph knew most well – the God of "Terrible

Thought, Shall I Alone" was replaced by the God of "I'm H.A.P.P.Y." and "Jesus Wants Me for a Sunbeam", and He opened the curtain of fog just a smidgen to allow through one small shaft of light in the shape of his best friend, his only earthly friend.

Archie Truman.

CHAPTER SIX

Walking in the Counsel of the UnGodly

Archie Truman was two months younger than Joseph, a good four inches shorter and about as far away from Joseph Kirkland's uptight rigidity and God-fearing gaucheness as you could possibly get. He was an unclean, underfed wee skelf of a boy, a dirty shilpit elf of a boy, always dressed – come wind come weather – in his trademark thin greasy anorak, shorts and sandshoes, all of them worn and frayed. All of *him* was worn and frayed. There was barely a square inch of him that wasn't scratched or bruised. His fingernails were black, his cheeks shiny from layer upon layer of grime mixed with smeared snot from an endlessly runny nose that had dried hard on his face like varnish. He looked like a wooden marionette with his Andy Pandy retroussé nose, his big round pale blue puppet eyes that were painted forever wide open, fixed in a state of utter astonishment, and thick tufts of carrot-red hair that seemed to have been drilled into his skull in oddly cut clumps. He walked towards Joseph like he walked through life, in a loose-limbed string-cut swagger, kicking the hell out of whatever lay in his path: tin cans, stones, people.

His six-year-old sister, wee Maggie, skipped along at his side. Where else would she be? She had the same blue eyes, red hair, the same turned up button nose, but unlike her beloved big brother, wee Maggie was well-fed, well-groomed, immaculately turned-out, and dressed to fight the weather. Archie saw to all that, always, without fail.

"Look at me," he said, walking backwards until the fog had completely enveloped him, "I'm the Invisible Man," and reappeared, "Did you know the Invisible Man was naked?"

"Archie!" said wee Maggie, giggling now, "That's rude, so it is Joseph?"

"He was! Bare bum, everything! He couldn't make his clothes and shoes and things invisible so he had to take them off. Except his specs. He had to keep them on or else he'd end up bumping into folk." Wee Maggie was still giggling at *naked* and *bums*, so Archie had to say it again, "It's just you couldn't see his *bum* even though he was *naked* because his *bum* was invisible. Imagine that. Imagine having an invisible *naked bum*." Wee Maggie imagined and giggled even more. So Archie wiggled his bum, trying to send her off into hysterics, "I wonder if the Invisible Man did invisible jobbies..."

This was Archie's main business in life, to see his wee sister happy and laughing, *all the time*. And this was what Joseph needed in *his* life; happy-go-lucky Archie, devil-may-care Archie, a down-to-earth, of-this-earth Archie Truman. He glanced around in case Mrs Chaddock or anybody else from the Hall might see him talking to Archie Truman.

Joseph Kirkland, the Fake Friend.

"There's no school the day, Joseph!" said wee Maggie, breathless with all her chuckling.

"Aw, that's a shame," said Archie, "and there was me going to go in as well."

Wee Maggie folded her arms like a wee wifie and looked up at him, frowning, "Archie! You were not!" and again to Joseph, whose name she could not say often enough, "He was not, Joseph,"

"Was so!"

Since Archie arrived in Kilhaugh, he'd only seen him in school the once or twice. He'd drop wee Maggie off at the gate, disappear, then pick her up after. Nobody ever said anything.

A woman showed up with a Primary Two girl ages with wee Maggie. Joseph didn't know her, and assumed she was one of the Overspill from Glasgow moved into the new scheme.

"Hello you two," she said, and in a flash Archie had switched from rascal urchin to responsible elder sibling.

"Hello, Mrs McCreadie."

"Oh I love your bunches, Maggie, did your mummy do that?"

Wee Maggie opened her mouth, but Archie intercepted, "Yes."

Wee Maggie opened her mouth again to protest but Mrs McCreadie had read the situation at once, maybe it was all too familiar, and swiftly changed the subject: "Would you like to come to Lizzie's to play?"

Wee Maggie straight away grabbed the girl Lizzie by the hand and stood by her side.

"Can I, Archie?" she said, beaming, knowing the answer.

"Okay, but I'll come and get you at twelve."

"Och there's no need, Archie," said Mrs McCreadie, "I've a couple of bridies that need eating. I can bring Maggie round the back of four."

"It's okay, I'll come and get her," said Archie, polite but firm. He produced two buttered digestives wrapped in brown paper from his anorak, "Mind your play piece."

The look that Mrs McCreadie gave Archie was a look that Joseph knew well. Pitiful.

The moment Mrs McCreadie disappeared, Archie the reckless urchin was back. The world his playground. The fog his smokescreen.

"Let's do something!" he said, "Let's... let's... I don't know... let's... let's just..."

Archie looked like he might explode with the sheer excitement of it all, of everything, of life in general, and the limitless possibilities of fog-bound mischief in particular. He looked around, quickly assessing where maximum amusement might lie. Up the hill? Down the hill? The main street? The braes? The scheme? The building site? The woods? The Sappie?

The social stratification of Kilhaugh had a textbook clarity. Forming a triangle around the outskirts of the village were *the outcasts*; the inhabitants of Kilhaugh's two children's homes, the Robert Munday Home for Orphans and Unfortunates and the Borstal (for bad boys). Gran was fond of reminding Joseph how *fortunate* he was not to be in the former and how, if he didn't watch the company he kept, he might end up in the latter, along with the company he kept. There were dreadful rumours about both of them, but they were nothing compared to the stories surrounding the third corner of this triangle of pariahs, the Robert Munday Mental Asylum. Sir Robert Munday, the wealthy Victorian industrialist, whose family hailed from Kilhaugh, had left his money and his name to a number of Kilhaugh institutions and constructions; the Robert Munday Memorial Bridge, the Robert Munday Memorial Hall, the Robert Munday Home for Orphans, etc., and the Asylum – or Munday Mental – where Archie's neighbour worked as an auxiliary.

"She says they stick all your food in a liquidiser: toast, tea, eggs, milk, sausages, Rice Krispies, the lot, and then they make the loonies sook it through a big straw! Can you imagine? It'd make you boke, but she says the loonies don't know any better."

Joseph mentioned it to Grandpa; it was one of the few occasions he'd seen him get angry,

"It's wrong, son. Wrong! Poor sowls. *We* know better. No… it's just wrong."

Then there was Kilhaugh village proper. On the top tier was *Up the Hill*: the big houses with their high walls and hedges, manicured lawns and private woodlands. Every big house was unique, each with its own architectural quirk or folly: faux turrets, faux battlements, faux gargoyles, mock Tudor, mock Gothic, mock Scots Baronial, faux this and mock that. This was where the posh folk lived: a variety of minor aristocrats, rich industrialists, doctors, clerics, company directors and wealth-inherited eccentrics, and it was in these houses that

Gran got down on her knees three or four days a week to do her scrubbing.

Right in the middle, on the main street were the shops and the shopkeepers who lived above them; *J. Webster & Sons* – Grocers, *W. Rattray & Sons* – Newsagents, *D. Underwood & Sons* – Butchers, *B. Goodwin & Sons* – Ironmonger, and so on like a pack of Happy Families with all the female offspring removed. Then there was *Down the Hill* with its odd mixture of picket-fenced post-war prefabs, red-roofed houses built for heroes, and a few old stone-built terraces, built for the families of workers at Agnew's Paper Mill, now owned by the council, where Joseph's grandparents lived. At the very bottom of the hill, where the swamp used to be – where the swamp still was in the opinion of some – were the new schemes where Archie lived: rows of identical two-up-two-downs, and pebbledash three-storey affairs thrown up to house – in the opinion of many Kilhaugh worthies from up and down the hill – the barbarian hordes of the *Glasgow Overspill.* And beyond where the swamp dwellers lived, down in the back-of-beyond, in Kilhaugh's deep south, in a clearing in the woods beside a wee loch known as *the Sappie*, for a few months each year, were the lowest of the low: the tinkers. Nobody mixed with them.

"We could go to the prisoner-of-war camp, play commandoes!" said Archie. "Or we can pretend we're like those folk stuck in the fog on the ship in *the Lost Continent?* Mind? And they're surrounded by that creepy seaweed that eats folk? You know there's plants that can eat folk? I don't mean Triffids, I mean real life. They've got teeth and everything. Imagine?"

Real life, wild imaginings, things he'd seen on the news, the pictures, things overheard, were all of a piece. Archie was obsessed with the pictures. Joseph had never been to the real pictures, due to them being *Gateways to Hell*, though Gran did, for reasons best known to herself, turn a blind eye to Saturday Morning Picture Club at the Munday Memorial Hall. But the blind eye was only turned every second week, which meant he missed every other episode of the serial, and had to rely on Archie and wee Maggie to fill him in. Archie's Uncle Tommy ran the Regal Picture Palace in Templeton. Archie got in for free, and he gave Joseph a blow-by-blow account of all the films he saw, or at least most of them,

"Wee Maggie only sees the U's but Uncle Tommy lets me see *all* the films." He sniggered a dirty snigger but said no more. Unlike Uncle Tommy, Archie practised censorship. He'd only known Joseph two years but he understood how far he could go with this boy who was so different to himself he might well be from another planet.

"Or the coal sheds," said Archie,

The coal sheds were special. This was where Joseph and Archie first met, the very day the Trumans had spilled out of Glasgow and into Kilhaugh.

"Or along the railway line? Or down to the Lele? Or the building site?"

Right from the beginning, despite knowing it was dangerous and wrong, Joseph had allowed himself to walk in the counsel of the un-Godly Archie Truman and dealt with the guilt later. And on any other day than today he'd happily have done the same.

"The workies won't even be there in this weather. The new flats don't have their stairs yet but they've got these big ladders so you can get right up through all the floors. There's hundreds of stuff lying around, so there is. I went by the other night and they had this thing that can cut through concrete. It was still plugged in. We might even get rope. I've found a great new place for a swing. You'll need to see it, so you will. Honest it's even better than the one over the cemetery. And the workies have always got ginger bottles. We can get money! Oh! Hold out your hands." He fished out a load of sweets from his anorak pocket, "Ta da!" Opal Fruits, Bazooka Joes and Blackjacks were, as always, shared out equally. Joseph shared what he had – cold toast – and Archie, best friend and diplomat, made a big deal of it. "I love cold toast. Mmm. It's really buttery. Oh! And here." He gave Joseph a book of matches with a picture of a monkey king. Archie was always giving him matches. Joseph had to take out his Bible to make room in his pocket for the stolen goods.

One: Habits, things you do that you shouldn't be doing.

The sweets were either stolen from Rattray's or bought with money stolen from his mum's purse or his dad's pocket. Joseph opened an *Opal Fruit*, strawberry, his favourite. By rights it ought to taste bitter, it would serve him right, but it didn't, it tasted sweet and delicious.

"What's the book?" said Archie, sniffing snot back up his nose, gasping for air as he chewed on three *Blackjacks* at once.

"The Bible." He didn't usually carry it around, "I've to learn the names of the books."

"Can I see?"

Joseph had never seen him with a Bible. Archie rubbed the corner of a page.

"It's dead thin. Like the paper my dad uses for roll-ups."

"It's Bible paper. They make it at Agnew's."

"There's probably some in the house. My dad's always knockin' stuff from there."

Joseph had a vivid picture of Archie's dad smoking a roll-up made from *the Bible,* then remembered overhearing him outside Agnew's and pictured him doing something even worse. Archie flicked through the Bible stopping here and there, moving his lips. He wasn't sure if Archie could read. He always had comics but you could tell those stories just by the pictures.

The two boys armed themselves with long sticks and sauntered along the banks of the Lele. Sometimes it was a raging torrent, but today it was a frozen trickle. They went down past the big pipe where Agnew's Mill belched its billions of gallons of waste water, but this too had been reduced to a dribble. They were hoping to find some rats. This was usually a good place for rats. Archie stabbed at the fog with his sword, "There was a man on the telly talking about rats. He said we're never more than three feet away from a rat." He narrowed his eyes, held his stick like a bayoneted rifle and looked around. "There's probably millions all around us," he whispered, "but we just can't see them. Imagine if they all came at us at once? God. That must be the worst way to die, eh? I'd rather get bitten by a poisonous snake or burned alive or get eaten all in a oner by a lion or one of those plants or something than get eaten alive a wee bit at a time by rats."

They chucked rocks onto sheets of ice, shattered frozen puddles and icicles with their sticks. Joseph felt a sudden overwhelming urge to unburden. Archie was perfect. God and Jesus meant nothing to him,

"I went and told my Gran I've been Saved."

Joseph's family situation, the religious goings-on at the Hall; these weren't subjects of conversation. Neither did Archie express uncalled-for thoughts or opinions on Joseph's home life. And anyway, everybody Archie knew had "trouble at home".

"What do you mean?"

"It's when we ask Jesus – or God – into our hearts." It did feel odd, talking about this to Archie, but good as well, necessary even, "And then … that's you… *Saved.*"

Archie slurped syrupy Blackjack saliva back and forth between his teeth, like an old- timer cowboy chewing a lump of baccy and squirted a gloopy black jet onto the ice.

"Right." Archie had no idea what Joseph was on about, but what did that matter, "Well that's good then, eh? I'm going to have a strawberry, a lime and a *Blackjack* all thegether. It'll be like one of my mum's cocktails." He did a whiny mum's voice, "*It's just fruit juice Archie.*"

As they scrambled up the embankment, towards the main street, Archie impaled a lump of brown and white dog turd on the end of his stick. Joseph persevered, he needed him to know, "But I haven't."

"Haven't what?"

"Been Saved. I just said I was. But I haven't. Not yet."

The catastrophic nature of this lie was totally lost on Archie, but he understood that this *getting saved* business was important to Joseph, and that was more than enough,

"What is it you need to get saved from anyway?"

Hell. And he would have said it, if three ghost boys hadn't appeared, chanting, H*ello! Hello! It's one-eyed Holy Joe!*

The ghost boys ran like mad as soon as they saw who "one-eyed Holy Joe" was in the company of. Archie disappeared after them into the fog, wild-eyed and roaring, wielding his dog turd club like a caveman while the coward Joseph Kirkland, just stood there, helpless, hopeless, useless, as always – letting the fearless Archie fight his battles, as always. The caveman and ghost boy voices were muffled but audible.

"Aye run Lamont! You and your smelly wee pals!"

"No as smelly as you, ya fuckin' tink!"

"Watch it!"

"Ma jacket..."

"Ya clatty bastard!"

There were squeals and yells and more language and eventually Archie reappeared, laughing, flushed and energised, "I got Marty Logan on the leg." He chucked his turdless stick into a hedge, broke off a fresh one from an overhanging branch and carried on like nothing had happened, "So, you just need to say them words and that's it?" Joseph nodded. "Well just say them, then that'll be you." Archie smiled, "I'll go first if you want. Then I'll be Saved and all."

That was Archie all over, always wanting to fight Joseph's battles. Even this one.

"Jesus and God..." shouted Archie.

"No! You can't. It's not... you can't"

"Is it like a magic spell?"

"No, it's..." And as he was thinking *yes maybe it is like that, a powerful magic spell,* a pair of huge glowing yellow eyes like a giant low flying owl, swooped towards them, screeching to a halt inches from the boys, trapping them in its glare and from inside the giant owl came the deep honey-rich tones of a country western singer,

I'll tell the man to turn the jukebox way down low

And you can tell your friend there with you he'll have to go…

"You're in the middle of the road, ya eejits!" a man shouted over the music.

The big yellow eyes were the fog lights on Uncle Mathew's latest money maker, Kirkland's Mobile Grocers. Uncle Mathew was Gran and Grandpa's youngest, *sent to test a mother's love*, according to Gran. She passed that test too. She'd always love him no matter what. As would God and Jesus. Uncle Mathew had been saved.

"Matt, can I have a packet of crisps?" said a girl's voice in the back of the van.

Uncle Mathew had recognised who the bespectacled figure in the duffle coat was and he

hissed at the girl, "God sake!" the way he'd hissed at the girl in the lane, but he managed to switch his smile back on for Joseph, "No school the day?" Uncle Mathew saw Archie half in half out of the fog, "That manky wee nyaff a pal of yours, Joseph?"

Archie laughed a plausibly cruel laugh,

"What? Me and Holy Joe? Ye must be jokin'!"

"Want a skelp son?… No? Then beat it."

As Archie drifted away, another song by the same honey-voiced singer began: Th*is world is not my home, I'm just a-passing through…*

Uncle Mathew groaned, and jabbed the rewind button on the eight track several times. A thick greasy lock fell from his quiff and slid down over his forehead.

"So that's you, eh?" he said, fixing his errant lock in the mirror, adjusting the collar of his leather jacket, "Ready for the holy dookin'?" Joseph didn't respond. "Gran's been singing your praises. What d'you think she'd say if I told her

I'd seen you with Jimmy Truman's brat?" Joseph looked in the window, hoping to catch a glimpse of the girl in the back. Uncle Mathew thrust a tube of Smarties in his face, "There you go. Don't say I'm not good to you." The engine faltered. As he revved it up, he joined in the song, directing the words at Joseph:

"*And you can tell your friend there with you … he'll have to go…*"

As he drove off, full-blown laughter erupted from the front and back of the van. Archie re-emerged from the fog,

"God, it's like the rats. You think there's nobody there cos you can't see them, but they're everywhere, so they are." He sniggered in Joseph's ear, "D'ye hear the lassie in the back? That was Tommy Maxwell's big sister. She just turned fifteen in October …"

That was as far Archie got because Joseph Kirkland was away in a deep dwam and the *unco Joseph Kirkland* had taken his place. Archie watched and waited. It was fine. He'd seen it before. What Archie could not see were the white sparks, the wee electrical explosions going off at the back of Joseph's head that made him feel light-headed and *not quite there*; not an altogether unpleasant sensation. Then the lift doors opened, and there he was, the same old Joseph. The whole thing lasted seconds.

"Away with the fairies, so you were," said Archie, kicking a stone as hard he could, not caring where it landed. He kept kicking, at nothing now, just scuffing his foot off the ground. "You know, you don't need to do anything bad, so you don't. See if there's anything bad needing done, like knockin' sweets or comics and stuff, or like if you want a wee Matchbox car or something? I can do it for you. I can even set fire to stuff for you, so you don't have to. Unless you want to. Hardly anybody'll see us in this fog anyway." He moved backwards a few steps to prove the point. "And if they do we can be like spies, you know, just pretend you don't know me. *Archie who? Truman? Never heard of him.*"

Archie looked around for inspiration, "I know." And he took a small key from his shorts and presented it to Joseph, "Ta da!" As though it was the key to solving all Joseph's problems, "Let's go down the drains."

There were parts of Kilhaugh Joseph didn't know existed before Archie spilled out of Glasgow. For example, on the pavement in front of the shop windows on the main street were iron grilles that led down into the drains. Archie had barely set foot in the village when he discovered an entrance gate down by *Ramsay's* the newsagent. Some things Archie did on a daredevil whim, but he planned this carefully, breaking off the rusty old padlock and adding a new one he'd stolen from *Goodwin's* the ironmongers so only they could have access.

The gate grinded like a dungeon door. Inside it was high enough for two eleven-year-old boys to walk upright and light enough to make their way around without stumbling. Most days if you looked up through the grilles you'd see folk standing outside the shops. Today the fog hovered an inch or two below the grilles like a low cloud obscuring everything up above. The ground was a thick carpet of twigs, leaves, bottle tops, sweetie wrappers and fag ends. And in amongst it all, hopefully, money – loose change and small trinkets fallen from the pockets and purses of window-shoppers. Joseph and Archie spent fifteen silent minutes rummaging through the debris with their sticks. They found two thrupny bits, a sixpence, a shilling, three pennies, an unused bright red lipstick and a one-cent piece.

"That's American money, so it is," said Archie, and they both looked up as if expecting to see a pair of cowboy boots standing right there on the grille above. "What actually happens to you?" he said, painting a red lipstick gash on the back of his hand, "when you get saved?"

Joseph could just not answer. Archie wouldn't have pursued it. He was just being a pal, making conversation. But weren't you meant to spread the Good News? *What actually happens to you, when you get Saved?* Yes, he could answer that. There was no ambiguity.

On several occasions Joseph had stood with Gran, Uncle Andrew and the others, on the street outside the Hall in Templeton – it was a pointless exercise in Kilhaugh – stopping passers-by, handing out tracts with titles like, *Stop Friend! Think! Jesus is Coming Soon!*

(Are You Ready to meet Him?) and *Where Will You Spend Eternity?*

"If you're Saved, you go to Heaven when you die," said Joseph, applying a lipstick gash to his own hand, "And if you're not, you... might go to Hell."

Might? What was this *might*? There was no *might* about it? *Sorry.*

"Right," said Archie turning this over in his head, "But... what about when you're still alive? Folk that are saved I mean... do they... look different?"

Joseph thought about Jenny. Yes, her behaviour had changed right after being Saved, but... he couldn't put it into words.

"Maybe," he said, "I don't know. I don't think so. I think you look the same."

Archie looked disappointed, like he'd just sat through a rubbish ending at the pictures. Maybe that's what he was thinking, *This is rubbish, this religion.* Joseph must try harder,

"Some folk call it being 'born again' but we don't say that, we just say..."

"*Born again*? I know them! We had some near my bit in Glasgow, so we did. They had long hair and rainbow tee shirts. Like hippies. My Grannie calls them *happy clappies*."

Joseph footered with his spectacles, he needed to keep a hold of the thread,

"After you're Saved it's like... you're *born again*... and then... then you belong to the Lord... that's God... or Jesus... and then after... you're not the same... and everything you do... or say... or think... *everything*... is for the Lord, always... till he calls you home."

That uncontrollable convulsive excitement once again began bubbling up inside Archie,

"Know what that's like, Joseph? It's like… it's like… it's like that film, *Invasion of the Body Snatchers*, so it is. Mind I tellt you?" Archie came closer, speaking in the hushed tones of someone passing on a state secret,

"These things like big peapods arrive in this town from outer space. And they end up all over the place, under hedges, in the street, in your house, under your bed, in your wardrobe, in the airing cupboard, behind the settee, even in the toilet. Everywhere. All over the world as well. And you don't even know they're there. But when you're near one you get all tired and you end up falling asleep, even if you don't want to, you can't stop yourself. And when you're asleep, you start to dry up and shrivel away to nothing and die, like… mind when my newts escaped and I found them weeks later under the bed and in the chest of drawers? As dry as leaves? Mind? And empty? Like their insides had been sucked out? Like that. But at the same time as you're asleep and shrivelling up, inside this big peapod *another you* is growing. A kind of *vegetable you*, all covered in gooey slabbery stuff, and it's identical to *the real you,* except it's nude, but that doesn't matter because you're as dried up and dead as a dry dead newt now. And then when the thing gets out of its pod, it cleans off all the slabbers and puts on your clothes and then… that's it! That's you. It looks like you and it's even got your voice and everything. But it's not you. But everybody thinks it's you. The thing is as well, you don't notice anything is weird because… because… because you're one of the vegetable people as well! See what I mean? That could be a wee bit like being *born again,* so it could? A wee bit like being *saved*," and seeing a look of alarm on Joseph's face, Archie added, "But in a good way."

"Does everyone in the film become one of these… vegetable… people?"

"Some folk who aren't aliens try to kid on they're aliens to survive. But the real aliens just know. They've got these special powers. They can talk to each other just with their thoughts. And they can tell if you're a human just kidding on you're an alien. I don't mind how exactly, but they just can."

Archie had got straight to the heart of it – of exactly what Joseph was frightened of: being replaced with a vegetable version of himself. More or less.

"What happens, in the end?"

"Ach it was one of those films that ends before you find out. But I mind there's this one man and he's trying to warn the folk that are left, those that are still human, about what's happening. You see him standing in the middle of traffic, and his eyes are all mad and staring, like this..." Archie did the mad staring eyes extremely well, "... and he's stopping cars and lorries and screaming at folk, trying to tell them about the aliens. *They're after us! They're here! You're Next!* and all that. But they just think he's a loony or drunk or something and of course the harder he tries, the madder he looks and the less folk believe him. And then... that's it. It's really good but."

"What about that one there?" said a man's voice.

Joseph and Archie froze. They were directly below the grille outside Hambledon's Television and Radio Rentals.

"No. That's far too big," said a woman's voice. "We don't want it to dominate the room."

It was Mister and Mrs Sangster. He hadn't reached the Robert Munday Home after all.

"We could get a cabinet built like yon one Samuel had made for Sarah."

It was odd to hear Gran and Grandpa referred to as *Sarah* and *Samuel.* Gran had allowed a television set into the house in 1953 so they could watch Billy Graham's live Scottish Crusades, but as Auntie Abi explained, it had never been more than an unwelcome visitor,

"It's the same nine-inch Ekco they've got the now. Oh your Gran did not like it one iota. Honestly, she'd gaup at it like it was some disgusting, dangerous beast, *Dad will you do something about that… monstrosity?* So your Grandpa builds this big solid wood cabinet around it, hangs a pair of heavy doors on it. Very proud of that cabinet, so he was. Then a few days later she comes home, finds your Uncle Mathew watching football on it. Well, you can imagine. *Dad, I want a lock put on that thing*! So your Grandpa goes and fits this big sturdy lock on it. Of course she's still not satisfied, and flings a green throw over it and then sticks a big yellow vase on top of that. And that was her, happy. The beast had been tamed… or disguised."

The sway of Mister and Mrs Sangster's long heavy coats shifted the fog a little so you could see the soles of their shoes. You could also see up Mrs Sangster's skirt.

"I can see her knickers," Archie whispered, and snorted a loud snottery snigger.

"Did you hear that?" said Mrs Sangster, gathering in her skirt.

"Is there somebody down there?" said Mister Sangster, stamping on the grille.

"Everything okay?"

A third pair of shoes had arrived on the grille.

"I think there's somebody down the drains, Duncan," said Mrs Sangster.

PC Carmichael was down on his knees now, face pressed against the grille.

"I can't see anything. Keep an eye here. I'll away down and have a gander."

Archie was already at the entrance waving like mad at Joseph, *hurry up, hurry up,* but Joseph was trapped on the wrong side of the grille with no way to get past without the Sangsters seeing him. Anyway it was too late, Carmichael would be at the entrance any second, so now Archie was waving like mad for Joseph to go back again, deeper into the mirk.

Archie ran straight into Carmichael. As he knew he would. He tried – half-heartedly – to wriggle away. He nearly managed it. With his scrawny wee frame and greasy anorak, he wasn't easy to get a grip of.

"How many times have I warned you?"

"I dropped my money down the drain sir."

"Oh aye," he dug his fingers into Archie's stick-thin arm, "what money's that then?"

"My mum gave me money for messages."

Carmichael was hurting him but so what. He didn't flinch. He showed his share of the coins.

"Messages?" He laughed, a mean laugh, "Aye, right, you mean drink? Who's with you?" "Nobody."

"Nobody?" He looked into the drains, saw nothing, and didn't fancy going in to find out, "Right, well get up them stairs. And I'm warning you. See if I catch you here again, it'll be Kilhaugh Borstal you'll be heading for." Archie showed no fear so Carmichael slapped him, "You hear me? I've my eye on you. I know all about you and your family. Okay?" Still Archie did not react, so Carmichael slapped him again, harder. "I said, *Okay*?"

It wasn't the first time he'd been slapped, it wouldn't be the last. Yes it hurt but he couldn't care less. He'd had far worse. He could kick Carmichael in the balls, right now, it would be so easy, but there was wee Maggie to consider, and Joseph, so he chose the far more difficult option,

"Okay," he said, shoulders shaking now, allowing the tears and snot to run down his face.

"Good," said Carmichael, satisfied with what he believed to be a victory, "Now beat it."

Archie ran. Carmichael closed the gate, snapped shut the padlock and pocketed the key.

"Just some wee toerag from the scheme."

"Thank you Duncan," said Mister Sangster, "The Overspill could be running around like Apaches in this fog and we'd never even know."

"It's a rascal's paradise right enough. Hear Templeton's fine though. Seems it's just Kilhaugh that's got it."

Carmichael continued on his beat and the Sangsters, having decided that they could not justify a new television set, large or small, left their spot outside *Hambledon's*.

The fog closed in, descending an inch or two into the drain. But it was okay. Archie would be back soon with a spare key. Or something. Some plan. The Books of the Bible, that's what he should be doing. Taking every available opportunity. But he couldn't, not here. It was too silent – the kind of silence where you hear things. Sure enough something rustled. A leaf probably. Or his own feet shuffling. Or a rat. He'd never seen rats down here, but it was near Agnew's so why wouldn't there be? Some of them were enormous, like that one Archie killed.

He'd dropped a boulder on it from the bridge. Joseph felt sick but still he'd clambered down the embankment to see it up close. That rat was on its back, all its insides out, its yellow teeth still set in a snarl. They looked at it for ages, poking its entrails with sticks, just to see.

"That's what *we're* like inside," said Archie, "We're just animals so we are. Just meat."

Archie will come back when the coast is clear. That's exactly the kind of thing he'd say as well, *I'll lie low till the coast is clear.* Like Kit Mossman the black hat outlaw in Grandpa's cowboy books, who was really a good guy. Archie was an outlaw too. And a good guy. He'd lay down his life for you, take a bullet for you. Like Kit Mossman. Like Jesus Christ our Lord, who died on the cross so that we... Joseph felt that familiar shiver of fear. He opened the book of monkey-king matches, struck one and extinguished it on his tongue. A wee soreness. Nothing much.

When Gran was wee, her mum had held a match under the tip of her tongue,

"For uttering a profanity," she said proudly – of the punishment, not the profanity – "And she made me thank her for it. And I did thank her for it. And I never did it again."

He was cold and tired. How long had Archie been away? Minutes? Hours? Was it dark yet? It was hard to say down here. Maybe he should shout. He could make up a story about how he ended up here. That would be no problem for a liar of Joseph Kirkland's stature. That might even be part of Archie's plan, *I made Joseph do it*, he'd say. *I locked him in there.* But the Coward Joseph Kirkland never shouted. Maybe he *couldn't* shout. Maybe he didn't have it, the shouting muscle, or it had withered through lack of use.

He thought about *The Invasion of the Body Snatchers*, about waking up and not being himself anymore and how that might actually be okay because if he was a totally different person, he wouldn't *know* he was a totally different person. He'd just...

The first thing was the whining, then the paw pads and the pink tongue tip poking through the grille, then the amber eyes, and finally a couple of short sharp urgent yelps. *Come on! Come on!* like one of those heroic Saturday Morning Pictures dogs – *Lassie or Rin Tin Tin* – that crossed mountains and raging torrents to save their masters and mistresses from all manner of dreadful perils, *Get yourself together boy, it's time to make your escape!* Then the black dog was gone, the padlock was hanging loose and the gate was wide open.

On the way home he heard more gossipy whispering from behind the curtain of fog,

I hear the Kirkland boy's been "saved" / And how would you know that?/ A wee bird / A wee bird perched on a stool at the telephone exchange?/ Wee sowl / She's a thrawn one that so she is / Sarah Kirkland? Och away. / A Holy Willie if ever there was one / I was at school with Sarah. / She's a good heart so she has. / Aye, and a scowl that could curdle milk...

The laughter and the admonishment faded away, and then a little further on,

Somebody said the tinkers are back / At this time of the year? /That's odd / What's not odd these days? / You still stocking up / You could build a house with the tins I have in that cupboard / You think it'll come to that?/ Who knows? / We'll be the last to know / Four minutes / For goodness sake, what are we meant to do in four minutes? / The Okey Cokey?

There was the vaguest outline of a budgie cage hanging on a stand on the lane, just a soft pencil sketch. It was clean as a whistle, complete with fresh lining paper, millet spray, cuttlefish bone and a box of *Trill* on the pavement below. Joseph looked up to the sky, or to where the sky used to be, for signs of life.

CHAPTER SEVEN

Fly Away Peter ...

"Why is the budgie cage out on the lane? I'll tell you why the budgie cage is out on the lane. Because a certain somebody was smoking their pipe out the window this morning and that same somebody forgot to close the cage door."

And all this out the side of her mouth for Grandpa's benefit. She needn't have bothered. Grandpa was slumped in his chair, his hearing aids in the bedroom, his teeth in the bathroom and his thoughts somewhere else entirely. His eyes were pink and wet, "Wee boy."

"In a world of his own, so he is. The pair of yous are."

"Pretty wee boy."

"Ach him and his filthy weeds. Umpteen times I said this would happen." She turned to Grandpa, "Didn't I say?" then to nobody in particular, "Well. That's that. That's what happens. You can take it to the jumble sale. There's no point it staying here." The fingers of her right hand wrestled with the left, tying themselves in knots, "It'll just upset him. I've cleaned it. No doubt somebody'll want a budgie cage. Somebody as daft as him."

"I could go and look for him."

She stared at him, not because of what Joseph had said, but because her grandson saying anything at all unprompted was such a rare occurrence.

"Outside? In that? You can't see the end of your nose in that."

"Maybe he'll come back."

"A wee tame thing like a budgie? Out there? In the wild? They're not from here you know, they're from… ach… well wherever it is, it's warmer than this."

"Australia."

"Oh. Australia indeed?" She folded her arms under her bosom, lifted her nose, "And where'd you learn that? Your Miss *O'Donnell* no doubt?" And then immediately added, "See that nice plate I got from your cousin Sam? From when he was in *Hong Kong*," as though name dropping foreign places was what this conversation was all about.

The streetlamp came on as usual but it could barely make a dent in the fog. Joseph looked for a while, even took off his specs in case that might help. At one point he thought he saw a flash of yellow, but it was his eyes playing tricks, showing him the thing he wanted to see.

Come back Peter.

He spread out his Scripture texts on the candlewick bedspread, scripture side down. *Texts* were the size of bubblegum cards. On the front was a picture: a locomotive, a sailing ship, a flower, etcetera, and on the back, a line or two of Scripture. *No! The Scripture is on the front – the picture's on the back. Remember! It's about the Scripture, not the picture.* Joseph had over a hundred, which he kept in a barley sugar tin Grandpa had given him. Most of them he'd got at Sunday School or the *Sunbeams Club* as a reward for a Bible reading or a right answer in the Bible quiz. Others were swaps and a few he'd inherited. He closed his eyes and picked one at random, like he did with Bible verses. It was one of the ways God or Jesus told you things you needed to know. He chose a ship, the *Cutty Sark* – also the name of the scantily dressed witch in "Tam O' Shanter" – *weel done Cutty Sark* – which he should not be remembering. He squinted at the line of Scripture and put it back, wishing he hadn't seen it.

"What did it say?" It was Jenny, Uncle Andrew and Auntie Ishbel's daughter. "Dad says if it was up to him he'd have Scripture on both sides and do away with pictures altogether."

She was leaning against the door, strumming her bottom lip with her finger. She was four and a bit years older, desperate to leave her childhood far behind and in need of a member of the opposite sex to practise on. Joseph would just have to do. She let down her ponytail,

"It's always so hot in here," she said as she languidly undid the top three butterfly buttons on her blouse. Then she languidly sat beside him on the bed – the perfume she wore was so sweet and thick he could taste it – languidly tousled his hair, languidly ran her finger down the back of his neck, making him shiver, making him feel awkward and uncomfortable, taking great delight in all of this, as was her way these days.

"I think it was..." she wiggled her fingers over the texts like she was working a spell. "... that one." She turned over the *Cutty Sark*, and read the text, "Psalms 31,18; *Let the lying lips be put to silence*. In-ter-es-ting. Pick another. "

"I don't want to play anymore."

"You don't want to *play* anymore? Is that what you think this is? Play? Tut tut.." She lay her pale pink forearm against his swarthier forearm, "Look." She waited for a reaction, but Joseph remained blank, and eventually she laughed. It was just Jenny being Jenny. She was older, that's all, and a girl, and that was that.

Through in the living room, Gran was on the harmonium: *Rock of Ages, cleft for me / Let me hide myself in Thee...*

Jenny hummed along as she walked around the room, a desultory walk, all swaying hips, tilted head and affected disinterest, sighing and wiping non-existent dust from the scripture samplers, riffling through his *Heroes of the Cross* books with mischievous witchy fingers, still trying out this new body of hers, seeing what it all felt like, seeing what it could do, what it was capable of. She did a half spin and stopped, poised, looking over her shoulder. Grandpa's imaginary cameras were trained on her now,

"Gran said you've to do your Books of the Bible." And

before he'd a chance to respond she took a breath and rattled through them, Old and New, at breakneck speed:

"*Genesis Exodus Leviticus and Numbers Deuteronomy Joshua Judges* Ruth and *Sam-u-el Sam-u-el Kings Kings Chronicles and Chronicles Ezra Nehemiah Esther Job Psalms Proverbs Ecclesiastes Song of Solomon Isaiah Jeremiah Lamentations Ezekiel Daniel Hosea Joel Amos Obadiah Jonah Micah Nahum, Habakkuk Zephaniah Haggai Zechariah Malachi Mathew Mark Luke and John Acts Romans Corinthians Corinthians Galatians Ephesians Philippians Colossians Thessalonians Thessalonians Timothy Timothy Titus Philemon Hebrews James Peter Peter John John John Jude and Revelations*."

Joseph's heart sank. How would he ever …

"Peter's gone," he said, a clumsy attempt at changing the subject.

"Peter?"

"He flew away."

She shrugged, *so what, who cares*, and knelt down, her face close to his, "So, Joseph Kirkland… you've been Saved."

"Do you think he might still be alive?"

Gran had moved on to something a little more upbeat, *What a friend we have in Jesus / All our sins and grief to bear*.

Jenny ignored his question. She put her hands on his knees, and spoke to him like he was a wee primary one, "Know what happens when Mister Agnew Baptises you?"

"Yes."

"Yes?"

"I've seen it getting done."

"*Seeing* isn't the same as actually being in it," she moved in a little closer. "For starters, he holds you under the water longer than you think. A *lot* longer."

He must have heard about this before. Otherwise why would he have dreamt it?

"You know a girl actually died getting Baptised?"

A wave of nausea washed over him, "No."

"Years ago in Templeton, nobody you know. There was

loose wire or something in the pool. I'm not sure which bit killed her – the electrocution or the drowning. The preacher had rubber waders like Mister Agnew wears, so he was all right. Must have been horrible. Like getting the electric chair. They say that smoke and flames shoot out all the holes in your body and your eyes pop out. Don't mention it though. Folk still get really upset about it. Some folk think it was just an accident, but other folk say it was because the girl had lied about being Saved. That's a terrible sin, so it is. Imagine? Lying about something like that? God can do that. Drown you. Electrocute you. Make you burst into flames. Anything. Just like that..." She snapped her fingers, "To teach you a lesson. Or teach other folk a lesson. The Bible's full of it, lessons being learned and not being learned."

Gran shouted from the lobby, "That's your tea ready!"

"I'm just coming, Gran!" Jenny said, and she quickly did up her buttons, tied back her hair, and switched off her woman.

Joseph crammed the electrocuted lying girl image into his *Cupboard of Terrible Unthinkable Thoughts* along with the countless other things he avoided thinking about, such as the possible Damnation of Archie who was also *at that age*, and wee Maggie, when she reached that age. And also, if Jenny knew about Joseph's lie – how could she know? – then how many other folk knew or were suspicious? Gran? Could they tell when someone was just pretending? Was it a special power, like Archie's *Body Snatchers*? He put the texts back into the barley sugar tin. He would have liked a barley sugar right now, something sweet to take this bitter taste away.

After tea Gran and Jenny went off to the Friday night Bible Meeting. "I've marked the passages I want you to read to him," said Gran, half in, half out the front door. Joseph nodded. "You and your nodding," she said.

Jenny laughed, "Noddy! That's what we should call him."

"One of these days that head's going to fall off with all that nodding," said Gran, ignoring Jenny's reference to popular children's literature. "You've a tongue in your head, learn to use it, properly. And mind get him to drink: water, tea, juice, it doesn't matter."

Grandpa's funny "chai" song was playing in Joseph's head... *Heh chai wallah / You're a real swell fella / With your ye-lla umbr-ella...* as he made him his special milky sweet tea, pouring it back and forth from mug to beaker to froth it up and cool it down... *And your awfie nippy nippy / Sweet ma-sa-la chai!* But Grandpa was in no fit state to drink tea, even from a child's beaker.

There were no passages marked in Grandpa's Bible. Gran did that sometimes – think she'd done something, then get angry at Joseph or Grandpa for disobeying her or forgetting, then get angry at herself when she realised it was she who'd forgotten. Still, he ought to read something so he opened the Bible at random. It was the opening page of *The Book of Nahum*. He knew nothing of *The Book of Nahum*, it had never come up at Sunday School or Bible Quiz.

"The Burden of Nineveh..." was as far as he got when Grandpa tapped him on the wrist,

"Howdy pardner!" he said, his voice thin and wheezy. He attempted a naughty conspiratorial wink but his eyelid was glued with sticky sleep.

Joseph felt a twinge of annoyance. Grandpa should be helping him, not leading him astray, even if he was sick. *Be careful of the company you keep.* Did he need to be careful of Grandpa's company as well now? He should just read him the Bible anyway. It would do them both some good. But how could Joseph resist?

He reached deep under the mattress and pulled out a lurid library paperback with a black- clad cowboy on the cover, legs astride, hands on his holsters, standing against a backdrop of a huge desert sunrise,

Joseph began:

UNDER A BIG BAD SKY
A Kit Mossman Story
by Zachary T. Mayfield

The oven-hot sun was hanging high and everything in Little Fury lay silent and still except for the buzz of an occasional horsefly. Sheriff Skinner was doing what he always did on a Sunday, watching life go by from the comfort of an old rocking chair on the porch. But when he saw Miss Victoria Burnham and Miss Sarah Newman arrive in their buggy at a speed these old spinsters had never travelled in their lives, his lawman instincts told him that they were bringing a mess of bad news with them,

"Ladies," he said, tipping his hat, "What brings you to Little Fury?"

Grandpa had his hearing aids in, but still he watched Joseph's mouth.

Miss Burnham burst into tears, leaving a shaking Miss Newman to do the talking, "Sheriff Skinner, I know you think we're nothing but a couple of eccentric old fools but we have never in our entire lives come to you for help, so please give us the time of day, because what we have to say might affect us all."

"Oh for goodness sake, Sarah," said Miss Burnham, through her tears, "forget the penny dreadful melodrama and spit it out."

"Poor wee birdie," said Grandpa and Joseph carried on:

"Sheriff," she continued, "this morning, we decided to go down to the river a little ways to bathe our feet, it being such a fine morning and all..."

"I don't think the Sheriff need know our bathing habits," interrupted Miss Burnham.

Miss Newman gave her a hard stare and carried on, "We saw three men take their horses to water. Charles, I swear on papa's grave, one of them was Babe Reno. The others were Wilbur Driscoll and Cyrus Hatfield."

Charles Skinner's heart missed a beat. This wasn't possible. Reno, Driscoll and Hatfield were in the county jail waiting to be hung for the killing of Tom Skinner, the Sheriff's own brother and Jacob Newman, Miss Sarah's nephew.

"Now look here ladies, I ain't doubtin' you saw somethin', but if the men you saw are who you say they are, then they must be ghosts..."

"Joseph," shouted Gran from the lobby, "are you in your pyjamas?"

He shoved the cowboy book back under the mattress and grabbed the Bible: "God is jealous, and the LORD revengeth; the LORD revengeth, and is furious; the Lord will take vengeance on his adversaries ..."

He looked up at Gran, feigning surprise at her being there.

"Remind me again ..."

"*The Book of Nahum*," he said, "Chapter one, verse two," as though quite familiar with it.

Gran looked at the pair of them, not knowing what to think. This grandson of hers, who she would never fathom; this husband of hers, of forty-eight years, toothless, deaf and draining away. There were other thoughts too, but she shook her head to get rid of them, as Joseph was wont to do, and shuffled out the room.

"The cowboys," sighed Grandpa, "That's us, eh son?" He lifted his hand like it was a Colt 45, "Pieu... pieu..." the sound of distant gunshots.

Joseph did his Gentle Jesus, adding Peter to the list. Tomorrow he'd look. Amazing things happened sometimes. *Heroes of the Cross* was full of tales of survival against the odds. And what about the miracles? Lazarus and all those blind folk, lepers, mutes and cripples? If he found Peter, that would be a sign. And if he didn't that would also be a sign.

There was a light rat-a-tat-tat of gravel against the window. He'd been wondering when Archie would make an appearance.

He was standing under the street lamp, in his pyjamas, shabby dressing gown and slippers, immune to the cold. At least he had slippers on this time. When he saw Joseph he did that wee skip and dance of his, for no reason except it was late, there was fog, he was alive and he was happy to see Joseph safe and well, so how could he not skip and dance?

"Look at me!" he whispered, moving in slow motion like he was floating, all smiles, till he bumped into the budgie cage almost knocking it over, and swallowed a curse word.

"Peter flew away," said Joseph.

"Oh no!" Archie looked around as though Peter might be right there beside him.

"I'm going to look tomorrow."

"I'll go and look the now."

Hold on, I'll come with you.

But of course Joseph did not say that, and Archie had long stopped asking Joseph to accompany him on his nocturnal escapades. There was no point and he didn't like to make Joseph feel bad. Archie's mum and dad probably had no idea he was out and about at night, and even if they did… But Joseph Kirkland was a different story. Archie unhooked the cage from its stand: "I'll take it for a wander. He'll maybe see it and fly inside. *Home sweet home,*" he said in a wee high voice, and now he did a bird dance, flapping his hands and chirruping away. "How'd you get out the drains? I came back with the other key but you were away."

"Somebody opened it."

"Who? Carmichael?"

"No, I don't think so…"

"But there was only one other key. Whoever it was must've picked the lock. God I'd do anything to learn how to pick locks. I wonder who it was."

Joseph really did want to tell Archie all about his encounters with the black dog, and the bearded, smoking cowboy in the tweed jacket,

"I don't know," he said, the *Liar Joseph Kirkland.*

CHAPTER EIGHT

The Kilhaugh Mappa Mundi

It was the wee small hours and Joseph was still wide awake. His Bible was everywhere, glowing in the corner of his open eyes, burning white hot through his closed eyelids. His soul was troubled, no two ways about it, yet the one book that promised to ease those troubles was the one book he was too scared to look at. What he wanted right now was a simple story with simple earthly obstacles and straightforward earthly resolutions; a *Kit Mossman* story, a *Lassie* film, something from *The Hotspur*.

He got out his crayons and pencils and unfurled his would-be map of Kilhaugh on the floor, keeping it flat with a *Hero of the Cross* on each corner. *Heroes of the Cross* was a series of biographies of the great Scottish missionaries, Sunday School prizes, *Presented to Joseph Kirkland for Perfect Attendance, Presented to Joseph Kirkland for Bible Reading* and *Presented to Joseph Kirkland* for other Hall-related good deeds and accomplishments. Of course they were not *just* adventure stories, set in far-off lands filled with tropical diseases, dangerous beasts and heathen cannibals, though there was no denying that they were that as well. One or two were weren't so unlike the *Tarzan* serial at the Saturday Morning Pictures, especially *David Livingstone* with his fighting lions and freeing slaves and exploring dark interiors and all. They wouldn't help him sleep though. There was too much Bible in them.

Sorry.

His Kilhaugh map was almost blank, just a big potato-shaped village outline and two sets of parallel squiggles running diagonally across, representing the Lele and the main street. Miss O'Donnell had shown them lots of different maps: real, fictional and somewhere in between – the *Henricus Martellus* map that Columbus used to discover the New World, Daniel Defoe's *Robinson Crusoe – Island of Despair* map, the *Hundred Acre Wood* map from *Winnie the Pooh*, the map that Captain Scott used on his *Terra Nova* expedition to the South Pole, and the medieval *Hereford mappa mundi.*

"This map was made in the time of the Crusades," said Miss O'Donnell, "but it's not so much a map of the world as *a map of the imagination*. You see at this time people hadn't travelled much of the world, they had no idea what was out there, so they had to make it up, or at least take an educated guess. What I'm trying to say is, *geographically*, the map isn't correct by today's scientific standards, not at all, but as a *spiritual* map, a *map of the soul*, well, that's something else. Can anybody tell me what's at the centre of this map?"

They scratched, yawned and fidgeted, but Joseph was immersed. This was his territory.

"Jerusalem."

"*Jerusalem*. That's right Joseph. Jerusalem was the spiritual centre of the world back then, and not just for the Christians who made this map, but also for the Muslim folk they were fighting, and the Jews, and lots of other religious groups as well."

A *Spiritual Map*. This is exactly what Joseph needed right now. A *Map of the Soul*. The first thing to go into his map should be the Hall, Joseph's very own *Jerusalem*, right in the centre. He drew a box with a cross on top, then he rubbed out the cross in case Gran mistook for a Catholic chapel. It was better plain anyway, more like the real thing. He coloured it yellow, the nearest to a gold crayon he could find.

Miss O'Donnell had actually been to the Holy Land,

"Do you know," she said in the quiet voice she used when she wanted to reel you in, "that underneath Jerusalem, there are all these secret tunnels that that were used back in the time of the Bible, and in one of them there's a pool where King Solomon himself was anointed." She turned out the lights, switched on the slide projector, and there it was, larger than life on the classroom wall, King Solomon's pool. It was like he was looking at it through a window, it was so vivid, so close, like he could climb inside and bathe in it.

Gran had said only the Hall, the Doctor's, the Police Station and the School should go in, but if that was all he did the map would remain almost empty. He drew a row of wee boxes for the shops – even Gran used the shops – and after a moment or two of *Should I? Shouldn't I?* added a dotted line for the drainage tunnels. Only he and Archie would know what it meant. Around the potato-shaped perimeter he added lots of wee arrow-head trees: the low woods and high woods above the braes that surrounded Kilhaugh. Beyond all that, in the margins, outside Kilhaugh proper, Joseph wasn't allowed to go.

"This area of the mappa mundi," said Miss O'Donnell's, her eyes all wide with the wonder she wanted them to feel, "is known as *The Sea of Darkness* – the dangerous uncharted territories, filled with dog-headed cavemen, like werewolves, and headless warriors and so on. You'll find all sorts of strange terrifying creatures in these early maps; dragons, demons, cannibals, boiling oceans and raging infernos." She looked around; *werewolves, dragons, demons and cannibals* had grabbed their attention. "Back then folk were afraid of what lay beyond their own everyday world – most folk still are – but they were even more afraid for their souls, of what lay beyond this life. So these fires, these creatures, were expressions of those fears too. Are you all still with me?" Joseph was. One hundred per cent. "Why don't you draw some strange things in your maps? Things that you find frightening."

Drawing wasn't his best thing, but what if he drew the dense grey fog? There would be terrible creatures too but because of the fog you wouldn't see them properly. And *Body Snatcher* pods! Why not? What could be more terrifying? At the top of the map, above the Hall, he drew a big cloud with sun rays shooting out of it: *Heaven.* And at the foot of the map – what else – the fires of Hell. The map should be colourful: blue for the Lele, green for the woods, yellow for Heavenly sunbeams and those good places that the Heavenly sunbeams shone upon. Red for fire. He shivered, not with fear but with excitement. Something big and important was starting.

He started drawing these arched doorways: two big ones on the outskirts of the uncharted territories; some wee ones next to places like Hambledon's Television & Radio Rentals, Faulkner's Public House, Moretti's Cafe and Kilhaugh Borstal and a big fancy arched doorway at the bottom, leading into the fire. He coloured these red, because these were *Gateways to Hell* – places that tempted and corrupted and took you far away from God. Yes, there would be an awful lot of red archways on this map.

CHAPTER NINE

The Munificence of Mrs Merryweather

"Not again. Oh for goodness sake. Of all the times to wet the bed! And Benjamin Mutch on his way! As we speak!" She ran around in her exclamation-marked panic with her carpet sweeper and her duster, "He's coming in from Templeton! On foot! In this weather! The man must be well into his eighties! Mister Sangster's just off the phone. Mrs Sangster taken not well! Worried it's catching. Honestly, see that fog. Mind you're well wrapped up. And there's me just after saying *oh that's fine, Benjamin Mutch can have Joseph's bed, Joseph can have the settee.* At least the rubber sheet was on, or we'd have the mattress to contend with. Not that I'd say no to the man. Of course not. But och, look at the state of this place. I'd be black affronted if he was to arrive right now." Then remembering the sin of pride, added, "Aye well, take me as you find me, that's my motto. But I could just have done without the pair of you and all your falderals. Oh, have you not heard the latest development? Your Grandpa's decided he's not getting out of bed for his breakfast this morning, says he's *not hungry*. Not hungry. When's the last time he *was* hungry? Ach… "

Joseph could've been no more than a year old when Benjamin Mutch had last passed through Kilhaugh. He was famous among Gospel Hall folk, and beyond. *Scotland's answer to Billy Graham*, said some, though Gran shunned the very premise of such comparisons, *They're preachers, not personalities*. Benjamin Mutch hailed from the North East, or so folk said, but there was a lot of mystery surrounding him. He was said to be an ex-fisherman, an ex-alcoholic, an ex-convict and a legendary evangelist. He wandered from town to town, village to village, the length and breadth of the country, spreading the Good News, giving his testimony and surviving on the hospitality of labouring brothers and their families. It was after hearing his testimony that a young Auntie Ishbel, a once staunch Catholic, was Saved and converted, and a hitherto impossible marriage to Uncle Andrew became possible.

"Aye, say what you like about Catholics," Gran liked to say, "but see once they're Saved? My, they could teach us all a thing or two about faith, so they could, unlike a few others I might mention," and she did, "like your wishy-washy Episcopalians to name but one, or your once-a-week Church of Scotlanders; neither one thing nor another, so they're not."

Would Benjamin Mutch have the same transformational effect on Joseph? It was as though he had been sent. Maybe he had. Why not? Is that not how these things happened?

Prophets, dreamers and messengers; there was no end of them in the Scriptures.

"It's good he's staying though," said Gran, "He can speak to dad. That's something that's needs doing, just to be..." She was thinking aloud, a habit that Joseph had inherited, and was quite discomfited when she saw him staring at her. "What have I said about you and your gawping? Anyways, he'll be giving his testimony at four, a special one for the children, so don't forget." She went to the airing cupboard for clean sheets, "Och no, they're still not dry," and went straight back into her panic, "I can't hang them outside in that weather!" It was a desperate situation and it called for a desperate measure, "You'll need to go next door and ask Mrs Merryweather."

What was the world like before it became wrapped in this icy grey shroud? It was only two days but already it felt like this was how Kilhaugh had always been, would always be. He wondered if Archie had found Peter. It was a possibility. You never knew with Archie.

He knocked on Mrs Merryweather's door several times before she eventually appeared. She was bleary-eyed, her dressing gown flung on, but her usual cheeriness was undiminished.

"It's yersel son, whit can ah dae ye fur?" and she immediately collapsed into a phlegmy coughing fit. Joseph waited till the worst of it was over.

"My Gran says I've to ask you if you've any spare sheets."

If she was surprised or guessed the reason, she didn't show it: "Of course son, come away in."

Joseph occasionally went round to Mrs Merryweather's to pick up or hand in parcels and sometimes washing if Gran or Mrs Merryweather was out and it was raining. Although she never said anything, Gran didn't like Mrs Merryweather taking in her washing. *Half an hour in the Merryweather house and they smell like they've never been washed at all.* Gran rarely went round herself, and if she did, maybe to hand in a bowl of soup if Mrs Merryweather was ill, she wouldn't cross the threshold. It was an awkward neighbourliness then, on Gran's part, but neighbourliness nonetheless. Gran and Mrs Merryweather had known each other since they were teenagers, but Gran had never once been inside her house, despite there being a long-standing open invitation. No such invitation had ever been extended to Mrs Merryweather. Joseph himself had never once been further than the front step.

"Ye cannae stay ootside in that," she said, and when he hesitated, "Ah'll no eat ye," she laughed and coughed, "honest tae God."

The first thing that hit him was the smell, like a waft from out the front door of *Faulkner's*. And something else. He made a face, didn't wipe it off fast enough, and felt bad about it, but Mrs Merryweather didn't seem to take offence.

"Ah know, stinks tae high heaven, so it does. That's cats fur ye. Have ye met *Snap*, *Crackle* and *Pop*? Daft names, ah know. They'd be runnin in tae see ye, but they're sleepin'. That's aw they dae since that fog arrived. Ah wid tae if ah could, just take tae ma bed till it aw blaws ower. Ah tell ye son, if yer tae come back as an animal come back as a cat. No a care in the world." She looked beyond the front door, "Aye, there'll be nae washin days fur a while eh? Pit yer sheets oot in that, ye'll be bringin in sheets a cardboard." There was more laughing and coughing. "Whit size ye after?"

"It's for *my* bed," and then, as if it might matter, "Benjamin Mutch is staying."

"Aye, so ah heard," and she added a wee Grandpa-style conspiratorial nod and a wink. "Ye're in fur a rare treat there, so ye are. Ah play fur the other side, but even ah was impressed last time he wis here. Saw him in the street. Oh my…" She puckered her lips, narrowed her eyes, folded her arms beneath her bosom and gave a wee shake of her hips, all in one fluid, slightly inappropriate movement, "Very Charlton Heston, so he wis. Till he opened his mouth. Ah could barely understand a word he wis sayin… vera braid." All this drew a blank look from Joseph. "Right, sheets. Away and sit yersel doon."

The layout of the living room was identical to Gran's, but the décor was not. Gran's tended towards Gospel Hall austerity, Mrs Merryweather's was its antithesis. The wallpaper was floral, white and yellow daisies against a bright pink background. Not that you could see much of it. Every wall was a gilded riot of Catholic gift-shop kitsch. Almost every square inch was taken up by colourful pictures and statuettes of Jesus and the Virgin Mary, Saint this, Saint that and Saint the other, and a variety of Popes past and present. The display cabinet was also similar to Gran's, but again, not its contents. The Merryweather cabinet was jam-packed with wee bottles of Holy water, Holy relic replicas, a Vatican snow globe and other cheap and cheerful Vatican memorabilia. The theme continued onto every available flat surface with Vatican coasters and a Vatican ashtray on the coffee table, a Vatican fruit bowl on the dining table and a detailed plaster model of the Vatican itself on top of the television set. Even the settee was adorned with papal cushions, a papal throw and papal antimacassars. Joseph was dazzled. How was it possible to have all this shimmering colour in one room? You could almost believe all the colour in Kilhaugh was in here, being kept safe and sound from the colour-eating grey fog outside.

On the mantelpiece between two golden candlesticks was a gold-framed photograph of a middle-aged Mrs Merryweather aside a tall, handsome priest. They were standing in front of a cave. They looked happy. He had his arm around her, holding her close to him,

"Ma eldest, Vincent, God rest his soul." She handed Joseph a cellophane-wrapped set of daffodil-yellow sheets and pillowcases, "Aye. Taken far too soon," She frowned at the black and white wedding photograph beside it, of her younger self with a short fleshy man with greased-back hair, "Unlike him, who outstayed his welcome. God forgive me, but it's a fact." That said, done and out the way, she sighed, smiled and returned to Vincent, "He used tae take me tae Oor Lady of Lourdes every other year. Six times ah've been. That's where the wee bottles of Holy water come frae, the real thing so they are. Ah'd say take wan fur yer Grandpa, him being no well, but ah don't think yer Gran would thank me fur it. Ha ha. And the Vatican five times. Twice when his Holiness wis there. Wan time ah was as near tae him as ah am tae you. 'The boss', that's whit Vincent cried him, terrible eh?" She chuckled up some phlegm and swallowed it, "He wis a lawyer ye know. Ma wee boy, a priest *and* a lawyer?" She shook her head, "Ah don't know where he got it fae, his brains. No fae me. And no fae his dad that's fur sure. Or his faith." She was lost for a moment, "Ach well. Life goes on, eh son? Life goes on. By the by, here's a wee bit tablet for yer Grandpa, ah know he's a sweet tooth. Ah made some yesterday for the jumble sale but ah think ah went a bit mad, ah've enough here to build a tablet chapel. Is there somethin' the matter son?"

Joseph had become distracted by the bedlinen. "They've never been used, still in their cellophane and… och they're no smellin are they…" She bent down to sniff them and saw what Joseph saw, a larger than life colour portrait of a Pope printed on the pillowcase. "Oh my Goad," she said, laughing and coughing, "Ah'd love tae have seen Sarah Kirkland's face if she'd fund those oan yer bed. Ah'll away and get ye somethin mair… appropriate."

Joseph stood in the garden hugging the beige flannelette sheets. The cold grey fog seemed that much colder now, that much greyer, after being in Mrs Merryweather's house. He went down onto the lane to see if Archie had brought the budgie cage back; he hadn't. At that moment a rusty old Bedford van rolled up and slowed down almost to a stop, but when Joseph approached it to see who was inside, the van carried on down the lane.

CHAPTER TEN

Ecclesiastes, Song of Solomon, Isaiah, Jeremiah

"That's for flour for the bread for the Breaking of Bread," said Gran, handing him a sixpence, "Mrs Agnew's taken ill now as well, so I said I'd do it." She had puffed herself up, just a little, but quickly caught herself on and expelled her pride as best she could, recalling her scorched childhood tongue maybe. If Joseph could have eliminated just one sin from his Gran's long list of sins, one that might have allowed her to relax in life just a little, the sin of *pride* would surely have been a contender.

"And here's a half-crown for the jumble sale tonight. Just clothes mind. For out and about. But nice." She sniffed at Mrs Merryweather's sheets which were hanging over the kitchen door, grimaced, and gave them another spray of lavender air=freshener, "Beggars can't be choosers I suppose. And a good coat if you see one. And some proper shoes. Make sure you get in early, there's bound to be some good quality whatnots from up the hill. And mind Benjamin Mutch's testimony. Make sure you're presentable. Not that that's important. But nevertheless."

She'd made no mention of the budgie cage, or the Saturday morning pictures. This was his week as well. Usually she gave him thruppence, though she'd never actually mention it was for the pictures, *There's thruppence*, she'd say, *for whatever.* He couldn't ask. Not today. Not after... Archie would have money of course, but Archie's money would be...

There was no one around outside, or at least no one he could see, "Gen-e-sis, Ex-o-dus, Lev-it-icus and Num-bers ..."

A discarded yellow Cadbury's Flake wrapper rustled in the gutter near the entrance to Agnew's Mill and it made his heart jump, then sink. He started again and got as far as Proverbs without any hesitation. His best yet. As he did the next four, Ecclesiastes, Song of Solomon, Isaiah, Jeremiah over and over, he was drawn, as he often was, down the steep slope into the Meadows.

The Meadows was a large expanse of unkempt land, wild with bracken, bramble bushes, broom and nettles, long grasses and trees where you might find birds' nests. Small ponds where you might find frogspawn. Secret dens where you might find a stash of comics hidden by Archie Truman. Elsewhere you might see foxes, rabbits, hares, feral cats and, if you were lucky, you might see a solitary deer wandering down from the high woods. A path ran through the Meadows, leading to the Sappie and the low woods. Grown-ups rarely used it. It was too muddy, too thick with nettles, sticky willy, burrs and thorns that stung, stuck, snagged and ripped. The Meadows wasn't huge but when Joseph was there on his own, or with Archie, he felt so cut off from Kilhaugh Gospel Hall and from the outside world he might as well have been on some remote island.

At the foot of the slope there were two large moss-covered boulders which locals called the Sleeping Bairns. Folk sometimes joked that they were nosy children turned to stone by the witches for keeking in on one of their clandestine midnight rituals, but despite the fact there actually had been a witch trial in Kilhaugh – in the late sixteenth century, one of the very last in Scotland – the story had surprisingly never found a place among the night terrors and day terrors that haunted Joseph Kirkland's imagination.

He took some millet and budgie seed from his pocket and placed it on top of one of the Sleeping Bairns, then called out in a sing-song voice, all the things Grandpa would say, "Wee birdie! Bonnie wee yellow birdie," like Grandpa would say them, "Coo wee Peter, coo. Wee yella birdie."

If Peter came back right now, Joseph would be Saved. He'd ask God and Jesus into his heart right here and now. *Promise.* He closed his eyes tight to make the prayer, the offering, whatever it was, this thing he was doing – *it's not a magic spell* – stronger, and when he opened them, there in a clump of crisp frozen stinging nettles, lay a small dead bird with a downy yellow breast.

A blue tit. Perhaps a cat had taken it, played with it, got bored, and left it to die. Or a hawk. Joseph often saw hawks up behind the high woods when he used to go out for walks with Grandpa, when Grandpa was well.

"They'll take anything these hawks," said Grandpa, "a rabbit, a wee lamb... a wee boy!" And he'd grab his grandson by the shoulders, "Look out!" The sort of scary games Archie played with wee Maggie. *Nice* scared. Not *real* scared. Not... *Satan, Hell* and *Bible* scared.

The blue tit was completely intact, its yellow breast pristine. Surely a hawk or a cat would've torn it to pieces for food or the fun of it. Its freshly frozen eyes still shone and the thought crossed his mind that it might not be dead after all. The blue tit was, together with blackbirds, magpies, crows and robins, one of the few birds Joseph could identify. *Sly wee skellums,* Grandpa called them because they stole the cream off the top of the milk bottles, but brave too, because of the risks they took. Once Joseph found a dead one on the front step. *The cat that got the bird that got the cream,* Grandpa said, before launching into, *I know an old lady who swallowed a fly...*

Joseph picked up the bird in a dock leaf and laid it on a Sleeping Bairn alongside the seed and the millet. He considered it all, his shrine, his altar, of dock leaf, millet, mossy stone, dead bird. He added twigs and dry leaves and then lit a monkey-king match but his kindling was too frosty. He'd come back later with Archie, with petrol or white spirits or something, to get it going, cremate it properly. In the meantime there were other distractions to be had.

He placed the sixpence for the flour, for the bread for the Breaking of Bread, on his thumbnail, closed his eyes and flicked it a few feet into the long grass. Then he searched, experiencing a few seconds of mild *will I find it, will I not* panic, which was all a part of it. This fog made it harder than usual, but he found it. He held the icy cold coin against his tongue, closed his eyes, and flicked again, further, found it, flicked it further still, found it… and so on, again and again, flicking and finding, flicking and finding… until he lost it. Then he closed his eyes, counted from ten backwards and did all the other things he always did to find lost coins, this time adding promises of his forthcoming Salvation,

Please let me find it. If I find it then I'll…

"Look who it is Hamish, it's Joseph." It was Mrs Hendry from up the hill, one of the ladies Gran cleaned for. She was walking her wheaten Cairnie, Hamish, "Remember Joseph? He's the clever boy who found you when you went missing. Have you lost something?"

"It's money my Gran gave me, for the messages." *That's the truth.*

"Oh for goodness sake, you'll never find it in this," she said, and reached into her bag for her purse, "How much was it?"

"Half a crown." He glanced over his shoulder. Such casual lies now. Such a skilled liar.

"There you go. Hold on to it this time! How's your grandfather?"

"He's in his bed." Mrs Hendry wanted more. "The budgie flew away."

"Oh dear," she said, not knowing what else to add to this apparent non sequitur, "Well give him my best. And your Gran. I'm never there when she does the cleaning," she laughed. "It all seems to get done by magic. Like the elves and the shoemaker."

Please God let her not tell Gran about the half-crown. Sorry.

The moment Mrs Hendry was out of sight, Joseph found

the sixpence, right where she'd been standing. He could still run after her. Pretend he'd just found Gran's half-crown and …

Once he heard Benjamin Mutch's testimony. Then. That would be it. That would be him. All this deceitful carry-on. It would finally stop.

CHAPTER ELEVEN

My Cup's Full and Running Over

Joseph was only in Websters for flour for the Breaking of Bread but his eyes were on the jars of boilings and trays of penny chews. He'd an extra halfcrown now, he could buy sweets for Archie and wee Maggie for the pictures. But wouldn't Mister Webster wonder? *See yon Kirkland boy? Never has sweetie money. Yet here he was, Master Moneybags...*

"Hello son, what are you doing in here?" It was Auntie Abi, lovely funny Auntie Abi, beaming at him, hugging him. Where Gran was all brittle and bony, all angles and edges, dumpy wee Auntie Abi was all roundness and softness. She hadn't been to the Meeting for long and weary but she'd been Saved when she was eleven, so...

"Gran asked me to buy flour," he said. "She's making bread."

"Did she say what kind?" said Auntie Abi, heading to the shelves with the flour, "I know that big sister of mine likes her wholemeal, keeps her regular."

"It's for the Breaking of Bread."

"Breaking of Bread? Right, that'll be a white loaf then." She handed him a bag of flour, "Is that not usually Mrs Agnew's job?"

"She's not well."

"Och, that's not so good. Nothing serious, I hope."

"Mrs Sangster's sick too."

When she saw Mister Webster listening from the counter she obligingly brought him in, "Us auld yins'll be dropping like flies in this fog eh, Mister Webster?"

"Aye," he said, "there'll be a traffic jam all the way to the Kilhaugh cemetery!"

"Book now and avoid disappointment! They should put that up at the Co-op." They laughed. Gran wouldn't have. *Humour? Is that what it is?* He wondered, *what had Auntie Abi been like before being Saved?* Because if she was like this now, all cheery, all…

"Benjamin Mutch is staying."

"Aye, news travels fast with Mrs Merryweather on the end of the line. He must be as old as Methuselah," she chuckled. "Looked like him too with that beard. How'll he get here?"

"Gran said he's walking."

"From Templeton? Mind you, that's his style. Turns up unannounced, *wherever he's needed most.* Like Mary Poppins. Don't you dare tell your Gran I said that!" He wouldn't, and he'd never seen *Mary Poppins*.

"Ach she'll be in her element running about like a blue-arsed fly," said Auntie Abi, and Joseph looked away, pretending he hadn't heard her use language. "Och you, you're such a good boy, so you are," she pulled him in close, "too good for this world."

No, I'm not. I'm not a good boy. "Peter flew away."

"I know, poor wee thing. And poor Grandpa. He doted on that wee bird. Oh, is this your day for the pictures?" He nodded, "Did she mind and give you money for it?"

Joseph shrugged. *It's true, she didn't.*

"Well here's a shilling for the pictures and some sweets, and here's another to get yourself a wee whigmaleerie at the jumble sale, and if that big sister of mine asks, say bad Auntie Abi made you do it." She smoothed his cheek with the back of her hand. "I see Benjamin Mutch is doing a children's talk? I don't imagine your Gran'll want you missing that. Especially now." She leaned in to him, "About all that, son. You're not feeling under any pressure are you? … Yes? … No? Well, whatever, I'll be there anyway. How could I not? And suffer the wrath of Sarah Kirkland?"

"Can I have a wee word, Abi," said Mister Webster, waving her over. They whispered and glanced at Joseph. Whispering, glancing, nothing odd, it's how it was.

"Well that's me," she said, adjusting his scarf, footering with the toggles on his duffle coat, "I take it you'll be out playing after the pictures?" He shrugged. "Well, just mind you stay away from the Sappie eh? Especially in this weather. I know how you like to wander."

Across the road outside the Hall a small printed sheet had been pinned to the notice board.

AN URGENT CALL
In Your Own Interest
You Are Earnestly Invited
To Come and Hear
The Renowned Evangelist and Missionary
Mister Benjamin Mutch
Everybody Welcome
Children: 4.00 pm / Adults: 6.00 pm
DO NOT MISS THIS OPPORTUNITY!

Underneath someone had scrawled...

It might be your last! ☮

CHAPTER TWELVE

Tarzan and the Heathens of the Dark Interior

There was usually a bit of a queue outside the Robert Munday Memorial Hall but this morning it was only Archie, wee Maggie and half a dozen others.

"Sorry I couldn't find your Grandpa's budgie. I looked for ages, so I did." The dark shadows under his eyes were proof. "We can go after. I put the cage up in the tree house. He might even be there now, you never know."

So he'd gone down to the Sappie. Alone. In the fog. At night. All night, possibly.

"Archie said about the budgie Joseph," said wee Maggie. "I cried." She threw her arms round Joseph's waist. "I'm going to look too, Joseph, after the pictures."

Archie was always scathing about the Saturday Morning Pictures, *They just show ancient stuff* or *I've seen this a million times*. He'd been spoiled by his umpteen free trips to Uncle Tommy's Regal Picture Palace. True, the Saturday Morning Pictures comprised scratchy old silent shorts, antique cartoons, a pre-war Tarzan serial and a cheap as chips short feature. But for Joseph, starved of popular entertainment, this was a fortnightly feast of imagination. Usually. This morning there might as well have been a red neon *Gateway To Hell* sign right above the main entrance to the Munday Hall. Of course Gran hadn't given him money for the pictures. Because this week of all weeks she'd be expecting more of *a boy who's just been Saved*.

Sorry.

Archie made a big show of Joseph having bought cinnamon balls to share and how good they were, even though wee Maggie didn't really like them.

"They're awful nippy, Joseph."

"My Grandpa says they're good for when it's cold." *I'll give the money back.*

Old Mister Jackson opened the doors. He groaned when he saw the numbers,

"This it? Hardly worth ma while turnin' on the projector."

"Would you like a cinnamon ball, Mister Jackson?" said wee Maggie, holding out the poke, "Joseph's Grandpa says they're good for when it's cold."

"He's no wrong there pet," he said, immediately charmed. "Ah'll take the one. How is yer Grandpa, son?"

"He's in his bed, Mister Jackson."

"Where ah'd like to be. Well, give him my best. And mind tell him Jimmy Jackson's no forgotten whose turn it is doon the Legion."

Joseph held out his ticket money.

"Yer pal's already paid. Ye take after yer Grandpa, too slow aff the mark when it's your round. I'm kidding ye on. Away in so ah can shut the door or ye'll no see the film for fog. And mind keep yer coats on, it's like the South Pole in there."

As usual Archie had made a beeline for the front benches, and said what he always said, "Feels like you're actually right inside the film when you're sitting here, so it does.

Maggie, mind tell Joseph what happened in *Tarzan* last week."

This is how it was. Wee Maggie's body twitching with excitement at the responsibility of faithfully recounting the episode of the story that Joseph had missed.

"It was brilliant Joseph," she said, sniffing up some snot.

"I hope you don't have a cold coming on. Did you put on that vest I left out?"

She ignored old mother Archie, she was too busy thinking about the important task in hand: "Mind how it finished with Tarzan trapped in a net hanging from a tree and underneath was the bad hunter with the wee moustache and the two black men and the hunter all ready to shoot? Well, just then this big lion jumped out of nowhere and killed the two black men and oh Joseph it was horrible! The poor black men were screaming! They tried to fight it but…"

"Och, you don't need to say about the black men! Just tell him about the hunter."

"But the lion *did* kill the black men, and they *were* screaming and…"

"I know but… they're just … they're not even really in it. The black men are always getting killed. You can't go telling him about every time a black man gets shot or eaten or drowned in quicksand or something or we'll never get to the proper story."

"Okay," but she was frustrated, because it wasn't right, and she couldn't say why, "the lion killed the bad hunter too."

"It was rubbish so it was. The lion didn't even have any teeth."

"Liar Archie!" she said, outraged by this. "It did so have teeth, Joseph."

"Aye, rubber teeth."

"They were not rubber. Joseph they weren't," she added, gripping Joseph's wrist.

"Were so. They probably got special wallies made for it, lion wallies, like dad's wallies."

He turned his lips inwards so he looked like a toothless old man, gurning away till wee Maggie dissolved into fits of laughter. Joseph loved all this, was mesmerised by it, always. Archie and wee Maggie, the pair of them, doing things just for fun, for no other reason than to make each other smile and laugh. Mister Jackson turned out the lights, "Right everybody, wheesht!"

"Get to the end," said Archie.

Wee Maggie whispered more hot breath than words into Joseph's ear.

"So Tarzan got out the net and you're thinking *oh it's okay*, but then he sees the hunters have robbed the elephants' graveyard and oh the elephants get really upset and go mad and stampede towards the village and, oh Joseph, all the poor village folk, the mums and dads and wee ones, they're all just going about making the tea and having a nice time but..."

The countdown leader flickered, the *Looney Tunes* intro began, "Quick, get to the good bit!"

"I am! Tarzan tried everything so he did, even his Tarzan cry and then just when you think he's going to get there and save everybody he falls into quicksand and he's sinking and you're going *oh no, oh no he's going to die, oh no* ... That's how it finished."

Everyone laughed at Sylvester the cat going through his eternal cycle of humiliation, mutilation and extraordinary near-death experiences. Everyone laughed as he and the canary Tweety Pie found new and horrifyingly elaborate ways to kill each other. But even when Sylvester was shot in the head or fell off a hundred-foot cliff with his tail tied to an anvil or got squashed by a steamroller till his eyes popped out or was thrown into a red-hot oven, he could never die. He merely went through the agonies, then came back to life and the whole violent routine started all over again. No one ever found peace in *Looney Tunes* world.

"Tarzan's next," said wee Maggie, stating the obvious, simply reminding him she was there, the three of them were all there, together, and wasn't this just so good.

The eyes of the LORD are in every place, beholding the evil and the good. Proverbs, Chapter something Verse something. When I get back I promise I'll read about the missionaries John Paton or Doctor Livingstone who were in the jungle too, labouring for the Lord...

He felt at his feet for the bag of flour for the bread for the Breaking of Bread, making sure he hadn't left it somewhere, because right now, nothing was certain or solid or where it should be. He pulled up his duffle coat hood so Archie and wee Maggie couldn't see his face, sank into the bench and let his eyes roll backwards. The wee electric spark show inside his head began almost at once.

CHAPTER THIRTEEN

Hide-and-seek

It was just before midday when the pictures finished. Wee Maggie went off with a new wee girl from the scheme whose name Joseph couldn't catch.

"I'll look for Peter round at my pal's bit," she promised, as she skipped away.

"She's tons of pals, so she has," said Archie, puffed up with pride. "Anybody who's ages with her that she likes, she just goes waltzing right up to them, *Hello, I'm Maggie, what's your name?* And that's her, best pals."

Joseph Kirkland and Archie Truman did not waltz up to folk and ask to be their friend and folk did not go out their way to make friends with Joseph and Archie. *We're the awkward squad!* Archie was fond of saying. And they were. And they were fine with that. Archie had Joseph, Joseph had Archie. It was enough. More than enough.

They stopped outside Faulkner's. Archie quickly sized up the wooden fence that led into the back yard, took a run at it, and vaulted over the top like a commando, barely touching it. No sooner was he over than two men came out front of the pub. One looked fine but the other was staggering and slurring his words, which only got worse when the cold hit him.

"… shit-hole this place, so it is." It was Mister Truman, Archie's dad.

"The state of you Jimmy," said the other man. "The time of day as well. It's nae wonder ye got yer jotters."

"They're aw *Holier than fuckin' thou* in *Holy* Kilhaugh. A preacher tae? Turn the other cheek? Aye! Right. Andrew fuckin' Kirkland wouldnae turn his fuckin' erse cheek!"

The other man went back inside, unconcerned with Mister Truman or what might befall him. They were drinking buddies, not friends. Mister Truman stood there swaying, shaking his head, muttering to himself or to God or to demons in the fog or to who knows what, "Bastards… so they are… ah mean whit… whit's … whit… ach…" and so he continued, trying and failing to remember why he was angry, who he was angry at. He licked his lips. The thirst was on again. He patted all his pockets from top to bottom for money, patted them again in a different order, then cursed the world and all its contents, and peered into the fog, unsure which way to turn. Then he leaned forwards at an absurd angle and staggered off, following whatever direction his body took him, not really walking now, more a perpetual falling over.

If he'd hung on a moment longer, he'd have seen a Cossack vodka bottle materialise over the fence, like a cartoon thought bubble from inside his own head, or a wish granted.

"Told you it'd be easy," said Archie and he tucked the vodka bottle under his anorak. "Honest to God, Joseph, we can do anything in this fog and nobody'll see us."

That's not true.

They headed down the Meadows to cremate the dead bird that was waiting for them on the makeshift altar. Archie knew all about cremations,

"Two grandas and a gran. It's dead creepy, so it is. They pull a red curtain round the coffin, then there's music like in a Hammer horror film, and when the curtain opens again it's gone, like one of David Nixon's magic tricks. Know what actually happens but? The coffin just goes down into the cellar. Then the workies get it and rip off all the fancy bits, like the brass handles or even the actual coffin if it's expensive wood, and flog it down Paddy's Market or somewhere – honest – then they shove the body in a furnace and one of them presses this big red button and whoosh, a hundred flame-throwers shoot out the sides and that's you, burnt to a cinder in five seconds flat. Can you imagine it?"

Joseph Kirkland had no problems imagining it.

The offering of leaves, moss, twigs, millet spray and budgie seed were all still there, plus one tiny yellow downy feather, but the blue tit was gone.

"Maybe it was only playing dead," said Archie, "they do that sometimes."

They both looked up at the sky but there was still no sky. Or everything was sky. Archie yawned and shivered and tapped Joseph on the shoulder, pulling him back from the edge of the dwam he was on the brink of falling into.

"We could have a wee nip to keep us warm," he said, a cheeky glint in his eye, and lifted the big bottle to his lips. "Maybe we should eh? Have you ever tried it? It's dead burnie."

"I saw your dad," *Sorry. I didn't mean to say that.*

"At Faulkner's?" Archie kicked a stone. "Bet he was stotious," he said. He tried to feign indifference, but he wasn't indifferent, not at all. "Was he?"

Joseph shrugged and Archie set about thrashing every thorny bush within reach of his stick, kicking every stone that lay in his way, then quite matter-of-fact, "Think I'll end up like him?" There being no more stones, he began kicking the ground, "My gran says my dad's like that cos my granda' was like that. But all my family are like that. They all like a drink. Even my gran likes a drink." He tried to snap off a branch. "*Ye'll end up like yer dad*, she says, whenever I get up to something." The stick was green but he twisted it, until sinew by sinew it broke. "Wee Maggie won't be like that but. She's too smart, so she is. Bet she ends up marrying a prince or a film star or something, or somebody from up the hill or maybe even ..." He knew Joseph was shy, so he didn't say it. "Bet she does as well."

He threw the vodka bottle from hand to hand, up into the air, swinging it around like an Indian club, then stopped and presented it to Joseph,

"Want to burn something?"

On a tree at the end of the Meadows nearest the schemes was one of Archie's rope swings. It wasn't his best effort but it was made with thick heavy rope with a big seat knot instead of a stick. Archie climbed up, untied it and got himself into a nice comfy place on the fork of a high branch where he could watch his friend go about his business.

Joseph poured the vodka a wee bit at a time into the knot, letting it soak in. The whole process took a while and when the knot was completely sodden he held a match to it. Archie began an ululating war cry as Joseph started swinging the burning knot around his head, slowly at first, letting out more and more rope, then faster and faster till all Archie could see was a great circle of fire and Joseph Kirkland in the centre of it, his one eye flaming bright behind his spectacle lens. It was a rare treat for Archie to see Joseph Kirkland like this, in his fiery element, truly glorious.

"Faster!" shouted Archie, nearly falling out the tree with excitement.

Joseph leant back and put his whole body into it. The momentum helped him maintain his balance, and the faster he went the slower everything else became. There was no dizziness. He was a part of this now. In frosted bushes and low-hanging branches wee hidden creatures flapped and scurried away. *Do your Books of the Bible, Joseph!* Was that Archie shouting? *Do your Books of the Bible!* So he did, chanting like a playground skipping game, chanting to the beat of the burning rope, ecstatic, "Gen-e-sis, Ex-o-dus, Lev-it-icus and Num-bers, Deut-er-onomy, Joshua, Judges, Ruth and Sam-u-el, Sam-u-el, Kings, Kings, Chron-icles, Chron-icles, Ezra, Ne-hem-iah, Esther, Job, Psalms,

Proverbs, Ecclesiastes, Song of Solomon, Isaiah, Jeremiah, Lamentations…"

Archie wanted to drop by wee Maggie's pal's house to see if she was okay, which was as just well because she was not happy at all. The pal's mum wouldn't let her go and look for Peter, *It's no weather to be out looking for a budgie,* and she'd been crying non-stop, feeling she'd let Joseph down. The mum looked like she was glad to see the back of her, just to get some peace.

The tree house was next to the Sappie. It was just a platform of nailed down planks and a knotted rope to climb up. Archie shimmied up no bother even with wee Maggie on his back.

"Look at me, Joseph," she shouted, "I'm Tarzan's monkey."

Joseph could barely get off the ground. Archie was made for these kinds of shenanigans. What was Joseph made for?

"Take off your duffle coat. You're too bumphled up."

He followed Archie's suggestion and managed it, but clumsily and only with Archie helping him up the last couple of feet. Peter's cage was empty. Of course it was. They sat in a huddle looking at it. Joseph's teeth were chattering.

"Here," Archie gave Joseph his anorak, "I don't need it anyway."

Once the little warmth from Archie's body had left it, the anorak offered no protection.

They resumed their vigil, staring at the cage, all of them believing in the possibility of Peter's return, of being able to *will* Peter to return.

"We could say a prayer," said wee Maggie.

"When have you ever said a prayer?" said Archie.

"We say prayers at school. We say the Lord's prayer. Our father who arts…"

"When?"

"When the minister comes and at assembly."

"She's full of surprises this one, isn't she?" Archie often used old folk's expressions, an old folk's tone of voice, when he spoke of, or to, his wee sister,

"Can *you* say a prayer, Joseph?" she said, for Joseph Kirkland must surely be an expert on such matters, "It'll work better if you do it."

"I'll get your Bible," said Archie and he dreeped down to the ground, put on Joseph's duffle coat and clambered back up. He looked at Joseph, still in his anorak. "You're me and I'm you," he said and reached for Joseph's specs, "Can I?"

The moment he put on the specs and clutched Joseph's Bible to his heart, Archie's eye lost its sparkle, like he'd switched off a light. The transformation was complete. Joseph looked at his dour, dead-eyed doppelganger; was this really what he looked like to the world?

"Hello Joseph," said wee Maggie to Archie.

"Hello Maggie," said Archie, a bit too posh.

"Joseph isn't posh."

"He's posher than us. What do we do now?"

The Bible wasn't something to play games with. But if their intentions were…

"You need to close your eyes," said Joseph, "… then… just… open the Bible anywhere and… point at a line of Scripture and… just read it out."

"You go first," said Archie and handed the Bible to wee Maggie.

"Do I make a wish, Joseph?"

"No. It's not a wish." *It is, exactly that, a wish.* "Just… think about something you want to happen, something good, but not for you, for other folk. Or if it is for you… it has to be to do with… trying to be a better person. Or… if you're sad or worried… or… if you don't understand something… something you want to know the answer to… you can ask it about those kinds of things."

"Oh it's like the *Magic Robot*, so it is, Archie. Have you

ever played it, Joseph? It's great so it is. You ask it questions, anything, and it always points at the right answer!" She was all excited now, holding the Bible in outstretched arms, face skywards, eyes closed, "Who will I marry when I grow up?" she shouted and spun around like *the Magic Robot.*

"She's good at this, so she is!" Archie was loving every minute. "You don't need the Bible to tell you, I know the answer to that."

"I don't want you to tell me, Archie. I want God and Jesus to tell me!"

This is not right. This is not right. We really should not be doing this.

Wee Maggie stopped spinning, threw open the Bible and stabbed a line of Scripture, but before she'd a chance to read it, Joseph gently took it away from her.

"Can we not play hide-and-seek instead?"

Hide-and-seek in this weather was fantastic and impossible; a few steps in any direction and you were invisible,

"Watch out for those crocodiles in the Sappie," said Archie.

"There aren't any crocodiles in the Sappie," she squealed, and looked around like there might just be crocodiles in the Sappie.

Archie might be a daredevil with his own life but not with his wee sister's. She wasn't allowed to hide on her own and when it was her turn to seek, Joseph or Archie went with her. For Archie and – to a lesser extent – Joseph, some sense of geography remained even with everything obscured by the fog. They knew the nooks and crannies, rocks and boulders, bushes and trees where they'd built swings or played commandoes and cowboys and Indians, where they'd ambled endlessly and aimlessly, together and alone. Wee Maggie had only ever been led, but after a few rounds her confidence grew,

"Can I have a go on my own?"

"All right, but just a wee go. Me and Joseph will hide nearby."

"Okay, but no cheating Archie. And mind shout *in den 1,2,3* or it doesn't count. Make sure he doesn't cheat, Joseph! He always cheats."

"She's the hide-and-seek police, so she is."

She put her hands over her eyes and counted loud and slow,

"One… two … three …

By *five* Joseph could barely hear her. By *eight* he was hiding behind a bush and couldn't be sure if she'd said her *Here I come ready or not*! He waited, just a second or two but enough to wonder why Auntie Abi had told him not to go to the Sappie and what was all that whispering between her and Mister Webster? Grown-ups were like that. When something bad was in the air, they never just said, *Right, here's the thing.* No, it was all, *Don't talk to this person or that person, Don't do this, Don't do that, Don't go here or there,* and never a *Because.* You never knew. And you couldn't ask.

Her scream was dampened by the fog, but even so. It was one of those short open-throat screams of a child who has just woken itself up from a nightmare only to discover it hadn't woken up at all. Joseph could feel the place in his own body where that scream came from; he'd screamed that scream often enough.

Oh please, please not wee Maggie, please don't make her a sign.

Pictures of wee Maggie were forming now, pictures that he did not want to see, built from half-heard news stories, warnings from grown-ups, apocryphal tales, the Bible and things overheard. You never knew when someone great or small would be taken. Kilhaugh was filled with the broken bones of children, with blindings, cracked skulls, severed fingers, spilt blood, and with tragic fatalities. A stumble or a trip might lead to a collision with a vehicle or a fall from a precipice. You never knew when it would… He tried to shake these thoughts from his head and when they still wouldn't shift he prayed his usual prayer, but really prayed it, out loud, like Gran prayed, for the highest stakes.

"Gentle Jesus meek and mild look upon this little child pity my simplicity..."

There was Archie now, vague and wraithlike – Archie who every day promised wee Maggie in word or deed, *I'll always be there for you,* whose only ambition was to stand between his wee sister and jeopardy; whose own recklessness was in fact a lure, designed to attract all danger away from her and towards himself; *Heh Mister Menace! Heh Doctor Danger! Don't look at her, look at* ME! He was flailing around in the fog, not playing hide-and-seek now but a frenzied game of blind man's buff. He had fresh scratches and grazes on his face, hands and knees and a new rip on his anorak from charging through thorny bushes, low-hanging branches and tripping over roots and stones and anything else that got in his way, and he was shouting, high and sharp, trying to cut through the fog, "Maggie! Maggie! *Maggie!*" reaching an almost hysterical pitch now, "Maggie! MAGGIE!" while at the same time, for wee Maggie's sake, desperately trying to sound calm and normal, "Maggie! Maggie!"

A big hand grabbed Joseph by the wrist, and pulled him towards the water's edge. There was that earthy smell again, that tree-sap, nettle, damp-dog, tweed and petrol. Then warm fur pushing against his bare legs. It was him. Them. Joseph didn't resist. The hand let go and there was a petrified wee Maggie sitting stock-still on a boulder right at the very edge of the ice-fringed Sappie, her face in her hands, crying, not for her mum and dad, but for *Archie*.

Seconds later Archie was there, holding his wee sister close. The little colour he had, had drained out of him, but even so, it was important that he made a joke of it all, "I better get back," he said sniffing and shaking, "and shout *in den 1,2,3.*"

"Caught you," she said, grabbing him tight, "I win." And she laughed and sniffed and shook and sobbed and laughed and sobbed again, as she told as best she could what had happened, "Oh Archie, I was right beside the water, and I tripped up and I thought I was going to fall in but somebody grabbed me and he had this deep voice and he said, *You'll sit there and you will not move,* just like that, but I couldn't see him and I thought it was you Archie, doing a funny voice but it wasn't anything like one of your funny voices..." And once more she began her shaking and sobbing.

Archie lifted her up. She wrapped her arms and legs around him.

"Course it was me, ye daft wee monkey, I was doing my Tarzan voice...listen...*Maggie must sit...not move.*"

She did not believe, but wanted to believe, and so she made herself believe. "I just got a fright," she said, wiping her nose on his anorak.

"Thanks very much. That was just clean on as well."

She laughed, and wiped her nose on him again, and again.

They walked in silence, wee Maggie quiet in Archie's arms. Archie's legs looked like they might buckle, but he didn't put her down till they got back to their house. Joseph wanted to tell him about the man and the dog and all, reassure them that he was certain this man was good, that he was not any kind of bogeyman. *I will. Just not now.* Wee Maggie was safe. That was enough to be getting on with. It was a good sign. *Thank you.*

"See you the night at the jumble sale," whispered Archie.

He went in the back way, trying not to make a sound, a thief breaking into his own house. The door had barely closed when the shouting and the swearing and the slapping began, "You take money out your da's pocket?"

"No."

Slap.

"Don't lie ya wee shite!" *Slap.* "What've ye done wi it?"

"Empty yer pockets now!" *Slap.* "Now!"

"Maggie, upstairs! And ye can stop yer bawlin or you'll be gettin it too."

"She didn't do anything."

Slap.

"Shut it! Where's ma fuckin' money?"

"Ah don't have it."

Slap.

"Thievin' lyin' wee bastard, so ye are."

Joseph had so much money now. He could knock on the door, say something. Lie. He was good at the lying now: *Oh here's your money Mister Truman. I saw this half-crown falling out your pocket outside Faulkner's*. But, no, the Coward Joseph Kirkland could not lie when it really mattered. Anyway, Archie wouldn't want him to; he wouldn't want Joseph to be party to this; it would make him feel ashamed.

When he got in Gran was on her knees scrubbing the toilet, continuing her meticulous *take me as you find me* panic-ridden preparations for the arrival of Benjamin Mutch.

"Did you mind and get the flour?" He nodded. "What kind did you get?"

"Auntie Abi said white."

"Oh, did she indeed? It's been that long since she broke bread I'm surprised she remembered." She mopped her brow with her apron, "That's Mrs Hendry not well now. They think it might be pneumonia. One minute she's out in that fog walking her dog and the next …"

Isn't this what Joseph had prayed for? For Mrs Hendry not to say anything?

"Mind and wash your face before you go up to the Hall, and not just a cat's lick either."

I'll be Saved. I will. This afternoon. Once I hear Benjamin Mutch's testimony. Then. That'll be it. That'll be me.

CHAPTER FOURTEEN

The Testimony of Benjamin Mutch

Benjamin Mutch's reputation went far beyond the front door of the Hall. He was known, *by those who need to know*, the length and breadth of the country, in towns and villages, in the highlands and the islands, in the big cities and their slums. So as well as the usual Sunday School folk, others had turned up, including a couple of mums and children from the scheme. Some folk from the Hall had mixed feelings about this. Yes, God loved all sinners. Yes, they'd like to increase their numbers. But all the same.

One of them was just a toddler. It would have no idea what was going on. But toddlers didn't need to know. They didn't need to ask God or Jesus to Save them. There was Scripture on all of this. There was Scripture on everything. That was the point: if you needed to know – and everyone needed to know – how a life ought to be lived, then look no further. No, a toddler didn't need to worry, it could just toddle about in its own wee carefree world and if it died, it went to Heaven anyway, because how could a toddler be blamed for something it couldn't even understand? It was the same for folk at the Munday Mental or folk who'd died before Jesus's time. Now if Joseph had been born long before Jesus or had died when he was a toddler or... But no, here he was, at that age. He understood fine well. Joseph Kirkland had no excuses.

"Joseph," said Mister Agnew. He was holding his hand out. *What?* Did he want Joseph to shake it? He gripped the hand of *Joseph the Ditherer*, *Joseph the Interloper*, folded his other hand over it, and looked him in the eye, searching him, reading him, like a body-snatcher alien might do with its special thought powers, *So, Joseph, you're one of us now? Or so you say.*

Uncle Andrew and Auntie Ishbel were next. Uncle Andrew had *Labourer for the Lord* written right through him like a stick of seaside rock: the mutton chops of austerity, the rigid military bearing he'd somehow gained from being in the Red Cross in Poland during the last months of the war and the haunted look from what he'd seen there. He was a handsome man, like Grandpa had been handsome, aristocratic even, a minor Royal disguised as a commoner. He held out his hand too, a worker's hand, and gave Joseph the same searching look Mister Agnew had given him. And over his shoulder, Jenny too, searching him with her eyes, questioning him with her grin. Is this how it would be now?

Auntie Ishbel was a good few years younger and youthful in a way Uncle Andrew had never been. She smiled at Joseph and kissed him like she always did. There was no searching. Her eyes were sparkly and mischievous, like Jenny's eyes, but not ulterior like Jenny's eyes. Was that sparkle the residue from her years as a Catholic? Had her childhood been as golden and glittering as Mrs Merryweather's front room? Imagine that. She must've loved Uncle Andrew like nothing on earth.

Benjamin Mutch walked straight out of the Old Testament. From the moment he appeared and began his slow ascent onto the platform, Joseph Kirkland was bewitched. He was all that Joseph had imagined. All he'd hoped for. More. Much more. He was *Abraham, Jeremiah, Isaiah*, all of them, all the prophets. He was even carrying a shepherd's crook for goodness sake, the kind they'd have used in the "Parable of the Lost Sheep", the kind Moses himself might have used to part the Red Sea. If anyone was to be the Saving of Joseph Kirkland it must surely be this man. Joseph felt the cold lead dread subside, a little, enough, and sighed the sigh of a drowning man who'd just seen a ship on the horizon. SOS indeed.

Oh, this hollow-cheeked old man was just perfect. He was as tall, thin and craggy as a sea stack, with a long beard and wild mane of hair as white as foam on a breaking wave. He was magnificent, magnetic.

He wore the uniform of the North East evangelist; tweed suit, Fair Isle v-neck jumper, grey flannel shirt, green knitted tie, brown brogues. All of it, all of him, had seen better days, but it was in his milky opal eyes, filmed with cataract clouds, that his splendid decrepitude was most apparent. His long life of long walks and Saving Souls had clearly taken its toll.

He stopped directly on top of the trapdoor and raised himself up to his full considerable height: "Ah've been stravaigin up an doon the kintra frae Muckle Roe tae Melrose an back again, an noo here ah am in Kilhaugh aince mair,"

Joseph had cousins in the North East but Benjamin Mutch didn't sound like any of them. Like anyone Joseph had ever met. And neither was this the boom or bellow of those itinerant fire and brimstone preachers Joseph had witnessed at the Templeton Hall. This was a high hoarse whisper that everyone heard because everyone wanted to hear. Benjamin Mutch looked around and quietly chuckled. Chuckling. In the Hall.

"Ah've no been here fur lang an weary. Mmm. Ah wunner why the Guid Lord in His wisdom has led me here…"

For me. You've come for me.

"Weil noo. Ah've some muckle guid news an ah've some muckle bad news, as they say. Ah'll gie yese a' the bad news feerst eh? It has been written that *the fearfu' an unbelievin an the abominable an the murderers, an the whoormongers, an warlocks, an idolaters an a' the liars shall hae their pairt in the loch which burneth wi fire an brunstane: which is the saicant deith.*" Benjamin Mutch considered this, let it sink in, for his own benefit as much as anyone else's. The heat in the Hall played its part. "This is the wey it is. This is the wey it will be. But! There is guid news." He chuckled again and shook his big, bearded, lion-maned head as though not quite believing it himself, "An it's gey guid. Gey guid. The guid news is that *God sae luved the warld that he gie'd His ainly begotten son* – His *ain son* – think aboot that noo, eh – *that whosoe'r believeth in Him shouldna perish, but hae e'er-lastin' life.*"

Joseph was shocked. Not at the descriptions of Damnation and Salvation, which he'd heard often enough, but at Benjamin Mutch quoting scripture in Scottish words. Nobody used Scottish words in the Hall, not like this, and certainly not when quoting Scripture. Gran had little time for Scottish words, which she considered uncivilised and common: *It makes good words and profanities sound the same.*

"Gentle Jesus, meek an mild, leuk upon this little child. Hou mony o ye chant that in yer bed at nicht afore ye gang aff tae sleep eh?" Nobody answered. "Noo listen, yase'll need tae say somethin or ah'll no ken yer there. Wi ma eyesicht it's foggier in here than it is oot there." Was Benjamin Mutch making a joke? Nobody laughed, and he chuckled again, then a few hands went up. "An there's nae point pittin yer hauns up neither. Ah canna see them. Bawl it oot! Wha chants their *Gentle Jesus?*"

There was a muted chorus of *Me. I do. I say it.* Benjamin Mutch nodded sagely. Everything he did he did sagely.

"Weil mind add Benjamin Mutch tae yer list o them ye askit the Lord tae Bless."

He scratched his beard, licked his lips, closed his eyes and muttered to himself. Some folk looked at each other like he'd gone doolally. But when he opened his eyes they were clearer, his voice stronger, "Ah wis in the jyle at the time, at the tap end o a vera lang preeson sentence. Oh whit a dork an drearisome place it wis tae. Ah wis that lost in there. Och dinna misunnerstaun me, ah wis lost lang afore ah went tae the jyle. Ah wis as far awa' frae the Lord as it's possible fur a maun tae be. Ah kent the Deil but. Oh aye we were weil acquaintit, masel an the Deil. Ah didna ken Jesus Christ oor Lord though. But ah soon fund oot that he kent me. It wis a chaplain frae ain o the Halls up North wha telt me whit ah needit tae hear. Ah usually avoidit these fowk like the plague, but this yin – oh a richt dour man so he wis, wad hae gien Haly Wullie a run fur his money – he saw this tattoo o a blue fish oan the back o ma haun." He held out a pale liver-spotted left hand. "A bit faded wi salt waater and years o wandrin hither an thither, back an forrit, but yese can still see it eh? Onywey, this chaplain, he kent ah'd been a fisherman an he says tae me, *Benjamin, ye ken the vera feerst follyers o Christ had picturs o a fish drawn oan their hauns?* An ah says *Oh, is that richt?* Because tae be perfectly honest wi ye, ah couldna be bathered wi a' this releegious clishmaclaver. Weil he gie'd me a Bible, the feerst ah'd e'er held. The same auld tattered Bible ah'm haudin in ma haun noo in fact. *Read this Benjamin*, says he, an he merked it at *Mathew's Gospel* chaipter fowr. *The Lord's waitin fur ye Benjamin*, says he. Weil that wis me. Oh ah cursed the maun an his God, yasin words ah couldna repeat here in Kilhaugh."

Disappointment registered in the eyes of the Sangster twins who'd loved to have heard him repeat the words he couldn't repeat in Kilhaugh.

"Och ah wis a thrawn crittur back then. Ragin' at the warld so ah wis, worse wi a drink in me but wickit wi'oot it. Weil ah took his Bible because ye ken in the jyle ye tak onythin that's gaun free. But ah wis that determint no tae read it. That nicht tho, ah wis in ma peter – ye ken a *peter* is whit preesoners ca' their cell – an ah wis sharin it wi anither puir sowl. Auld Joe wis his name. Been in an oot the jyle a' his days. Auld Joe couldna read nor write an we had nae books in oor peter, so Joe, he says tae me, *Whit ye got ther Benjamin? A Bible*, says I, an he says, *Will ye read me a wee bit o it?* An ah thocht, ach whit fur no, ah've naethin else tae dae. So ah opened the Guid Beuk for the vera feerst time, at the place yon dour man frae the Hall had merked, an this is whit ah read," Benjamin Mutch again closed his eyes. He knew the scripture off by heart and recited it as if he was remembering his own life story, "Then wis Jesus led up o the Spirit intae the wilderness tae be temptit o the Deil. An when he'd fastit forty day an forty nicht...." as if he was there right now in that wilderness and was simply reporting on events. "Frae that time Jesus began tae preach, an tae say, Repent: fur the kingdom o heaven is at haun. An Jesus, walkin bi the sea o Galilee, saw twa brethren, Simon cried Peter, an Andra his brither, castin a net intae the sea: fur they were fishers. An he saith untae them, 'Folla me, an ah will mak yese fishers o men.' An they straightawey left their nets, an follaed him." His eyes sprung open. "Weil, ah nearly slammed the Guid Book shut there an then because ah didna want tae be remindit o the fishin days. But auld Joe, he insistit ah cerrit oan. An when ah got tae the end, ah dinna ken why but ah leuked at auld Joe, an ah leuked at the fish tattoo oan ma haun an ah got up oan a chair an keeked through the wee barred windae high up oan the cell wa' that leuked oot ower the North sea, the vera sea that fur mony years ah yased tae fish an which had been the source o a' ma troubles. An there wis a storm blawin that nicht. My, whit a tempest it wis tae, the likes o whit Jonah himsel micht hae witnessed. Weil, the wind blew the salt waater in through the wee windae but ye ken ah couldna say whether it wis the salt waater ah wis tastin' or ma ain teardraps. Fur ah wis greetin like ah'd ne'er gret afore. No greetin' like a bairn mind. Mair, howlin, like a woundit beast, screichin oot that wee windae intae the nicht, *Oh Lord if yer ther, please hear me.* Ah couldna haurdly speak fur greetin. *Ah ken ah'm a filthy rotten sinner, there's nae gettin awa' frae it. But Lord if ye see fit, then ah'm askin ye, please come intae ma hert.* An at that moment a muckle great waw cam crashin oan tae the rocks an the waater hit against the preeson wa' an the spray cam through yon wee windae an waashed ower me. An ah kent. Richt there an then ah kent that ah had been foon. Efter that... efter that..." He was speaking in a whisper now, "...ah wis calm. Ah went tae sleep an ah slept like a babby. An when ah waukent... ah heard things different, ah saw things different, ah felt things different. Ah wis different… a different maun."

A different man? Different, how? *Invasion of the Body Snatchers* different?

"Ah had been SAVED. Weil the follaein Sunday ah wis baptised, in a tin tub in the jyle, bi yon maun frae the Hall, an whit a glorious day that wis. But that wisna the end o ma journey. In fact, ah wid say it wis ainly the beginnins o it. Ah read scripture evra oor o evra day in ma peter, or daunderin roon the yaird, readin tae masel or tae onynody wha'd listen. The Guid Beuk wis ayeways in ma haun. Bible Benjamin! That's whit they ca'd me. An whit fur no? At nicht ah cerrit oan readin auld Joe scripture an evra bit o scripture ah read tae him it wis that fittin ye micht hae thocht it had been scrieved jist fur me an him. Weil, efter mibbe twa weeks o this, auld Joe wauks me up in the middle o the nicht. Oh his een were fu o bodement, pished wi' dreid so he wis. In the jyle ye ken the nicht is the time ye feel it maist, the desolation an despair. An he says tae me, quiet as a moose, *Benjamin, ther's somethin ah need tae say an ah waant you tae hear it,* an ah says, *Joe ahm a' ears* an he gets doon oan his knees an he closes his een an he says, *Lord, it's Joseph here. Ah've ne'er spak wi ye afore but here ah am noo, a sinner, an aboot as coorse as they come. But ahm askin ye tae come into ma hert like ye did wi ma guid pal Benjamin here.* Weil, see when he opened his een, maun there wis a licht in them ah hidna seen afore an his sowl wis mair lichtsome tae an ah kent that this wisna the same maun, that the auld sinner Joe had died a deith. "

"Weil boys an girls ah served ma time an eventually ah wis liberatit. An ah thocht tae masel *whit'll ah dae noo?* Weil, as an auld lag, ma options were gey limited eh? There wis aye the fishin boats. But ah wis that feart. Feart that goin back oan the boats wad mean goin back oan the drink. Feart ah wid turn back intae the maun ah had aince been. Weil ah thocht aboot it richt enough. An then ah remembert auld Joe an the scripture yon chaplain had merked oot fur me a' those years afore an ah realised in a flash that aye ah wid tak up the fishin again. But no fishin fur the cod or the herrin. Na, ah had mair muckle fish tae catch. Ah'd be a *fisher o men*. An the mair ah thocht aboot it the mair ah realised that ah already wis a fisher o men, fur had auld Joe no been ma vera feerst catch?"

Leaning heavily on his stick, Benjamin sat down. "Onybody ony questions?" Silence. "Naebody? Weil, ah'll tell yese the feerst question ah'd be askin if ah wis a bairn sittin doon there listenin tae some bletherin auld lag up here. Ah'd be askin, *whit were ye in the jyle fur Mister Mutch?* Eh? Dinna tell me that's no whit yer thinkin! Weil ah'll tell yese. Ah wis in the jyle because ah murdert a fella fisherman in a drunken rage. An no wi a knife or a gun or a rope but like a beast, wi ma bare hauns, these same hauns that haud the Guid Beuk."

He held up those murdering hands and Joseph's mouth fell open. All the children's mouths fell open. It had of course been spoken of, but to hear this confession out loud, to see those killer hands!

"Oh ah wis drunk a lot in them days." His eyes were wet. "Aye, tak a leuk evrabody, tak a guid leuk. Whit ye hiv afore ye is a convicted murderer. Oh ah've repentit. Ah'm still repentin. Ah've served ma time but ah'll be repentin till the end o ma days. The panel that pit me awa is naethin compared tae the panel ah'll staun afore oan judgement day. But here's whit ah hiv tae say tae yese a'. The Guid Lord wis crucified tae deith oan yon cross so that sinners sic as me, aye *even sic as me,* wad no perish but wad hae e'er lastin life! Weil, whate'er sins ye micht think ye've committed ah'm shair they're naethin compared tae mine. An like me ye can be Saved, but *ainly* – an ah'm talkin tae the aulder bairns amang yese – if ye repent an gie up yer life tae Him. There, ah've said whit ah cam tae say. Noo, pick up yer chorus beuks…"

They'd sung this chorus many times, but never in the presence of a real fisherman turned murderer turned missionary:

I will make you fishers of men, / Fishers of men, fishers of men,
I will make you fishers of men, / If you follow Me.

Benjamin Mutch answered questions about life as a missionary, about his eternal wanderings from village to village, town to town, *labouring for the Lord*. Most of them had read *Heroes of the Cross* and Benjamin Mutch sensed their disappointment when it became clear that his missionary work had not taken him far beyond the Scottish borders.

"Ah suppose yese are askin yerselves whit fur did he no gang ower tae dorkest Africa or dorkest India or dorkest Papua New Guinea or dorkest some ither place ower the sea? Eh? Places whaur they'll eat yese as soon as leuk at yese! Places whaur *the real heathens* live eh? Weil ah'll tell yese!" He rose to his feet again. His evangelical armoury was extensive. He could do avuncular warmth and wit, child-friendly H.A.P.P.Y., but he had the Old Testament big guns too:

"Because in the een o the Lord yin unsaved sowl is like ony ither! Because dorkest Africa is nae dorker than dorkest Glesga or dorkest Aiberdeen! Nae dorker than dorkest Barra or dorkest South Uist. Nae dorker even than dorkest Kilhaugh. Evrawhaur has a dork interior." He swept the Hall with his shepherds crook, "An dae yese ken whaur's the dorkest interior o a'?" He punched his heart, "In here," and tapped his skull, "an in here. This is whaur ye'll fund the Deil an a' his works. This is whaur ye'll fund murderin drunkards like me!" He was stabbing at the air now, "This is whaur ye'll fund puir lost sowls... like Joseph."

His shepherd's crook was pointing directly at Joseph Kirkland.

CHAPTER FIFTEEN

The Boulder-Headed Devil Dog

The jumble sale wasn't for another hour or two. He'd plenty of time to get the cage. He'd forgotten all about it, what with wee Maggie and the hide-and-seek business and everything. Anyway he needed to be by himself, to think, or not think, about all that had happened, or not happened. He was still *not Saved*. That had *not happened*. Not even in the presence of the extraordinary Benjamin Mutch, a real missionary, a *Hero of the Cross* even. He could help Save and convert staunch Catholics like Auntie Ishbel and hardened criminals like "auld Joe" and convicted murderers such as himself, but could he help Save Joseph Kirkland? No, that was beyond even Benjamin Mutch's powers.

Joseph had heard testimonies before and though they were never anything less than astounding, and each of them unique, they all had something in common. These men had all found God, or been found *by* God, as a consequence of serious illness, near-fatal car crashes, shipwrecks, air disasters, acts of war or alcoholic lives that had all but ended in the gutter. Joseph knew it was wrong, but he couldn't help but be envious of these men. He felt sure that if he were to experience some extraordinary life-threatening event, some catastrophic disaster, then he too would turn to God or be found by God.

Sorry. No. I don't want that. I don't want that. I don't want that.

Joseph tried his Books of the Bible but he couldn't concentrate for all the other thoughts demanding his attention. Such as, where in the grand scheme of things did Joseph Kirkland's sins rank? The lies for example.

Lying about money was one thing. Lying about day-to-day goings-on another. But lying about being Saved was lying of a different order. He tried to convince himself that it wasn't God or Jesus he'd lied to, that it was Gran, and anyway, Mister Agnew says you can't lie to God *because He just knows. Also… Benjamin Mutch is a murderer! How can there be anything worse than being a murderer? And he still got Saved. He's even a Missionary for goodness sake, going about the country Saving folk. God and Jesus forgive you for anything. Anything. If you're Saved.*

With all this thinking Joseph wasn't thinking at all about where he was headed, but somehow he got to Archie's tree house without falling over or falling down anything. He took off his duffle coat and peeled away his woollen mitts and socks which were stuck to his skin with a glue of congealed weeping eczema from all the heat and scratching. Ah, yes, this was what he needed, soothing icy cold fresh air.

He started climbing up the knotted rope and was pleased to find himself getting most of the way up, but he wasn't good at things that required physical coordination and no matter how much he twisted and contorted his body he couldn't manoeuvre himself off the rope onto the platform. This is what happened. There was just too much gawkitness about him. And now he was stuck, suspended there, neither up not down, and without an Archie to help him.

There was a loud angry bark. He looked down half expecting to see the black dog emerge from the mist. There was a dog there but it wasn't the black dog. Of course not. The black dog wouldn't bark angrily like that, not at Joseph, not now they had been introduced and played and so on. No, this was a great muscle-bound thing, a dirty white beast with bloodshot eyes and an enormous head like a boulder. Both its ears were torn and it had scars around its flabby drooling muzzle. Joseph was good with dogs. They took to him. But not this dog. He'd seen this dog once before with a friend of Archie's dad.

"They used them for fighting round my bit when we were in Glasgow," said Archie. "They train them special to kill each other. It's terrible, so it is. They even file their teeth to make them extra sharp. Folk bet on them. My mum used to scream at my dad for losing his wages on the fights... *see you and yer dugs ya big effin eejit, whit've ah said?* ... but then once in a blue moon he'd come home with a nice big pile of tenners and fivers and ten shillingses and they'd be all lovey-dovey and go out and spend it all on drink or get their pals round for a wee night which was great because there'd be a sing-song and me and wee Maggie would maybe get to stay up late and have our own wee night with crisps and ginger and... ach..."

The dog had stopped its barking but it was still growling, snarling, sniffing around his duffle coat and mitts. Especially the mitts with their stink of weeping bloody eczema. Joseph should have said hello to it when he'd met it that day, maybe given it a treat, a biscuit or something, made friends. That's what you do with dogs. Any animal. Then they remembered you.

The wolf also shall dwell with the lamb, and the lion... no, the leopard... shall lie down with the kid, and the calf and the young lion and... and something... and a little child shall lead them. Isaiah chapter something, verse something. He should remember it better, he loved that bit of Scripture. He liked to think that's what Peace on Earth would be like, with all the animals, the hunters and the hunted, the murderous killer animals and the meek and mild animals, all great pals thegether.

Joseph's way with dogs, maybe that was part of all this. If he could make friends with a dog like this, a trained killer, then...

"Hello," he said, as nice and calm as can be. But the dog snarled again, fixing Joseph in its bloodshot stare, curling its lips, baring its pink-red gums, its teeth made for ripping, which looked like they had indeed been filed. "Hello boy."

Joseph whistled, clicked his tongue, made kissing noises, went through his entire repertoire of dog-befriending noises, even some budgie-befriending noises too, "Good boy, good dog." But this wasn't a good dog at all. It was a boulder-headed Devil dog.

Joseph knew he was out of reach. Just. This dog was solid muscle with jaws and teeth like a bear trap. It would bite if it could, but it probably wasn't a jumper. He lowered his foot half a knot, just to see. The dog snapped at him and before he knew it Joseph had hauled his whole self up onto the planks for the first time ever without Archie Truman's help.

And just as he was thinking such things as, *What am I going to do? If only the big black dog would appear like in a Lassie film,* the big black dog did appear like in a *Lassie* film. At least Joseph had thought it was big when he'd first seen it but now compared to the boulder-headed Devil dog, the black dog looked such a scrawny wee mutt. It would be okay though because you could see that despite its bulk, its strength, its battle scars and its teeth, the boulder-headed Devil dog – except when it was in a ring – was a house dog with soft-edged house-dog instincts. If it wasn't fighting it was lying on a hearthrug getting fed dog biscuits and chocolate drops and *Kennomeat* from a fancy dish. But the black dog belonged exactly where it was, on frosted ground, in the fog, in the wild woods, catching its food, eating raw bloody kill meat, and when it pulled its lips back into a full-toothed snarl Joseph saw the wolf in it. The boulder-headed Devil dog attacked first, lunging and snapping, but the black dog had already vanished back into the fog. Joseph wondered if it had run away scared and he honestly couldn't have blamed it for that, but no, a second later it reappeared right behind the Devil dog, jumping on its back and biting into a ripped ear. It was smart this black dog. It had tactics. But the fighting Devil dog had tactics too, of course it did, it was a fighting dog wasn't it? It bucked that hard it shook the black dog off and faster than Joseph had given it credit for, spun round and caught the black dog's back leg in its jaws. The black dog pulled but this just made it worse because the Devil dog could lock its jaws and pulling only sent those iron trap teeth even deeper into its leg. The black dog pulled anyway and now blood, its blood, was trickling out the side of the boulder-headed Devil dog's mouth.

Peter's cage. He could hit that big boulder-head with it, hurt it, maybe even kill it. *Sorry*. He'd never killed anything. Okay he'd captured and drowned the odd wasp in a sweet watery jam jar. Archie had killed loads: birds, rabbits, rats, squirrels, you name it, with catapults and air rifles and all sorts. Benjamin Mutch had killed a man and had been forgiven for it. Joseph held Peter's cage above his head like a caveman and threw it at the dog, "BASTARD!"

Oh my. He had never used language, not any swear word, even on his own just to see what it felt like. It felt good. The cage hit the devil dog's shoulder and it loosened its grip for a moment, not out of pain, but surprise, maybe the shock of hearing Joseph Kirkland use *language*. But the poor black dog was in no fit state now to take advantage of this hiatus and the Devil dog knew it. It let go of the leg and moved towards the neck.

"Please no!" *I'll do anything*. And the Devil dog paused again, its jaws open around the black dog's neck, like a gladiator, *So Joseph Kirkland wants to make a deal?*

The bearded man arrived in rolled-up shirtsleeves like he'd been just called away from his work. He launched himself at the boulder-headed Devil dog, landing a hammer punch on the back of its head. The dog's front legs buckled a little. He punched it again harder and this time it relaxed its grip and the black dog collapsed in a heap, its leg a gaping bloody mess. The Devil dog quickly came to its senses a little and turned its bulk around to face the man but it was sluggish now and the man was poised and ready, his leg pulled back like a shotgun trigger. With all his strength he kicked the boulder-headed Devil dog under its chin with the toe of his steel-capped boot. Joseph heard an awful grinding crunch and the big Devil dog's lower jaw hung there useless now and its face looked that stupid. It went over slow and heavy like a big tree being felled and lay there motionless, making this low pathetic whimper. It was sad. The man looked sad too, then turned his back on it – there was nothing to fear now – and tended to his own dog, walking around it figuring out a way to lift it without causing it even more injury. He saw Joseph's duffle coat and glanced up,

"You can use it if you want," said Joseph.

The man said nothing, just grabbed the coat, spread it out on the ground and eased his dog onto it. He gathered it up at its corners and was going to lift it, but instead he went and took another close look at the boulder-headed Devil dog. Its eyes were glazed now, its fighting days gone forever. He stroked the big boulder head once, affectionately almost and vanished into the fog. A minute later he was back with a length of scaffolding. He looked up at Joseph, *If you're going to look away, look away now*, and when Joseph did not the man just gave a nod, swung the metal pole above his head like it was a great two-handed Crusader's sword and brought it down upon the boulder-headed Devil dog's skull. Blood trickled out of its mouth again but this time it was the Devil dog's own blood.

The man came over and placed his boot on the end of the rope to keep it taut. Joseph didn't need asking and clambered down over the man, whose arms, legs, body were as solid as tree trunks.

The man lifted up his wounded black dog all wrapped up now in Joseph's duffle coat, and walked off fast, taking a route through the woods that Joseph didn't recognise. He hadn't asked Joseph to follow him but he had his duffle coat, so... After a wee bit the man stopped.

"You'll pick me a handful of those leaves," he said, nodding towards the foot of a tree. Joseph pulled up some big leaves. "No. The wee ones. With the red spots. Like spiders."

The man's voice. Was is it Scottish? It wasn't that nasally Kilhaugh drawl or Glasgow or wherever it was Benjamin Mutch was from. Not a preacher's voice either, but it was a serious voice though. Joseph picked four or five of the wee spidery plants.

"A good handful. There's more over there. Quick mind."

Joseph scurried over to the next tree, grabbed some handfuls. He didn't know what do with them so he loaded them into the front of his jumper. And so they carried on through the woods, the man stopping along the way and ordering Joseph to pick up this leaf or that stalk or a strip of that bark from that sapling. He never gave the plants names but described their colour, shape, size and smell, "Here's what you're looking for. Small, five points like the fingers of a newborn." Joseph picked a plant that fitted the description. "Now smell it." It smelled like Mrs Merryweather's house. "Cat's piss? You know why it smells of cat's piss?" Joseph shook his head. "You like stories?" Joseph nodded. "They've all got stories. That one's a good one. Pick some more."

The man had started singing, a sleepy sort of tune. Joseph couldn't make out any of the words, if they were in fact words. The singing was quiet, just for himself, or maybe it was for the dog, which hadn't moved or made a sound since he'd picked it up. They made one more stop beside a moss-covered tree trunk that was lying half in and half out the Sappie.

"You'll be careful with that… that's good stuff that."

Joseph ripped several clumps of frosted green moss and shoved it in his jumper with the rest of the foliage and stuff. As they walked Joseph considered the boulder-headed Devil dog lying dead now beneath the tree. What would happen to it? Maybe he and Archie could come down tomorrow and bury it or bring petrol and cremate it, although they'd never cremated anything that big before. He should definitely put these things in his map though. The tree house. The dead Devil dog.

This tent.

CHAPTER SIXTEEN

The Kingdom of Caleb

It was a bow tent and it appeared to be have been woven from fog.

The sheets of dirty white tarpaulin were held tight from all sides by guy ropes that stretched off into nothingness. Joseph hadn't been invited to enter and the heavy tent flaps closed so quickly behind the man, he didn't have time to see inside. Joseph believed this to be a tinker's tent. He saw them every spring when they came by for the tattie howkin or when they went round the doors selling bits and bobs or repairing this and that. Sometimes they'd bring their children on their rounds, but the children would never speak, just give you a hard stare, give everybody a hard stare. And no wonder. The local teenage boys often went down to their camp with the sole purpose of picking fights with the tinker boys to prove some man-boy teenage point. Gran thought the Kilhaugh boys were worse because *they should know better*. Most folk were quite open about their animosity towards tinkers, but Gran's thoughts on the matter were more ambiguous. She'd never actually say she didn't like them, just, *Mind and stay away from those tinkers*, or *They're not like us*; that sort of thing and if she saw one coming to the door she'd say, *Get away from that window* and she wouldn't answer the door no matter how long they chapped. Joseph did answer the door to a tinker man. Once. But Gran had yanked him away and shut the door that fast he didn't get a proper look at him or hear a word the tinker said. *Never EVER open the door to them again. Do you hear me?* Grandpa rarely said anything about them, though he did have an expression, *tinker-fix* that he'd use for something that had been mended well or needed to be mended well. *That's a nice wee bit of tinker-fix* or *we need to do a bit of a wee tinker-fix on that.* Gran didn't like that expression.

Grandpa did say that it was the same extended tinker family that came by every year – *They're more like a tribe than a family*. Joseph had never seen this man among them. So maybe he wasn't one of them.

The man came out the tent, wiped his hands on his trousers, and without a word or look of gratitude or anything else he took the plants from Joseph's jumper and went back inside. Moments later he was out again with the duffle coat. He hung it from the wing mirror of the rusty old Bedford van, parked alongside the tent, the same van Joseph had seen on the lane, then he ripped up a clump of frosted turf and wiped off as much dog blood as he could from inside the coat.

"Caleb," he said, handing Joseph his coat, still avoiding looking him in the eye.

Caleb. What kind of a name was *Caleb*. A tinker name? A Bible name?

"You'll give me your name now," he said, busily tightening a guy rope that didn't look like it needed tightening. Joseph considered a false name; Archie's old get-out-of-trouble name, *Donald MacFarlane* was at the tip of his tongue. "Joseph Kirkland."

This *Caleb* looked at Joseph now, not blinking, not smiling but like he might be looking at a strange new plant and wondering; *What are its properties? What qualities does it possess? What good might this Joseph Kirkland thing do?*

"Well," he glanced towards the tent, "Joseph Kirkland's got a friend for life now." He called inside, "That right?" The dog answered immediately with a weak yelp and Joseph felt the hint of a smile crease his face. This was something. It wasn't Joseph's own dog. But still...

"I need to go," said Joseph, and because he didn't want the man – he couldn't yet call him *Caleb* – to think he was just making excuses, he added, "I've got to go to the jumble sale." He didn't want to go. He wasn't sure where to go.

The man stood behind him, walked him forwards, then

placed his big hands on the side of Joseph's head like blinkers on a horse. Joseph did think this was odd but then who knew tinkers and their ways, and who knew what was odd anymore. He whispered in Joseph's ear, "Now listen, Joseph Kirkland. We don't like to be the centre of things. We don't like it when folk pay us too much attention. You hear what I'm saying."

"Yes."

"Good. Now look. You'll see the line of the plants. You'll see the way the grass is growing, different from the grass over here, and that bush too all over to one side. You'll see how they grow different to the others. That's the line. The one that'll take you back to your folk and your jumble sale and all the rest of it."

Joseph didn't like to say but he could not see any of this. Maybe the man was taking a lend of him, even though he didn't seem the sort. But then the blinkers were gone, the man Caleb was gone and there was no sign of the tent. Joseph followed some vague, barely there at all path or line or whatever it was he was following, but he did have a feeling that he *was* following something. He stopped and put his duffle coat back on. It was still warm and smelling of dog, and still damp with dog blood.

CHAPTER SEVENTEEN

I Will Make You Fishers of Men

The Episcopalian Church jumble sale was a major event in the Kilhaugh village calendar. It drew Episcopalian and non-Episcopalian locals and a few hawk-eyed dealers from far and wide.

The collecting began weeks in advance with Church worthies and helpers trawling up and down the hill – mostly up – for the flotsam and jetsam of the great and the good, and the leavings of the recently deceased (by accident or natural causes). The volunteers came back with cars bursting with ancient wooden golf clubs, cribbage boards and lacrosse racquets, curling stones, mounted antlers, stuffed badgers, pheasants, foxes and weasels, barometers, chestnut roasters and copper-bottomed jam pans, prints, poorly painted paintings of thoroughbred horses, sleek-coated pedigree hounds and their sleek-haired, red-coated pedigree masters, walking sticks, shooting sticks, bundles of *The Scot*, *The Countryman*, *Country Life*, *Farmer's Weekly*, *Horse and Hound*, *The Lady*, and other journals dedicated to posh living and rural pursuits, none of which would ever be found in any house on or below the main street. There were also great bundles of what seemed to be DC Thomson's entire comic catalogue: *Beezers*, *Beanos*, *Sparkys*, *Victors* and *Hotspurs* which Joseph longed to buy but couldn't.

"If you want anything, just say," said Archie, who would happily purchase them on Joseph's behalf with stolen money, and keep them at his place or plank them in a den; Joseph's own secret library of banned literature. Just as he'd done the year before. But things were different this year.

"It's okay," said Joseph, knowing that Archie would buy them anyway, and off Archie went to pilfer or procure clothes and things for wee Maggie, who was currently unknotting a tangle of dolls and knitted dolls' clothes. Neither of them mentioned the earlier encounter with the mum and dad. Archie didn't seem any the worse for it, but then the blacks, blues and yellows of a parental battering would've been hard to find beneath the existing camouflage of blood reds, browns and purple bruises that Archie accumulated through his general day-to-day living.

Joseph sifted through mountains of good quality men's and women's clothes in tweed, cashmere and silk, and handmade shoes and hats made by proper tailors, cobblers and milliners with Royal Crests and Coats of Arms. There was nothing his size or which Gran would deem *suitable*. He was just about to move on to the piles of mass-produced, produced for the masses – rayons, nylons and terylenes – when he saw it hanging from a nail on the wall behind Mrs Urquhart and Mrs Brown.

"Can I help you, Joseph?" said Mrs Brown, the Episcopalian minister's wife, who Joseph had never actually spoken to as far as he could remember.

"How much for that?" he said, pointing at a complete ensemble consisting of a small Harris Tweed suit, Fair Isle sleeveless v-neck jumper, flannel shirt, green woollen tie, and a pair of small brown brogues. Joseph Kirkland's name was not written on it, there was no light shining on it. But there might as well have been. It was a child-size version of Benjamin Mutch's entire missionary wardrobe.

This is it.

"You mean this lot?" Joseph nodded. "The whole lot?" she said, not quite believing it but then when he nodded again, "Mrs Urquhart, could I have a wee word?"

Mrs Brown and Mrs Urquhart huddled together like sheriff court lawyers and exchanged whispers. They looked at the tweeds and brogues, looked at Joseph, resumed their huddle and exchanged more whispers,

"They're here to be sold," whispered Mrs Brown.

"I know, I know but…" whispered Mrs Urquhart. "They're awfully old-fashioned, son."

"Have a wee look round," said Mrs Brown. "See if there's not something else."

"I'm sure I saw some nice windcheaters and anoraks over there."

"And baseball boots as well, if I remember correctly."

"Something a wee bit more *with-it*."

"Exactly, more *with-it*."

The ladies laughed at themselves using language they never used, but the promise of being *with-it* was never going to work with Joseph Kirkland. He was standing his ground, inscrutable, the two half-crowns resting on his outstretched palm.

"It's a lot of money for something you don't know will fit," said Mrs Urquhart.

"Could I try them on?"

"Folk don't try things on at jumble sales," said Mrs Brown.

Joseph didn't budge. The ladies shrugged and shook their heads, *oh, what to do?*

"There's that big mirror on the stage," said Mrs Urquhart to Mrs Brown, "you know, the one the Operatic and Dramatic Society use? I suppose he could use that. Hold on a wee minute," and she got an old cardboard suitcase from under the table, "It'll be easier to carry."

Joseph walked up the side stage steps, clutching his suitcase, like he was off to join the army. Or the Crusades. He was. *Onward Christian Soldiers, Marching As To War…*

Behind the heavy dark red stage curtains was a clutter of vaulting horses, medicine balls and Indian clubs used by the Life Boys, an organization Gran might have approved of had it not held its meetings in Kilhaugh Episcopalian.

"You've enough daftness in your life without them and their falderals."

At the back corner he found a big full-length mirror with white light bulbs around it. He stripped down to his vest, pants and socks, flicked a switch on the side of the mirror and there he was in all his glory: Joseph Kirkland. *That Kirkland boy.* There wasn't a long mirror in Gran's. He couldn't mind when he'd last seen all of himself, when he'd last seen for himself how unlike Gran and Grandpa or Uncle Andrew or Jenny he was; how unlike any of them, with their blue eyes and their fair hair and their peely-wally skin. But these were fleeting, half-thoughts; Joseph was well used to being different. He began singing, "*I'm H.A.P.P.Y.*", in a jerky breathy murmur, "*I'm H.A.P.P.Y.*," moving his arms and legs, jiggling them around, like a puppet, like Archie often did when he was excited, "*I Know I am, I'm Sure I am…*" letting his head go floppy, wiggling his fingers; in something that was not quite a dance, more a collection of wee jumps, hops and spins – and all for no reason other than… here he was seeing himself, all of himself, all working "… I'm H.A.P.P.Y."

He put on the flannel shirt first. It was exactly his size. Then the green tie. He was good with ties; Grandpa had shown him. Then the Fair Isle jumper, the tweed jacket and trousers. Just right. Finally the brown brogues. A perfect fit. It was like the whole lot had been made to measure. He packed all his own things, his *old* things, from his old life, into the suitcase. Except his Bible. He needed that to complete this… thing.

The Bible was still in his duffle coat pocket. The leather cover was sticky with the black dog's blood. He got a wad of damp paper towels from the toilet at the back of the stage. The blood wiped off the leather easily. Then he opened it. *Oh please, no.* The dog blood had seeped inside onto Mister Agnew's list, onto the edges of the Bible pages themselves. You didn't really notice it when the Bible was shut because the paper edges were stained red anyway. But when you opened it, *No, no, no*. The wet paper towels had made it worse, made the blood seep in deeper. *Genesis*, *Exodus* , *Leviticus*, *Numbers*, *Deuteronomy*, *Joshua*, *Judges* and on and on and on; all of them had a ragged dog-blood border like the dangerous uncharted territories in Miss O'Donnell's *Mappa Mundi*. A Bible stained with the blood of a black dog. What might that even mean? This could not be a good thing. But then he caught himself again, complete with Bible, and he was stunned by what he saw. *Yes. That's me now. It doesn't matter that I lied. None of it matters. It'll be okay now.*

He tried on an assortment of gestures and serious expressions. He tried stroking his chin but he'd really need a beard for that and promised himself that one day he'd grow one, a long one, for that very purpose. But in the stabbing the air with his finger, in the pointing at imaginary people with outstretched arm, in the sage nods, the tapping the Bible and in the holding it aloft, in all that he looked the part. The hubbub of the jumble sale allowed him to read some scripture aloud – but not too loud. He tried to vary his tempo and modulation to achieve the most powerful effect: "For God so LOVED the world... for God SO loved the world... for GOD SO LOVED the WORLD..."

His voice was thin and thowless. He needed practice in this department but there was no doubt in his mind what he looked like: a miniature missionary, a small Benjamin Mutch, *I WILL be Saved.*

He looked the part. Now he would become the part. And then that would be it. God would see. Joseph Kirkland was a serious boy, serious about being Saved, and about Saving others, and before he knew it he would himself be Saved. Just like that.

He marched back towards the red curtains, filled with excitement, desperate to reveal his new self to the world. Where was the opening? He found himself flapping and tugging the curtains this way and that in such a frantic and undignified way that when he finally tumbled out onto centre stage in his tweed suit, brogues and patched specs, suitcase in one hand, Bible in the other, and a look of open-mouthed surprise on his face, he looked less like a small missionary and more like a small music-hall comedian. For a brief moment the rummaging, haggling and chatter came to a halt as all heads turned towards Joseph as though they were waiting for him to perform his novelty act. Was he going to whip out a ventriloquist's dummy from that suitcase? But when nothing happened, apart from his right leg starting to tremble, there was a bit of a sniggering and snorting, some disappointed sighing, some *Well, what do you expect of the Kirkland boy?* kind of whisperings, and the jumble-sale din resumed.

"So, you're taking them then?" said Mrs Urquhart, still not sure about this transaction.

"Five shillings mind!" said Mrs Brown.

"You're keeping them on?"

The ladies again shook their heads again, *oh what to do?*

"Where's your own clothes?"

Joseph looked down at the suitcase,.

"Och you can keep that," said Mrs Urquhart, "Nobody's going to buy it."

Joseph held out the two half-crowns. He could not wait to be rid of them. Mrs Brown gave him one of those sad-eyed looks that Joseph was used to,

"We'll call it half a crown, and say no more about it."

"It's okay," he said, shoving the money at them. *Please take it.*

"Do the words 'gift horse' and 'mouth' mean anything to you? Away you go now, before we change our minds."

"Look at you!" said Archie. He was carrying two bales of American and British comics and two bags of girls' clothes and shoes,. "Gentleman Joseph."

"I'm going to be a missionary," said Joseph, quite the thing.

"A missionary?" Archie was unfazed by this revelation, "How?"

"I'll tell you tomorrow." He needed to be away. Now.

"Can I be one too?" Archie said, handing him an old *Captain Marvel* comic.

"I don't know. Maybe. I can't take the comic. I have to go."

"I'll put it in the den. For later."

There he goes again. *Temptation*. Archie did it all the time. He didn't mean to but he did. Joseph was determined to resist. He'd chosen a path. He had to stick to it. But it was *so hard*.

"Okay." He didn't have to read it. It would just be there. *Liar*.

"Can we play at missionaries tomorrow?"

Wee Maggie was there now, "Oh Joseph, you look so handsome. You look like a posh person from up the hill."

"He's going to be a missionary."

"A missionary?"

"We can play Tarzan as well," said Archie. "Imagine Tarzan was a missionary? He'd be a great missionary, so he would!"

"Oh, can I play at Tarzan and the missionaries too, Joseph?"

So hard.

The missionary Joseph Kirkland walked out into the night, full of purpose, swinging the suitcase that contained his old self and half-humming, half-singing, I will make you fishers of men, fishers of men, fishers of men, I will make you fishers of men, if you follow me…

There was a woman with a dog. They were standing in the middle of the Memorial Bridge. Mrs Arnold from up the hill. Joseph had never spoken to her, had never tried "to borrow" her dog, though he'd seen them both often enough out for walks. It looked a nice dog – a big jowly face, black like the other dog but fatter, older, grey around the muzzle, something of the Labrador about it. Mrs Arnold was wearing a long brown fur coat that reached almost to her ankles and a matching fur hat and leather gloves. She looked lost. Or far away. Or … She must've felt the vibrations on the bridge and looked up, but when she saw Joseph Kirkland standing there in his missionary clothes she grabbed hold of the railing like she was in serious danger of falling over the side. She looked like an animal herself now in all that fur and leather, a frightened animal. Her dog was fine though, even wagging its tail, panting, smiling its big dog smile. The poor woman though, she was petrified, the way those shepherds were when they saw the Angel that said unto them, *Fear not: for, behold, I bring you good tidings of great joy, which shall be to all people.* Joseph shook his head, he wanted to shake the scripture right out of it this second and looked around to see if there was someone else or something else that was scaring her, but no, no, it was just him. Maybe she had trouble at home. You never knew with folk, what went on with them in their own houses. Should he go and get someone? Uncle Andrew was just up the road, or the doctor or… But the dog was fine, still wagging its tail and that was important because dogs could tell. Those shepherds were fine too, once they'd heard the Good Tidings and understood…

"It'll be okay… if you're Saved," said *Joseph the Missionary*, delivering the Good News she needed to hear, that everybody needed to hear, "Everything'll be okay then."

Had *Joseph the Liar*, *Joseph the Hypocrite* really said that? Out loud? He held the suitcase tight, as rigid with fear as she was, and then bolted past her. *Don't look at her. Don't look her in the eye. Don't let her touch you. Because if you do…* And he didn't stop until he was safe inside Gran's house.

CHAPTER EIGHTEEN

Heroes of the Cross

"Joseph Kirkland! Whatever possessed you?"

What she really wanted to do was shout at him, give him a proper row, give him a right good slap on the thigh with her slipper, which she hadn't done for long and weary, not that she'd ever made a habit of it. But what with Benjamin Mutch taking a nap in Joseph's bed and Grandpa asleep as well…

"Look at you! I mean in the name of the wee man. I told you to buy something for every day, not Sunday best."

"I'll wear it every day. I'm…"

But Gran wasn't anywhere near ready to hear another side to this: "I don't understand you, Joseph, I really don't. I send you out for one thing and you come back with something else all thegether. You're worse than Jack and the Beanstalk and his… ach…" She caught herself in time and looked at Joseph like it was him who made her do it, quote fairy tales instead of scripture. And hadn't Jack been proven right with his magic beans? "And who sold you this lot?"

"Mrs Brown and Mrs…"

"The minister's wife? Aye, well, no surprise there then."

Joseph was confused, the way Gran was behaving towards him, like she was black affronted. Why? Why wasn't she pleased that he'd eschewed windcheaters, anoraks and baseball boots of the riffraff teenager in favour of Fair Isles, tweeds and brogues, clothing that looked like it belonged in the Hall? He put his hand up, which he'd never done before and it was such an odd thing to do that it threw Gran off her stride. Oh, this odd boy and his strange antics.

"What?"

"I'm going to be a missionary."
"*What?*"
And right on cue Benjamin Mutch tottered in. Gran did a double take. Benjamin Mutch and Joseph Kirkland were dressed so alike the former might've been an old Joseph Kirkland arrived in from the future or the latter a young Benjamin Mutch come back from the past.
"Whit's a' this aboot missionaries?"
Gran tittered, a nervous titter that got caught in her throat and ended up as a Mrs Merryweather coughing fit. Benjamin Mutch gave her a whack on the back which she
wasn't expecting, but it did the trick,
"Joseph's a bit of a dreamer," she said. "Got it into his head that he might be a missionary. One day. Now, if we want to get to the Hall we better make a move," and she made a big theatrical sweep towards the door, which she hoped would drag Benjamin Mutch in its wake, but he was anchored to the spot.
Even leaning almost at right angles on his shepherd's crook Benjamin Mutch towered over them. He looked Joseph up and down, scratching his beard like he was thinking of bidding for a sheep but wasn't sure if this one was worth the time or money. "Joseph, aye," he said, trying out the name, "Joseph," seeing if it fitted this awkward-looking beast, "Ah hae in mind anither Joseph," he said. "No Joseph the stepfather o Jesus, an no auld Joe frae the jyle. Na, the Joseph ah'm thinkin o wis a bit o a dreamer tae. Ridiculed fur it, so he wis. But his dreams bore fruit. An if ma memory serves me richt, did he no also git himsel a new set o claithes? Ye'll ken wha ah'm referrin tae, Mrs Kirkland?"
"Genesis chapter thirty-seven," she said trying not to look too pleased with herself.
"Clearly ye've spent yer days wisely."
"Well, I don't know about..."
"It seems yer grandson here hae plans tae dae likewise."
She opened her mouth to say something, closed it and

opened it again to say something else, "He's only eleven years old, Benjamin."

"We were a' ainly eleeven year auld, Mrs Kirkland. Jesus Christ oor Lord wis ainly eleeven year auld. Ane year later He was *in the temple, sittin in the midst o the doctors, baith hearin them an askin them questions.*"

They recited the rest in unison, Gran in "proper" English, Benjamin Mutch in *rude* Scots.

"An a' that heard Him were dumbfoondert at His unnerstaundin an answers." He walked over to window and looked out, "If ah haed listened tae the Lord when ah wis eleeven, ah mebbe widna hae endit up whaur ah endit up."

After they'd gone, Joseph unpacked his suitcase and put away his "civilian" clothes. He wouldn't be needing these for a while. Maybe never. He unfolded his map and added a wee triangle beside the Sappie. Caleb's tent. *Red or yellow?* He would decide the colour later.

The shape of Benjamin Mutch was still visible on the bed and there were lots of his white hairs on the pillow. Joseph had himself an odd notion. He gathered the hairs up in a wee tumbleweed ball in his hand, went through and lit the cooker and sprinkled the hairs a few at a time onto the flame. They fizzled, sending up wee puffs of acrid smoke. His appetite whetted and with Grandpa asleep, and Gran and Benjamin Mutch not due back for a good while, he got the tin of lighter fuel from under the sink, went into the toilet and skooshed a criss-cross pattern around the enamel bath.

I know. I'll stop. I will.

He switched off the light, it was better that way, and threw in a match. The fuel trail ignited. It was beautiful, but too quick. He was still feeling the urge. He wiped off the scorch marks with Vim, went back to the kitchen and poured a spoonful of lighter fuel straight onto the ring to make a wee ball of fire. *One more turn. Two. Three and no more. Four. Five and no more. Six. Sorry.*

He stuck the spoon inside the flame for a few seconds, pulled up his shirt and held it against his stomach.

Had Grandpa aged in the past fifteen minutes? Was that possible? He looked awful but then again the bedside lamp was orange. Maybe he would look better in daylight.
He really was going to read Grandpa the Bible, the pages had been properly marked this time, but then that touch of Grandpa's hand on his wrist, that pathetic attempt at a wink:

"Sheriff Skinner," said Miss Victoria, "we might be in our twilight years, but we're sound enough in mind and eye to know what we saw and sound enough in body to come here and tell you 'bout it."

There was only one way to get this sorted out. The sheriff hollered into the jailhouse, "Elizabeth!"

Seconds later a pretty young woman, appeared: Elizabeth Skinner, only days from her seventeenth birthday and in full beautiful bloom. Seeing the ladies, she curtsied,

"Afternoon Miss Victoria, afternoon Miss Sarah. Yes daddy?"

"Send a wire to the county jail, ask 'em how the Reno trial is farin?"

"Course," said Elizabeth and she curtsied again and went back inside.

"You must be mighty proud of the way she's turned out," said Miss Victoria.

"Her mamma did enough before she passed, I won't take no credit," He looked uncomfortable with this line of conversation and steered it towards safer territory, "You ladies care for some lemonade while we're waiting?"

"Why thank you, Charles," said Miss Sarah, "if it's no trouble."

"No trouble at all."

He wished he could do the American voices, like Grandpa, but if Joseph did it... well he couldn't.

Moments later a breathless Elizabeth Skinner came running out: "Daddy! They're saying Reno, Driscoll and Hatfield were freed three days ago."

"Freed? What you talking about Elizabeth?"

"One of the witnesses was shot on the morning of the trial and now the other three have refused to testify. The judge said he had no choice but to set 'em free."

Joseph wondered how long it would be till the gunslinger *Kit Mossman* arrived on the scene, head to toe in black with his ivory-handled pistols in their death's-head holsters.

"*Well, looks to me like somebody needs a helpin' hand*," he'd say and he'd sort everything out and make sure the right side won. Like he always did. Then he'd ride off into the sunset and not look back…

Grandpa had slipped back into something like sleep.

What'll he be like he's dead? Sorry.

He'd never seen a dead person. How different would he be? Grandpa coughed another rattling cough then lay still, almost not breathing, then another rattle, then nothing. Then more nothing. Joseph felt bad for wanting something to happen. Anything. *The thing* even. Watching Grandpa dying – and he was dying – was sad at times. Scary at times. And intense at times. But not scary and sad and intense *all the time*. No. Mostly, and it wasn't Grandpa's fault, not at all, but watching him dying was mostly just boring.

Sorry.

He saw to Grandpa's catheter. There was so little heat left in him, so little moisture, the bag was cold and the liquid thick, dark and as orange as marmalade.

He arranged his missionary clothes on the chair in such a way it looked like a small person was sitting there, and put down the plastic sheet on the settee, just in case, and a blanket on top of that. Tomorrow was going to be so big. It's when it would start properly. All this. *The Missionary Joseph Kirkland.* A Hero of the Cross. Maybe. One day. Who knew? Folk never knew. How could anybody know the road that had been chosen for Joseph Kirkland?

His thoughts turned to Mrs Arnold on the bridge, how she'd looked at him and what he'd said – *It'll be okay, if you're Saved. Everything will be okay then* – sure now that he had actually said it out loud, and not knowing what do with these thoughts, put them away.

He went into a drawer in the sideboard and removed a polythene bag full of documents.

"For when the time comes," said Gran at every opportunity, "it's all here: hymns, purvey, insurance, telephone number for the Cooperative and all the rest of it." *All the rest of that earthly nonsense.* "Uncle Andrew will make the arrangements, this is just so you'll know."

What he was really looking for lay beneath these documents, a small leather album with a dozen pages of photographs, black and white mostly. There was a small faded picture of Gran and Grandpa in their early twenties, blond-haired – nearly everyone in the photographs was blond haired – just married, him looking happy, her looking worried. There were some less faded photos of Uncle Andrew and Uncle Mathew as children, a newborn Jenny, a toddler Sam, and some others. There were none at all of more recent get-togethers, and none at all of Joseph, but then Gran wasn't keen on photographs, or mirrors.

"Mister Agnew says *photographs and mirrors encourage vanity and an unhealthy obsession with the earthbound body.*"

There was also an envelope containing a few unmounted snaps. One, the one Joseph was looking for, was a beach photographer's monochrome postcard of a boy, a toddler, sat upon a seaside donkey. Behind him, her hand on the small of his back, making sure he wouldn't fall, was a young woman. They were both laughing.

The photograph had been garishly, ineptly, hand-tinted.

The woman's yellow wavy hair – the same yellow as her flower-patterned dress, the same yellow as the sand – was *too* yellow; her rosy red cheeks *too* rosy, her blue eyes too blue, her red lipstick, her pink arms and legs, all too red, too pink, too much. The boy had also been badly coloured in. Nothing could be done with his black hair but there had been a poor attempt at tinting his skin the same salmon pink as the woman's. What's more, the wash of blue on his eyes had bled into the whites making the boy look bizarre, like a sunburnt alien. The background of sea, sky, boats, seagulls, swimmers and paddlers, all distant and blurred, had also been ludicrously tinted. It looked like a Primary One *First Reader – A Day at the Seaside* or *My Summer Holidays*. But despite all this, the messy artificiality, the other-worldliness, it held Joseph in its thrall. He sniffed it, out of habit. There had once been a faint scent of rosewater. Now it was no more than a phantom scent, but it still had the power to transport, "It's okay… wee man… wee soldier… she won't let you fall…"

CHAPTER NINETEEN

Navigating the Dangerous Uncharted Territories

"Joseph. Wake up, son. Benjamin's moving on first thing. He wants a wee word."

It was the early hours. Benjamin Mutch was sitting up in Joseph's bed drinking tea from Grandpa's mug, wearing Grandpa's grey-striped pyjamas, buttoned up to the neck like a prison uniform. On his lap were his Bible and one or two *Heroes of the Cross*.

"Quite a library ye've got here. An a' aboot the missionaries, eh? *Paton, Moffat, Livingstone*. Ye read them a'?" Joseph nodded. "Aye? Weel yer a better reader than me." He prodded his Bible. "This is a' the reading ah dae an ah struggle tae unnerstaun this at times. Ach, ah'm shair we a' dae, eh?"

"They're Sunday School prizes."

"Guid fur you. That's braw. Hard life these men led, Joseph. Hard men as weel, maist o them. Terrible hardships. Thankless tae. A'richt, some o them micht hae wandert frae the straight an narra. Like yer maun Livingstone here, wi his maps an explorations an a' his ither bletherations. Noo if yon maun had been as concernt wi his Scripture as he wis wi his maps he'd mibbe hae saved a few mair sowls."

Joseph was taken aback at this attack on the legendary Doctor Livingstone. Benjamin Mutch laughed a wheezy laugh. "Dinna look sae shocked, son. Ah'm no sayin Livingstone wisna a guid maun, jist that he wis flawed, easily led astray. Like the rest o us. We should aye be carefu' o turnin' fowk intae heroes, Joseph. Fur the next thing ye ken, we're turnin them intae saunts an ither heresies."

"Miss O'Donnell got us to make a map. For school."

"*O'Donnell* eh?" He narrowed his eyes, "Is that richt? Weil let's hae a look at it."

He spread it out on the bed.

"It's not finished yet."

Benjamin Mutch scrutinised it, scrutinised Joseph too, his motives maybe.

Three; why are you doing the things you're doing and saying the things you're saying?

"This map. Tell me aw aboot it,"

"In olden times they used to put Jerusalem in the middle of their maps so they'd mind that God was in the centre of their lives." He paused. He rarely spoke this much, not all at once.

"Cerry oan, yer daen a grand job." He pointed at the small yellow square in the centre, "So that's Jerusalem?"

"No. That's the Hall. Because ..." he searched for the phrase that Miss O'Donnell had used, "... that's where the *spiritual centre* is. In Kilhaugh. So..." Unable to explain it properly he went on to safer ground, "You can't get gold crayons. So it's yellow. I'm going to colour in the rest too. Those wee bits are Gateways to Hell. I'm going to do them red. I'll draw more of them. When I think of more."

"Guid stuff. Guid stuff. An this schuil teacher's name is O'*Donnell*, ye say?" Joseph nodded. "And whit are a' these swirly lines alang the sides an oan tap an doon ablow?"

"That's going to be Hell at the bottom with its fire. And over there and there, that's places I don't know. Or I haven't been to. Or I'm not allowed. Because there might be things there that... I'm going to draw different monsters in those bits and... But they might not be real places. Some might. But others might just be..." again he could not find the words "... places where folk don't know God. Miss O'Donnell called it *the Sea of Darkness*,"

"Uncharted territories."

Joseph shivered, his body was so tense. His voice shook with it too.

"Miss O'Donnell called them that as well."

"Us auld sailors, we ken a' aboot uncharted territories." He removed his spectacles and rubbed his eyes, "Weil noo, this is a piece o wark, Joseph Kirkland. This is a map. This a *guid thing*. An the teacher's name is *O'Donnell*, ye say? Weil, weil. Mind ye feenish this. This can be a tool tae help ye in yer mission. Ah'll hae a word wi yer graun. She's a guid wummin, nae twa weys aboot it, but you bein a missionary, ye ken, it'll tak a bit o gettin yased tae. When'll ye stairt yer mission work? "

"Tomorrow." *I will.*

"The morra? Awricht. An how'll ye stairt?"

"Just… talk to folk."

"Talkin' aye, talkin' tae fowk is aye a guid stairt. Ah'll be daen the vera same thing masel somewhaur or ither. An whit'll ye say tae them?"

"I'll show them the map. I'll say… here's what'll happen if you get lost. If you wander away from God. I'll point to hell and I'll say… look… this is where you might end up."

"Guid boy. Ah'll tell ye whit, Joseph, if ah e'er decide tae tak oan a prentice, ah'll ken whaur tae leuk."

Oh yes please.

"Noo, wha' will ye speak tae feerst?"

"Archie Truman." No hesitation.

"An wha's this Erchie Truman? Is he a freen?"

"He's a boy from school. From the scheme." *I didn't say he's not my friend.* Joseph chose a phrase Gran was fond of, which covered all manner of unmentionable conditions, emotional, physical, psychological, criminal, "He's got trouble at home."

Benjamin Mutch threw his head back and laughed.

"Oh aye. Ye mean his mither an faither tak a drink?"

"Yes."

"If ah've heard that tale aince ah've heard it a thoosand times." He leant in close and with the utmost urgency said, "Save him, Joseph. Show him yer map. Save this Erchie Truman. It's the greatest thing ye can e'er dae fur him." He launched seamlessly into scripture, "*Ah will bring the blin bi a wey they didna ken. Ah will lead them in paths they hav'na kent. Ah will mak the mirkness licht afore them, an crooket places straight.*" Again, it was so seamless that Joseph didn't know when Benjamin Mutch had stopped and scripture had begun. This was another trick Joseph must learn.

"Yer weil on yer wey Joseph. Better than yon ither map reader, *Doctor* Livingstone. Ye ken hoo mony puir sowls he Saved in his hale career?" Joseph shook his head. "Tak a guess!"

"A thousand?"

Benjamin Mutch laughed and clapped his hand together,

"A thoosand? Aye, a thoosand tak awa' nine hunner an ninety nine! Yin! *Yin solitary sowl*! An *he* lapsed!"

They filled in the map and talked about the lives of the missionaries. To the Gateways to Hell that Joseph had already drawn, Benjamin Mutch suggested others, "Ony Catholic schuils or chapels!"

Saint Adrian's Primary was outside the Kilhaugh boundary line. He would've put Saint Rita's chapel in but he'd never been there and didn't know exactly where it was, "Jist fling them intae the dangerous uncharted territories."

Joseph added rough-drawn outlines of fire-belching dragons and boulder-headed demon dogs into his fogbound uncharted territories. The small ovals were the body-snatcher pods. Thankfully Benjamin Mutch didn't ask him about those.

"That's the ticket Joseph. That'll pit the fear o God intae them."

"Is it wrong that it's made up? That dragons are just in stories?"

"The Lord kent weil the power o stories, Joseph. *Why speakest thou untae them in parables? Spak ah tae them in parables because they seein see nocht an hearin they hear nocht, neither dae they unnerstaun.*" He pointed his big bony forefinger at the triangle beside the Sappie. "Whit's this here? Anither o the Gateways tae Hell?"

"No. I don't know. Maybe. It's a tent."

"A tent?"

He couldn't lie, not to Benjamin Mutch.

"Down by the Sappie. There's a man. He lives there."

"In a tent? ... Och ye mean tinkers? Are we talkin' *tinkers* here? At this time o year?" Joseph nodded. "Aye we can hae tinkers oan yer map. Whit fur no?" and he handed the red crayon to Joseph, for a tinker's tent must surely be a Gateway to Hell.

They carried on a while, Joseph colouring in the fires of Hell and the dangerous uncharted territories, Benjamin Mutch doing the golden rays of Heaven till eventually he nodded off. Joseph took the yellow crayon from the old man's hand and added a thick protective golden border around Caleb's Hell-red tent.

Gran was waiting for him in the living room, "Go and kiss your Grandpa goodnight before you go back to sleep"

She'd never had to ask. But Joseph kissed him, the heaving wheezing bag of bones that was for the time being still Grandpa.

"I'll not be at the Meeting tomorrow," she said, "I'll leave the bread out for you. Don't forget it." He turned to go. "And mind say your prayers." His nod wasn't enough this time. "Did you hear what I said?"

She was like a scared child. Like wee Maggie lost in the fog playing hide-and-seek. Or Mrs Arnold on the bridge. Or all the others.

CHAPTER TWENTY

Joseph Kirkland's Second Dream

It's a bright and sunny blue sky morning and Joseph is standing in the lobby looking through into the living room. Gran and Grandpa are sitting side by side on the settee. Gran's busy writing an airmail letter, to Sam probably. Grandpa's still in his dressing gown and Peter is perched on the end of his finger cooing away. They pair of them seem happy and contented in each other's company. It gives Joseph a nice feeling. Safe. Secure. He leaves them there and goes through to his bedroom. But Gran and Grandpa are there too, looking out the bedroom window. They have their backs to him. But it's them. There's no doubt it's them. Joseph screams because he knows that in this dream screaming is the only way to wake himself up before they turn around and *oh please no,* they must never turn around.

CHAPTER TWENTY-ONE

The Breaking of Bread

Early Sunday morning, Kilhaugh's new young missionary marched across the Memorial Bridge thinking of the souls he might Save, the first being Archie's. The second, his own. He looked the part, all brogued and tweeded with Bible, map, tin of scriptural texts, a carrier bag of freshly baked bread for the Breaking of Bread dangling by his side: the full evangelical mission kit.

It was cold, but he could hardly put a duffle coat or a balaclava and mitts over his tweed suit. He'd be too bumphled up. And it would not look right.

It wasn't long past eight o'clock, the Meeting was ages away but he needed to be outside in the open without walls, ceilings and floors, with his thoughts. He tapped out a rhythm on the barley sugar tin like a Salvation Army tambourine.

"*Gen-e-sis, Ex-o-dus, Lev-it-icus and Num-bers, Deuteronomy, Joshua, Judges, Ruth and Sam-u-el, Sam u-el, Kings, Kings, Chronicles and Chronicles, Ezra, Nehemiah, Esther, Job, Psalms, Proverbs, Ecclesiastes, Song of Solomon…*"

He sensed someone on the other side of the bridge,

Please let it not be Mrs Arnold.

A small hooded figure was slouched over the railing throwing things into the water or ice or whatever it was today. Was that an anorak it was wearing?

"Archie?"

The figure turned around. No, it wasn't an anorak at all, it was a tunnel-hooded parka and at the end of the tunnel was the round, sneering, thin-lipped broken-toothed face of Eddie Lamont. Lamont walked towards him, clapping a slow handclap. Joseph knew what was coming but what could he do, he wasn't a runner.

"Hello! Hello!" he chanted, "It's one-eyed holy Joe!" It was an early morning croak of a voice, a child smoker's voice, but half-hearted, as though it was too early for this kind of carry-on. But he was Eddie Lamont. It was his sworn duty to torment Joseph Kirkland whatever the time of day, whether his heart was in it or not, so he grabbed the tin of texts,

"Gie's a barley sugar, Holy Joe." He opened the tin and laughed, a forced, humourless laugh. Joseph reached for the tin but Lamont rapped him on the knuckles with it. He riffled through them, picking one at random, a ship, the *Mayflower*. He read it in what he thought was a parody of a preacher, starting loud and dour, ending in a bleak diminuendo, "*And whosoever was not found written in the book of life – was cast into the lake of fire.*" Actually it was not unlike Mister Mayhew, a lay preacher in Templeton. He barked another fake laugh, "Ma da' says that's all you lot talk about, hell and damnation."

Joseph reached for the tin again and this time Lamont slapped his face. It wasn't that sore but because of the cold, tears welled up anyway. Lamont was delighted: "Aw, the wee baby. Nae manky wee schemie psycho pal tae look efter ye the day, eh?" He went to slap him again and missed, which annoyed him, so he hit him on the side of the head with the tin instead. It made a hollow drum sound which made Lamont laugh even more.

"Ye want it? Take it?" There was no point but he tried anyway and Lamont slapped him again, hard. His face was almost completely numb now, anaesthetised by the cold and the slaps.

"Again!" Joseph didn't move so Lamont slapped him for not moving. "Ah said *again*!" Joseph obliged with a listless effort, missed and got yet another for his trouble. "Ye need new specs Clarence. C'mon yer no even tryin'." Joseph didn't move. He was tired. He just wanted to lie down. "Ye feart, Holy Joe? D'ye no want it?" Lamont shrugged, he was getting bored; this game was rubbish now. "Oh look there's a picture of a butterfly on this one. Let's see if it can fly." He scrunched it up and flicked it over the bridge. "Fact, let's see if they can aw fly," and he tossed the tin high up into the air. The texts fluttered out like real butterflies and disappeared down into the Lele along with the tin. The Coward Joseph Kirkland's heart fluttered too but of course he did nothing, except feel a tiny bit of shame, and he was almost too tired even for that.

With both hands free Lamont could really go about his business. But he looked awkward, a bit embarrassed even, fighting somebody who wouldn't fight back, and he hated Joseph all the more for it. A slap and a push and Joseph was on his back. Joseph tasted something metallic. He'd cut himself often enough, accidentally and on purpose, to know that taste.

"Whit's that?" Lamont snatched the bag with the bread, "Aw brilliant! Here birdies, come and get yer breakfast, birdies..." He threw the loaf into the river. Yes. This was more like it. He only now took in the tweed suit and the brogues and all. "Whit ye dressed like that fur? Eh? Think yer some wee Laird frae up the hill?" he put on a posh voice, "What ho old chap." He laughed and said it again, "What ho!", he couldn't believe how funny he was being. "That's what yous are like. Think yese are aw better than everybody else, mindin' aw yer p's and q's and..." And because he couldn't think of what else to say he kicked him, hard on the thigh. Joseph curled up in a ball, put his hands over his face but Lamont sat on his chest, pinning Joseph's arms to the ground with his knees. He yanked the Bible out Joseph's pocket and tried to hit him across the face with it but he caught his finger on the sharp corner of his specs- "Bastard!" – broke them in half and went on to twisting Joseph's ears and nose and pinching his cheek. Lamont's repertoire was limited, what else to do with his tediously passive new toy? He spat on Joseph's face, rubbing it hard with his sleeve, "Who's yer da, the coalman?" Lamont carried on with the insults, then went back to the slapping and the pinching, but Joseph couldn't hear or feel anything now because the wee electric light show had begun again. He was no longer there.

Lamont's screams brought Joseph back to earth. He was on his back, kicking at the snarling black dog, trying to keep it at bay with Joseph's Bible. Even with a big bloody bandage wrapped around its hindquarters, the dog was putting on a good old wild wolf show. It grabbed Lamont's sleeve. The boy was whimpering now, terrified. A short sharp whistle and the dog limped over to its master's side, wagging its tail; it had been fun but the game was over.

"You'll drop that now," said Caleb, a picture of calm.

Lamont dropped the Bible, but he was not at all calm, he was sobbing and shouting,

"That dog's mental, so it is!"

Caleb picked up the Bible and wiped it on the grass, not even looking at Lamont.

"She didn't draw blood, did she? No. She was just playing with you son. You go on your way now."

Eddie Lamont was off into the mist like a shot, not towards the chapel, homeward bound, spitting jets of venom in his wake.

"Dirty tinks!" he screamed. "Yer gonnae to get it so yese are. Ma da'll kill ye, ya bastard. The pair a yese." He was barely visible now, "Dirty fuckin' tinks!"

Caleb helped Joseph to his feet. He held him firmly by the chin and looked at his face, quite unconcerned, "Maybe you'll bruise, maybe you won't." He picked up the broken specs and put them in his pocket. He looked at this new brogued and tweeded version of Joseph Kirkland; it was the first time he'd seen him since the jumble sale. "Very…conspicuous." He frowned, "Maybe too conspicuous for your own good," then turned and walked off in the direction of the Sappie.

Joseph trailed a few feet behind, almost tripping over the dog as it weaved in and out of himself and Caleb in a kind of hobbling eightsome reel. Joseph stroked her head and her velvety ears, which was exactly what she wanted.

"Some men might take exception to their dog going daft on someone other fella," said Caleb without looking around. Joseph stopped stroking, "You're fine. It was the dog I was talking to."

She stuck her muzzle in Joseph's palm, licking it, pushing him forward, in case Joseph was having second thoughts about following Caleb. He wasn't.

Joseph's thoughts turned to the bread for the Breaking of Bread and the Scripture texts. He'd tell Gran what happened. It would be okay. She'd sigh, look at him, shake her head. But she'd know it wasn't his fault but the fault of *the Lamonts, that lot, the Overspill*. What could you expect? The texts had taken him years to collect, but this past while each seemed concerned with reminding him of his faults and follies. It felt like a burden had been lifted.

"Sorry," he said out loud.

The dog looked up at him. If Caleb heard too, he didn't react.

But Joseph did feel lighter. Maybe God and Jesus were saying, *Listen Joseph, you don't need this tin of texts now. You're on a different path now. They're just another thing to weigh you down. You've got your Bible and your map and your tweed suit and all, and that's plenty to be getting on with*. Maybe.

They cut down through the Meadows. They'd just passed the Sleeping Bairns when Caleb froze mid step on a held breath, his head cocked, and alert, like an animal out hunting or being hunted. He disappeared into some bushes. Joseph followed, just in time to see him remove a rabbit from a snare. It was alive, barely, but not for long. Caleb didn't need to check this time whether Joseph was happy to bear witness. In one swift expert manoeuvre he grabbed it by its ears, lined up the side of his hand with the base of its neck and gave a short hard chop. The rabbit flopped like an empty glove puppet. Caleb sliced it across the throat with a knife that seemed to have slipped down his sleeve into the palm of his hand, and carried on walking, leaving a trail of blood spatter on the white frost which made Joseph think of Hansel and Gretel and that stupid trail of breadcrumbs which always annoyed him each time Grandpa told it. *Of course the birds will eat them!* A trail of blood though… The black dog's amber eyes shone bright with excitement, or blood lust. Joseph's eyes were shining too. Here was something.

They passed by Archie's tree house. The cage was gone. The boulder-headed Devil dog was gone too. The black dog sniffed the frosted ground around the tree where the fight had been. Joseph wondered if Caleb had buried it there. He wanted to ask but couldn't. He felt the need to say something though, and his lips moved, searching for the something. The black dog looked up at him, providing the answer.

"What's her name?"

"Mirky."

Mirky. What an odd name for a dog. He wasn't sure if he liked it. If it had been Joseph's dog he'd have given it a proper black dog name: *Blackie, Black Bess, Daisy Dubh, Shadow.*

"The name I gave her anyway." He looked round at Joseph, "She'll have her own name for herself. And for me. And you now, no doubt. Her saviour. Go on then. Put your hand on her head. Ask her, *What's my name?*" Nothing in his eyes suggested jokes. "Out loud, in your head, makes no odds to her."

The dog was already sitting waiting. Joseph crouched down, put a hand on her head, and thought hard and slow, *What's my name Mirky?*

Mirky looked at him, tilted her head to the right, and to the left, blinked like she'd had a sudden revelation, and then made a long melancholic whine that ended in a sharp yelp.

"That'll be your name then. Don't forget it. She doesn't like being asked twice."

It was the first time they'd seen the other smile.

The inside of the tent was a smoke-filled grotto. In the centre on a slab of grey slate, a wood fire smouldered. Occasionally it flickered into flame, breaking the murk and sending light and shadow up into the bowed tarpaulin-draped branches, illuminating details in all the bits and pieces that hung there: pots and pans, bunches of drying leaves, tins, bottles and jars filled with who knows what, and soon enough the dead rabbit, hanging by its hind legs in the far corner, dripping and draining into the earth. Mirky sniffed around the blood puddle then sat herself down and gazed up at the rabbit like it was a deity, willing it to fall. The blood ache seemed less acute now, she knew she'd be getting her share soon enough.

Among the objects were a number of small carved wooden figures hung from strings of various lengths. Joseph wanted to look at them up close but he couldn't, not yet. And all of it, the wooden figures, the bottles and jars, the pots and pans, the dead rabbit too now, swayed and spun in the hot air rising from the fire, gently clinking and bumping against one another like one of those cradle toys that folk use to pacify and hypnotise their babies.

Hanging over the fire was a small cauldron, a real cauldron: the stuff of fairy stories, used by witches and warlocks to cook up evil spells and cook up lost children. This was just the sort of shadowy half-lit place that should have encouraged Joseph's imagination to play tricks, and call to mind some of the darker hymns and passages of the Bible. And so it did, a little, but Joseph, he couldn't have said why, was confident he would not be eaten by this man.

"Sit," said Caleb, pointing at an upturned bucket beside the fire.

Joseph's frozen face had begun to thaw and was throbbing

now. Caleb was sniffing at bunches of leaves, poking around in this jar and that tin. He grabbed a handful of something and a handful of something else and spread the whole lot on a piece of muslin. *Magic*. He was making a spell right enough. He added a little liquid from a bottle and mixed it all together with his fingers, the way Joseph mixed Grandpa's tobacco, and tied it in a bundle.

"You'll hold it to your face, where it hurts."

The poultice smelled mulchy and pungent, not completely foreign but not something he could put a name to either. Caleb noticed the eczema on Joseph's wrists and without seeking consent rolled down his sock and took a look at his red raw ankles too. He nodded as though he'd expected as much, scanned the tent for some other things and not seeing them, shrugged and disappeared into a shadowy corner.

Mirky hobbled over to Joseph and rested her head on his foot.

"My Grandpa's budgie flew away," he said, because it was important and because he felt he should say something, "Peter. It was his cage up in the tree."

"It's gone son, the bird." said a soft voice from the smoke and shadows, "You know that. But there's Mirky. Right there. *Look at me*, she's saying, *Look at me, I'm alive and kicking.*"

"Hello Mirky," said Joseph, "hello girl."

Between stroking Mirky and whatever was in the poultice, the throbbing quickly turned into something more vague, and together with the smell and the warmth and the swaying clinking wooden figures and jars, he drifted away, but not into one of his bright white spark picture palaces – some other place that was calm like sleep.

When he came back his spectacles were on his lap, mended, *tinker-fixed*, and Caleb was down on his hunkers loading a big lump of dough into a tin,

"You're in luck," he said "today's my bread day too."

He pulled the slate with the fire on top to one side, to reveal a hole, scraped some red hot embers from the fire into the hole, put the tin inside, heaped some more burning embers around the sides and shoved the slate and fire back into place. Joseph had never seen the like. He wondered if bread baked in a hole in the ground by a tinker would be suitable for the Breaking of Bread. But soon enough the smell of it began to rise up, and it was good. He wanted to know how to do this, make bread in a hole, make potions and poultices from plants. And make a tent like this too, with bowed branches and old tarps. And those wee wooden figurines turning in the hot air, what were they all about? What was any of this about?

Oh, I wish Archie was here. He'd love all this. He wouldn't be shy about asking anything. He'd say, "Joseph said you can pick locks mister. Will you show me how? Please!"

Caleb poked the fire with a stick, added another lump of wood. Then he got up and ran his fingers through the strings of the wooden figures like he was playing a harp, untied three of them and dangled them in front of Joseph. They were about two inches long, unpainted, rough-looking things, not pretending they were anything other than bits of wood, but full of movement and character. There was a fox, a roe deer and a pretty smiling mermaid with long hair. The fox seemed to be sniffing the ground and the deer had its head turned, alert, like Caleb when he found the snared rabbit. But it was the pretty smiling mermaid that really caught his imagination. She had her arms outstretched, inviting an embrace or asking to be rescued. No. It was her that was doing the rescuing. *A drowning sailor or…*

"Put her in your pocket," said Caleb, "she's yours now."

The two of them sat in silence, on opposite sides of the fire. There was no hint of unease. Joseph was able to take in all of Caleb's lustrous leather-grained face now. It was covered in lines. Some forked off and led into other lines, other tributaries, some faded away into nothing and others ended suddenly in dead ends. There were deep lines across his face and forehead and circling his tree-trunk neck, and wood grain lines on his claw-like, hard as resin fingernails. There were the thick lines of his rope-veined hands and the red veins that threaded the whites of his dark brown eyes. But they were sharp too, those eyes, focused, not bleary like Archie's mum and dad, and not misted and milky like Grandpa's eyes or Benjamin Mutch's. Caleb didn't seem to mind being stared at. Maybe, like Joseph, he was used to being scrutinised. Or maybe he was making an exception for Joseph's scrutiny, just as Joseph was making an exception for his.

"You'll give me something now," said Caleb. "A thing for a thing, eh?" He looked serious. Joseph looked blank. "So. What do I get then... Joseph Kirkland?"

What was this? Had some unco, unbreakable tinker bargain been struck because he'd accepted the gift of the wooden mermaid? *They're not like us.*

"Something you've made."

"I don't have anything."

"It doesn't have to be a hard thing. Something of yourself will do."

Something of yourself? What sort of thing was that to say? *Something of yourself.* Had he been wrong about this man with his wooden dolls and his warlock's cauldron?

"A song maybe. Or a tale or a verse. Like your friends do on their Halloween."

Any sort of public performance or display was anathema to Joseph. And also he wasn't allowed to do Halloween. *Dangerous nonsense.* The year before Archie and wee Maggie had gone out, Archie as the Devil with cardboard horns and face stained red with beetroot, which made him look the part but took an eternity to come off. Wee Maggie went as a Casper the Friendly Ghost with a bed sheet over her. Convinced they would not be recognised they knocked on Gran's door. She didn't recognise them. She didn't have to. No one was welcome at Gran's for Halloween and certainly not a boy dressed as Satan. They managed to rattle out two lines of their home-made blasphemous party piece…

I'm the Devil
and I'm a wee ghost
we turn the Souls of the Damned to toast

… before Gran slammed the door in their faces.

"I can show you this," he said, unfolding his map. Caleb's eyes widened and he cooried in till Joseph felt him close and the map lay across their laps.

"You made this?"

"Benjamin Mutch helped me colour it in."

"Did he now?" Caleb took it in inch by inch.

"I can't give it to you."

"?"

"I'm going to be a missionary."

Caleb leant back amazed, and waved his hand, "Tell!"

The floor belonged to Joseph now. Joseph wasn't sure about this at all, but Caleb was insistent, "Come on now. You come into my tent, a tent that flimsy it would fall to pieces if it wasn't for the stories keeping it all together; then you tease me with your talk of maps and missionaries. You want to drive me mad with curiosity? Come on! The Story of Joseph Kirkland the Missionary. What'll his business be?"

"I'll… he'll… he'll… travel the world."

"He'll travel the world? Will he indeed? Good for him. I'm getting to like this Joseph Kirkland fella more already. And what'll he do in the world?"

"He'll Save folk."

"He'll travel the world and *save* folk?" He leant back even further scratching his head in astonishment at this information, whistling under his breath. "Now that's a business and a half. I mean, let's face it, there's times we all need to be saved. Where in the world will he travel exactly, to do his saving? Or will he just see where the wind blows him?"

Is he making fun? No. "Africa and India. And faraway

islands. And… places like that. Where most folk have never been or… maybe places that folk don't even know exist."

"Except the folk who already live there, eh?" He laughed, waving the question aside, and prodded the map, "Right now, this map. Tell."

Joseph began. Hesitantly at first, despite having been through this already with Benjamin Mutch, "It's not all real. I mean… there's the village, the things that you can see, like the shops and the school and all. Then there's things that some folk don't know about. Like the drains and the tree house. The yellow is gold, for places you know for sure are good, that are close to God. The red bits are the Gateways to Hell. That's places where folk are bad, or … misguided. Gran says Mrs Merryweather is misguided, *a poor misguided Catholic*, she says. These bits here are *dangerous uncharted territories*. These are things that I don't know or places I haven't been, like Saint Rita's, but invisible things too. I think. Places where Satan might be. Or might not. But if Satan is there then he might trick you, pretend to be somebody else, and take you away from God or… It's hard to explain. You just don't know. So you need to be careful. You need to think, *Oh maybe there's monsters there, maybe the Devil's there, maybe God's not there*, you need to think about these things, just to be on the safe side. That's why there's fire and smoke and monsters, to mind us to be careful. Of everything. All the time. What you do. Who you're with. What you say. Even what you think… because… all these things can take you away from God. There's loads of things." *So many things. So many things.*

Joseph felt stupid, inarticulate, just blabbering now. How on earth would he ever be a missionary if he couldn't talk to folk, explain to them…

"This," said Caleb, tapping the map, "That triangle."

"It's here."

"Here?" said Caleb, stamping his boot on the ground. "So it is." He ran is finger over it. "So I'm on a map now, am I?

Joseph Kirkland's map. This is something, eh?" He let out a breathy whistle, "I have to be honest with you... I'm not sure if it's a good thing or a bad thing. It's a new thing, that's for sure." He touched the triangle, "Why is my tent red *and* gold, eh?"

"Benjamin Mutch says tinkers are far away from God."

"Did he? Well, they say that man's a powerful storyteller." Joseph looked at his feet. "You feel that yourself Joseph? That we're far away from God? The pair of us, right now?"

"I don't know. I just thought. If I put gold around it too, then ... I don't know."

Caleb laughed, a big belly laugh, but joyful, not...

"Hedging your bets eh? Thinking *Oh, I'm not sure yet about this Caleb Skeely fella*. Mm? *This Caleb Skeely fella's neither one thing nor the other*, eh? *I'll make him a bit Hell red and a bit Heavenly gold*, till I get the measure of him, eh? Quite right, quite right, you don't know me from Adam."

Caleb Skeely. A magician's name.

"So that's the story of this map. Okay. Good. We can keep adding to it. That's the way it goes. Now. Here's a story of another map, a miraculous map," and he rubbed his hands together, because that's what magicians do when they are about to work a spell,

"There was once a boy. Jack was his name. Ages with yourself. But this was many years ago before your time, before my time. A brave boy, so they say. Well he's out on the road one day while his mum and dad were away you see, picking your people's tatties or mending their who knows what. Oh they could mend anything, so they could. From the slide on an old trombone to the engine of Lady So-and-So's Rolls Royce. But he was a daydreamer their son, this Jack, and so he walks and he walks, dreaming of this, that and the other thing – of giants and dragons and elves and brownies and selkies and witches and the like, and before he knew it he's walked for miles and got himself completely lost. He has no idea where he is. Except that he's on top of a wee hill surrounded by woods. Woods that go on forever, which they did in them days. Well, he thinks, 'That's me, I'll never get out of these woods.' And he's hungry and thirsty now because he's had nothing since breakfast, and he starts to cry. And why wouldn't he? Even the bravest cry sometimes and anyone who says they don't are either liars or have had their hearts turned to stone. So anyway, Jack sits down and he starts his lamentations, 'Oh poor me, oh poor Jack,' resigning himself to his fate.

"What happens after that? I'll tell you. This boy Jack, he hears a voice, a nippy wee voice. And it says, 'Stop your weeping and wailing!' Well he does exactly that and he wipes his eyes and his nose on his sleeve, and he sees right in front of him a tiny wee old wifie. She couldn't have been bigger than his foot. And this wee wifie, she wags her finger at him and she says, 'How can a body sleep with all that noise!' And Jack says to her, 'Mistress, I'm awful sorry for waking you up, but I can't help weeping and wailing. You see I'm lost and can't get home to my mother and father, and I've had nothing to eat since breakfast.' Well the wee wifie, she scratches her head, and the wee bit beard on the end of her chin, and says, 'I can't have you sitting on my roof,' for this was her home you see, her being one of the fairy folk. 'I'll tell you what I'll do,' she says, 'I'll make you a map. And this map will help you find your way home. But to make this map, I'll need a wee bit of something from your home.' Well poor Jack's heart sinks down into his boots, 'Mistress I've nothing but the clothes I'm wearing,' he says. So the wee wifie looks him up and down, 'What about a piece of that homespun shirt,' she says. Now Jack's mother had put a lot of hours into making that shirt, but he's mad with worry and so he tears a wee bit of homespun off his shirt tail and gives it to her. The wee wifie folds the bit of shirt then folds it again and then folds it a third time and sticks it in her mouth. She chews it and chews it and then she spits it out onto the ground in front of her. 'There be your map,' she says. Well Jack could barely hide his disappointment. It wasn't a map at all, it was just a slabbery bit of chewed-up, spat-out shirt tail. But Jack was that desperate, so he picks up the slabbery bit of shirt tail and he unfolds it and he unfolds it and he keeps on unfolding it till it becomes twenty times bigger than the wee bit of shirt tail he'd given to the wee old wifie. And when he's finished unfolding it he turns it over, but there's nothing there. 'This isn't a map,' says Jack, and he starts to cry again. 'Of course it's a map, ye daft big gowk,' says the wee old wifie. 'Look closer and tell me what you see.' So Jack looks closer and what he sees is a wee picture of a tent, like this one we're in now. 'But how is this going to help me to get home?' says Jack. Well the wee old wifie looks this way and that to make sure nobody's listening and says, 'Wrap the map around your eyes like a blindfold and say these words,

Let me no wander /Let me no roam,

Let me no stray / From the road that leads home.

"'Then whatever way you go, the map will take you home.' Of course Jack is over the moon and thanks the wee old wifie and is just about to wrap the map around his eyes when she stops him. 'Just one thing', she says – there's always just one thing with fairy folk – 'The map will only work the once. When you've finished with it you must promise to give the map as a gift to some other body you come across who's lost. A gift, mind. You must not sell it! Because if you even try to sell it, you'll lose all sense of direction and find yourself lost for the rest of your days and longer. Promise me that, and promise me you'll make the next person who owns this map make the same promise.' Well of course Jack promises and he wraps the map around his eyes and he says the words that need to be said,

Let me no wander / Let me no roam,

Let me no stray / From the road that leads home.

"And even before he's taken the map from his head he can smell his mother's rabbit stew and hear her voice saying, 'Jack, that's your supper out son.' He was home. Well the days and years went by and Jack is true to his word. He never uses the map again, even when he's a wee bit lost and had a mind to. But he does tell stories about the map. How could he not? If you've a story as good as that, you're duty bound to tell it. Soon enough the story of Jack and the Miraculous Map was famous. Then one day Jack is on the road and he bumps into a right old rascal of a man, one of those who takes a lend of folk for profit. And the old rascal he says to Jack, 'Son, will you help me, I'm lost and can't find my way home.' Jack's a good lad mind, and an honest lad, who minds his debts and his promises so he says, 'I can help you,' and he gives the old rascal the fairy's miraculous map and tells him all that the wee old wifie had said and he makes the rascal promise, and of course the rascal promises and then he ties the map around his eyes like a blindfold, says the words that need to be said,

Let me no wander /Let me no roam,

Let me no stray / From the road that leads home.

"And pouf, the rascal disappears. 'Well', thinks Jack. 'That's him home then, safe and sound.' But the rascal reappears again right away at the other side of the road. And Jack realises that he's been tricked. 'Ha ha ha,' laughs the rascal, 'this map will be my fortune,' and off he runs. And what does the rascal do? He sells the map for profit! And how does Jack know this? Because a while later, in another part of the country, Jack came across the same rascal and what a sight he was, boots worn thin, beard long and tangled. 'Excuse me sir,' says the rascal to Jack, for he'd forgotten who Jack was, 'Could you show me the way home?' Well Jack was a forgiving lad so he shows the rascal the way but the rascal just turns around and walks off in the opposite direction. So Jack taps the rascal on the shoulder and says, 'Your home is in that direction!' But no sooner had the old rascal set off than once again he starts to wander off in the wrong direction. Of course after this happened six or seven times Jack realises what has happened. He felt sorry for the rascal, but he'd brought it upon himself and there was nothing he could do. Well, Jack lived a good life with a wife and children, and he travelled the world and many extraordinary things happened to him which I'm not going to tell you about right now. But every now and again Jack would come across that rascal, an old man now, in bare feet and a beard so long it was tickling his toes, and he was still trying to find his way home."

Joseph stayed a while inside Caleb Skeely's story till the tent began to rematerialise. Caleb emptied the bread from his fiery pit onto some newspaper. Joseph had uncertainty written all over his face. Caleb laughed, "It's bread Joseph, just bread. It'll do the trick. And talking of tricks, I've a trick that'll maybe help you mind your books of the Bible."

CHAPTER TWENTY-TWO

As Thin as Bible Paper

Some halls referred to folk like Mister Agnew as a *lay preacher*, but even this was too much title and office for Kilhaugh. Here he just was plain Mister Agnew, a *labouring brother on the Lord's work.*

"If Paul came to our meeting here today," said Mister Agnew, "I like to think that he would feel quite at home, that he would recognise what we do here as being no different from those first simple assemblies they held in folks' houses back in his day."

He made no comment about Joseph's new attire, and he made no comment about the bread or about the newspaper it was wrapped it in, *The Morning Star*, a communist paper.

"Mind I want a wee word with you after Sunday School."

Joseph sat at the back. He had never been there for the Breaking of Bread. He felt his stomach lurch when Mister Agnew broke off that first bit from Caleb Skeely's tinker bread: "*And when he had given thanks, he brake it...*"

Who knew what might happen with this bread... or not happen?

"*Take, eat: this is my body, which is broken for you: this do in remembrance of me.*"

Mister Agnew passed half the loaf and a plain china cup of sweet red wine, around the circle. There was no thunder and lightning, no flickering lights, nobody turned into a toad, nobody vomited. Caleb Skeely's bread had *done the trick*, just as he said it would.

A new person had turned up at Sunday School. A wee girl from the scheme who'd attended Benjamin Mutch's testimony. So it had clearly worked for some. She was sitting between Jenny and wee Ivan Chaddock. Ivan and the wee girl were staring at Joseph,

"Ask him," said Ivan.

"I don't like to," said the wee girl, all shy.

"She wants to know how you know when you're Saved, Joseph."

"Yes, how *do* you know, Joseph?" said Jenny.

"You just do," said the *liar Joseph Kirkland.*

"How?" said the wee girl.

"You just... feel it."

"But *how?*" said the wee girl.

Even as Joseph was telling himself to stop right there, to just do one of his shrugs or blank looks, anything at all, he dug himself deeper into his unHoly hole,

"It's like you're somebody else," he said, listening to himself with incredulity, not even avoiding eye contact, he was that shameless. "A brand new you, better than the one before."

Doubting Jenny Kirkland looked at Joseph like he was a fool. A damned fool.

Uncle Andrew let his big Bible fall open in his hand and with thumb and forefinger began to lightly rub the corner of a page. Ah yes. It had been less than a year since he'd done this lesson. He looked down at the new wee girl. This was for her benefit. She looked bewildered. That was good. Bewilderment was a good place to start: a shadowy place from which she might be enlightened.

"Aren't the pages of the Bible incredibly thin?" he said, as though he himself had just discovered this fact. "But also... incredibly strong. Those of you who have a grown-up Bible like this one, open it up at random, and feel one of the pages."

They did as instructed – though of course there was no such thing as *random* when it came to a page of the Bible.

Joseph blurred his eyes so he wouldn't see what page he'd chosen.

"At the mill we call this *light offset paper*, though I prefer to call it *Bible paper*. Where else do you think you might you find paper like this?"

Joseph should remember this. But nobody else seemed a hundred per cent confident either.

"Telephone directories?" said a cautious Sangster.

"A good try, but no, not telephone directories. Anyone else?" He was looking at Joseph, who panicked and was about to say the thing that had popped into his head, but fortunately the wee girl from the scheme said it first, "Comics?"

"An interesting answer," said Uncle Andrew, but gently, it was the wee girl's first time. "But no, we would never use expensive *Bible* paper for something like *comics*. People throw away comics after they've read them, don't they?" The wee girl nodded. No one else moved. It was a loaded question; good folk, Godly folk, Saved folk, would *never* read comics in the first place. "Of course they do, like they do with newspapers. Who wants to read yesterday's news, eh? But! Would you throw away the *Bible* after you'd read it?" The question required no answer but everyone shook their heads just in case. Ivan nudged her and the wee girl followed suit. "No. Because the Bible is *never* yesterday's news. Okay, I'll tell you where you might find this kind of paper being used – in one of the bigger *Oxford English Dictionaries* or in very important legal books. And what do these books have in common?"

After the wee girl's blunder, no one was willing to risk it.

"They are all concerned with *Information* or *Instruction* or *Law*. But only one of these books is concerned with all three of these things. Which book is that?"

"*The Good Book*," said Joseph.

"*The Good Book*." Uncle Andrew and held it up triumphantly. "Well done Joseph." He pulled a text from his pocket and handed it to Joseph like he was giving a chocolate drop to a dog, "Good boy."

This text was the beginning of a new collection, but he dared not look at it.

"The Good Book is more important than all the other books in the entire world, all stitched together. Why? Because this book isn't concerned with the word of man; it's concerned with the *Word of God*. In this book you'll find everything you will ever need to know. What a gift He has given us! What a gift! And all to be found in pages as light as a feather and as strong as steel. Unbreakable. Like his love for us. Like his promise to us. Boys and girls, let us sing out loud the Good News: *Jesus Loves Me. This I know, for the Bible Tells Me So.*"

Auntie Ishbel came in right on cue on the harmonium.

Jesus loves me! This I know / For the Bible tells me so. Little ones to Him belong / They are weak, but He is strong.

As Joseph sang he couldn't resist taking a peek at the scripture text. *Please*. It was a steam train, *The Flying Scotsman*, and on the back... on the front... *He that Believeth and is Baptised shall be Saved, but he that Believeth Not shall be Damned. Mark 16:16.*

The wee sparking white light show came on with a speed and intensity that took Joseph by surprise and he did nothing to resist it. It began at the back of his head...

Yes, Jesus loves me!

... and washed over him in great big delicious waves, *Yes, Jesus loves me!*

As Joseph fell to the floor, *The Flying Scotsman* fluttered to the ground just as the rest of his texts had fluttered into the Lele, and a big beaming smile lit up his face.

Yes, Jesus loves me! / The Bible tells me so.

CHAPTER TWENTY-THREE

A Chorus of Whispers

Joseph is in bed. The overlapping voices – Gran, Auntie Abi, Uncle Hector, Auntie Ishbel, Uncle Andrew – sound strained from the effort of trying to remain quiet and reasonable.

The Sappie? / "I want to be Baptised in the Sappie" is what he said. / The Sappie? / Didn't he Ishbel? / … / With all due respect… / Ishbel! / … / We've never seen him look more certain of anything, have we Ishbel? / … / And there's nothing in the Scriptures that says … / I cannot believe we're actually… / John the Baptist… /… he'd just taken one of his turns … /John the Bap… / It's the Sappie, no the banks of the River Jordan / Language! / But… / …and it's been done before / In the Sappie? / You were a wee girl, you'll not … / In December? / … one of the Chaddocks… / What about his chest? / …Betty, I think… / Has anybody spoken to the Doctor? / Benjamin Mutch has clearly … / That's another thing, that tweed suit… / He's decided … /A missionary? / It won't be the first time that Benjamin… / For crying out…! /Language! / Who are we… / His family! / It would be a sin not to… / His family! That's who we are!

In the middle of the dangerous uncharted territories, Joseph draws a golden-haired mermaid.

He's different now, he's… / In this world… / …but not of this world. /Aye and he looks like it too. / … a solemn young man, I'll grant… / Child! And too solemn. / Serious. / Too serious. He's Saved, fine… / Language / The Sappie? In this weather? / … and Ishbel's going to make lentil soup. / In the name o' the wee… /

Language! / So you are Ishbel? / … / It's high time you spoke to him. / We should all lower our voices / Aye let's whisper. / Sshh / Sshh yourself, all he hears is whispers / Enough! / Who knows what goes on in that head with all this whispering. If he's old enough to be Saved, he's old enough to hear the truth. (Silence, punctuated by the clinking of Apostle spoons on bone china) Ishbel. How's Sam finding life on the submarines? / I think he's just happy to be posted up the Clyde / Not on a banana boat … / Careless talk costs lives, Ishbel! / Did I say, there might be some news? On the romantic front.

Tomorrow. Tomorrow, I'll Save Archie.

CHAPTER TWENTY-FOUR

Joseph Kirkland's Third Dream

The good folk of Kilhaugh were in their nighties and pyjamas when they began to slowly rise up into the blue morning sky. Joseph was also in his pyjamas but his feet were firmly on the ground. At first when they were just an inch or two above the ground, and it was barely noticeable even to themselves. Joseph assumed that any second he'd feel something too, a weightlessness perhaps, or some overwhelming pull upwards. *Something*.

They were a good two or three feet above the ground now and rising. It was starting to dawn on folk what was happening and they began to laugh. Not hysterically. In quite a light-hearted way, as though it was all quite natural – *Oh here we go! And we're off!* – like they were taking the whole thing in their stride. But still Joseph remained earthbound. He felt the first quiver of panic and began doing this awkward little hopping thing to try to lift himself off the ground. Nothing too obvious. He didn't want to draw attention to himself.

"Morning, Joseph!" said Miss O'Donnell, hovering above, "I thought you'd be the first."

"Joseph Kirkland!" said Gran, looking down at him, annoyed.

"This is the business, eh son?" said Grandpa as though the whole thing was hilarious, "Ho ho. Here mum, maybe Joseph can tie a piece of string to my big toe and kid on I'm a kite, ha ha." He tapped Gran on the shoulder, "Fency a dence, Mrs Kirklend?"

"Och you," she said, blushing and smiling and fluttering her eyelashes, before letting herself be waltzed off into the clouds.

Joseph tried another wee jump but it was pointless, his legs were like lumps of lead.

"This is brilliant, so it is," shouted Archie, "Comin' up?"

"Look at me, Joseph," shouted wee Maggie, flapping her hands like tiny wings.

The sky over Kilhaugh was filled with folk now. *Here we go. Whoo hoo,* they cried, howling, laughing like children on a big ride at the shows. Joseph did another pathetic wee hop and a skip, a last desperate attempt. And then they were all just wee dots. He'd never felt so abandoned. He was going to scream, to wake himself up when he smelt cigarette smoke,

"You can't go. He doesn't know your name. That's the problem."

It was Caleb Skeely, sitting on a wall smoking a roll-up. Mirky was dozing on the ground below. Caleb didn't seem at all concerned that they were still earthbound. He gave Joseph a friendly wee nod, like everything was normal, and as it should be, and as soon as he'd done that, just that wee gesture, it felt like it too, like everything was normal, and as it should be.

CHAPTER TWENTY-FIVE

Mister Brunstane's Lesson for Devious Boys

Outside was the same but the trains were running, so Miss O'Donnell would be in school. She was a part of all this. Maybe she would help Joseph make sense of it all.

Gran looked at him, running her tongue around her gums as if trying to dislodge a bit of breakfast toast from her dentures. What was on her mind? *Saved? It doesn't look that way to me?* or *A tweed suit? For school? What on earth?* She refrained from making any comment, which wasn't easy for her. But she'd a lot on her plate with Grandpa and the extra cleaning work. Maybe this was how it was going to be now. And hadn't Benjamin Mutch endorsed it? Some folk were singled out by God to be part of extraordinary events and you never knew who or why or… anything. And neither you should. To question the Lord's plan would be…

Joseph looked in on Grandpa before he left. The covers were that flat the bed looked empty. Uncle Andrew, Mister Agnew and Mister Sangster were already there. They'd decided to have the early morning Working Men's Prayer Meeting by Grandpa's bedside instead of at the Hall. Mister Sangster was reading from the Book of Revelations, "And there shall be no night there; and they need no candle, neither light of the sun; for the Lord God giveth them light, and they shall reign forever and ever."

Grandpa looked neither asleep nor awake, like he didn't know what was being read to him. It might've been *Under a Big Bad Sky* for all he knew. He'd have preferred that.

Sorry.

But he would've.

Joseph was first in the playground. He was just thinking, this is as good a good time as any to try Caleb Skeely's Books of the Bible memory trick, when out the corner of his eye he saw something yellow in the gutter above Mister Scrivener the janitor's window. Sometimes you got nests up there. *Daft*. A budgerigar would not build a nest! And didn't Caleb say... But might it be possible that Peter could've sought sanctuary in an empty nest, like what were those birds... cuckoos? Imagine if he had though? That would be almost a miracle.

It wasn't that high, even for Joseph, and there was plenty in the way of window ledges, drainpipes and brackets and suchlike. There was a nest, but there was nothing in it, except for some withered downy feathers, none of them yellow.

In class the children snickered at the sight of him, but Joseph was used to it. He knew he was odd and awkward, a square peg in a round hole. Tommy Maxwell and Marty Logan, best friends with Eddie Lamont, weren't just laughing though. They were giving him the evil eye. Maxwell drew his finger across his throat and Logan held a finger pistol to his head.

"Enough!" said Miss O'Donnell, "I think young Master Kirkland looks quite the gentleman." Miss O'Donnell always had the friendliest of jokes in her eyes and when the children laughed again it was mostly free of mockery. Until Joseph, unprompted, announced, "I'm going to be a missionary."

Of course there was another explosion of laughter and a chorus of *Hello hello, it's one-eyed Holy Joe* from Maxwell and Logan. Miss O'Donnell nipped it in the bud, and she'd have been justified in taking Joseph to one side and giving him a kindly *Do yourself a favour*, but she seemed genuinely impressed.

"A *missionary*? Well, I have to say that you look like you're halfway there already. I was about to say a few words about what the life of a missionary might be like, but Mister Maxwell and Mister Logan seem to know already? Thomas?

Martin? Would you like to share your expert knowledge with us? No? Well let me tell you. The missionaries that I know of, men *and* women, endured the kind of horror and hardship that we'd find unimaginable. If they weren't traipsing across sun-scorched deserts in wagons with pregnant wives, sick children and new-born babes in tow, they were crossing oceans in rickety wee boats you wouldn't take out on the Sappie, and getting battered by waves the size of tenement houses. And on their days off you'd find them hacking their way through a hundred miles of jungle teeming with cannibals, lions, gorillas, poisonous snakes and goodness knows what tropical diseases. Take Edel Quinn for example. She was a young missionary from outside Mallow, which is the town where I come from in County Cork. Edel Quinn did her mission work while she was suffering from malaria and tuberculosis. Can you imagine? Most of us can't get out our beds with a dose of the cold. So there we go, there's the life of a missionary. And Joseph here is telling us he's going to *be* one? Well, hats off to him I say; he's a braver boy than most I've met. And who knows, in years to come your children might be sitting where you are now listening to their teacher – it might be me, God willing – telling them all about the extraordinary life of Joseph Kirkland, the Missionary of Kilhaugh."

The wonderful Miss O'Donnell who knew everything had defused the bomb of ridicule. Even Maxwell and Logan looked at Joseph, not with grudging respect, but at least grudging curiosity; might there be more to *Holy Joe* than meets the eye? The eternally excited Mary McPhee had her hand up, "When will you start being a missionary Joseph?"

"I imagine when Joseph's left school, Mary. Isn't that right, Joseph?"

No. That's not right. I've already begun. Thankfully he had not said that out loud.

"Talking of missionaries," said Miss O'Donnell,. "Did you know that Doctor Livingstone tried to find the source of the River Nile using a two-thousand-year-old *map?*" It was a neat segue into the map project. Everyone looked down at their desks.

"Nobody has done any work on it? No one? Not a scratch? I think that fog might've seeped into your heads." The children laughed.

"I've got a map miss," said Joseph.

"Have you now, Mister Kirkland? Maybe we've another Livingstone in our midst."

Miss O'Donnell was taken aback by Joseph's map. She liked Joseph Kirkland. Oh, there was no two doubts about it; he was an odd boy, but up until now his oddness had been of the quiet, unadventurous, even timid variety. But with his tweed suit, his talk of missionaries and now this map, was some hitherto unseen flamboyant eccentricity about to reveal itself? She got everyone to gather round because this map, with its dragons and dog-headed demons and mermaids and red gateways, whatever it all meant, was an impressive piece of work.

"Oh my. Would you like to tell us what it's all about, Joseph?"

Now Joseph, like Caleb Skeely preferred shadows and fog to the bright glare of attention, but if he was to spread the Good News, he was going to have learn to stand in front of folk and tell them all about it. And also, after telling first Benjamin Mutch and then Caleb about his map, he felt a little more confident.

"Well... this is my Jerusalem..."

But before he'd a chance to utter another word there was a loud knock on the door and Mister Scrivener stuck his head round: "The headmaster says Joseph Kirkland's tae go tae his office."

The *tap tap tapping* of Mister Scrivener's walking stick echoed along the corridor. He couldn't have walked more slowly if he'd tried, but Joseph was in no hurry. Mister Brunstane's office was at the far end of the school. The corridors were painted a sage green and reminded Joseph of Templeton Eye Infirmary. His mouth went dry and he licked his lips as he recalled the black ether muzzle that was clamped to his face, *Just count from ten backwards Joseph*. He'd got as far as eight, then dreamless oblivion. Later that night he went to the toilet and despite being warned not to, removed the patch, only to discover a congealed bloody hole where his eye had been. The nurse found him sitting on the toilet floor in a right state. She couldn't help laughing, *Ya daft wee boy*, and she poured on cup after cup of warm salty water over the wound until his eye reappeared.

"They think they cannae be seen," said Mister Scrivener, *tap tap tap*, "but they can be seen awright," *tap tap tap*, "Aye, yon fog might be thick, but ah'm no!" ... *tap tap tap*.

The hospital green turned to dark brown as they entered the dimly lit passageway to Mister Brunstane's office. Joseph didn't know this part of the school. The walls were lined with row upon row, year upon year of class photos, some too high to see, going back to the late eighteen hundreds. He scanned the generations of Kilhaugh children. Gran and Grandpa were born and bred in Kilhaugh; they'd be up there somewhere. In each picture, variations of the same faces looked out into the future. There were the fearful, the fearless, the angry, the confident, the meek and the mild. There were the robust and the fragile weakened by disease or damaged by trouble at home. There were the smug, the pompous, the entitled and gilded, and there were the Blessed. There was the look to a big bright future, there was the tragedy waiting to happen. And there, there and there were the shamed, the hopeless and the confused. Every class had an Archie, a wee Maggie, a Maxwell and a Logan, an Uncle Andrew and Uncle Mathew in the making, a Gran and a Grandpa. It was as though every year Kilhaugh Primary was replenished with new versions of itself. Except there were no Joseph Kirklands among them. And no Caleb Skeelys.

Like all the others, the class of 1940 stood rigid, shoulder to shoulder, arms folded or hands clasped, with gas-mask boxes around their necks. One or two appeared on the brink of laughter, others looked nervous, some scared. Of what? Bombs? The headmaster? The future? One wee fair-haired girl, third from the left on the second row, stood out. Her posture was less formal, her body, her face, her eyes, all of her, wide open and challenging the viewer, *This is me, it's all I am and it's more than enough for anybody*. How could you not want to be friends with this girl? And yet, nobody was shoulder to shoulder with her, instead they were very obviously giving her a wide berth. Joseph felt a tug at his sleeve,

"Joseph, what are you doing here?" It was wee Maggie, clutching a pile of beanbags.

"Mind yer ain business," said Mister Scrivener, from the shadows, "or the headmaster'll be wanting tae see you as well."

She didn't need to be told twice and scurried off.

Joseph found himself standing in front of a big bright red door, and on the door was a brass plaque engraved with the words *Mister William Brunstane, Headmaster*.

As soon as the door was closed the echo of the corridor was replaced by no sound at all.

The office was heavy with dark wood and leather, and thick with carpet and cigarette smoke. The headmaster was a huge man draped in yards of black suit. He sat behind a great tank of a desk, empty apart two packets of Embassy Regal and an ashtray piled high with fag ends.

"The truth," said Mister Brunstane, belching smoke, "that's all I want. Nothing else interests me. You were *seen*. Is that understood?"

Joseph was so taken by this voice, so rich and smoky, so deep and luxurious, a voice so in love with the sound of itself, that Joseph had difficulty hearing a word it was saying.

"Do you understand the difference between *truth* and *lie?*"

What lie? The lie?

"You were *seen.* I'm not interested in your *buts* and *becauses.* You were *seen.* And where is your school uniform?"

"I'm going to be a missionary," said Joseph, out loud, taking himself by surprise.

Mister Brunstane was also surprised. He'd heard many excuses from boys and girls. He took a drag of his fag and studied Joseph Kirkland, like a police inspector might study a suspect. He nodded. This boy did indeed look like a small missionary. However…

"That's not what I asked. I *asked*, where is your school uniform?" He was met with a blank look. Mister Brunstane did not like this boy. This boy was elusive. "The records show that in all your time here, you've never once been called to my office. So, I ask myself, how can it be that the Kirkland boy has managed to avoid me all this time? Is it because he is a *good* boy? … Is it because he is an *honest* boy?"

No.

"Or is it because he's a *devious* boy?"

Yes.

Mister Brunstane extinguished his fag, took his jacket off and hung it round the back of his chair. There were big patches of sweat under the arms of his yellow Bri-nylon shirt.

"Your school reports do not indicate that you're a genius," he said, cracking his knuckles, "but neither do they suggest that you're an imbecile. Therefore the fact that you are standing there looking like an imbecile, *pretending* to be deaf, *pretending* to be an imbecile, suggests that you are *not* an honest boy. Not an *honest* boy at all. Ergo, you are… a *devious* boy."

He opened a drawer in his desk, took out a key and held it out to Joseph.

"I'd like the devious boy to take this key and open that

cabinet by the door. There you will find my special lady friend, Black Betsy. She *loves* devious boys."

The long slim cabinet was designed to house just one item, a well-worn fork-tongued black leather Lochgelly tawse hanging from a nail hammered into the back wall.

"Bring Black Betsy back to Mister Brunstane, boy."

Mister Brunstane stood towering over him in the middle of the room. Joseph was perplexed more than afraid, and as was often the case, he just wished he could comprehend, even a little, what was actually happening right now.

"Black Betsy is going to give you *a wee reminder*. To help you distinguish between truth and lie, straight and crooked, honesty and deviousness. Hands out. *Straight out*. Right on left, left on right, it's all one."

A straightforward instruction. Something that Joseph actually understood. Mister Brunstane lined up the tawse, threw it over his shoulder, took a step back like Caleb had done when he'd put down the Devil dog, and then with the fast shuffle-lunge forward of an Olympic shot-putter brought it down hard on Joseph's palm with a percussive thwack. The pain was hot and electric and Joseph instinctively snatched his hand away.

"Hand *back*. I'll tell you when I'm finished."

Joseph swapped hands.

"You *are* a devious boy. The *same* hand."

He hit him again. And again. On the same hand. And again. Tears welled up in Joseph's eyes. He so needed this and it appeared that Mister Brunstane, flushed with exhilaration, needed it too. As he whipped Black Betsy back into position for one final run a tiny bit of eczemic scab flicked off Joseph's wrist and landed on the cuff of the headmaster's sodden shirt.

"So," said Mister Brunstane, breathless, triumphant, "what do you have to say for yourself now?"

Joseph's lips were trembling so much, it was an effort to reply, "Thank you very much, Mister Brunstane."

Like many confronted with Joseph Kirkland for the first

time, the headmaster experienced confusion. Then face turned purple and the tiny red veins in his nose and cheeks became so swollen and inflamed they looked like they might erupt.

"And again. Hands out."

It was playtime when Joseph got back to class. Miss O'Donnell was on her own,

"*Seven* times? He hit you *seven* times?" She saw the eczema on his wrist, bleeding from where the tawse had clipped it. "Jesus, if ever a man needed the shite beaten out of him, it's him." Joseph had never seen her angry and as for the language– "I'm sorry Joseph, God forgive me, but... that's beyond the pale." She went to cool a flannel under the cold tap, but there was no water, so she tried the hot, which drizzled cold, and held the damp cloth to his palm, "What did you do to make him so angry?"

"I don't know, Miss O'Donnell." The coolness was so soothing. He closed his eyes, "I'm going to be Baptised in the Sappie," he said, and when he opened his eyes Miss O'Donnell had such a concerned look on her face, "Oh Joseph, son."

It could have been the words or the tone, or something else entirely, but either way Joseph wrapped his arms around his Miss O'Donnell and held on. She stroked his hair and for a few seconds all his cares were forgotten, until he remembered where he was and who he was, and who she was.

"Sorry miss."

Mary McPhee charged in: "Miss O'Donnell! The pipes have burst. We're all getting sent home."

CHAPTER TWENTY-SIX

The Saving of Archibald Truman

Archie and wee Maggie were already there, barely visible at the school gate, waiting for him. Had Archie been expecting the pipes to burst? Or arranged it even? Who knew with Archie. Wee Maggie had already told him all about the encounter with Mister Scrivener, "What happened?"

"I got the belt.

"*You?*" Archie was incredulous. And impressed. "But you're always a goodie two- shoes."

"Can I see?" Wee Maggie had never been belted, "Oh you're bleeding Joseph!" She was close to tears, "Look, he's bleeding Archie…"

"God! How many did you get?"

"Seven."

"*Seven?*"

"Oh Joseph, it looks really sore,"

"*Seven?* What for?"

"I don't know."

"Bastard!" said Archie.

"Bastard!" said wee Maggie.

"Maggie!" he hissed, looking around. Archie didn't care two hoots what the good folk of

Kilhaugh thought about him, but wee Maggie, that was a different story. "Mind what we said about language?"

"You said it first," she hissed back.

"That's different." Wee Maggie drew in her chin, folding her arms like a wee old wifie. Archie snickered, "And you've got a voice like a foghorn, so you have."

So of course she made a loud nasally noise, like she imagined a foghorn might sound, stuck her tongue out and ran over to Lizzie McCreadie.

"I've never even had seven. I don't think you're allowed seven." Joseph was a picture of passive acceptance, but that was fine because Archie was raging with enough righteous indignation for both them, "I wouldn't've let him. I wouldn't've." Archie couldn't just talk about his violent, murderous fantasies, he had to be inside them, acting them out, " I'd've kicked him in the balls," he said, kicking Mister Brunstane in the balls, "or grabbed his Black Betsy and belted him across his stupit face," he said, belting Mister Brunstane across his stupid face. He stared malevolently at the school. "See if he ever belted wee Maggie. I'd kill him, so I would. I bloody well would." He looked at Joseph, and mouthed an apology, for the language, "I would though, I would so."

I know.

"Come and we'll throw a brick through his window?" He was on a roll now, looking around for an actual brick. "We could do it, so we could. Nobody would even see us in this. We could smash it to smithereens. Imagine if we did though?"

We this, *we* that, *we* the next thing. But if he ever did any of these things it would be Archie alone who would take the big risks, like he always did. Then, like he always did, he'd take the blame, but if there was glory, he'd share that with the Coward Joseph Kirkland.

"Imagine?" said Archie, his face contorted now with gleeful dark imaginings, "His big beetroot face all coughing and spluttering and choking. He'd maybe even choke to death." He threw his head back and laughed, blowing a big yellow-green snot bubble and wiping it on his sleeve. "Imagine he actually died but? And nobody would ever know we murdered him. And it wouldn't be murder anyway. It would be like something that just happened."

Joseph saw the picture too and it thrilled him and horrified him, but mostly thrilled him.

Sorry. "Is wee Maggie coming?"

"No, she's going back to Lizzie's."

"How, are your mum and dad not in?"

"No it's just..."

There he goes again. Joseph should not have asked that. He should really know better. Archie kicked the ground, really not wanting to talk about it, *really* wanting to talk about it,

"I don't like her being there when they're... och." And snap, with the kick of a stone, he was back. Bright-eyed beaming Archie. Everything-coming-up-roses Archie. Doing his wee skip and spin. His Archie Truman spell-dance to banish the blues and send them on their merry way, "Where'll we go?" And he birled around again, like a weathercock, to see which way the winds of waywardness were blowing.

They headed for the old prisoner-of-war camp that lay just outwith the village, towards the Robert Munday Mental Hospital. The fog was as thick out here as it was anywhere in Kilhaugh. On the other side of the drystane dyke a giant pylon skeleton quietly hummed. Archie was in seventh heaven, "Think it's like this all over the world?" and he held his breath, because he could. "Let's do dogfights. What do you want to be? Can I be a Messerschmitt? You can be a Spitfire. Spitfires always win anyway."

So they played dogfights, which Joseph usually loved, for Archie's *rat-a-tat-tat* machine-gun noises and his brilliant crash landings. Today though, he couldn't allow his heart to be in it. He badly needed to get on to a more solemn matter: the Saving of Archie Truman.

They went to the POW camp a lot, hail, rain or shine. They'd play commandoes or re-enact escape stories from the pictures. The camp was pretty dilapidated now. Doors were falling off their hinges, timber walls were rotting and most of the corrugated iron roofs were dangerously thin with rust. Johnny Delaney, ages with Joseph and Archie, had fallen through one the year before and broken his arm. Archie insisted, *You could actually see the bone sticking out!*

A couple of the huts were used by Betty Howie's farm to store straw and bits of farm equipment. Sometimes they'd find a stray sheep or a cow, but mostly rats and mice, alive, dead or dying from poison. And lots of discarded beer and spirit bottles. The walls, inside and out, were covered in fresh and faded graffiti. There were obscene cartoons, political and sectarian slogans, declarations of love and hate: *Make Love Not War, League of Empire Loyalists, Drop Acid Not Bombs, Mary T Loves Billy C, Keep Britain White, Billy C Loves Isabel T, Fuck the Pope, Billy C is a Shite.* Or folk just needing to make their mark, *A.T + J.K Were Here.*

"It's like smoke," said Archie, waving a hand through the fog, "Like there's been an attack, like the Russians have actually dropped the bomb and everything's gone *whoosh*. This is where we should come if they do, eh? Come on and we'll get stuff just in case? Like they said in the leaflet? We could get tins of soup and beans and semolina and things. And comics. It'll be great so it will. We could survive here for ages so we could. Till it was safe and everything. Come on and we'll do it? Actually get stuff and plank it and not tell anybody?"

"What about wee Maggie?"

"I know but she'll go and tell her pals, then everybody'll know. I mean when it happens, if it actually happens, she can. We can bring her dolls and books, make it nice and clean, like a wee home from home. It'll be a nice surprise when she sees all the arrangements; she'll be all, *Oh look at all this*." He made an explosion noise and collapsed to the ground, squirming and staring goggle-eyed at the back of his hand, "Oh no! I can see my own skeleton!" Then all of him came to a sudden stop and he looked at Joseph, deadly serious, "That's actually what'll happen, Joseph. And then that'll be it so it will. That'll be us. Kaput."

A couple of years before, when Joseph was off school after his eye operation, he'd gone with Gran to see a Civil-Defence film at the Munday Memorial Hall organised by the Women's Guild. Gran wasn't in the Guild, neither were most of them there, but the place was packed anyway with mums and aunties and grannies and so on. Gran never attended public events, social or otherwise, unless they were Hall-related. She sat at the back, awkward and uncomfortable, till Auntie Ishbel turned up with Mrs Sangster and a couple of the others. Joseph sat on the floor at the back playing with the wee ones and their wooden blocks, building towers and knocking them down, and building them again, catching glimpses of the film. In one bit, a family were calmly taking the kitchen door off its hinges, leaning it against the living room wall alongside a few other doors. The women laughed at this, fidgeting nervously too, but laughing. That's when Gran started her head shaking and her loud sighing and *tut tut tutting*, until she was sure she'd got their attention,

"Do you honestly think that hiding under a kitchen door with a hundred tins of corned beef is going to save you?"

"Archie calling Joseph. Archie calling Joseph!" Archie was standing on a crate, shouting into an imaginary walkie-talkie, "Come in Joseph." Joseph was away with the fairies again. "You okay?" Joseph nodded and that was enough. Archie threw him a Sten-gun length of wooden fencing, "Let's play."

Joseph needed an opportunity to bring up the missionary business and the business of Archie being Saved. But it was hard not to get caught up in the business of killing Nazis hiding in the huts. Armed with machine guns and beer-bottle hand grenades they ran for twenty-five minutes solid, hearts palpitating with manufactured fear and genuine excitement, zig-zagging from hut to hut, tiptoeing over cowpat landmines and mowing down the enemy. Joseph wondered which POW hut the Jerry Baptists and Mennonites who built the Hall had been in. He wouldn't want to shoot them. Archie smashed a bottle hard against a wall, and another and another. It made a fantastic clatter but after a while it wasn't enough.

"I could run and get petrol," he said with such urgency, he might really be at war. Archie was made for war. Fearless, ready to die for those he loved. "We could make proper hand grenades. Want me to? I'll be dead quick."

Of course Joseph wanted him to. Petrol grenades were always brilliant and satisfying, but right now he was meant to be labouring for the Lord. "It's okay, we can just pretend."

So they carried on playing heroic commandoes, escaping POWs and Nazi guards with all the German they knew, *Hände hoch Tommy, Achtung* and *Schweinhund.*

"Think we got them all?" said Archie, collapsing breathless on a bale.

"Mmm?" Joseph had his hand on his Bible like a gunslinger. *Do it. Now.*

"The Nazis. Think we killed them all?"

"I think so." *I will. I'm going to.*

Archie handed him some sweets and they lay a while in silence. Every so often Archie looked over at Joseph with a big chocolate grin on his face, and written all over it, *This is great isn't it? You and me. This. So it is?* And Joseph smiling back, *Yes it is.* In the end it was Archie who brought it up.

"So what'll we have to do if we're missionaries?"

Finally. Joseph had to get this right. Make Archie understand.

"You know *Onward Christian Soldiers Marching as to War?*"

"A wee bit."

"That's what missionaries do. We'd be like soldiers." Archie immediately reached for his stick Sten gun. "Except we wouldn't have guns. We'd have Bibles. And it wouldn't be Nazis we'd be fighting. It would be the Devil."

Archie grabbed the other stick gun, and held them up high to form a cross.

"This is what we'd need to do if it was Dracula we were fighting."

Dracula, the Devil. It was okay. Not completely the wrong of the stick.

"And I'd have to go all over the world," said Joseph, "spreading the Good News."

"Oh." Archie looked like he'd been slapped. Why had *we* turned into *I* all of a sudden? "Where would you go?"

"I don't know. Lots of missionaries start off in Glasgow, just to practise, but then I'd have go to Africa or India… and places like that."

"Oh. Right." He turned his back on Joseph and began picking bits of straw out of the bale and flicking them into the air. Archie taking the huff was a rare event. He sighed and sighed

again, like Gran, making a great deal of it in case Joseph wasn't getting the message.

"It's not like I'd be on my holidays," said Joseph. "It wouldn't just be exploring. I'd be going to Save folk. Folk who are far away from God and Jesus or who don't even know who God and Jesus are."

"But you're *not* Saved!" said Archie, back still turned, still in a huff, "You said you lied you were Saved! How come it's okay for you to go to Africa and places and not me?"

"But I will be Saved. I'm doing good works." *Good works aren't enough,* Mister Agnew was always saying that, *For by thy grace are ye Saved through faith: it is the gift of God: not of works, lest any man should boast.*

"What do you mean *good works?*"

"I'm going to Save folk, like a proper missionary."

Archie footered with some more bits of straw, "Who are you going to save first?"

"I don't know yet." *Come on Archie. Come on.*

Archie spun around and snatched the bait. "Going to pick me Joseph?" he said, looking his best friend in the eye, "*Please.* Going to save *me?*" Joseph rubbed his chin, where a Benjamin Mutch style beard would one day be. "*Please* Joseph, *please.*"

"But you need to really want to be Saved. You can't just…"

"But I do. Honest. Promise."

"Okay."

"And then can we both be missionaries thegether?"

"I think so. Yes." *Maybe we could.*

Archie sprung from the straw bale fit to burst, blinking like mad, scratching his head. What did it matter if he didn't understand all of it... any of it... It was enough to be with Joseph on an adventure, any adventure, *every* adventure. Archie was clapping now, making these squeaking sounds as though his body did not know what to do with this amount of excitement. Might this *really* be possible? Not just pretend? Might he *really* be a missionary with Joseph in faraway lands? With wee Maggie somewhere in the picture too? Far away from everything, from *that house*, far away from all that otherwise lay ahead. *Really*? He unwrapped a bar of Turkish Delight and gave half to Joseph,

"God Joseph, this is going to be so good, so it is," and wedged the other half into his mouth, "So... do missionaries... just save... anybody?"

"I think so," he said, licking his half of Turkish Delight loving its rose-water sweetness, "If they want to be Saved."

"What... even... murderers?"

"Yes."

" Nazis?"

"I think so."

"I wouldn't save a Nazi... even if God paid me a million pounds," and he smashed another bottle.

"Want to see my map?"

Archie was suitably astounded. He pointed to the scheme:

"See if it was my map, I'd make my house a Gateway to Hell. Honest I would. I'd draw a golden force field around me and wee Maggie's room but that would be it." A little darkness had descended but in another dazzling display of emotional acrobatics, Archie whirled and jumped and clapped in one spontaneous expression of joy. When Archie Truman was this brilliant, the darkness didn't stand a chance.

"I can't wait to go to darkest Africa!" he said and jumped up onto the straw bale and did his best Tarzan cry, "Let's go down the Sappie and play *Tarzan and the Missionaries.*"

Joseph looked at his breathless bright-eyed friend and considered the possibility that Archie, wonderful, all-accepting Archie Truman, was some kind of a genius.

In *Tarzan and the Missionaries of the Dark Interior*, Tarzan – played by Archie Truman – joined forces with celebrated missionary and explorer Joseph Kirkland – played by Joseph Kirkland – to Save the Heathen Hordes of the Dark Interior. Tarzan's methods were unorthodox, "Down on knees savage! Make sign of cross!" he cried, swinging down from his tree house to confront a heathen cannibal.

"We don't do that in the Hall, the cross..."

"Or Tarzan feed you to crocodile..."

"My Gran says it's a Catholic thing..."

"...or stick you in quicksand if you not say magic words..."

"And you can't torture folk into getting Saved... they need to..."

"Tarzan *make them*. Man-eating savages thank us when go to Heaven."

"You need to be Saved as well, mind."

"Great Joseph Kirkland give Tarzan magic words so Tarzan saved."

"Not *pretend* Archie. I mean it. You need to say it. And mean it. Or He'll know."

"Who?"

"God. Or Jesus." He was a bit exasperated now, and nervous, all these games, this frivolity, "And they're not *magic words*."

Tarzan, sensing the missionary's anxiety, dropped his mask and transformed back into Archie Truman.

"Sorry," he said, with a sheepish grin, "I'll do it right. What do I need to do?"

"You just ask God or Jesus to come into your heart." *See? It's so easy.*

"Okay... so is it God or Jesus I've to ask?"

"Em... both... ask both of them. Say you want them to come into your heart and Save you. Just... say that."

"Okay." He closed his eyes like he was making a wish," *God and Jesus I want you...*"

"No, wait!"

How could Archie just say it quite the thing? All cheery and fearless? This was *it*. This would be him. Changed. Forever. He'd be a different Archie after this. He needed to realise the full significance... not... go into it like it was all kid-on.

"Mind you need to *really* want to be Saved."

"I do."

"Not just because I'm asking you to."

"I'm not."

"Or just so's we can go to Africa or..."

"I know, I know how to do it, watch this, watch," Archie put on the lowest, most trembling, most melodramatic voice he could muster, "God... and... Jesus... this is how the priest did it in *Dracula Has Risen from the Grave*... I... Want..."

"*Please* Archie, you can't think about Dracula or the pictures and things."

"Okay, sorry, I'll do it right..."

"And you're a sinner mind... you need to think of all the bad things you've done."

"What... *all* of them?"

"Well... some of them anyway. So's God can forgive you. That's the whole..."

"How about the comics and sweets from Ramsay's? That was the last bad thing."

"Okay, well... just say sorry for that then." *This isn't right.*

"Oh, and this as well." Archie fumbled deep inside his anorak pocket and pulled out a small tartan penknife. "I meant to give it to you before, it was stuck in the lining. I thought it would be good for being a missionary, for making spears and skinning things and… I don't know… you can use it for all sorts of stuff."

Joseph took the knife. How could he not? He'd always wanted one. He dragged his thumb across its pristine cutting edge, felt the sharpness of its tip. But it was stolen! This is what happened when you *walked in the counsel of the unGodly*, you ended up going down blind alleys, taking wrong turnings, getting further and further away from God until…

"Right," said Archie, looking suitably solemn now, "here I go."

"You know you'll be different after?"

"I know."

"I mean it."

"But I want to be different."

"I mean *really* different."

Archie stopped, folded his arms and scowled.

"Look, if you don't want me to get Saved, I won't!"

"No, I do, I do, I do want you to." *I don't want you to.* "Okay. Say it." Archie barely had time to open his mouth, "Maybe clasp your hands first."

"Want me to kneel down as well?"

"No. Yes. Yes… that would be good."

"Here? Beside the water?"

Perfect. Archie got to his knees, hands clasped, eyes closed, face heavenwards,

"I'm going to say it now Joseph. Okay?"

"Okay."

His eyes flashed open.

"Actually, come and we'll say it thegether?" He patted the frosted grass. Joseph knelt beside him. He felt nauseous. "You and me, eh Joseph? Imagine? Missionaries thegether, eh? *Kirkland and Truman Save the World*! That'll be us. Come on and we'll say it really loud so's God and Jesus actually hear us up in heaven? Right, after three… one… two…"

Joseph felt a cold tingle of fear and looked over his shoulder.

But Archie Truman was ecstatic. His eyes weren't closed, his hands weren't clasped; he was all wide open in a perfect picture of supplication.

"Three! GOD AND JESUS!" he cried, long and loud, with all the eye-popping, spastic passion of a body needing to be Saved, of a baby begging to be born, "I… WANT… YOU…" – he pushed every puff of air from his lungs, draining his old self dry – "TO …. COME… IN… TO… MY… HEART!" Until his withered remains collapsed in a heap and there was nothing left of the old Archie Truman.

Had it happened? Was the transformation taking place right now? Archie's *Body Snatchers* moment? Sluggishly, its head hung low, the thing that had once been Archie Truman pushed itself onto its knees and turned itself around for the big nightmare reveal. The thing was blissful, it was beaming …

"Is that us then?" it said, wiping its nose on its sleeve and searching its pocket for wine gums.

It was still Archie Truman. It would always be Archie Truman. This was the thing, the wonderful thing; the dreadful thing.

CHAPTER TWENTY-SEVEN

From Genesis to Malachi

The newly Saved Archie Truman was full speed ahead on sugar and curiosity, "So will I have to get a fancy tweed suit and brogues and things too?"

Joseph was carving a big letter 'J' on the tree house tree trunk with his new penknife. It was one of many *AT + JK* commemorative carvings and scratchings that could be found on trees, fence posts, boulders, tarmac and concrete all around Kilhaugh.

"We should do the date as well," said Archie, "for folk in the future, so they'll know this was the day it all started. They'll go *Oh that's them two that are away saving folk in darkest wherever-they-are.*"

That wasn't a bad idea. And maybe a notch too for his first Saved soul, who was talking twenty to the dozen now, "Yeah, I'm definitely going to get a tweed suit and stuff and I'll have my hair all nice and Brylcreemed like yours, so's I don't look like a midden – that's what my Grannie says, *oh my goad yer a right midden, so ye are* – then that'll be me, that'll be us… give us a shot of your bible." Joseph handed it to him. "What's the red stuff?"

"Blood,"

"Blood?"

"From a dog."

"*Dog blood?*"

"From the tinker's dog."

"What tinker?"

The Liar Joseph Kirkland lied, but only by omission. He told Archie only that section of the story concerning the boulder-headed Devil dog, and nothing of the visit to Caleb

Skeely's tent. Archie wasn't just there in the story with Joseph and Caleb and Mirky and the Devil dog, he *was* Joseph and Caleb and Mirky. He was up the tree throwing cages and experiencing the joy and shame of swearing, he was down on the ground, grinding his teeth, biting the bite, clenching the fist and kicking the kick, and administering the *coup de grâce;* the whole epic battle.

"Bloody hell. Joseph, BLOODY HELL. Know what? I think that was the Lennox dog. Big stupid dirty white slaiverin' thing? Stephen Lennox mind? In wee Maggie's class? She was saying Stevie was greetin' in the playground this morning cos his dog ran away. I'm telling you, see if I was the Lennox dog I'd run away, so I would. If I was Stevie I'd run away. I thought my dad was bad, but his dad's totally mental. Everybody knows George Lennox where I come from. My grannie says they're just evil so they are, the whole family, especially the dad, been inside for all sorts. Knows all sorts too. She says she wouldn't be surprised if he was actually Bible John. Imagine if he was? And know what the dog was called? Cassie! Short for Cassius Clay. You saw them all the time, shoving it into a van and driving away somewhere. Poor thing. God, Joseph. And the tinker just punched it?"

This story had it all: fights, death, tinkers, wild beasts, the possibility of murderous vengeance, and at the heart of it all, the most unlikely protagonist in the whole world, his best pal Joseph Kirkland. Archie laughed, it was so unlikely, "George Lennox will actually kill that tinker if he finds out."

The blood drained from Joseph's face. He knew he shouldn't have said, not even to Archie.

"Where's its body?"

"I don't know. It's gone."

"Maybe he buried it?"

"Maybe."

"Or ate it. He could've but. Tinkers eat anything, so they do. They just cook it up in their big stews: rabbits, squirrels, hedgehogs, weasels. It wouldn't bother me; I'd eat it. I'd dunk my bread in it, so I would, *mmm yum, hedgehog and weasel.* I'd make a great tinker." He licked his finger and drew it across the Bible, hoping to find traces of blood, "Bloody hell Joseph… sorry… but George Lennox's dog?"

"I need to do the Books of the Bible now."

Joseph didn't simply recite the Books of the Old Testament, he plucked them from thin air and popped them into an invisible bag as he journeyed in his mind's eye through Kilhaugh's nooks and crannies. This was the memory map trick that *Caleb the Tinker Magician* had taught him.

The Book of Genesis was on his bed, *The Book of Exodus* on the front step, *The Book of Leviticus* in a crack in the wall in the lane, *The Book of Numbers* was wedged into the gate of Agnew's Paper Mill, and so on and so forth. Archie shadowed him, not the words, but the choreography of Joseph Kirkland's Old Testament map dance, loving that he was witnessing some brand-new oddness in his friend who was already so beautifully odd. In the real world Joseph's dance ended on the Munday bridge, and in his imaginary world, in Caleb's tent where he collected *The Book of the Malachi*, the final book of the Old Testament.

Yes. He clenched a fist, which for Joseph was as good as punching the air.

"Did you get them all?" Joseph nodded, and Archie did punch the air. "Yes!"

"All the ones in the Old Testament anyway." And then, quite the thing, without really thinking about it, "I'm going to the Hall tonight. You and wee Maggie can come too if you want… Don't tell anybody, but we're packing boxes of Bibles to smuggle into Communist countries."

Archie stopped dead. What? *WHAT?* He took a step forward and for a moment Joseph thought Archie was going to hug him, but instead he ran back to his end of the bridge, just behind the curtain of fog, and started jumping up and down with all his might but there was so little of him, so little might, Joseph could not feel the slightest reverberation.

"Can you feel it, Joseph?"

"Yes."

CHAPTER TWENTY-EIGHT

Visions of Hell

A figure wrapped from head to toe in animal fur was coming out of the library with a fat old dog by her side. She stopped in the doorway. There was so much fur and so much dog, Joseph couldn't squeeze past, but Mrs Arnold would not budge.

"Excuse me," he said, so quietly only her dog could've heard.

Her ladies' brown brogues were toe to toe with his. He'd forgotten you could get ladies' brogues. A lot of up-the-hill ladies wore them, tweeds too. He dared to glance up at her face. There was that look again. Terror, or something, but whatever it was, right then he felt the cold terribly and visibly shivered, actually said *brrr..*

"I'm sorry, son," she said, trying to force a smile, trying to sound okay but not looking or sounding at all okay, quite the opposite, "I'm not meaning anything. It's Joseph isn't it? "

She was probably a friend of Mrs Hendry. This was about the half-crown. These folk up the hill, they all knew each other, had cups of tea and biscuits thegether.

"Can I ask you," her hands were trembling, "these clothes… the shoes, and all?"

"I bought them at the jumble sale."

"Yes… And… they fit you so well. But… I was just wondering son…"

"I'm going to be a missionary."

Mrs Arnold looked at him, maybe seeking some sign of contempt, or juvenile cheek, and seeing none shook her head, the way Gran did, but not angry… confounded.

"A missionary," and like Gran she sighed, a loud warbling sigh, almost a cry really, "I see. And… and what…I'm not really… what will you…?"

"I'll Save folk."

"Of course, of course," she nodded, tried out a number of smiles, but couldn't find one that was suitable. "That's what missionaries do. What a…what a… what a…what a…" She stammered so much he wondered if she would ever finish her sentence "… what a…what a … *great thing* that is, Joseph. What a *great thing*. To… to… to… *Save* somebody." Now she was just nodding, nodding more than even Joseph nodded, "I'm not wanting to scare you, son; I'm really not, that's the last thing I'd want, to scare you…" she should really stop saying that, "but… would you mind if I …? Just for a second, son." And without waiting for a reply, she put her arms around Joseph and drew him close, "That's it. That's it. That's it," she said, over and over and over, pulling his face into the frost-damp bear fur, or fox fur or mink or whatever dead animal it was, while the dog sat and watched. It was only a few seconds, and when she let go, she looked so embarrassed.

"I'm so sorry," she said, trying to smooth his hair with one hand and wipe her tears with the other, but she was wearing these leather gloves, "I don't know what you must be thinking. Let's… let's pretend this never happened, eh?" She tried a laugh and when that didn't happen either, she grabbed the fat old dog by the leash and left.

Joseph was already pretending it never happened, making himself not think anything except, *I wonder what animal her coat was made of.*

Visions of Hell was in the oversize section. It had caught his eye many times but he'd never dared look at it. The librarian, Miss Marlow, frowned at this heavy tome and at Joseph in his new get-up. She'd have heard all about the latest goings-on from her sister, Mrs Merryweather.

"You know you're only meant to get books from the junior section."

"It's for Sunday School."

Of course, she'd be thinking, *the Kirkland boy would read a book like this, wouldn't he? What else would he be reading? Except the Bible and I can see that sticking out his pocket.*

"Mind look after it," she said, stamping his ticket, "you're the first to take it out."

Joseph wasn't listening; he was looking at *Under A Big Bad Sky* on the returned book trolley, wondering how it got there and hoping against hope that there were two copies.

Gran's house was cocooned in a fragile silence. Joseph stopped in the lobby, stopped breathing even, for fear of breaking it. His first thought was of Grandpa. *Has it happened?* Then Uncle Mathew appeared and shot him a *what are you doing standing there* look and waved him into the living room.

Uncle Mathew never took his beloved leather jacket off when he was at Gran's and he never sat still, always pacing, always ready for the off; *You and your pacing*, Gran would say, *You'll wear a hole in that carpet*, and she'd smile. Not that he ever stayed long. He always had something needed doing, someone needing seeing, somewhere needing going. "Here's your hat, what's your hurry?" she'd say and again. She'd smile, but the smile would collapse the moment he turned away. Grandpa would say nothing. He'd just sit behind his paper, mumble-singing bits of Arthur Askey, "I'd like to be a busy little bee, being as busy as a bee can be" or something home-made and pointed, "He's a ducker, he's a diver, he's a naughty little skiver, deedle eedle deedle idle, deedle o."

"Your Gran's up the hill cleaning," said Uncle Mathew and he'd barely slumped into Grandpa's chair when was on his feet again, looking out of the window. Was he was looking for Peter? No. He took a comb from his back pocket and leant this way and that, searching – unsuccessfully – for his own reflection.

Joseph felt bad. He'd hardly thought about Peter at all in the past few hours.

"He might still be alive," he said, accidentally out loud.

"Who?"

"Peter."

"What?" He looked Joseph up and down, the tweed suit, the brogues, the whole thing, it was the first time he'd properly looked at him and he didn't like what he saw.

"What are you like? I mean... as if this family wasn't daft enough as it is."

He was pacing again, patting his pockets, sticking his hand in, making sure whatever he was looking for was still there or still not there. Joseph hadn't sat down either.

"By the way, what were you doing hanging around with that Truman boy?" Joseph feigned deafness. "You're not too old for leatherin' by the way. I *said*... why were you hanging around with him?"

"I wasn't." *Sorry.* "He was just there."

"Aye right. You hear his dad was blind drunk over at Agnew's? Again. Threatened your Uncle Andrew, so he did, asked him for a square go." He chuckled, "Can you imagine? A *square go* with Andrew?" He chuckled again. "Had to get Duncan in." PC Carmichael and Uncle Mathew had been friends since school. "Anyway, he got his jotters. I tell you, I'd have given him more than his jotters. Duncan caught his boy down the drains for God's sake. Mind you, that's where they belong, in the effin' drains, with the rest of the vermin." He saw the huge *Visions of Hell* book under Joseph's arm, "What's that?"

"It's just pictures."

"Just pictures? Oh aye. What kind of pictures? Pictures of *ladies*?" and he threw Joseph a goatish wink that was totally wasted on him. "I'm kidding you. Show me." Joseph handed it over, "Name a' God. What's this?"

"It's pictures of Hell."

"I can see that, smart-arse. What have *you* got it for?"

"I just wanted to see."

"See what? *Visions of Hell*? Do you not get enough of that

at the Hall? Or here?" He rubbed the discoloured circle of carpet with his foot. "I've had about enough of this, so I have. Baptisms in the Sappie… missionaries… I mean look at the state of you, for God's sake! Most of the village already think we're a bunch of bloody weirdoes." He thrust the book back into Joseph's hands, "Well you can take it back to the library afore your Gran sees it. That's the last thing we need… Are you listening to a blind word I'm saying?"

Joseph was not listening to a blind word his Uncle was saying. He was too busy gauping at him, thinking, on the brink of mouthing, *Even Uncle Mathew has been Saved. How? How can Uncle Mathew be Saved? What must he have been like before he was Saved, if this is him now?* Eventually he managed a nod.

"Anybody ever call you *Noddy*… well they should…" he took a pack of Players cigarettes from his jacket and headed for the door, mumbling under his breath, "Fuckin' *Noddy*."

Visions of Hell was filled with drawings, woodcuts, etchings and paintings by Blake, Caravaggio, Goya, Géricault, Bouguereau, Bosch, and other artists whose names meant nothing to Joseph Kirkland. Their *visions* however meant a great deal. The cover alone was a nightmare kaleidoscope of tangled, eviscerated, yet still living, naked bodies, severed limbs and screaming heads, human-insect hybrids and gloating dwarves who whipped and branded cowering naked men and naked women. On a red fleshy hillside among pools of molten lava stood a ruined castle shaped like an ogre's head, creatures crawling out of its eyes, ears, nose and mouth, while from bone battlements, satyrs threw more writhing naked bodies into glutinous pitch-black lakes. There were smoke-belching volcano factories, peopled by countless tiny tormented naked folk being poked and prodded by pitchfork-wielding demons. Elsewhere a muscle-bound naked giant devoured naked children from a steaming cauldron, and a leathery bat-winged angel dragged a screaming naked man across a crumbling bridge that spanned a chasm like a gaping wound, while underneath, eight-foot skeletons pulled fishing nets full of the perpetually drowning naked damned from the gory sea. And all of them, all clinging to life while at the same time begging for a gift of death, which, like Sylvester in the world of *Loony Tunes*, they would never receive.

Uncle Mathew was right, Gran should not see this. Apart from anything else, she would not approve of the nakedness.

Joseph was hungry and Uncle Matthew hadn't come back in. Maybe he was having another fag. Or he'd things to do. Joseph heated up the lentil soup, his favourite of Gran's soups, got a big crusty doorstep from the back of the loaf and dunked it in.

"Caleb Skeely," he said, just like that, and looked over his shoulder, just in case Uncle Mathew had appeared. Or Caleb Skeely. He was the sort of man who could well appear out of thin air. He was probably there by the Sappie, watching Archie Truman not getting Saved. Joseph would've liked to be sitting in his tent right now, with Mirky at his feet. And Archie. The two of them listening to stories and dunking Caleb's earth bread into something good from that cauldron, rabbit soup, anything, even boulder-headed Devil dog soup.

Grandpa was lying on his back, arms straight down his side, like he was standing at attention at the cenotaph with his British Legion pals. His hearing aids were on the bedside table, on top of his Bible. They were ugly-looking things when they weren't in his ears, wee flesh-pink plastic body parts, like those flayed beasts in the *Visions of Hell*. Joseph had always wanted to try them on, just to see. Not today. He reached under the mattress and slid his hand up and down. Grandpa was almost weightless.

When Joseph was wee and Grandpa hale and hearty, he'd bend his knees and arms so Joseph could climb up onto his shoulders while he sang one of his made-up songs:

We're going up the Grandpa mountain
We're going up up up the Grandpa mountain
And we're not going to stop
Till we reach the very top
Of the bony auld crookit Grandpa mountain.

"Again Grandpa," Joseph would say.
"You and your daft songs," Gran would say.

Under a Big Bad Sky was not under the mattress. Grandpa's hand fell lightly onto Joseph's head and slid down, resting on the smooth roundness of his cheek. He liked it when Grandpa did that, *Joseph the seal pup*, he'd sometimes say. His hand was a block of ice.

"Grandpa. I met a man. I think he's a tinker. I'm not sure. But he's nice. He tells stories. And he makes things. From wood. See." Joseph wasn't sure if Grandpa had heard a single word, but still he took the mermaid, and caressed it like a blind man.

"She was that good, so she was." His voice was like the rest of him, barely there: "It was just the weight son, the weight of it all. She just couldn't bear it. If I could've had just one toatie wee bit of magic on the end of my fingertips, I'd have magicked her a pair of wings, so I would." As the bedroom door opened, Grandpa folded his hand over the mermaid, "Fly away ma darling, fly away ma wee one…"

"Is he still going on about that budgie?" Gran shook her head and walked back out again. She'd had enough of him and his budgie nonsense. It was high time he got over all that.

CHAPTER TWENTY-NINE

The Damnation of Archibald Truman

Archie and wee Maggie were standing on the edge of the pavement, just up the road from the Hall. They were examining a dead thing that had been run over several times and reduced to such a mangled mess of bone, flesh and fur that it was impossible to know for certain what it had once been.

"I think it's a rat," said Archie, prodding it with a stick; wee Maggie hid behind him as though the dead thing might leap back to life at any moment.

Archie couldn't have known about Uncle Andrew sacking his dad. Not if he was like this, all normal, gleeful even, or else putting it on for wee Maggie's sake.

"I think it's a squirrel, Joseph," she said. "What do you think it is?"

"A cat, maybe."

"Oh no! Not a pussy cat, Joseph. That would be too sad."

"I still think it's a rat."

"It's too big for a rat, isn't it Joseph? And anyway, where's its tail?"

"Maybe its tail's still alive, maybe it wriggled away like the man's hand in *The Beast With Five Fingers*."

"Oh don't, that's horrible Archie. Archie's horrible, isn't he, Joseph? Why can't you be nice all the time like Joseph is nice?"

"Some rats are huge so they are. I saw one under the bridge once and it was like a wee dog, so it was; it was that big. Mind, Joseph? That one I killed with a boulder? I got it on its tail with a half brick first and it just stood there, and looked up at me, like *I'm going to get you for that.*" Wee Maggie giggled so he had to do it again, even better, so he screwed up his face, stuck out his two front teeth, "I'm going to get you Archie Truman, so I am," he said in a squeaky rat voice, and shuffled towards wee Maggie, making nibbling noises, "Then I'm going to get your wee sister and nibble her toes... and nibble her nose..."

"Stop it, I don't like that," she said, but wanting him to keep going. So he did.

"And nibble her nice new clothes... and everything."

"We'd better go in," said Joseph.

Wee Maggie took Joseph's hand as they crossed the road, "Joseph, Archie says he's been Saved. Can I get Saved as well?"

"I told her Joseph. I told you. You need to wait till you're older."

"Archie says you get special powers."

"I did not say that," and he gave her a friendly dunt.

"Did so," and she dunted him back, harder. "He did, Joseph. He said it's like when what's-his-name *Captain Marvel* shouts 'Shazam!'"

In her new jumble sale outfit Wee Maggie looked like a Ladybird picture book cover: *A Wee Girl Goes to Church* – pink dress, patent leather black buckle shoes with frilly topped ankle socks and a green coat with a black velvet collar.

"She's like she's from up the hill, so she is!" said Archie as proud as punch.

Archie was just the same dog's dinner, reheated. The glaze of snot, sweat and grime had simply been smeared across his face in a different direction by an anorak sleeve. Wee Maggie didn't notice. They were from such a different world to Joseph's. Was it really a good idea to bring them into the Hall? It wasn't too late to make some excuse; they could turn on their heels and go somewhere else, anywhere else.

There were about a dozen in the Hall, children and grown-ups, including Uncle Andrew, Auntie Ishbel and Jenny.

Archie looked and felt like a fish out of water, but he stood ramrod straight, chin out, trying to act all *Take us as you find us – or else!* But it was so obviously an act. Wee Maggie looked the place up and down, "Where's all the pictures and statues and things, Joseph?" she asked, too loudly, as if a robbery had taken place and she was the first to discover it.

Alerted to the presence of strangers, everyone turned and stared. There had been trouble in the past from some of the teenage overspill. Wee Maggie sounded like a younger version of it. Then there was the business at Agnew's. Kilhaugh's jungle drums beat fast and loud over such incidents; surely they must've heard. Wee Maggie sensed something and hid behind Joseph.

"Welcome," said Uncle Andrew, and he meant it, the children would not be blamed for their father's iniquity.

Jenny looked at Archie and wee Maggie like they were something nasty brought in on the sole of a shoe and at Joseph like he was the shoe, but as ever she switched on her beaming smile before anyone else saw it. Wee Maggie got straight to the point,.

"Joseph saved Archie. He's going to Save me as well. Aren't you, Joseph? When I'm bigger? And I'm going to be Baptised in the Sappie too, aren't I Joseph?" She finished her speech with a curtsey.

Auntie Ishbel was amused and enchanted by wee Maggie, how could she not be?

"Maggie, isn't it?"

"Yes," and she curtsied again. She was surprised that this woman knew her name and decided immediately to like Auntie Ishbel, because she was certain Auntie Ishbel liked her.

"And you must be Archie." Archie's face went red. "As Mister Kirkland said, you're

very welcome. That's Mister *Andrew* Kirkland by the way, not Mister *Joseph* Kirkland, our young missionary, who seems to have got off to a flying start."

Four benches had been rearranged in a square. In the middle was a big table stacked high with Russian and German Bibles. The children were split into groups, with Joseph, Archie and wee Maggie working together on the boxes that were to be sent to East Germany.

"Has Joseph told you about what we're doing tonight?" asked Auntie Ishbel.

"He says we're smuggling Bibles into Communist countries," whispered Archie, and he bit his lip as though he might already have said too much, revealed something top secret.

"We are indeed. Have you heard the hymn, *Onward Christian Soldiers?*"

Archie answered by proudly quoting the words of his learned friend,

"Joseph said missionaries are like God's soldiers, but they've Bibles instead of guns… so you did Joseph?"

"That's right," said Auntie Ishbel, impressed at Joseph's mission work so far. She looked over her shoulder as though she herself might be under surveillance, "and *we* are His secret agents. We're going to disguise all these Bibles, to make them look like the kind of books folk are allowed to read in East Germany. So…"

She ripped open a parcel. Joseph knew what was next. It would be full of fake German book jackets. Last time it was drab inoffensive car and clock manuals; *Motorrad – Wartung*, *Fahrzeuge Reparaturanleitung* and *Uhren: Restauration und Reparatur* and the time before that, *Medizinisches Wörterbuch* – medical dictionaries. They changed each time, *to keep them on their toes*, Mister Agnew would say with a sly wee nod, like they were running some covert secret service operation. Which they were.

"*Winnetou der Apache Krieger*, von Karl May," said Auntie Ishbel in an excellent German accent. She was holding up two garish book jackets; one with a picture of a rifle-toting Apache Indian chief in white buckskins sitting bareback on a piebald horse, and the other, *Winnetou und das Halbblut Apache*, von Karl May, featured the same eponymous *Winnetou* on a precipice in what looked like Monument Valley.

"Don't ask me why," she said, "but East Germans love westerns. It seems this Karl May chap is one of their biggest sellers." She laughed and handed a bundle to Joseph, "I know, the Bible dressed up as a cowboy book, it's hard to credit."

"What would happen if one of them got caught with a Bible?" asked wee Maggie.

A Sangster twin answered from the Russian side of the table.

"You get put in prison," he said with relish, "and tortured."

"Or killed," said the other Sangster twin with even more relish.

"The communists work for Satan," said the first.

"Those who've been Saved have nothing to fear," said Uncle Andrew without looking up. "The wicked will get their punishment on the Day of Judgement."

"Good," said Archie and slammed another book into the box as though he was squashing a wicked communist on the Day of Judgement.

"Good," said wee Maggie, and slammed in another.

Smuggling! East German Communists! Cowboys and Indians! Prison! Torture! Secret Agents! The Devil! … Archie had no idea. If he'd known Joseph got up to things like this, he'd have come to the Hall a long time ago, "This is brilliant Joseph. It's like James Bond or something."

Joseph relaxed a little. *Maybe …*

After half an hour or so, Jenny was asked to say a prayer. Joseph was expecting *the Evils of Communism*, and she did cover that topic, but prayers were not meant to be too scripted so she added some local newsworthy additions of her own, "Lord, we pray for those who are sick in body, in mind and in heart. We pray for Mrs Agnew, and for Mrs Hendry, and we pray for my grandfather, Mister Samuel Kirkland." She half opened her eyes, and saw that Joseph, Archie and wee Maggie had their eyes open too, "Lord, we pray for those who struggle with alcohol, and with violent tempers. We pray for those who steal, Lord, and who would lead us astray with lies and deceit. We ask, Lord, that you remind them that though they may deceive others, they can *never* deceive You. But Lord, we've been blessed this evening, by the arrival of Archibald and Margaret Truman," Archie and Wee Maggie repressed a snigger at hearing their proper names spoken aloud. "We pray that the names Archibald Truman and Margaret Truman will be found in the Book of Life, for it is written that in the last days *whosoever was not found written in the Book of Life was cast into the Lake of Fire*. We also pray ..."

By the end wee Maggie's face was a picture of perplexity and alarm.

"What did she mean about the *Book of Life*, Joseph? And about going into *a lake of fire?*" Joseph shushed her but she was not to be shushed, "Are yours and mines and Archie's names in that book?"

"We'll talk about that later, pet," said Auntie Ishbel, "just you and me," and she looked daggers at her daughter over on the Russian side of the table.

Uncle Andrew handed out *The Good Shepherd Pamphlet of Popular Hymns & Choruses*.

"Let us sing the Lord's praises, page sixteen, *Rescue the Perishing*, by Blind Fanny Crosby, and inspired by... which Book in the Bible?"

"Isaiah!" said a Sangster twin.

"Isaiah!" repeated Uncle Andrew and his eyelids fluttered like a Biblical Rolodex, "Chapter One, Verse Eighteen: *Though your sins are as scarlet, they shall be as white as snow*."

They sang, *Rescue the Perishing, care for the dying.*

Joseph felt dreadful. This was a mistake. He must get Archie and wee Maggie out of this.

Snatch them in pity, from sin and the grave.

Especially wee Maggie. It was the heaviness of it all, the darkness of it all. He was used to it. It was part of him, he was part of it. Who knows, maybe he even needed it. Archie was probably immune. But not wee Maggie. She'd be suffocated by this. Yes, they needed to be Saved, but not here; why couldn't they go to somewhere else and be Saved… Kilhaugh Episcopalian or the Church of Scotland… Saint Rita's even. Once again the wee magnesium flares flickered at the back of his head. He tried, a little, not to give in to them.

"Joseph," Wee Maggie nipped his ear lobe, "Are you okay Joseph?"

"He was just away with the fairies. Weren't you, Joseph?" said Archie. "You never seen Joseph away with the fairies before?"

Jenny was all smiles as she went around the groups, seeing how they were doing. "So, you've been Saved, Archie? By the missionary Joseph Kirkland?" She taped down the lid on one of the boxes. "I hope you don't mind me asking, but are your mum and dad Saved as well?"

Archie said nothing. You didn't grow up in Archie's world and not learn how to read folk. He could see right through this false girl. She was not befriending them.

"I was just thinking, it might've brought them some comfort." Jenny paused to let this sink in. "You look a bit confused Archie." He didn't, but she carried on anyway, "Sorry, did your dad not say?"

"Say what?" Archie knew he was being led by the nose into a trap, but curiosity got the better of him.

"Say what?" said wee Maggie, not understanding what was going on, but feeling it acutely all the same.

"Just that he went to work, drunk," she sighed like a disappointed parent. "Again. Only this time he threatened my dad. With a hammer. They had to get the police."

Joseph looked for Uncle Andrew or Auntie Ishbel to intervene, but they were through the back getting the tea things. Wee Maggie welled up. Jenny closed in for the kill, "Sorry, I thought you knew he'd got the sack. Oh dear," she sighed again. "No job. No money. And the thing is..." this was for wee Maggie's benefit now, "see, if they think children aren't being looked after properly – they get put in the Robert Munday Home – not out of badness or anything, for their own good."

Archie snarled at her, "She is being looked after."

"Archie!" wee Maggie's voice trembled. This Jenny girl was older. She knew things: "So that won't happen? So it won't?"

"Course it won't. She's just being daft, so she is."

"And I hear you're only one step away from the borstal. I hope that doesn't happen. Or your wee sister might end up in the Munday on her own."

Archie's eyes had hardened, the blood drained from his face, his voice was flat and empty, "She's looked after fine."

"Know what I think, Joseph? I think your friend hasn't been Saved at all. I think him and his wee sister are both heading straight to Hell."

It was over in seconds. Archie pulled Jenny to the ground by her hair, his p's and q's going right out window, "Ma wee sister isnae going tae hell ya fff....." and he punched her in the face to stop himself saying the "f" word, "Don't you even *say* that ya..." and he punched her again, harder, to stop himself saying the "f" and the "c" words.

It was wee Maggie who dragged her big brother out of the red mist and into the fog.

Inside a shocked Uncle Andrew was trying to stem the blood from his daughter's nose and lip with his hanky, "Jennifer, are you all right?" Auntie Ishbel was looking at her like she deserved everything she'd been given, and Joseph was busy wiping yet another spatter of blood off his Bible.

CHAPTER THIRTY

You in Your Small Corner and I in Mine

Joseph ran home, lied to his Gran that he was feeling chesty, kissed his unaware Grandpa goodnight, and went to bed. He was halfway through his Gentle Jesus when the phone rang.

"No! ... Oh, Ishbel, is she all right? ... yes ... mhmm ... yes ... mhmm ... What was Joseph thinking? ... I know, but all the same ... in bed ... Aye, says his chest was bothering him, more like his conscience ... But Ishbel ... but ... I promise ... If that's what you ... No I won't say a word ... dad? ... Ach, I'm at my wits end, so I am ... I can't help it, he could go at any moment ... Aye, I've spoken to Mister Agnew but ... Ach it's hard to know what dad hears and what he doesn't ... I just need to be certain Ishbel, I just need to be sure ... I'm that scared Ishbel, I'm that scared, pet."

Later, when Joseph was sure they were both asleep, he stood by the door and watched them, like a mother might watch her newborn: the erratic rise and fall of bedcovers, then nothing, then something, as though over and over they were slipping off a steep promontory into the sea, only to be lifted back to safety by a wave, but just for a moment, until they started to slip again, Grandpa always slightly in the lead, but ever so slightly.

There was not one but *two* ghost children standing beneath the street lamp, like they'd drifted in from the past to issue a warning or seek assistance. He'd expected Archie to come by, but wee Maggie was a first. Both were in their dressing gowns, wee Maggie reinforced with scarf, mitts and woolly hat. Archie mouthed an exaggerated, *sorry*. Joseph opened the window and said something he'd never said to anyone before, "Do you want to come in?"

It was a six feet sprauchle up a drainpipe to the bedroom window. Archie shoved a game but

ungainly wee Maggie as far as he could and Joseph pulled her up the rest.

Once inside they stood, stiff and awkward in a triangle. The two guests took in as much as they could without turning their heads. This was uncharted territory for Joseph; literally so for Archie and wee Maggie.

"I like your room Joseph," she said, breaking the ice with a whisper. "It's dead tidy." She spied his *Heroes of the Cross*, "Can I see your books?" When Joseph nodded, she picked one up and studied its cover, "Why's the Chinaman on the boat tying books to folk's heads?"

"He's not a Chinaman. He's Scottish. He's William Burns, the missionary. He's just wearing Chinese clothes as a disguise. The Chinese folk swimming away have just been Saved. See, it's Bibles he's tying to their heads, to smuggle into China…"

"Archie's sorry about hitting your cousin, Joseph, and for using the two 'b' words and the 'f' word and…"

"I never used the 'f' word…"

"Yes you did, Archie. I heard you. We heard him, didn't we Joseph? Archie wants to know if he's still saved."

"I was just going to say that," said Archie,

"Even though your cousin asked for it, so she did, Joseph. Because what she said was worse, so it was. Even if it was God's honest truth she was saying, and I bet it wasn't, but even if it was, she was just saying God's honest truth to hurt me and Archie, and hurt you as well. And that's not right, so it isn't Joseph."

Joseph and Archie looked at wee Maggie, amazed by her ability to negotiate with ease through the impossibly tangled maze of rights, wrongs, whys and wherefores, and get to the plain and simple decent human heart of it all.

"Am I… still saved?" asked Archie.

Wee Maggie had picked up the David Livingstone book. If Archie wasn't Saved then Joseph Kirkland and Doctor Livingstone were even: Saved one, lost one.

"I don't know. Maybe. I think so."

"Can I still get baptised in the Sappie with you?"

"I'm not sure. I don't know if Mister Agnew will …"

"You could baptise him Joseph," said wee Maggie, "so you could."

"You need to be a priest like that Mister Agnew to baptise folk, don't you?"

"You mustn't call him a priest," Joseph shot an involuntary glance at the bedroom door. "He's not a priest. He's just labouring for the Lord. He's just ordinary… like you and me."

"So does that mean you *can* baptise Archie?"

Joseph caressed the wooden mermaid in his dressing gown pocket, *Missionaries can Baptise folk. It's not a bad thing. Maybe it's even a good thing. No. It's daft. I'm not even Saved. But I nearly am. And if I got Archie Saved properly …*

"Yes, maybe…"

"There's no school," said Archie. "We could do it tomorrow?"

"Right after our breakfast," said wee Maggie, "Oh, this is so exciting, isn't it Joseph?"

Archie was first down the drainpipe. Wee Maggie had one leg out the window when she saw the Pre-Tribulational Rapture picture, "Is the lady supposed to be flying?"

"She's going up to Heaven."

"Oh," Wee Maggie considered this, or considered something, "she's really pretty, isn't she Joseph? I like her dress. I'd like a dress like hers."

Archie called up from below, "Maggie, will you hurry up."

Joseph couldn't see the ground for fog as he lowered her

into her brother's arms, like an upside-down Indian rope trick. She looked up at him,

"Will me and Archie go up to heaven, Joseph?"

"Yes."

Because to think otherwise would be unbearable.

CHAPTER THIRTY-ONE

The Bible Designed To Be Read As Literature

"Where are you off to this morning?"

"I'm going to practise my Books of the Bible." This was true. He still had to learn the books of the New Testament, which should be a lot easier, as they were more familiar. But he also had to go to the library and return *Visions of Hell*. Uncle Mathew was right, it was best if Gran didn't see it.

"Well mind you've your balaclava and scarf. I don't know why I bother knitting, and I've heard Mister Chaddock's taken not well now." She took a bite of toast, chewing it slowly. He could hear her brain working, trying to turn the toast into words, trying to keep her promise to Auntie Ishbel and not mention last night's events at the Hall.

"And mind, I'm up the hill cleaning after Doctor Baranaski's been. If she gets here. She'll be run off her feet with all this. Auntie Ishbel's coming round for a bit. I'll wrap you up a couple of buttered digestives." She stared into the bottom of her cup like a fortune teller, did her sighing and her hand wringing, but there was nothing in that cup to bring her comfort.

Mathew, Mark, Luke and John, Acts, Romans and Corinthians, Corinthians Galatians... Baptise Archie in the Sappie? How could he have agreed to this? What had he been thinking? He slowed down as he approached the Memorial Bridge. The last thing he needed was another strange or violent encounter. Then again, mightn't a Baptism allow Archie to redeem himself in the eyes of God... in the eyes of Uncle Andrew and Gran, and folk at the Hall? But what about that girl, the one who was electrocuted in the Baptismal pool in

Templeton? If it really happened. Or did Jenny make it up? It didn't matter whether she did or whether she didn't, it was exactly the sort of thing that could well have happened, that God could well make happen. He couldn't risk it. Not with Archie.

Uncle Mathew was having frothy coffee with PC Carmichael in the window seat of Moretti's. *A winnock bunker in the east / There sat auld Nick in shape o' beast.* Joseph would have to unlearn all this Robert Burns. It was bad that bits of *Tam o' Shanter* were still popping into his head like that, instead of lines of Scripture, especially now. He strode on, head down, willing himself to be swallowed up by the fog but Uncle Mathew clocked him and chapped the window, *You! In here. Now!*

Inside was a warm fug of chip smoke, cigarettes and hot-drink steam, a homely – not Joseph's home – comforting, smell. A sinful smell.

"What's all this about Jenny getting a doing at the Hall last night? See if it wasn't for your Auntie Ishbel your pal would be..."

That's all Joseph heard, because this music had begun blaring out of the jukebox ...

Goin' up to the spirit in the sky / That's where I'm gonna go when I die...

Two long-haired, bearded hippies were standing next to it. One was a cousin of the Sangsters, from a non-Hall side of the family. They were wearing Afghan coats, long shirts, and beads, looking like they might have walked right out of the Holy Land two thousand years before. It was a look that oddly enough Gran did not approve of.

Uncle Mathew and PC Carmichael looked at them in disgust, wafting their hands in front of their noses, making a big thing of it so the hippies would see, but the hippies looked like they couldn't care less.

When I die and they lay me to rest / I'm gonna go to the place that's the best....

"It's everywhere now," thought Joseph, "in everything." Only he wasn't thinking, he was talking.

"See what I've to put up with, Duncan?"

The hippies were singing now, and smiling beatifically at PC Carmichael and Uncle Mathew, giving them a peace sign.

Gotta have a friend in Jesus...

Uncle Mathew and PC Carmichael didn't like this, it looked like cheek, so they took it out on Joseph, poking him in the chest, blowing fag smoke in his face, and singing in silly squeaky voices, ridiculing the song, the hippies, ridiculing Joseph... *So you know that when you die / He's gonna recommend you / To the spirit in the sky...*

"Heh! Leave the boy alone for goodness sake," shouted old Mamma Moretti in a Scots-Italian as thick as lard. She waddled out from behind the counter.

"Just a bit of fun, Mrs Moretti," said Carmichael.

"That right? Well if tormenting weans is your idea of fun, Constable, you and yer friend can take yersels off tae another café."

Uncle Mathew and Carmichael laughed, two naughty bully boys at the back of the class.

"There isn't another café, Mrs Moretti," said Uncle Mathew.

"Aye that's right, and ye'd do well tae remember! Joseph, come over here, son."

Old Mamma Moretti was dressed from head to toe in mourning black. Her husband, Victor "old man" Moretti had died suddenly three months before. But Mrs Moretti had been wearing black long before that, for as long as Joseph could remember.

"She's from a huge Italian family," Auntie Abi had told him. "Every time she's about to come out of mourning, she gets word from Italy that somebody else has crossed the Jordan. That's what happens when you get to our age, son. Your Uncle Hector keeps his black tie hanging over the door these days."

"Here," Old Mamma Moretti gave Joseph a Fry's Five Boys, "for yer Grandpa."

Every Saturday evening for donkey's years old man Moretti's ice cream van had stopped on the lane, its chimes playing *That's Amore* loud enough even for Grandpa to hear. He'd shuffle out the door, Joseph by his side, singing along, *When the moon hits your eye like a big pizza pie / That's amore*.

As soon as Grandpa hit his mark at the counter, he and Victor Moretti would begin their well-rehearsed music hall double act, "Good evening, Signor Kirkland!"

"Good evening, Signor Moretti!"

"And what can ah do ye for on this fine evening, Signor Kirkland?"

"Oh I don't know, Signor Moretti. What do you recommend?"

"How 'bout a wee bit a baccy and a Five Boys for yersel, and a poky hat for the boy here?"

"By Jove, Signor Moretti, I think you've hit it on the napper."

And Grandpa would pose with the Fry's Five Boys, like the Fry's advertising poster of the boy and his five emotions,

"Fry's Five Boys – Desperation, Pacification, Expectation, Acclamation, Realization and..." without missing a beat the old would-be Vaudevillians delivered the punchline, "... Constipation!"

They'd laugh, gossip about the week's goings-on and the latest hatches, matches and despatches, while Joseph ate his cone. Every Saturday. Then one day old man Moretti got the flu, took to his bed, and the next day he was gone. The funeral was a big Catholic affair up at Saint Rita's, so of course Grandpa couldn't go even if he'd wanted to (and he really did want to). The day after he took to his bed too.

Miss Marlow looked amused when Joseph handed *Visions of Hell* in to the library.

"That was quick. Enjoy it, did you?"

Under A Big Bad Sky was back on the shelf. It might look odd to take it out again soon, but he could read it here, just the last few pages, see what happened, see how Kit Mossman saved the good folk of Little Fury. He could tell Grandpa. That would be a good thing to do.

On the main street Joseph caught wafer-thin glimpses of people. Sometimes not even people, just the red glowing tips of their fags dancing around like toatie one-eyed demons, that grew brighter with each inhalation. And as ever, snatches of conversation faded in…

It was that sudden / Her chest / Won't be the last / I hope Mrs Hendry's all right / What do you think of the news? / On the brink, they're saying / Ach we're aye on the brink of something or other / We'll all go thegether when we go, eh? / There's a meeting the night / Harry Worth's on the telly/ Oh! Is that tonight?/ You can't bury your heads in the sand forever / No? Just watch me. … and out.

Here was something. Outside W. Findrum's Fishmongers stood a circle of hooded men in duffle coats, oilskins, parkas and so on, arms hanging stupidly by their sides. They were staring at this great mountain of fish: mackerel, plaice, skate, cod, herring, all sorts, lying in the middle of the road.

Findrum's wasn't on Joseph's map because it had been closed for months, for good as far as he knew. Joseph watched as the men shifted a load of the fish onto a stretched out tarpaulin,

"Right, Peter, tak that corner," said a balaclava'd man who seemed to be in charge. "Andy, go ower that side. Jimmy, you staund aside me. You, stop yer ditherin. You and aw. If we don't get this shiftit pronto the hale lot will rot. Here,

Tam, chuck something at yon cat afore it gets ony ideas." Joseph looked, but he could see no cat. "That Joseph there? Come ower here son, gie us a haun, eh." Joseph couldn't see his face, any of their faces, for the balaclavas, hoods and hats. "Grab an edge o' that tarp. That's the wey. Right, efter three ...!"

The others must have been doing the serious lifting, Joseph could feel no weight at all.

"Ta Joseph. Strange days eh, strange days," he said, pointing at the pile of fish, "but who are we eh? Ah'm tellin ye, yer better aff no askin the why's and the wherfurs and just goin alang wi it, whitever it is." He rummaged around in the heap, "Ah ken yer grandpa likes a wee bit a fish," and he slapped a large cold grey skate into Joseph's hands, "The wings are the best bit. And if yer grandmither asks where ye got it, tell her it drapped oot the sky!" He roared with laughter. "Eh lads? Ah'm just tellin' the boy here, the fish drapped oot the sky!" The other men roared too.

He didn't want to go back to Gran's but neither could he walk about with a fish. He could plank it behind a wall or... but some animal would get it, that cat maybe, or who knows what. There was no one in the Hall. He wrapped the fish in a couple of sheets of the pink sugar paper that the wee ones used at *Sunbeams* and hid it under the bench at the back. It was fine. The heating was off so it was chilly as a fridge, and there'd be no one there till teatime.

He was feeling bad now for avoiding Archie and wee Maggie. But what could he do? He headed up to the far end of the village to the wee row of posh shops that only folk from up the hill used. There was a clock repair shop called *Le Petit Horloger,* that Joseph wasn't sure how to pronounce, a small ladies' clothes shop also with a French name, *La Mirage,* that was so posh it only had one ladies' coat and one hat on display. And Clerihew's the grocer, with tins of fancy soup, boxes of fancy tea, packets of fancy biscuits and other fancy foodstuffs in its window. He'd never once set foot in any of them. Why would he? He only ever came by this way if he was off to find a dog, and even then he never went near the shops.

There were slippery looking stone steps up the side of Clerihew's that Joseph couldn't mind ever seeing before. He could only see a few steps up before they melted away. Surely there was no harm, no wrongdoing. There was no *Private* or *No Trespassing* sign.

The steps were slippery right enough, covered in frozen green algae. He pulled himself up by the railings like a mountaineer, as much for fun as necessity. It would've been more fun if Archie had been doing it with him, maybe even with real rope or a pilfered washing line. The steps went quite a way and just as he was thinking, *am I near the top yet?* the railings gave way to a doorway with a hand-painted sign hanging over it: D.W. Mallison, Antiquarian Books & Maps. He knocked, which was an odd thing to do, but with these posh shops, you never knew what manners you had to mind. A wee bell above the door tinkled as he went in.

It was smoky inside, like in the Headmaster's office but more aromatic. There was a long corridor of dusty old books on tall shelves that reached to the ceiling, or stacked dangerously high on the floor. And right at the end, behind a desk, a stick-thin old man smoking a slim panatella. He was looking through a magnifying glass at an enormous atlas. Its pages were old and dry and yellow, like all the books in the shop, like the walls and the ceiling. Like Mister D.W. Mallison himself. For surely that's who this must be. Joseph's skin, eyes, tongue, everything, began to dry out too. He tried to make some spit to swallow, to stop the cough that was coming on, but it was no use.

"Sink," said Mister Mallison, without lifting his eyes from his book. "Cup on shelf."

His voice was posh and brittle and he spoke in a rapid disjointed way, in shards. Joseph didn't like to but the cough persisted. The water was bracken-brown. He let it run for a bit.

"Rust. Peat. Something. Marmalade. Won't kill you… Probably."

The water was ice cold and slightly bitter. He looked over the old man's shoulder at the gigantic atlas. The pages were so big they made a breeze each time one was turned over, creating wee clouds of dust that hung in the air, each speck illuminated by the brass desk lamp.

"Kilhaugh and surrounding area. 1597. Year Kilhaugh jumped aboard Great Scottish Witch Trial bandwagon. Witches, so-called, taken from…" He tapped the spot, "… here." Cigar ash fell onto the map, he didn't seem to notice. "Kirk Session house. Where Agnew's stands today. Roped together. Dragged along banks of *Lele*. Past *Sappie*. Through woods. Burned alive. Here."

There was a horseshoe there to mark the place. Everyone avoided walking over it.

"Poor wretches," said Mister Mallison, "Spinsters. Midwives. Herbalists. Eccentrics. Strangers. Travellers. Me. No doubt. If I'd been there." He spun around in his squeaky swivel chair to face Joseph, "You. Almost certainly." His eyes, unlike the rest of him, were moist.

"Like maps? Miss *O'Donnell*, squire, she likes her maps, mm? Her *Mappae Mundi*. Her *Ebstorfs*, her *Herefords*, her *Psalters*." Joseph looked around. "No. Unfortunately. Local mostly. Très populaire with Kilhaugh's landed gentry. Obsessed with boundary lines and blood lines. Fixated with marking their territory. Worse than pissing dogs."

Once again Joseph wished Archie was here right now, so he could share this place, this man, all of this. But Archie would steal something. He just would. He'd have to.

"Have it about your person perchance? The *O'Donnell* commission. The map." Joseph nodded. "Show." Joseph hesitated. Mister Mallison picked up a business card, "D.W. Mallison: Honest Appraisal Guaranteed." Joseph wasn't quite sure what this meant but he handed him his map anyway. Mister Mallison unfurled it and examined it with his magnifying glass. Joseph's name was written at the top, "Joseph Kirkland. Mm. Not bad. First attempt?"

"Yes."

"Incomplete," he tapped it with his cigar, upsetting more ash, "my bookshop."

"I didn't know it was here."

"Now you do," he put on a couthy Scottish voice, "will I also require one of yer wee red erchways?" His shoulders shook but there was no chuckle. "Now. This map. Impressive. A map for the Would-Be-Damned, mm? Or Would-Be-Saved. Steer them clear of pitfalls, pratfalls and perdition. Deliver them from evil. To places of safety. Good stuff, squire." He slammed shut his book with Joseph's map inside. "Let's haggle."

"I need it."

"Oh," Mister Mallison looked disappointed.

"I'm going to be a missionary."

"Are you *sure?*" he peered over his spectacles. "Might I suggest an alternative career? Kirkland's Cartography. Nice ring to it. No? All… right, squire. A swap. Book for a map." His eyes darted around the shelves and stacks till he found what he was looking for, then he scurried over to a long ladder, repositioned it, and scrambled up it, nimbler than Joseph had given him credit for.

"Oliphant's *Heroes of the Cross*. Missionary biogs. Interesting publisher. Oliphant. Apprentice to Creech. Publisher of *Rrrrabbie Burrrns*, don't you know. Suit you down to the ground, squire."

"I've got all of them already." *Robert Burns? Does Gran know that?*

"Really. O– kay. Ah. *Carlisle's Encyclopaedia of World Religions? Volume One, A to* M. Marvellous stuff. Gets to the heart of what religion *is*. N to Z is missing I'm afraid. So, if *Zoroas trianism* is your 'bag' … But *A to* M has more than enough to satisfy even the most restless of souls. Behold!" He flicked through random pages, "We have… Atheism, Baalism,

Buddhism, Catholicism, Confucianism, Druidism, Hinduism, Mormonism this *ism* that *ism... ism ism ism ism.* Tempted? No? My word. Tough nut to crack. Perhaps *mysticism* might be your *thing...*" He pulled out several more small dusty books, "*Anthony of the Desert? The Pietism of Johann Arndt? The Cloude of Unknowyng? A History of Heysachism* ... inner light, stillness of the soul... and... all that. Fit neatly into your back pocket... wouldn't want to ruin the line of your nice new suit."

"My Gran wouldn't like it in the house." He should leave. Now.

"Hide it under the mattress. Everyone's entitled to a secret. No? How about a Bible!"

"I've got a Bible."

"Show." Joseph handed it up. "Authorised King James. Very fine. Language second to none. Although Tyndale did the donkey work. And paid the price. Belt and braces execution. Strangled. *Then* burned. Quite humane. By sixteenth-century standards. Pages are stuck together."

"It's blood."

"Blood?" he blinked.

"It's from a dog... and from my cousin... she..."

"No. No no no no... although. There's some I know... would pay top dollar. But. A Christian missionary cannot take a Bible soaked in dog blood into the backwoods and boondocks of Ballynowhere. *Sorcery!* they'll cry! They'll have you roasting on a spit before you can say *Deuteronomy Joshua Judges*. You need a new Bible, sonny." He ran his finger down the spines of numerous Bibles, "Something... a bit more..." he pulled out *Good News for Modern Man*. "... fun?" He looked over his spectacles at Joseph, "Maybe not. Accessible then. *The New English*? No? Wilson's *Emphatic Diaglott?* Moffat's *New Testament? The American Standard? The Martin Luther?* Ah! Yes. *The Bible Designed To Be Read As Literature*. People *love* a good story. The barbarians will adore it. Don't worry. I can see you won't part with your precious map. Here! A gift. Quite a tome, mm? Can double as a pillow. On your travels. Yes? No? Sure I can't tempt you?"

The steps came out behind one of the big up-the-hill houses with turrets and battlements; *Castle-ettes*, Grandpa called them. *Where the well-to-do live*. Gran, who was fond of reminding anyone who was listening that she was *in this world but not of it*, seemed to accept that *in this world* there were folk who were her betters; *better educated*, who *knew better* and were *better at making important decisions, better at running the country*... in this world.

"It's of no consequence. We're all just passing through. Just marking time."

Grandpa bit his tongue on "religious" matters, but when it strayed into the secular world... "Folk are folk, son," or the political world, "See, when you look at folk, look them in the eye. Stand on a box or stand in a ditch, but never look up to folk, and never look down at them."

There was a wee dog, a Jack Russell or something, scampering around the lawn of this particular... Castle-ette. If he just pushed the gate open, offered it a bit of buttery digestive, it might... It gave a high-pitched yelp. No this dog wouldn't do, it was one of those yappy wee things. Its master would hear then that would be it, game up.

There was nobody around and it wasn't just the fog, it was always like this up the hill. You didn't get cars parked on the side of these up-the-hill roads or folk standing around on up-the-hill pavements having a chit-chat. The walls were too high – or embedded with broken glass – for leaning on and nattering.

Eventually though, a big old dog face, black with grey around the muzzle, appeared through a hole in a hedge. It was Mrs Arnold's dog. Joseph felt a shiver and was in half a mind to go, but it had big sad eyes, which he hadn't noticed before, so he decided it was lonely. He offered it a bit of digestive on the flat of his hand. It sniffed once, wolfed it down and licked up the crumbs. It had a collar on but no tag, which was good. *Oh, I would've brought it back right away* he could say, *but I didn't know whose it was.*

The dog was waiting for him at the gate. He gave it another bit of digestive. The fat old dog made a long low whine and began snuffling at his tweed suit, maybe thinking, oh this *boy has something good hidden away*, more biscuit or something. But when Joseph tried to coax the dog out, it ignored him and waddled up the driveway and sat down on the front step. Joseph followed. If Mrs Arnold came out and asked what he was doing there, he could say, *Oh I was just worried about your dog. It looked sad*, and it would not be a lie. He stroked its head and its ears and gave it more biscuit.

"Paw."

It gave him its paw and slapped its tail against the step. He should've brought string for a leash. He often had some in his pocket for eventualities like this. He didn't really like to but he took off his tie. It was a bit short, but it would do,

"Walk? Walkies?"

The dog was willing, but there was a light on in the living room and Joseph had to take a peek. There was a couple, in their late thirties, or forties, or fifties, older maybe; it was hard to tell with some grown-ups. They were sitting at either end of a great heavy polished dining table eating scrambled eggs on toast and drinking tea from fancy teacups. The woman was Mrs Arnold, so the man must have been Mister Arnold. They ate slowly without any conversation or even acknowledgement of the other's presence, just staring down at their food the way Gran sometimes did. Now and then Mrs Arnold rested her hands on the table, chewing and chewing her food, and not swallowing, like Grandpa, like it gave her no pleasure this food, it was just hard work, something that needed doing. Mister Arnold held the teapot out to her but she ignored it, ignored him. Mister Arnold looked tired. He was all slumped and hollow in the middle, like his insides had collapsed or had been removed. The dog began pulling now, it wanted its walk.

"Sit." The dog sat, sniffing again at Joseph's jacket and trousers. "My dog now," he whispered, and looked in the Arnolds' window again.

Mrs Arnold had put her knife and fork down. She'd hardly touched her scrambled eggs. She clasped her hands and closed her eyes as though she was only now going to Give Thanks. Mister Arnold's head suddenly became really heavy and fell into his hands, and they stayed like that, the pair of them. Joseph looked round the room at all their heavy posh things: heavy ornaments, heavy vases, heavy jugs, heavy gilt-framed paintings, heavy plump, plush furnishings. Above the fireplace there was a huge landscape of somewhere not unlike the braes behind Kilhaugh and on the mantelpiece, next to the clock, a framed colour photograph of a boy, ages with Joseph but with yellow hair and bright blue eyes and rosy cheeks, but natural, unlike the badly tinted photograph in Gran's sideboard. The yellow-haired boy was standing outside the house, this house, and he was wearing all Joseph's clothes; his tweed suit, his flannel shirt, his tie, his pullover, his brogues. Everything. The dog pulled again, nudging his thigh with its big head. *Come on now you,* it was saying, *let's go.*

"Okay boy. Good boy. You're my dog now."

It was the dog that took Joseph for a walk, along a path that led up into the woods. Joseph knew it well; a quarter of a mile on, over the brow of the hill was the old limestone quarry, filled to the brim with water the depth of which Archie and Joseph had often speculated.

"It's probably a hundred times deeper than Templeton baths," said Archie.

The quarry was one of the places *you must not go to under any circumstances*.

Today you couldn't even see the water. Grey sky, grey land and grey water were all one. The dog looked into where the water should be, and Joseph thought it might want a swim, but it would be too cold and the dog too old, and anyway, the slope down into the water was so smooth and steep it would never be able to scramble back out, not a fat old dog like this.

The dog started yanking on the tie. If it couldn't have a swim, it wanted to leave. But they'd just arrived. Joseph pulled it in close, tried to show it who was master. He wanted to stay a while, throw stones into the invisible water to hear the splash or hear the ice smash like glass. And also, he wanted the dog to be his dog for a wee while longer.

"Sit boy. Sit."

But the dog just pulled even harder, *I'm done with here, I want to go now*. Joseph wrapped his end of the tie around his fingers to get a good grip, but the dog was having none of it and a right old tug-of-war ensued, *heave ho, heave ho*, but in silence, *heave ho, heave ho*; the fat old daft old dog pulling with all its might this way – so hard it was in danger of choking itself – and Joseph pulling with all his might that way, *heave ho*, until he found himself pulling with all his might on nothing at all. He was falling, one hand clutching the tie, the other hand flailing around, snatching at everything and anything. There was a metal bar or pipe sticking out the embankment, the guts of some bit of old quarry machinery which he managed to grab and he came to a halt. He lay there for a moment, gasping for breath, his specs at a stupid comical angle, the soles of his brogues slapping the surface of the water. And there was the dog, sitting at the top of the slope looking down at him, adoringly now, or so it seemed, waiting for him. There were more bits of bent and twisted wire and pipe, which might do as handholds and footholds but they were shoogly and could easily work free and if that happened... His heart was going like the clappers. If that happened that would be it. That would be him. A prayer was at the tip of his tongue, a simple *Please God help me*, right at the tip.

The second Joseph got to his feet the dog started all this

blinking and sniffing like it was surprised to see him standing there. Then it turned around and toddled off, just like that. It took quite a different route back, through thick woods with low-hanging branches that snagged and scratched, and any gap that there was, was filled with foliage and fog. Joseph had no idea where he was; the dog must know a short cut. Once or twice it stopped and cocked an ear listening to footfalls only it could hear, and the rustling and rummaging of who knows what woodland creatures great and small, but not for Joseph's benefit. He felt all cold and clammy, a bit shaky, a bit swimmy, and thinking something might be happening and not wanting it to happen here in the middle of *this*, he called on the old dog to slow down, "Here boy. Tch tch.. Heel," and other dog words, tongue clicks, whistles and noises but the dog couldn't care less now whether Joseph was there or not. It was not Joseph's dog anymore. Joseph was a stranger to this dog now. He wished Mirky was here, not this fickle, unfaithful beast. Mirky would care. The fat disloyal old dog squeezed itself under a fallen tree trunk, and that was the last Joseph saw of it.

Joseph had to choose now; this direction or that. *Please, make it this way*. He found himself mumbling snatches of choruses and hymns; they weren't chosen, they just appeared, like Mister Agnew had said they would, "In moments of sadness, or danger or distress, the right words will come to you. And you'll have no idea how this happened. They'll tell you what you need to know. If you need warning, they'll warn you. If you need comforting, they'll bring you comfort."

You have wandered far away / Do not risk another day...

Lead kindly light,/ amid the encircling gloom...

No. These dense fog-filled woods were full of real or imagined – it was all the same – creaking, rustling, sighing and whistling, and these Bible-ish hymn words were not bringing any comfort at all. He ran fast and blind till he came to what he thought was the noticeboard of Kilhaugh Episcopalian, which meant he was safe back in the village. Except it wasn't.

And he wasn't.

Catholic Diocese of Templeton
Welcome to
SAINT RITA OF CASCIA

A large white building floated into focus, its front door wide open and from inside shone
a warm and welcoming golden light. It was so tempting. *Come inside, come inside.* How could Joseph Kirkland resist?

CHAPTER THIRTY-TWO

Saint Rita of Impossible Things

The dazzling light of a hundred... a thousand... a million... a zillion – who knew – flickering beeswax candles spiralled and spun off myriad golden statues, golden picture frames, golden candlesticks, golden goblets and golden all the other fabulous unco trappings that the astonished Joseph had no words for. The light was diffused through a filter of incense and candle smoke that took the edge off everything. And the colour, so much colour. *Too much colour.* Even *the brazen Episcopalian* was nothing like this. No wonder Kilhaugh was so dreich. How could it not be? Saint Rita's had hoovered up all available light and colour and any leftovers had ended up in Mrs Merryweather's living room, because if the inside of Saint Rita's reminded Joseph of anything, it was Mrs Merryweather's living room, on an astronomical scale. Had Auntie Ishbel really given up all of *this* for the Hall?

There was some sporadic low-key activity; a solitary body drifting in, kneeling, lighting a candle from a candle, whispering a prayer and drifting back out. Joseph stood in the shadows, anxious he might be recognised, but this was the last place anyone would expect to see a Kirkland and no one did. His gaze was hauled this way and that by the extraordinary riches that Saint Rita had to offer; Technicolor stained glass, high-vaulted midnight-blue ceilings frescoed with circles of dancing winged angels, crowned kings, enthroned saints and mischievous cherubs juggling with stars, and halfway down the aisle, a colossal metal contraption the size of a Russian sputnik hanging from a long purple rope. Elsewhere there were golden haloed nuns in various pious poses, men pierced with golden arrows, and more angels and still more angels with golden trumpets and golden harps, some with arms outstretched like they were trying to save someone from falling or drowning and... oh everything. Everything. And a Christmas tree. What would Gran say? *A Christmas tree! In their place of worship, for goodness sake!* It was festooned with tinsel and baubles and at the very top, yet another gold angel. He'd never seen the like. The fanciest, fantoosh Christmas window in Templeton could never have competed with this.

"Beautiful." The word had slipped from his lips before he could catch it.

The Lord couldn't care less about their fancy dancey gilded whigmaleeries and their fancy dancey pantomime preachers.

Sorry. But it *was* beautiful. It just was.

At the far end on either side of a monumental marble altar were two statues Joseph actually recognised: Mary cradling her deathly-white baby Jesus and across the aisle, a larger than life, blue-eyed bloody man-Jesus, hammered onto his cross thirty-odd years later. Joseph had imagined the scene often enough, on a weekly, sometimes daily – and recently, hourly – basis, but still it was shocking. Those thick iron nails. He'd never seen nails like these in Grandpa's toolbox and he had hundreds, all shapes and sizes. Did you get special nails for crucifixions in those days? Why not? It was someone's job to make special leather belts for belting children, why not special iron nails for crucifying folk?

Around the chapel walls there were fourteen wee cartoonish pictures featuring Jesus in His usual long hair, beard and robes, but everyone and everything else looked modern, like it might be happening today, right here in Kilhaugh. The first he looked at was of dead Jesus on what seemed to be a stainless-steel hospital trolley. There was a sheet over Him, but you knew it was Him because of His wounded hands and feet. There was a woman in a winter coat and a headscarf, just some ordinary wife, standing by the door, looking so upset. There were two policemen, a doctor, and one or two other everyday folk as well. It was hard to know what they were thinking. Another was of Jesus being taken down off the cross, but it wasn't

Calvary, it was like the bing or a dirt mound on a building site in a scheme and the crowd of folk, well they were just folk. Some of the men were holding half-bottles of drink and they looked like they'd just fallen out of Faulkner's on a Friday night. Others though looked inconsolable. And there were those two policemen again, one of them looking bored, like PC Carmichael. And that wife in the headscarf, looking like Mrs Arnold had looked on the bridge, desperate. In another, the same policemen were shouting at this red-haired man in a plaid shirt who was trying to help carry Jesus's cross. He looked like Archie might look when he was grown up. In fact this is exactly what Archie would have done if he'd been there? *Here, let me. I'll take that,* he'd say, and not give two hoots about the police.

And if all of this wasn't enough to take his breath away, there on a golden eagle lectern was a large silver box embossed with an image of the Last Supper and inlaid with rubies and emeralds and who knows, maybe diamonds, its pages also edged with gold. It was a Bible. Joseph had never seen such a thing. Gran would be appalled at the Good Book being tarted up to look like something you'd find at the end of a rainbow in a fairy tale. He should not be here, but here he was. He should at least make something good of it, practise his books. He opened the treasure chest, "*Gen-e-sis, Ex-o-dus, Lev-it-icus and Num-bers, Deuter-onomy, Joshua, Judges, Ruth and Sam-u-el. Sam-u-el, Kings, Kings, Chron-icles and Chron-icles, Ezra, Nehemiah, Tobit, Judith, 1st Macabees, 2nd Macabees…*"

What? *Tobit? Judith? Macabees?* He'd never set eyes on these. There were more; *Wisdom, Sirach, Baruch.* What on earth? He'd never heard anybody ever read from these books. But then, he'd never heard anyone read from *Haggai* or *Nahum* either. Neither could he remember reciting these at Sunday School, but then wasn't his mind always wandering? He checked his own Bible to see. Nothing. Was it just *his* Bible? A printing error? Surely it must happen sometimes. A human error. Was it possible he'd been carrying an incomplete Bible all this time? What might that mean?

"Joseph Kirkland. Whit in the name of a' that's holy are you doing here?" *Oh no. Please.*

"No that yer no welcome," said Mrs Merryweather, "And don't worry. Ah'll no say a word tae anybody."

Would she be able to stop herself? *You'll never guess who I met in Saint Rita's.* She dropped some coins into a wooden box, lit a candle, closed her eyes for a second or two and repeated the ritual. As she turned to leave she handed Joseph a small candle, "Here, light one yerself son." Joseph looked unsure. "Ye just light it and haud them in yer thoughts, the livin or the dead." Joseph shrugged his *yes, no, don't know* shrug. Mrs Merryweather laughed, "It's awright son, yer no signin' ye up tae anything, honest."

At one side of the Chapel there was a fancy wooden booth, a great dark heavy thing like the Hall's harmonium. Grandpa would appreciate this. He liked well-made wooden things, *A nice bit of wood. That's a grand chest of drawers that. Oh my, that's a lovely wardrobe.*

"Come away in, I won't bite," said a man's voice, a jokey-sounding voice. You could never be sure though, if grown-up jokes were meant to be laughed at. Except Grandpa. You always knew with him. "Not that door, the other one. Unless you're after my job."

Inside it was like a wee one-person railway carriage. It smelled like it too, of everyone and their everythings: peppermints, boot polish, lavender and sour milk, damp tweed, Bay Rum, tobacco, drink and sweat. But a calm place too and Joseph was content to sit in silence.

"So what's troubling you?" asked the man.

What's troubling me? What sort of a question was that to ask? Where would a person even begin? There was a wooden grille. Joseph could just make out a shadowy figure, "God's grace is infinite." The voice was still friendly enough, but it sounded like it was reading from a script now, "His forgiveness knows no limits." *Silence*. "Right, how this works is somebody has to speak. Mostly you." *Silence*. Again his voice was filled with jokes. "Fine. Makes a change anyway. Some of them in here can talk I can tell you. Have you seen all those donkeys out there without their hind legs?" There was a pause, for laughter, but it wouldn't be coming from Joseph Kirkland. "I'm famous for it myself." *Silence*. "Okay then, I'm thinking you're a stranger to these parts."

Did Kit Mossman not say that?

"Father Giordano," he said, "And by the way, I don't need to know your name."

"Joseph."

"Joseph?" He tried the name out a few times, like Benjamin Mutch had done, to see what he might glean from it maybe, "*Joseph. Joseph*... a good biblical pedigree there then eh?"

"Joseph Kirkland."

"Ah! Too much information now." Again he paused for a laugh that didn't come. "So ... am I right in saying this is your first time here?"

"I go to the Hall."

"The hall?"

"Kilhaugh Gospel Hall."

"Goodness me, is that right?" *Silence. Then more silence*, which Father Giordano felt obliged to fill, "I have to be honest with you, Joseph, I already guessed that. You kind of gave the game away. *Kirkland*. Scots and their names, eh?" He put on a comical suspicious voice, "*Would that be Stephen with a 'ph' or Steven with a 'v'?*" What are we like, eh? Well, whatever, we are extremely honoured to have one of the Kirklands of Kilhaugh in our midst. Rumour is, you're good people down there. Take your scripture very seriously. Some of my flock would do well to take a leaf out of your book. Been thinking about popping down myself, maybe steal a few trade secrets. Better go in plain clothes though, eh? I hear you don't go in for all this vestment and Vatican malarkey, all the Roman razzamatazz, mm?"

So this was a Roman Catholic priest? One of those *fancy dancey pantomime…*

"I hear they're good preachers too. Fancy it yourself? The old preaching?"

"I'm going to be a missionary."

"A missionary? You are not. Get out of here. Joseph Kirkland, I am *so* jealous. I always wanted to be a missionary. Honest. I only became a priest because my father was a priest and his father before him," he laughed again. "I'm joking by the way. Don't go repeating that, I'm in enough bad books as it is." Joseph didn't react. "A missionary now. That's… that's…

that's really something that is. And where would you go to…"

"I lied."

"Oh. Here we go. This is where I come in. What did you lie about, Joseph?"

"About being Saved."

"Saved? Okay… I… get you. Why?" *Silence*. "Let me guess. Were you perhaps … *scared* Joseph?" *Silence.* "Scared of being Saved? Scared of *not* being Saved?" *Silence.* "Of course they don't go in for baptising babies down at 'the Hall', do they? You lot have to have a good old think about it first. I tell you, Joseph, some things are a damn sight easier when you don't think about them. Truth of the matter is, between you, me and these four walls, sometimes I think I'm Saved and sometimes… I'm not so sure. Sometimes, Joseph, I even know what it means. It's so solid and real I can reach out and touch it. But most of the time I haven't the foggiest. And here's me, a professional! Top of the class at priest school and everything. Honest. What's that all about? Seriously, there's times I feel like *Oz the Great and Powerful* sitting here… you know… *not* so Great, *not* so powerful… hiding behind the red curtain pulling a fast one?… No?… It doesn't matter. The thing is… these are *my people* Joseph, the good folk of Saint Rita's. A right old bunch of odd socks they might be, but, there we go. That's family for you." He tapped on the grille. "You still there? It won't be the first time somebody's upped and left without me knowing." He chuckled. "So, what do you make of *Saint Rita of Impossible Things* then, Joseph?"

Saint Rita of impossible things?

"That's what we call her. You know, like *Alice in Wonderland*, or is it the other one, *Through the Looking-Glass?*" Father Giordano moved closer to the grille, "'There's no use trying,' says Alice, 'One can't believe impossible things.' And the Queen says, 'I daresay you haven't had much practice. When I was your age, I always did it for half an hour a day. Why, sometimes I've believed as many as six impossible things before breakfast.'" He laughed. "Doesn't that just say it all, Joseph? The gloriously ungraspable nature of it all? All these impossible things that we find ourselves believing. You know, when push comes to shove you'll find even the most diehard atheists down on their knees praying to... something ... anything... everything. *Lord – even though I know for certain thou art but a figment of my imagination – hear my prayer.* Ach, we need to be kinder to ourselves, eh Joseph? Ha. Good old Alice. Good old Saint Rita. Good old you, good old me. Good old the lot of us. So off you go now, Joseph Kirkland, refreshed and renewed, into the fog, into the great *Cloud of Unknowing*. You'll have no problem finding your way home. As long as you don't think about it too much."

CHAPTER THIRTY-THREE

Joseph Kirkland's Fourth Dream

Rat-a-tat-tat. Rat-a-tat-tat.

Mister Agnew was quite the action hero: shirt sleeves, tie loose around his neck, one foot on the harmonium stool, firing his Sten gun into the crowd of calm faithful and hysterical faithless. *Rat-a-tat-tat.* Gran sat at the back, bullets whizzing past her, shaking her head and tut-tutting at all the noise and nonsense, while she busied herself embroidering a new sampler with the words, *Follow the Yellow Brick Road.*

Rat-a-tat-tat. Rat-a-tat-tat.

Another handful of pebbledash rattled against Joseph's bedroom window. *Rat-a-tat-tat. Rat-a-tat-tat.* Before he'd got to the window the dream had begun to fade.

The second Archie saw Joseph, he launched into his jerky puppet song and dance routine,

Wee Wullie Winkie runs through the toon
Upstairs and doonstairs in his night goon.
Chappin at the windae
Greetin through the lock
Are aw the weans in their beds?
It's past eight o'clock!

"I sooked it out of Carmichael's panda car," he said, lifting a heavy jerrycan. "Hope he ends up breaking down in the middle of nowhere." He opened his mouth wide like he was at the doctors and exhaled loudly, "You should smell my breath, I ended up with a mouthful so I did. I should do fire-eating so I should. I'm away to plank it."

"My Grandpa's not well."

"Think he'll die?"

Oh wonderful Archie for asking straight out like that, without the pussyfooting.

"I think so. Maybe. I don't know."

"Sorry about not finding his budgie, Joseph."

"Sorry about not Baptising you and wee Maggie. It's just..."

"Och that's okay. I actually forgot. Wee Maggie never even mentioned it."

Archie was so good at telling lies, at telling good lies. Joseph's lies were never good.

"I found a new shop. It sells old books and maps and things. I'll show you. It's just this one old man there and..."

"Tut tut tut, Mister Kirkland," Archie wagged a finger at him, "you're awfully bad, so you are, leading me astray." He laughed. "See you in the morning." He picked up the jerrycan and was about to go but he saw something in his friend's face, "Oh no, I can't, sorry, I just remembered, I said I'd take wee Maggie to Templeton to see *Underwood's* Christmas window." He'd taken wee Maggie to see the shop window just a few days ago. Another good lie. "Och well, you just have the petrol for yourself. It's dead easy to get more."

As Joseph drifted off, he remembered the fish in the Hall, but it was only a fleeting thought and then he fell asleep, thinking about petrol.

CHAPTER THIRTY-FOUR

The Lord of Obstacles and Beginnings

There was no opportunity to give Grandpa the Fry's Five Boys from Mrs Moretti or tell him what happened at the end of *Under a Big Bad Sky* because Gran, Uncle Andrew, Mister Agnew, Auntie Ishbel, Jenny, Auntie Abi, Uncle Hector and Uncle Mathew, alone, in pairs or all together, never left his bedside. They prayed solemn prayers, sang serious hymns, read sombre passages of Scripture all the while waiting for this thing to happen.

Uncle Mathew looked bored with it all dragging on so long. Maybe everyone was bored. But then hadn't *The Hypocrite Joseph Kirkland* been bored just the other day sitting by his bedside? Uncle Mathew did nothing to hide the fact. When it was his turn to keep vigil he kept looking at his watch, then the door, then his watch, as though Death was running late. He looked disappointed, irritated even, at Death or Grandpa: *look at you, lying there, useless, still hanging on! You're doing it on purpose, so you are, just to annoy me.* He probably was.

Joseph picked up the jerrycan from the bushes beside the bridge and made his way up the braes. Oh my. The weight of that jerrycan, filled to the brim with petrol. And Joseph, filled to the brim with pyromaniacal possibilities. There was no question that he would start a fire. The question was *what kind of fire*? He was tempted to fling a match right inside, right now. Blow the whole thing up in a oner. Could he toss the match and run before it exploded? *No.* Just last year, the morning after Guy Fawkes night he'd ended up singeing his hair, his eyebrows and the end of his nose after igniting the big pile of gunpowder he and Archie had collected from dud fireworks. For Gran it was the perfect opportunity to preach, "You play with fire, you get burnt by fire. You think about that now."

For Grandpa, an opportunity to do a turn,

"Ho ho! You smell like Templeton knackers yard. *Clippety clop, clippety clop, this is a fine to-do / With my hair they'll stuff their mattresses /With my bones they'll make their glue.*

For Doctor Baranski, an opportunity to issue a health warning, "You're a lucky boy Joseph. You've only one good eye as it is. If it hadn't been for those spectacles, we might be calling you *blind* Joseph Kirkland."

Blind Joseph Kirkland. There was a name to remember. Like *Blind Fanny Crosby.*

Collecting gunpowder from duds had been Archie's idea. The two of them had scoured the village low and high. The best places were the public park where the big bonfire had been, or up the hill where folk had their own private bonfires and firework displays. There they found unexploded bangers, Catherine wheels, Roman candles and whizz-bangs, garishly decorated with stars, moons and ringed Saturns, like they'd been wrapped in the covers of those exotic American Sci-Fi monthlies – *Tales from Another Galaxy*, or *Incredible Science Fiction* – that Archie used to steal from Rattray's comic shelf till they cancelled the order. But the best and biggest, the likes of which they'd never seen, were found inside the high-walled gardens of the Hindoo Twins.

"Of course you know the 'Hindoo' Twins aren't Hindus at all," said Grandpa, "but they are twins, mind you. Sydney and Alfred. Henshaw. They must be into their eighties now. Their faither was Sir Arthur Henshaw, the munitions millionaire," he looked at his imaginary television camera, "*How to make a killing from bullets and bombs*. Ho ho, eh? Aye, you need big bucks to build a palace like Henshaw House. Anyways, when Sydney and Alfred were no much older than you, they were sent out to India to help run their daddy's *business interests* in Delhi. That's where I met them, donkey's years later, up in Mussoorie, a hill station where aw the peely-wally British sodjers went to cool doon in the hot summer. When the twins heard that I hailed frae Kilhaugh they invited me up to the Henshaw Haveli. And oh my goodness, what was it like! What were *they* like? With their fancy waxed moustaches, and all dressed up in their turbans and their Indian whatnots. But sickly wee men too. Fact they were that riddled wi' dysentery or malaria and who knows what, so it's hard to believe they're still alive. Anyway, that's when we started calling them the *Hindoo Twins*. Or *The MacMaharajahs*. Och, they never minded. Posh folk love all that fantooshery. But that wasn't the best of it. Out in the garden, which must've been the size of Kilhaugh public park, they had their own railway. A railway! A wee narra gauge. *The Great Mussoorie Express*. That's what they cried it."

Gran was busily ironing during, busily feigning disinterest, occasionally interjecting with a disappointed tut or an exasperated sigh or a disapproving headshake at his vulgar Scotticisms. But listening. Intently. To his every word. *Enjoying* his every word.

"A toy steam train. Just big enough for them and a few pals. And away they'd go, tally ho, chug chug chugging all aroon the garden. Happy as Larry. Mad as March hares so they were. Ho ho. That was the last time I saw them till nineteen forty-seven and the big *nahpoo toodle oo goodbyee*. I'll never forget the day they came back to Kilhaugh. Eh mum? July wasn't it? A scorcher so it was. But they hadnae just brought the Indian weather back with them, they'd brought the entire Mussoorie mansion. The hale kit and caboodle. All its Indian bric-a-brac, baubles and bagatelles. The Maharajah costumes, the big painted statues of Hindu gods and goddesses, everything."

Gran felt obliged to interject at with a *tut-tut*.

"And animals. My word, what a collection. Ho ho.

Would've put Doctor Dolittle to shame. Peacocks, bright green parakeets, chipmunks, a monkey... and an elephant. A real live Indian elephant. You know the difference atween an Indian and an African..."

"There was no elephant," said Gran, without looking up.

"No elephant?" He winked at Joseph, "Are you sure there was no elephant?"

"I'm sure."

"And they say you never forget an elephant. Well, elephant or no elephant, it was a real menagerie so it was, and the whole bazaar came rolling down main street Kilhaugh. Everybody was in such a funk when they saw it, so they were. We all turned out to see the show. How could we not?"

"Well I wasn't there. I can tell you that."

"*Roll-up rrroll up, the circus has come to town!*" Grandpa had put on his American showman voice: "*Come and see the strrrrangest things known to man. The strrrrangest things in all the land.* And at the front of the big parade, on the back of a lorry, there was their pride and joy, *The Mussoorie Express*. They'd shipped ower the entire railway. But, ach, their garden, big as it is, wasn't big enough to lay down the track, so that was that. I don't know what happened to it. Cryin' shame so it was. You never saw much of them after that. But see on the odd occasion, when they did make an appearance, oh boy, you'd know all about it; cycling down the street on these big grown-up tricycles, still dressed in all their MacMaharajah finery. Or maybe you'd catch a wee glimpse of their kites. Aye, they used to fly kites from the roof of Henshaw House. You'd see them from the village, every spring." He sighed a big sigh, "Nobody's seen them out and about for nigh on ten year. Age caught up wi' them, no doubt. But *Clerihews* still delivers a big box of posh nosh once a week. And they still have their fireworks. So there must be somebody there, eh? Unless they're ghosts. Eh mum? Ho ho."

Nobody was ever invited to the Hindoo Twins' firework display. There was no need. Their enormous rockets, imported from India, lit up the Kilhaugh sky for free.

That morning after, Henshaw House was littered with huge spent fireworks: "Look at the size of them," whispered Archie, crouching like a commando. "There's hundreds, so there is! It's like a battlefield, eh?" They rummaged around, shaking them for powder, "Joseph! Look at this one!" He held a large Roman Candle, with a picture of a four- armed woman sitting cross-legged on a pink flower. "And this one, look. A blue woman with *six* arms! She's like Spider-Woman or something, wow, eh? "

Joseph was getting cold feet, thinking about the wrongness of it, the trespassing, the consequences if they were caught. He shouldn't have come. But oh the promise of gunpowder. Archie was in his element, darting around the garden, Joseph on his heels. They took cover behind the menagerie of India-inspired topiaries; cows, monkeys, vultures and more. The real versions, if they had ever existed, had long passed away, or were indoors.

"Bonkers, eh?" said Archie, taking cover behind a horned-cow hedge.

Amazing.

Joseph had been inside lots of up-the-hill gardens but he'd never seen anything like this. There were the topiaries of course. Then there was the house itself. It was typical Scots Baronial, but with some fantastic Indian embellishments: floral, bird and animal fretwork, door panels and shutters in yellows, pinks and blues.

In my Father's house are many mansions: if it were not so, I would have told you.

I go prepare a place for you. John Chapter 14, Verse 2.

"It would be nice if one of them was like this."

"What?"

"Nothing. I was just..."

"You think the Hindoo Twins are working on a new secret weapon?" said Archie, who had already learned to ignore Joseph Kirkland's odd moments,

"I don't know," said Joseph, picking up another Roman Candle.

"That's how they made their mint. Weapons. See if they are, I bet it's something evil though, eh? I mean the atomic bomb isn't even a secret anymore and look what that can do, so imagine what the secret ones must be like?" When it came to war, weapons and conspiracies, Archie's imagination knew no limits: "It could be anything, so it could. You know, things you think, *oh no that's impossible, they'd never be able make something like that*, but then you find out they've actually gone and made it."

"Like what?"

"Like anything!" He looked around for inspiration in the trees, the burnt-out fireworks, his own hands, Joseph, the sky, "Wee robot insects maybe... that can fly and... and can eat through metal or concrete or anything. Or maybe toatie wee ones that get in your ear and eat your brain. Or ghost soldiers." He pointed at the colourful Hanuman on Joseph's Roman Candle, "Or soldiers that are half-man half-monkey. Or tanks... that can tunnel underground or through mountains. You actually get them. Or a big... a big... I don't know... like a... a huge anti-aircraft light like they used to use at night-time to look for German bombers, but even bigger than that and it actually sucks out all the light and makes everything pitch black!"

How did Archie do it? These flights of fancy? Then he remembered: "That's in the Bible."

"What... a light that makes things dark?"

"And insects too. God made it. For Moses. To help him fight the Egyptians. He gave him all these things. Ten terrible things."

"Weapons?"

"Kind of. Plagues."

"Plagues?"

"Boils and... and thunderstorms and... and these bugs and..."

"Bugs, what kind of bugs, brain-eating bugs?"

"I don't know, but they were terrible. And diseases too. Ones that killed all the animals. And other ones that killed the first child-born in every family. And the river Nile. He turned into blood. So all the fish died and all the Egyptian folk starved. There's more but I can't..."

"That's Biological Warfare, so it is. That's going to be even worse than the Atom Bomb. That's what they're all are working on. The Russians. The Chinese. The Yanks as well. Maybe that's what the Hindoo Twins are working on. Maybe if you pull one of those branches, a secret trapdoor will open up with stairs going deep down into this laboratory where all these mad scientists are making poison gas and... ach I don't know, you keep looking here, I'm going to nip round the back."

As soon as Archie had gone, Joseph sat down on the grass. He let his eyes sink into the back of his head and soon enough the wee electric discharges began popping in his brain like tiny firecrackers and for seconds, minutes, hours or days he was lost in that unthinking, un-breathing, disembodied space where he was spending more and more time.

And then he was back. By his side was a three-foot rocket in a drainpipe launcher. The fuse hadn't been lit. How had they missed it? It was decorated with a picture of a chubby pink man with the head of an elephant,

"Lord Ganesha, sah," said someone in a croaky aristo Indo-Anglian accent.

Joseph saw two pairs of curly-toed, purple-brocaded slippers. Above those, two pairs of turquoise silk pyjama trousers, above those two black duffle coats and balancing on top, were two tiny green-eyed, straggly-bearded heads, wrinkled and wizened as walnuts and wrapped in saffron turbans.

"The Lord of Obstacles," croaked another voice, or maybe it was the same voice, because the green-eyed, straggly-bearded, turbaned walnut-heads were identical. Even their skin, as thin as Agnew's Bible paper, as yellow as Psalm 23, seemed to be creased in the same places.

"Sometimes he removes obstacles from our path sah," said one.

"Sometimes he puts them there, sah," said the other.

"We all need a banana skin to slip on once in a while."

"Or a crocodile-infested loch to circumnavigate."

"Or a jungle filled with snakes, tigers and bears to hack our way through."

"To slow us down, sah?"

"Or stop us in our tracks, sah."

"Or stop others!"

"Indeed. A banana skin thrown in the path of an unwanted pursuer can be a welcome intervention, sah."

"Or just a ruddy good laugh!"

And they did laugh, like a pair of punctured squeezeboxes.

"Looking for gunpowder, yah?"

Joseph nodded.

"Good for you, sah."

"For purposes of blowing things to Kingdom come?"

"Or just a bit of a flash and a bang, yah?

"Sydney adores the display...."

"...and Alfred takes delight in destruction."

Joseph simply shrugged. He felt the need to pinch himself, bite his lip, confirm that what appeared to be happening was actually happening.

"Play it by ear, yah?"

"Excellent idea, sah."

They looked down at the Ganesha rocket.

"Quite the beauty, yah?"

"Of a mind to fire her, sah?"

"Tilt her a few degrees, sah, you may even hit the old chokey."

The two naughty old men-children once again dissolved into wheezing laughter.

"Well good luck on your adventure, sah, and to your young comrade-in-arms."

"We have some whoppahs lying around: Maroons, Gerbes, Tourbillions…"

"Henshaw Haveli has the whole ruddy arsenal."

"Your good name, sah?"

"Joseph Kirkland."

"Joseph Kirkland, sah. Be a good fellow, and strap us to this rocket."

"Send us over the black water to the banks of the sacred Ganga, sah."

"Has Joseph Kirkland the wherewithal to build such a rocket?"

Again, Joseph could only shrug.

"*The Pyrotechnist's Treasury*, sah."

"The firework-maker's bible. All you need to know, sah."

"Thomas Kentish."

"Friend of our father."

"*Mallison's Books and Maps*."

They sighed, then turned and began a slow synchronised shuffle back to the house.

"Go see her while you can, sah."

"Before she turns to dust."

"We are lighter than fuse paper, sah."

"Lighter than fuse paper."

It was the first and last time that Joseph would encounter the Hindoo Twins. The following year there were no rockets fired from Henshaw House.

Archie was already sat astride their rusting pride and joy, eyes blazing with wild imaginings, "All aboard the Great Mussoorie Express! God Joseph, this is what I want. My own railway!"

Joseph didn't mention the encounter with the Twins to Archie. As was often the case, he didn't know how to put it into words that would do it justice, and wasn't entirely certain the encounter had taken place.

They played a while. Train robbers, commandos, the French resistance. Archie fantasised about where they might fire the Ganesha rocket and how far it might go.

"We could tie things onto it. An Action Man. Two Action Men. Pretend it's us. Like voodoo dolls. Send them into space. Or a message, like stranded sailors do, but for aliens…"

"So the Aliens'll know we're here?"

"Yes!" Archie was always delighted by Joseph's rare contributions and he shouted it up into the sky, "JOSEPH KIRKLAND AND ARCHIE TRUMAN ARE HERE!"

And now, here he was again, a couple of days before his baptism, on his own, up in the braes in the freezing fog, with Archie's gift of petrol burning a hole in his imagination. Nothing, not the threat of eternal darkness or eternal damnation or PC Carmichael and Kilhaugh Borstal could keep Joseph Kirkland away from fire. Of course Archie would like to have joined him in his petrol adventure. But last night Archie saw Joseph drifting away on a raft full of demons and knew that the one thing guaranteed to purge them was fire. It's how they became friends in the first place. Two years ago, the day the Trumans left Glasgow and spilled over into Kilhaugh.

Joseph had gone through a hole in the fence into the coal yard behind the railway station. There was a *Trespassers Will Be Prosecuted* sign on the fence but Joseph wouldn't have seen it the way he was this day, and even if he had…

There was another boy there already, Archie Truman, as filthy as the coal he was loading into a tartan trolley bag, but Joseph was oblivious to him and his business. The keen-eyed feral Archie however was oblivious to nothing and when he saw Joseph appear out the blue, he stood rooted to the spot, staring at this odd bespectacled boy. Maybe Archie was thinking, *He's no out knockin' coal, he's too spick n span for aw that* or *Maybe he's a workie's son* or *Maybe he'll run n tell his da'*. But Archie quickly realised he'd nothing to fear, that this speccy boy could not even see him, which was incredible because he was standing right in front of him. Was Archie so filthy that he was invisible against the coal stack? There was a patch on this boy's specs. Was that it? He got the impression he could do a wee song and dance in front of this speccy boy and he still wouldn't notice. He certainly was odd, clearly away with the fairies. But interesting. Oh yes.

Joseph went into one of the old sheds behind the coal stacks, that workies sometimes used in the winter for a brew. Archie was right on his heels, stalking Joseph like he was a wild beast: a young deer or a hare, something harmless anyway. He wiped some soot from the window with his sleeve to get himself a better look at this boy and oh my goodness, he was definitely out of the ordinary, unless all kids in Kilhaugh were like this. Archie was always dirty and dishevelled, but this boy, he wasn't posh exactly, but he was well turned out. Clean clothes, combed hair, scrubbed face. Not peely-wally like himself, like most of them in the scheme. Oh the thoughts that would've been going through Archie's head right then.

Maybe he's foreign. Maybe he's a tally boy, wan a' they Moretti's frae that tally café. Maybe he's no aw there. Maybe he's no the full shillin'.

Joseph was scrunching newspapers into balls and flinging them into the brazier in the middle of the shed. He looked more focused now, more *there.* There was a big bucket of oily rags sitting in the corner and he flung them in as well. Archie could barely contain himself. He could see fine well where this was going and if he'd known the speccy boy even a wee bit, he'd have been in there like a shot, joining in, making suggestions, *why don't you add bits of wood… why don't you get some petrol or…* And then Joseph took a bottle of methylated spirit from his pocket and sloshed it over the paper and rags. Archie was impressed. The boy was well kitted out, he knew his stuff, he'd done this before. Joseph took out a box of matches, sniffed the sulphurous sandpaper and struck a match. It went out. He struck another, it broke. Archie was all fidgety, he had a lighter in his pocket and he'd a mind to go in and give it to him, just to get this thing going. The third match lit, the brazier ignited, and within seconds the flames were climbing the height of the shed and licking its roof.

The boy stuck his hand into the fire and held it there as long as he could, his face illuminated, ecstatic. Archie knew that look, that feeling. This was how Archie felt when he used to sit up on the tenement roof, or when he was making mad high rope swings under road bridges or dancing on a railway line as a train approached, or stealing stuff from Woolworths or firing his airgun from his bedroom window at passing car tail-lights or folk on bikes. But was the boy not holding his hand in the fire a wee bit too long? For goodness sake, now he was adding more paper, more oily rags, more meths, making the flames go higher and spread further across the tarry ceiling. Archie did not like this now, not one iota. *Okay. Enough.* But it wasn't enough for this daftie. What was he playing at? He'd done a good job. The fire was unstoppable. Uncontrollable. Brilliant. Now it was *make your getaway* time. Time to stand back at a safe distance and admire your handiwork. The shed was that full of smoke now, Archie could barely see him. The flames were coming out through cracks in the roof but – *och for God's sake* – he was still just standing there. *He's mental.* Archie chapped the window.

"HEH YOU, GLAIKIT!" but the boy didn't react. Maybe it was the roaring fire. Maybe this speccy eejit was half deaf as well as half blind or maybe he really was not right in the head.

"STUPIT! Bloody STUPIT BASTART !" He ran round to the side and kicked the door open, "HEH! YOU! Ye daft or somethin'? Yer gonnae get burnt so ye are!"

Whatever spell this boy was under could not be broken by shouting. Archie ran in through the choking smoke and dragged him out by his sleeve. He met with no resistance. Outside Joseph cleaned the smuts from his specs with a hanky and stared at the burning shed. Archie stared at Joseph. He was about to ask his name but heard the clang of the coal yard gate. Joseph was still in a dwam, so again Archie dragged him out of harm's way, behind the wall of old railway sleepers that banked up the coal stacks. Joseph opened his mouth to speak but Archie shushed him. A dirty-faced workie in manky overalls was standing in front of the burning shed, an inferno now, scratching his head. The workie trotted a few steps back towards the gate. Maybe going to phone the fire brigade or police or something but then the shed roof fell in, followed in quick succession by the back wall, and then the other three walls. The workie relaxed, lit a roll-up. What could be done now, anyway?

Archie whispered, "Stay where ye are. Ah'll just be a minute. Okay?"

Joseph didn't reply or attempt to follow. Archie ran in a wide arc round the coal yard, then casually sauntered up to the workie from behind, all wide-eyed and innocent, as though he'd just that moment come in through the front gate.

"Whit happened Mister?"

The workie looked him up and down, "You anything to do with this?"

"Me? Naw! Ah just saw the gate open there, and the fire, and ah got worried..."

But folk who looked like Archie, who sounded like Archie, were never innocent.

"That right? What's yer name?"

"Donald." There was no hesitation.

"Donald, eh? Donald what?"

"MacFarlane."

"You frae the village?"

"Naw. Edinburgh," said Archie, only now adding a wee East coast inflection, "Ma dad came here to buy a van off somebody like, I wis jist havin a wee walk like."

"That right? Well, Donald MacFarlane frae Edinburgh, see if I find out you had anything to do with this..."

"Ah didnae"

"Aye right. Well, beat it anyway."

Archie ran out and hid in some bushes. All he could think of was that daft speccy boy, and not wanting him to get caught. *Stupit*. Why should he care?

The workie watched the fire a couple of minutes longer and left, locking the gate behind him. The second he was gone Archie nipped back through the hole in the fence. Joseph was still exactly where he'd left him.

"Come oan," said Archie, leading Joseph out. "It's awright. He's away." Archie sniggered. "Hear me tellin that big shite I was Donald MacFarlane frae Edinburgh?" Joseph shot Archie a look, more discomfort than disapproval, but Archie knew right there and then that if he'd a mind to be friends with this boy, he'd need to mind his p's and q's. That was fine. He could manage that.

"Ah always say I'm Donald MacFarlane frae Edinburgh when I'm up to something. I'm telling ye, see if there *is* a Donald MacFarlane frae Edinburgh, he's gonnae get a fu… he's going to get a right old fright one day, so he is. What's yer name?

"Joseph Kirkland."

"Ah'm Archie Truman."

Archie had seen what this Joseph could do. Now Joseph needed to see what Archie Truman could do. He screamed like a wild man, leaping across the bonfire of burning shed, using bits of unburned wood as stepping stones and shouted over from the other side, "What else have you set fire to?"

He couldn't see Joseph for smoke and leapt back again, "See if you went fast enough, you could do it in your bare feet. I saw it in a film… there's these magicians in India that can do it." The smoke was stinging his eyes and he rubbed them hard with his sleeve, "I'm going to be in the circus, a trapeze artist or something when I grow up. Or maybe a commando. What are you going to …"

Joseph Kirkland was gone.

Archie would have ran home then, heart bursting, desperate to tell his wee sister Maggie, wasn't it good that he'd only been here a day and already they'd made a best friend. "His name's Joseph," he'd have said. "He's really… he's jist… he's dead polite. He's a bit mental as well but ye'll like him, so ye will. Ah know ye will. So yer no to be scared anymore, awright? Everything going tae be okay. Honest Maggie, ah mean it."

Joseph sniffed the top of the jerrycan. There was a good view of the cemetery from up here. *The Dead Centre*.

"Don't go spending good money on coffins!" Grandpa said, umpteen times. "I'm going to make my own. Easy-peasy. We'll keep it under the bed. Your Gran can pull it out now and again and give it a wee polish. And when it's my time, you can take me to the Dead Centre in a wheelbarra. Mind tie a red rag round ma big toe, for the traffic eh, or you'll have Carmichael the laughin' policeman chappin' on the lid wi' his bobby knocker."

A gnarly old tree grew out of the side of the hill at a dangerous angle. It had been blown over by the hurricane that hit the village a few years before. The thickest and longest of its branches spanned most of the way across the road at a height of about twenty feet. Halfway along was a long rope swing that Archie had built. It was looped over to keep it out the hands of others. There was no need. Only Archie had the nerve to build such a swing. Only Archie had the nerve to climb up and unhook it, and only Archie would ever dare swing on it.

The potential for serious injury was endless. There was the risk of slamming into the tree on the return journey. Or the seat-stick snapping. Or the rope fraying. Or the branch breaking. Or the tree itself uprooting. If the fall didn't kill him a lorry would finish him off. He'd be nothing but unidentifiable gore. Like the roadkill Joseph and Archie poked with their sticks.

"Just shovel me into a bucket and fling me over the fence into the cemetery."

Archie and Grandpa should've been friends. They'd've got on like a house on fire.

Anyway this was Archie's thing; climbing, building, stealing, fighting. Joseph's thing was fire. Suppose he did just throw a match in? Suppose he didn't manage to leap away. Suppose he was engulfed in flames? How long would it take to die? Minutes? Not an eternity. He should've brought rags to make a fuse. He could scrape out a furrow with a stick, pour in some petrol, like in the comics. It might be fine just doing wee splashes onto random bits of bracken and gorse bush, till he thought of something…

"*And then God appeared to him inside a big burning bush and…* " And what? He ought to know this. He'd read it often enough. Imagined it too. "*…and Moses asked him who he was and God said 'I am that I am'…* and then… then Moses got scared, so he hid his face."

No. Though Moses did get scared and why wouldn't he? Like those shepherds. God must've known folk would get scared. An angel. Just appearing like that. Out the blue. In a burning bush. Or in a field late at night. Goodness sake. Who wouldn't be scared? The Bible was full of folk getting terrible frights. Why couldn't God and the angels reveal themselves in ordinary ways? In a café, on a bus, in the daylight, when there was folk around.

He found the perfect biblical bush and drenched it with the entire contents of the jerrycan. It was magnificent. He lost himself in its flames. *Put off thy shoes from off thy feet, for the place whereon thou standest is Holy ground*, said a voice inside his head.

"If the Lord calls out to you, you'll know," says Mister Agnew.

"You will know," says Uncle Andrew.

"Mark my words," says Gran, "you'll know."

"You'll just *know*," says Jenny.

But how could you *know*. The voice just sounded like his own voice. He could easily be talking to himself. Again. As per usual. This was the thing. You never knew. Not for certain. There was always this ambiguity. At least with an angel appearing there could be no two ways about it. He took his shoes and socks off anyway. And it was nice. Standing there in his bare feet on the cold frosted grass. It made him feel clean. And fresh. And all brand new.

Peter was encased in a frozen puddle in the front garden. He was lying on his side. Legs out straight. Wings neatly tucked in. Eyes wide open.

Do budgies have eyelids?

The frozen water magnified him, making his bright yellow feathers brighter, more yellow. He should take him inside. Show him to Grandpa. Then bury him. He chipped at the ice with his penknife but it was too thick. He could leave him there till it thawed. But how long might that be? This weather was showing no signs of abating.

Gran's front door opened and who should come out but Mrs Merryweather. She saw Joseph on his knees. It must've looked like he was praying,

"Och son, come here," she said, flinging her arms open wide to receive him, "Och son." Everyone wanted to hold him or hit him. He let himself be held. "I'm so sorry for your loss, son."

CHAPTER THIRTY-FIVE

Under a Big Bad Sky

No one saw Joseph come in. He drifted through the house like one more ghost, observing all the comings and goings of family, Hall folk, neighbours. It was over. The waiting. The feeling bored. The feeling guilty about feeling bored. They were all in their element, immersed in the business at hand. All better, more generous versions of themselves, except Uncle Mathew who had a half-bottle in his pocket that everyone pretended not to see. Auntie Abi and Auntie Ishbel were in the kitchen, making hot buttery toast and tea for folk who needed that kind of comfort, which was most folk. "It's good of the Co-op to do it so quick," said Auntie Ishbel.

"Two days?" said Auntie Abi. "That's above and beyond."

"Oh, Sam phoned, he's still doesn't know if they'll let him away."

"Och, it's be a shame if he can't."

"They're all up to high doh with this Russian carry-on…"

"Did he say anything… well, of course he wouldn't would he?"

"We're going to need more bread," said Uncle Hector.

"That's a loaf and a half we've got through," said Auntie Ishbel, proud as punch.

"I wonder if I should make some scones and pancakes," said Auntie Abi, "to go with that raspberry jam Mrs Merryweather brought round."

There was a sense of relief, light relief, even festivity. For Gran, less so. She showed no outward signs of grieving. Or maybe this was it: all the desultory wandering in and out of rooms, the opening and shutting of cupboards, wardrobes and drawers. The searching for something or nothing in particular. A woman on a mission. Or a woman looking for a mission. She looked redundant.

"Take that down," she said, pointing at the sheet Uncle Mathew had just thrown over the lobby mirror.

"That's what folk do."

What folk? she might have answered, and quoted Scripture, and fought, but she let it pass.

"I've made an appointment at Jeanette's," said Auntie Abi.

"Ach, I've no time for all that."

"We'll find the time... just a wee shampoo and set."

Gran couldn't muster up the strength to agree or disagree. Things would be happening to her that she'd have no control over, wee things arranged for her by others, out of love and concern or long-held tradition. It's how it was and she wouldn't stand in its way, not for the next few days.

"It was very peaceful, son," said Auntie Ishbel, handing Joseph a slice of toast. "He just slipped away."

"No fuss," said Auntie Abi, "A wee smile on his face, you know the one, like he was about to tell a wee joke? And that was it."

"Just like him."

"Aye. He's still in his bed. Away and say your goodbyes, afore the Co-op get here."

Grandpa was the first dead person he'd seen. The first thing he noticed was the straightness and the tidiness of him; the fresh pressed pyjamas, the brushed and Brylcreemed hair. How convenient of Grandpa to have died like that, so neatly, like Peter. Joseph touched his hand. Not a tender touch. Curious. He just wanted to know what a dead person felt like. He didn't feel that different. No colder dead than alive.

"I found Peter. He was in a puddle out the front." He removed a crisp poke with the ice- encased Peter from his pocket, bits of grass still stuck to it. "He looks nice. Not like something killed him, an animal or... I'm going to bury him."

He got up and pushed the door to, smoothed Grandpa's cheek the way Grandpa used to smooth his, and whispered in his ear, "What happened is… Babe Reno… and the other two, Driscoll and Hatfield, they killed Sheriff Skinner. They ganged up on him at the river. So Miss Sarah and Miss Victoria went to Kit Mossman to ask him to help. At first he said, *No, I'm not coming. I just want to be on my own and be a farmer*, but Miss Sarah and Miss Victoria said, *Oh but you have to, Mister Mossman, you have to, it's your duty*, and Kit Mossman hummed and hawed, and they kept on going on at him and eventually he got really angry with them and shouted something like, *No! And that's my final answer. Go away*! But then a wee while after they'd gone he got all his black gunslinger clothes out the box, and his black hat and his death's-head pistols and everything, and he came. He turned up at Elizabeth Skinner's place and he said…" Joseph tried, unsuccessfully, an American accent, "*Well, it looks to me like somebody needs a helpin' hand*. And what happened after that is he went and got Driscoll killed in a cattle stampede and then stabbed Hatfield with a Bowie knife. Then he shot Reno when he tried to cross the river and Reno floated away. Face-down. And that was it. Oh, and Elizabeth Skinner fell in love with Kit Mossman. And I think he loved her as well, even though he didn't say. She cried when he went away. But he had to… just because. And that's how it ended. Him just riding away and not looking back until you couldn't see him anymore."

Like all Kit Mossman stories ended.

The family were all in the living room, sitting or standing, or in Uncle Mathew's case, shuffling. Gran and Mister Agnew were on the settee, going through the list of hymns from the plastic bag of arrangements *for when the time comes*.

"The three he mentions…" said Mister Agnew, holding up a sheet of blue airmail paper, "…are *Blest Be the Tie That Binds, There Is s Fountain Filled With Blood* and *Rock* …"

Gran was shaking like a leaf.

"Listen to me, Sarah," Mister Agnew patted her hand like a well-trained doctor. "I know what's been plaguing your mind, so I made a point of speaking to him a couple of days ago; when he was still compos mentis. I said, *Samuel*. I said, *Sarah needs to know*. I said, *She needs to know if you've been Saved Samuel? She needs to be sure*, I said, *that you've asked the Lord Jesus Christ into your heart, Samuel.* And Sarah, do you know, he held my hand tight, like I'm holding yours right now, and he looked into my eyes like I'm looking into yours, and he nodded, *Yes.*Yes." Mister Agnew nodded too, in case she needed to see what a nod looked like. Then he turned away and took a sip of tea, but it made him grimace. Maybe it had gone cold. Or maybe the milk had turned.

CHAPTER THIRTY-SIX

God Bless Those That I Don't Like

Joseph put the crisp poke with the frozen Peter out on the windowsill and began his Gentle Jesus. He added Mrs Merryweather and Father Giordano to his growing list of those to be Blessed, and gave a mention to Eddie Lamont, Mister Brunstane and Uncle Mathew in the *God Bless those that I don't like and God Bless those that don't like me* section.

"God bless Gran, God bless Grandpa..." He'd never God blessed a dead person and he wondered if there was anything special that needed saying or doing. Perhaps there was something about it in one of the new books he'd discovered in *Saint Rita of Impossible Things*. *Tobit*, *Judith*, *Macabees and Macabees*, *Wisdom* and the others. Who knew what might be in those books.

He couldn't sleep. Again. He turned this way and that, was too hot then too cold, the blankets were too loose then claustrophobically tight. Elsewhere in the house whispering unsettled people came and went. Nobody would sleep tonight. He went to the toilet just as a pink-eyed Uncle Mathew was coming out, fumbling with his half-bottle, trying unsuccessfully to shove it back into his jacket pocket. The toilet was the only place in the house that Gran ever allowed drink, and only at Hogmanay, *If you need a drink that much you can sit in there and have it... and I hope you enjoy it*. His face became ugly when he saw Joseph and his frustration at the unhelpful bottle turned into something else altogether,

"What you starin' at?" he slurred.

Joseph was a bit taken aback by the anger, the ugliness. He said the first thing that came into his head, a silly bit of cheek, the likes of which he'd never said to anyone ever, "I don't know, the label's fallen off."

Uncle Mathew wobbled slightly, then deciding that yes he had heard right, slapped him a backhander across the face. Oh all this hitting and hugging and hitting and…

"Ye think ah don't know you? Eh?" He was muttering now to himself maybe, in a low rasp, "Oh, ah know you. Ah know you awright. Aw aye. Ah know aw about you!"

This was it. Where it would all come out. The truth. The lies. About being Saved. About the half-crown. All the *Liar Joseph Kirkland's* lies.

"That's enough Mathew," said Uncle Hector, gently putting a hand on his shoulder. When Uncle Mathew tried to shrug him off he dropped his bottle and it smashed, the little that was left spreading out on the linoleum. Auntie Abi was there too now, straightaway down on her knees, picking up bits of broken glass. She spoke in a low voice. Everyone was keeping their voices down, because of Gran, "Darlin', away and get me a wad of toilet paper eh?" It was late. She was too tired for all this. "Time for you to go home, Mathew."

"Ah'll stay here as long as ah want. It's no Faulkner's we're in."

"No, but it smells like it. Just go home." Joseph handed her the toilet paper, "Away to your room, son, I'll be through in a minute."

He did as he was told, but left the door open.

"It's high time we got everything out in the open." He was slurring, over-gesticulating, trying to keep his balance as much as make his point, "Time we were honest."

"*Honest? You?*" she said, mopping up the puddle, "You should be a comedian, Mathew."

"Elspeth was ma big sister… it's like … she never existed."

"She existed. The proof is in that room."

"That's no *proof!* That's *evidence*… that she wisnae well…"

"Enough!"

"He should've been put away in the Robert Munday…"

"Mathew…"

"… wi all the other mongrels and mistakes."

He put his hand over his mouth when he saw Gran, trying to stop the unspoken words getting out, or trying to shovel the spoken ones back in. He should have wept and begged forgiveness like a wee boy, like a sinner. She might have forgiven him, she always did. But she didn't respond at all. She just stood there, small and fragile, framed within this gigantic doorway in her nightie, in her bare feet, trembling like a wee scared bird.

It had been a while since Auntie Abi had been in Joseph's room. She scowled at the samplers, the rapture picture and all the rest of it, "That was just drink talking." She tucked him in, "Want the big light left on?"

"I've got a candle," he said, showing her the candle stub Mrs Merryweather had given him. "Would you light it for me? For Grandpa."

She went into her cardigan pocket for a lighter, smiling a sideways smile, *are you pulling my leg?* "A *candle*? For Grandpa? That's... nice." Joseph didn't pull folks' legs.

Joseph looked into the candle, but however much he tried he couldn't get a clear picture of Grandpa. He could manage his hands, his long, bony nose, his big ears, the outline of his frame, all the composite parts, the shape of his face, even the back of his head, but not his face. Is this what happened when folk died? He dripped hot wax onto his stomach. It was good but not enough, so he stuck his penknife in the candle flame.

A few months before he'd been to see Doctor Baranski about his wheezy chest. She'd insisted on examining him, "Joseph, what are all these marks?... Did someone do this to you?" He did lots of head shaking. "Are you sure? You can tell me, you know... Did you do this to yourself?" He nodded. "Do you want to talk about it? ... No? ... Okay. Do you ever get the urge to... go further?" He felt sorry for Doctor

Baranski. Why couldn't he just say, *No, nobody did it to me. I don't know why I do it. It just makes me feel…*

"Will you please not tell my Gran."

Joseph felt the urge to go further right now. He was fantasising about dousing the bed and the curtains in petrol and watching the flames sweep across the ceiling in great fiery waves, like they had in the coal shed, but bigger. It would be like being inside a sea of fire. Like in the film Mister Conlon the Fire Chief showed him when Uncle Hector took him to the Fire Station for a so-called *special outing*.

"Your Uncle Hector says you like fires. That right, son?" Mister Conlon took Joseph into a small projector room, just the two of them, "See that? One wee candle left unattended on a windowsill. Nothing eh? Now look. See the curtains? The settee. And then just a few seconds later… completely out of control. Can you imagine being in the middle of that? An inferno. Can you?"

Joseph stood by the bedroom window. He so wanted Caleb and Mirky to appear. Would he ever see them again? *Please let me see them again.*

But there was Archie now, down on the lane, always reliable and bursting as usual with what for Joseph was impossible excitement. How did he manage it?

"I've got something brilliant for us tomorrow. I mean it. It'll be so good, so it will."

My Grandpa's dead, but he didn't say it. He wanted to enjoy the thrill of Archie, to know what Archie had planned for tomorrow that was so good and so brilliant.

"We're going to build a railway. A real one. Down the Meadows. I've worked it all out and everything, how we can do it, and I've found the stuff, it'll be like…"

Archie never got a chance to say what his railway would be like. As soon as saw the long black car roll up he tiptoed off into the mist like a silent movie clown. Two men in black coats got out, slid a big long metal box out the rear and carried it inside. It didn't seem that heavy, and when they returned with it a few minutes later, full, it didn't appear to be any heavier, and then they were gone.

Archie reappeared. He looked up at the window and he was all sad and confused and awkward, his face, his hands, all of him searching for the right gesture to accompany this brand new situation that had arisen between himself and Joseph, and not finding one, he put the palm of his hand to his mouth and blew his friend a kiss.

CHAPTER THIRTY-SEVEN

The Great Kilhaugh Railway Disaster

Everything is a sign. Peter and Grandpa, Caleb and Mirky and the Devil Dog, Mrs Merryweather's candle and Saint Rita's and that priest and those extra books of the Bible and Mrs Hendry and the money and Mrs Arnold and the quarry and wee Maggie getting lost and the tweed suit and the bookshop and the fish and everything. I just need to pay attention.

Last night was the first night Gran had slept on her own in nigh on fifty years, and now what a sight she was with her snow-white hair standing on end like she'd received an electric shock, her face hollowed out from lack of dentures, and her eyes red-raw from crying. She looked like a runaway from the Munday Mental. *Sorry. But she did.*

Uncle Andrew was in the kitchen organising the funeral and the purvey. This involved sifting through Grandpa's share of documents from the *For When the Time Comes* polythene bag, and going in and out the lobby to make telephone calls, "Sausage rolls, sandwiches, tea, coffee… biscuits… yes… not chocolate-covered… or wrapped… custard creams, gypsy creams… No, absolutely not, no alcohol… Hello?… Speaking… Did you get to the bottom of the smell in the Hall?… A fish?… And would that be Truman senior or junior, do you think? …"

He removed half a dozen small white cards from a wee brown envelope and laid them out on the kitchen table. On one side was printed, *Please Take Cord No 1* or *Please Take Cord No 2* and so on up to *Please Take Cord No 6*. He pushed *No 1* to one side and picked up *No 2*, passing it between his fingers in an act of prestidigitation that reminded Joseph of the tricks that Grandpa occasionally did and Gran always disapproved of.

The routine was always the same, his and hers; a double act. *The Sam and Sarah Show*, that's what Auntie Abi called it, or *Mister Gleesome and Mrs Gloom*,

"Ach you and your magic tricks," Gran would say, but she'd have to watch, despite herself, her face full of wonder, like a child. Then she'd catch herself, and get annoyed with herself for being in thrall, the way she got annoyed with herself for being playful. And she could be playful, as playful as Grandpa, sometimes – though not since Grandpa took to his bed. She would sneak up on Joseph behind the settee and tickle him under the chin, paralysing him with tickling. Grandpa loved all that, Joseph giggling, Gran's mischievousness. He'd look at her then, *Ah yes, there she is, there's the girl I married*, though he never said that, it might've sounded like disenchantment had set in.

"There you go again with your tricks," she'd say, her arms folded now, "leading me astray with all your daftness and frivolities. It's tricks Satan uses to make you think something's one thing when it's another. Why don't you tell the boy about real marvels, about the Lord and his miracles?" Then Grandpa would pretend to be chastised, and she'd get annoyed with him all over again for making fun of her: "Ach, I'm away to make a cup of tea," and then, "I suppose you'll be wanting one too..." and then "...and a biscuit no doubt for that sweet tooth of yours."

No, there had always been enchantment.

On the reverse of each card was a simple diagram of a coffin and on each of its corners a number, 1 to 6. He tapped each number with his fingernail: "Cord *1* me, Cord *2* Hector, *3* Mathew, *4* George Chaddock, *5* Donald Sangster, 6...?"

Nobody asked where Joseph was going. They'd other things on their mind and it was better for all concerned if he was out the way.

Kilhaugh was as cold, ethereal and monochrome as any day over the past week. There were more stumbling spirits around than before. Folk could no longer stay inside waiting for a change in the weather that might not happen anytime soon:

I've never seen the like / Another ice age / A fog age more like / Ye hear aboot auld Samuel Kirkland? / Och don't tell me / Aye / Been a long time comin' / A guid man / He'd a lot tae pit up wi / Even so… / He was aye up for a laugh / Aye / Well he didnae get much o' that at hame / No / Ye shouldn't speak ill o' the dead / It's wisnae the deid ah was talkin' aboot / Just watch what you say / I know, creepin' Jesus and the KGB / They say it was fog like this at the Kilhaugh witch trials / Oh, ye mind that do ye?… my, you're looking good for your age / I'm just saying, things happen for a reason / Aye, scientific reasons / True… but who knows what they're up to with their atomic this, that and the next thing…

He was getting to know his Books of the Bible well enough to let his thoughts meander, think about other things, like Archie's railway. But shouldn't he be thinking about Grandpa being dead? Grieving? That's what folk did, they grieved. They cried and sighed and remembered and prayed and made arrangements, and in Uncle Mathew's case, got angry and drunk, but even he was involved, even he was feeling *something*. The *Liar Joseph Kirkland* felt nothing.

"Sorry about your grandpa, Joseph," said wee Maggie, hugging him, her eyes welling up, "Was he really old?"

"Yes."

"We can do stuff for him today," she said. "So we can Archie?"

Archie agreed, "Everything we do the day we can say *it's*

for Joseph's grandpa. Even wee things. Look. *This is for Joseph's grandpa!*" and he kicked a stone. "Or... watch this. *This is for Joseph's grandpa!*" he yelled, running up a wall, clinging to the top and dreeping back down!

"*This is for Joseph's grandpa!*" said wee Maggie, doing a graceful ballet dance.

"She's good, so she is— We can make the railway be for him as well."

Joseph presented the crisp poke containing the ice-preserved Peter,

"Oh my God, please can I feel it?" said Archie sticking his hand in, "He's freezing."

"Can I feel him too?" said wee Maggie, "Oh, poor wee thing, he's so cold, Joseph."

"I bet if you kept him frozen you could bring him back to life in the future."

Joseph considered this for a moment: "I need to bury him."

"We could put him in a wee hollow under a boulder," said Archie. "Or inside a tree trunk and carve his name on it so folk know. There's a great tree for it in the Meadows."

"And put flowers beside it," said wee Maggie.

There wasn't much by way of ceremony. Joseph held his Bible but he couldn't think of a prayer. They closed their eyes for a few seconds, then he dropped the crisp poke with Peter inside the tree. Joseph carved the letter *P* on the trunk. There were no flowers around so wee Maggie made a bouquet of frosted leaves and twigs which she threw into the hole in the tree: "It'll be like a nest. I've got a song I can sing too, Joseph? Is it okay if it's not a hymn?"

It was the calypso that Grandpa used to sing, "*Yellow bird, up high in banana tree / Yellow bird, you sit all alone like me.*"

Wee Maggie couldn't resist a cue for a song and dance any more than Grandpa, and as they headed up towards the unnamed area of wasteland behind the railway station she burst into another, "The runaway train came down the track and she blew. She blew!"

"She's a song for every occasion so she has."

"What are you going to call the train? Joseph should give it a name because of his Grandpa." She slid her hand into Joseph's. "What'll you call it Joseph?"

"The Great Kilhaugh Express!"

"Yes!" shouted Archie, "that's exactly what I was thinking, honest to God I was."

Joseph unfolded his map. He'd drawn a railway line across the Meadows.

"That's it," said Archie, like the map was an official council document, authorising planning permission. "We're going to have to build it now. I mean we've got to now."

"We've got to!" shouted wee Maggie.

There was a mountain of old railway track, overgrown with thistles and nettles, which they cleared away as best they could with stick machetes. Eventually they managed to get near enough to haul out some lengths of the narrow portable track that the railway workies once used for maintenance. It might have been portable, but it was still heavy.

"Ach we'll be fine," said Archie, "Want to see the best bit?"

The best bit was a maintenance bogie, lying in the undergrowth, its wooden frame rotted away to nothing. All that remained was its iron skeleton. Archie handed his friend a lump of chalk and Joseph wrote, THE GREAT KILHAUGH EXPRESS in big letters along the chassis. Archie clapped his hands, "This is going to be soooo good!"

"Where are we going to sit?" said wee Maggie, "We'll fall through the bottom."

"We can put some planks on it or a crate or something."

"Oh, can we get cushions and stuff so it's really comfy?"

"Course. We can nip back home and get stuff out the cupboard. We can even paint it; make it look like something from the shows." The wheels screamed painfully when he tried to turn them, "Och, it'll be fine with a wee bit of oil."

It took them the best part of the morning to drag the track, a length at a time, to the Meadows. They'd have done it quicker if Joseph hadn't insisted they go the long way round to make sure nobody saw them. Nobody did.

"It's not stealing. It's just lying there rusting. And anyway..."

He didn't have to say what the *and anyway* was. He'd said it often enough. Joseph knew fine well. *And anyway, you can just say that wee toerag Truman made you do it. They'll believe you.*

They laid the track down the steepest part of the slope. It exceeded their wildest expectations.

"Wow!" said Archie, "It goes for miles so it does."

It did go on for miles, a good thirty yards at least, fading away two thirds of the way down before finally vanishing into the gorse bushes behind the Sleeping Bairns.

"You can't see the end of it," said wee Maggie.

"Maybe we'll disappear. Never to be seen again."

"Oh don't, Archie," she was giggling.

"Maybe it's a ghost train."

"Don't!" she shut her eyes tight, "I'm going to think nice things." She had a gift for that. "Oh Joseph, maybe we'll all end up in fairyland or something. Imagine if we did though?"

"Right, I'm away for oil. I'll meet you back up at the bogie."

It was rare for Joseph and wee Maggie to spend time together, just the two of them, and Joseph felt a shyness. Wee Maggie on the other hand was quivering with delight. She had Joseph all to herself and could ask him all the things she wanted to ask, but couldn't while her big brother was there,

"Is your Grandpa going to be buried or cremated, Joseph?"

"Buried."

That was that out the way.

"Are you really going to be a missionary and travel the world, Joseph?"

"I think so, yes."

"And Archie as well?"

"Yes." *I hope so.*

"Joseph?"

"?"

"Archie says I can come too. Can I? Really? Is he just saying that to be nice?"

"No. You can."

She was skipping and dancing wee pirouettes all around him, in and out, like Mirky.

"Can you get girl missionaries too?" and before he was able to answer she added another, "What happened to your mum and dad, Joseph?"

The buoyancy Joseph felt was so powerful it lifted his heels a full inch off the ground. *Wee Maggie*. He wanted to pick her up, like Tarzan's monkey, like Archie did. He bent down, till his face was close to hers and he was on the brink of saying something, there was such a strong urge to do so, to try to answer this question, and wee Maggie was the perfect person, but he really did not know where to start, so he answered the first question instead. "There's lots. Miss O'Donnell told us about an Irish girl missionary, Ellen something, and there's Mary Slessor, she's Scottish, there's loads of Scottish ones. She was in Africa and used to adopt babies that were abandoned by their mums and dads, especially twins because folk thought twins were cursed and they'd just leave them there in the jungle to die."

"Oh Joseph, there's twins in my class so there are, Leslie and Lorna and ..."

"But she'd say *no you mustn't do that, that's superstition*, and she'd read the mum and dad Scripture so they'd know it was wrong but if they still said no, then she'd adopt them. I've got her in my *Heroes of the Cross*. You can borrow it if you want."

"Oh can I? Oh I'd love to do that Joseph, rescuing babies in darkest Africa."

"There's loads of other women as well who weren't missionaries but they married missionaries, so they travelled the world as well and worked as nurses and doctors and teachers and ..."

"I'm going to be a teacher Joseph! Or a nurse. *And* I'm going to marry a missionary!" She was pirouetting again. She grabbed his fingers and spun, and before he even knew it he was part of her dance, "I'm going to marry *you* Joseph!"

"*Maggie and Joseph up a tree k.- i. – s -. s. – i. – n -.g!*"

"Archie!" she giggled, hiding her face in her hands.

"Is she going on again about how she's going to marry you? That's all she ever talks about, so it is – *you're* all she ever talks about!" He put on a high-speed wee Maggie voice, "*Joseph says this, Joseph says that, Oh I saw Joseph, Can we go and see Joseph? See when Joseph and me get married, will you be the best man? Maggie Kirkland sounds nice, so it does Archie? Joseph, Joseph, Joseph.*"

Maggie was delighted that it was all out in the open, because that made it more real and she celebrated with another gleeful giggling twirl.

With the frozen ground rock-solid and the wheels oiled it was a bit easier than they'd thought to roll the bogie up to the Meadows. Getting it lined up onto the flat section of track at the top of the slope was tricky but with a couple planks and the combined weight of all three of them, they managed to lever it into place. Immediately it began to move forward and Archie had to throw one of the planks down in front of it to stop it rolling away.

"*The runaway train went over the hill and she blew!*" sang wee Maggie, her arms and legs going like pistons. "*The runaway train went over the hill and she blew.*"

Archie joined in the actions, all elbows and knees.

"The runaway train went over the hill... the last we heard she was going still... and she blew, blew, blew, blew, blew."

"Mind jump off at the last bit like a train robber. Or we'll end up in the jaggy bushes!"

"I will," said wee Maggie, "I will. Promise."

"Maybe I should have a go first," said Archie, "I can be the test pilot."

"What about the cushions and everything?" said wee Maggie.

"Just to see."

"But I want to do it properly, all of us together."

"Just the once. To make sure..."

"But you said."

"Then we'll get stuff to make it nice."

He kicked the plank away. Now it wouldn't move at all. He started shoving it, one leg in, one out till it began grating and grinding its way forwards, rusty old iron on rusty old iron, an inch at a time. He whispered to Joseph, "Quick, get on."

"Maybe we should roll it down on its own the first time."

"Okay," said Archie, but then he jumped on, "All aboard the Great Kilhaugh Express!" he shouted, and began all this whooping and howling.

"Archie!" Wee Maggie was trotting after it, almost in tears, "That's not fair!" But she couldn't see a way of getting on, and it was right at the edge of the slope.

"You can get the next go."

"But you said!"

It trundled on, sluggishly. This wasn't good enough. Archie stood upright at the front, like a charioteer, arms out wide like wings to balance himself, and began rocking backwards and forwards to make it go faster, but Archie was so flimsy and the big iron bogie so heavy, how could he make any difference at all? As soon as it rolled over the brow of the hill though, off it went, not like a bullet but like some great unstoppable beast, a rhinoceros, or a mammoth, a behemoth even. Its wheels screeched against the track like nails across a blackboard. Wee Maggie had her fingers in her ears but Archie was in his element, doing his whoops and laughing like a mad thing and Joseph was wishing now that he'd got on too. Wasn't this just typical of Archie Truman! Taking it upon himself to be test pilot, one-man advance party and solo explorer of the dangerous uncharted territories all rolled into one. And wasn't this just typical of the Coward Joseph Kirkland to let him. But still, it was glorious. Archie was glorious.

Archie and his laughter vanished. Nothing. The whole journey would only have lasted a few seconds. He'd have jumped off into the long grass by now, *like a train robber, like a spy*. Joseph listened for the mad laughter to resume, waited for Archie to reappear triumphant, for the Archie Truman victory dance to commence. Then they'd push it back up the hill, get some planks and cushions to make it nice and all have a turn together. He couldn't wait. The three of them, oh what a racket they'd make. Still nothing.

It wasn't a decision, he simply found himself running down the hill, slipping on the icy grass, sliding down most of the way on his backside.

Please. Please God. Please Jesus. Please.

A bird took flight, which was unusual because in the past few days, since the arrival of the fog, the only living beasts that Joseph had come across were dogs and that cat, which he hadn't actually seen. Maybe they'd been there all the while: the cats and rats in the shadows, the sheep, cows and horses in the fields, the crows and squirrels in the trees, the rabbits, foxes and deer in the undergrowth, all keeping absolutely still and quiet, not wanting to be seen. It was a robin, the first one Joseph had seen this year. *What do robins mean?* Everything was dripping with meaning and with stories and with …

Caleb and Mirky were there now, at the foot of the hill, beside the Sleeping Bairns, just the faintest of outlines, but it was them. Of course it was them, of course Caleb and Mirky would be there, where else would they be, they were always there.

"You'll give me your tie," said Caleb, hard at it, stemming blood flow, "Now!" He sounded scared. *Please don't let Caleb be scared. If Caleb is scared…*

Caleb smashed a frozen puddle with his fist and packed handfuls of ice into the bloody parcel he'd made of his jacket. Mirky watched sniffing, getting close, and closer, excited by the smell, like she had with that rabbit. She couldn't help her nature, but when she got too close Caleb didn't think twice about giving her a good kick. Wee Maggie was there too now, ghost-white and mute, not a shiver in her body, despite the cold. Caleb grabbed Joseph's head in his big hands, like Gran often did, as if this was the only way he could be sure that this fey boy would understand./."Listen. You'll go up to the telephone box. You'll phone for an ambulance. You'll tell them we'll be at the doctor's. Now."

Caleb picked up this red-haired clown-white floppy boneless thing, this bafflingly incomplete stringless loose-jawed puppet thing that was wearing Archie Truman's clothes, and ran with it, the bloody parcel tucked under his arm. Caleb was always running with some bloody parcel.

Wee Maggie let herself be dragged along by Joseph, who moved so swiftly he barely left a mark on the frosted grass. Even the fog seemed to part for him. They squeezed into the phone box and Joseph tried to dial 999 but he was shaking now, and all fingers and thumbs.

"Hello Kilhaugh Telephone Exchange what number …"

"I've to ask for an ambulance," he felt – as he did a lot of the time with much in his life – that he was not part of these events but simply bearing witness to them.

"Who is this?"

"It's Joseph Kirkland."

"Joseph? Are you okay son? What's the…"

"It's Archie …" He spoke in short gulps, "… Truman …" as

though he had to come up for air for each word, "... Mrs... Merryweather... He's... had... an accident."

"An accident? Where?"

"A train... in... the Meadows."

"A train? In the Meadows?... I don't understand, son. A train?"

"Please."

"Okay. I'll get an ambulance, son. Whereabouts in the Meadows is he?"

"No... No... he's... I've to say... he's at... the doctor's."

"Okay Joseph, I'm doing that right now son."

Wee Maggie put her arms out and Joseph picked her up. She clung to him like she was in danger of flying away. Mirky was there now too, pressing herself hard against his legs giving him what comfort she could.

There was no one in at the Truman house, so he took her up to Faulkner's. Wee Maggie's head was resting on his shoulder, asleep maybe, a dead weight anyway. He looked through the fake-snow-covered window into the Saloon Bar at a lively, cheery scene, all tinsel and lights, a fake Christmas tree, a fake flickering fire. *All the things that make you forget what Christmas is really about*, Gran would say. Mister Truman was slouched over a pint and a short, his eyes half shut. Mrs Truman was stumbling towards the toilet. She bumped into a stool and held up her hands, apologising to everyone and no one in particular and anyone who did take notice looked at her with malign amusement, disgust or a mixture of both.

Where to go? Where to go? He carried wee Maggie to Gran's house, all the way making himself not think about Archie, or Grandpa or God or Jesus, but trying to think only about getting wee Maggie inside into the warmth. A siren sounded, so muted it was pitiful and a lazy hazy blue light appeared and disappeared at the top of the lane. Had no one told them this was an emergency? Maybe it wasn't a proper emergency, just a dirty wee bit of overspill from the scheme.

"Who's that with you?"

It was Uncle Mathew out for a cigarette. Mirky took one sniff in his direction and slunk away.

"Maggie Truman."

"What've you brought her here for?"

"Archie's at the doctor." He tried to breeze past all casual.

"What you playing at? You can't take her in there."

"She just needs..."

"I don't give a damn what she needs."

"Is that the Truman lassie?"

"Duncan?" he peered into the gloom, "What's happenin'?"

"Her brother's what happenin'. Built a fuckin' railway down the Meadows."

"A railway? You're having me on."

Carmichael laughed, as much out of incredulity as cruelty, "Stole some track and a bogie. Ran over his fuckin' legs."

"Heh... mind where you are Duncan."

Carmichael gave Uncle Mathew a graphic account of exactly what had occurred, which Joseph tried to obliterate by blowing a tuneless cheery whistle, more breath than whistle, across wee Maggie's ear. Carmichael finished and pointed his finger at Joseph,

"I'll be talking to you later by the way," and then to wee Maggie, "Right, you, in the car."

"But there's nobody home," said Joseph, "Her mum and dad are in Faulkner's."

"Disnae matter. I'm taking her up the Munday. Right, c'mon."

She clung to Joseph for all she was worth but still it didn't take much of an effort from Carmichael to prise her off. She made a low whining noise, like Mirky when she was injured. Joseph felt nauseas, which was fine, natural, but Archie would actually have done something. He'd have launched himself in there, punched and kicked or picked up a brick, or a broken bottle, or a knife or anything, and actually hit Duncan Carmichael, but the Coward Joseph Kirkland who wee Maggie loved and who she dreamed of marrying and travelling the world with, could not bring himself to feel such rage; all he could do was feel nauseas, and what good was that to anybody?

Wee Maggie gave up the ghost.

"Gentle Jesus, meek and mild, look upon this little child, pity my simplicity..."

He was on his knees, at the side of his bed, putting his all into this prayer but there was too much noise inside his head. The door of his *Terrible Cupboard of Unthinkable Thoughts* was rattling on its hinges, and threatening to burst open. He needed distracting. He emptied his pockets of all the accumulated paraphernalia – penknife, Bible, *Swan Vestas*, monkey- king matches, map, mermaid and Grandpa's hearing aids, which he'd taken – as a what? As a souvenir? – and scattered them onto the candlewick, as though together they might form an oracle that would make sense of everything. If only he knew how to read it.

CHAPTER THIRTY-EIGHT

Joseph Kirkland's Fifth Dream

It was the woman in the Pre-Tribulational Rapture picture, in that same yellow cotton flower-print dress except now she had on a bus conductress's hat, a ticket machine slung around her neck, and a big beaming smile that was all for him,

"Look at you, my wee man. Just look at you. Wee soul. All shiny brand new, so you are. My wee man. My wee soldier." She licked the edge of a tortoiseshell comb and ran it between her painted red lips. "A wee soldier so you are. That hair of yours, a mind of its own so it has." She combed his hair, carefully, making the parting perfect.

"All aboard the Great Kilhaugh Express!" she shouted.

The doors slammed shut before he could get inside and the bus began to move. He ran along behind it, but no matter how fast he ran he couldn't catch up with it; he never could.

This time there was a wee girl looking out the back window, terror stricken, but not pleading, because what was the point in that? She knew that the Coward Joseph Kirkland would not save her.

CHAPTER THIRTY-NINE

Keep Me Searching Till the Break of Day

Outside in the freezing fog, in the wee small hours, Joseph felt like he was in a dream, or in a film of a dream. No wonder, Archie loved walking around like this, late at night, in dressing gown and pyjamas, the whole wide world all to himself.

The Great Kilhaugh Express was still there, upright and partially camouflaged in the bushes, and there it would remain, a testament or a monument to... *something*... bravery, stupidity, childhood, the wicked webs we weave when we practise to deceive God.

Joseph was at the exact spot where Caleb had gone about his gory business. There were a few tiny blood icicles hanging from the gorse and long grass. They looked sharp as needles and Joseph had to touch one to see if it were indeed so. It melted instantly on the end of his finger. He tasted it. Tasted Archie.

Joseph and Archie were already blood brothers. The day after the fire in the railway shed they'd cut hands, mixed blood and ash from the burned-out shed and made binding promises.

"That's us for life now," said Archie. "See if anybody ever comes near you or ever does anything to you or even just says anything, then they better watch out cos I'll be chap chap chappin' at their door. And if something ever happens to one of us, we'll just know... we just will."

Joseph hadn't added anything in reply. Of course not. Joseph Kirkland just nodded his nod. Archie didn't push it. Even then, right at the start he knew: a blood brotherhood with Joseph Kirkland was likely to be a very one-sided affair.

He touched another icicle, wiping the sticky melted blood on the back of his hand.

I'm sorry. "I'm sorry."

Joseph continued his pilgrimage – because that's what this was now – past the tree where Joseph carved the first and only *Archie T + Joseph K*. Subsequent carvings were a little more circumspect and anonymous; *AT + JK*. Past Archie's favourite den, past the tree house Archie had built for Joseph, and where so many things had happened, to the grassy banks of the Sappie where Archie Truman had *not* been Saved.

There was a figure standing there now. It was wearing a World War Two sheepskin flying jacket, the kind American fighter pilots wore, trousers and long brown leather boots, and when it turned around Joseph saw it was wearing bright red lipstick too. She was beautiful.

Joseph had never seen her or her like. Maybe she was a relative of somebody from up the hill. No one else would dare go around dressed in such an eccentric outfit. She had set up a big ancient box camera on a wooden tripod, the brass lens pointing out into the middle of the fog-covered water. She was too involved with the camera's knobs and dials to know that he was there. Joseph wasn't even a hundred per cent sure she really was there until he got up close and smelled her perfume. Rosewater. And even then...

"Hello."

She jumped like she'd seen a ghost.

"Oh my God!" and seeing it was not a ghost, but a boy, with patched spectacles and a dressing gown, and all the rest, she quickly concluded that this boy might well be odd, but he was probably not a threat, "Hi. Well, you certainly got me a good one there."

She was an American. Joseph had never met an American in real life. There was an American flag on her flying jacket too. Archie and wee Maggie should be here, they knew lots of American films, they'd... *Oh Archie*.

"*Zachary T. Mayfield* is American."

"Excuse me?"

"He writes the *Kit Mossman* stories."

"Oh yeah… the cowboy guy… he sure is, though I believe he's from the *Wild* West. I'm from Illinois." Nothing registered on his face. "Chicago… Gangsters?… Al Capone? Saint Valentine's day massacre? Bang bang, you're dead? That kinda thing?"

"Billy Graham's an American too."

"Billy Graham? Em. Wow," she looked at him. "Right," as if it made complete sense that any small Scottish boy who referenced both Zachary T Mayfield *and* Billy Graham would be out in the freezing fog in their dressing gown and pyjamas, "Yup. He sure is."

He took a closer look at the camera, keeping his hands firmly behind his back so she'd know he wasn't going to touch it.

"I'm a photographer," she said, quite matter-of-fact, then added in a silly voice, "*You don't say!*" It was the kind of humour that was lost on Joseph at the best of times, but she was smiling at her own joke, so Joseph put on a smile too, out of politeness.

"It looks old."

"It is old. It was my grandad's. I know, it's crazy, everybody seems to be chasing the next big thing, Polaroid or whatever, you know, trying to speed things up, and I seem to be heading in the opposite direction. I wanna *slooow* everything down."

"What do you take pictures of?"

"Landscapes, mostly. Portraits, sometimes," she winked at him. "If I like the look of someone. I was visiting the Robert Munday Children's Home? My grandad was an orphan there, back in the day. Ended up in Chicago. It's a very long, very American story."

Oh wee Maggie please God let her be okay.

"But when I saw this fog had descended, well, how could I resist?" She waved her hand. It was Joseph's turn. "So, now you know why I'm prowling around in the fog with an ancient camera. What's your story? Dressing gown? Pyjamas? Come on, spill the beans."

But Joseph wasn't there. He was looking at Archie being carried to the doctor's and at wee Maggie staring out the back of the panda car. The lady looked concerned now, "Listen, I know it's none of my business, but do your mom and dad know you're here?... Want me to walk you home?... You live near here right?"

And in a flash he was back, "I live over there." He was pointing towards the other side of the Sappie, "In a tent."

"Ah! ... O...kay ... You're a ... gypsy?"

"A tinker."

"A *tinker.* Okay. Wow," she looked at him differently now, like Mister Mallison had looked at his map. Like a collector, "Listen, would you mind if I took your photograph?"

"No, I don't mind."

"Great. I'm Miriam by the way, Miriam McArthur. What's your name?"

"Joseph."

"Hold on, let's do this right," she took a small notebook and pencil from her pocket, "Okay. *Joseph...?*"

"... Skeely."

"*Skeely?* That's a new one. How d'you spell it?"

Joseph took a wild guess, "S.k.e.e.l.y."

"That a Scottish name?"

" Yes. No... It's a tinker name."

"That a fact? Well Joseph *Skeely,* if you could stand just over there, in the middle of that clump of frozen grass. Right there beside the water." Joseph repositioned himself. "Great. But facing me. Fantastic. Now, I'd like to keep this quite formal. Kinda like one of those classic portraits, yeah?... Sorry, ignore me. Just... stand tall, look straight into the lens and..." she made some adjustments "...and think of... something... anything... count backwards from a hundred if you like. It doesn't actually matter what you're thinking, so long as there's someone at home. You get what I'm saying?

The last thing we want is that dead-fish-eye look. Grrreat. Hold… it… right… there." She ran over and held the light meter up to his face. His lips were moving.

"Well there's certainly something going on in there, I can hear the cogs and wheels."

"I'm doing my Books of the Bible."

"Your what?" She was footering with her camera, only half listening.

Joseph took the Bible from his dressing gown pocket, "I need to know them off by heart."

"Sorry?"

"I'm going to be a missionary."

"Get out of here!" She stopped her footering and took a fresh look at him, "Wow. A tinker *and* a missionary… in his pyjamas… in the fog. This must be my lucky day. How old are you, Joseph?"

"Nearly twelve."

"Do you have an address?" He shrugged. "Of course. Wherever the wind blows you, yeah?" He shrugged again. "Well. You're definitely a piece of work, Joseph Skeely… that's for sure," she said, looking at the upside=down image of Joseph on the ground glass screen, and perhaps wondering, as Joseph himself sometimes wondered, *what kind of thing is this Joseph?* She smiled, "When it comes out it'll look kinda like you're walking on a cloud. In fact, hold on…" she scribbled into her notebook, "*Walking out of the late=night fog, bible in hand, came eleven-year-old Joseph Skeely, the Tinker Missionary.* How does that sound?"

Joseph ran around the outskirts of the Sappie, in and out the trees looking for Caleb's tent, but everything looked different. There were no vague, barely there paths or lines to guide his way now. *We don't like to be the centre of things. We don't like it when folk pay us too much attention.* And now there was the police and ambulances, maps, murdered dogs and now photographs in magazines. Everything he could possibly do to drag Caleb and Mirky out of the shadows and into the light, he had done. He felt further away than ever, from everybody, from God and from everything.

"It's a comforting thought, isn't it, that Lawrence Oates would only have felt the bitter cold for a very short time," Miss O'Donnell had said in response to a question from a concerned Mary McPhee, during a discussion about the map used by Captain Scott on his ill-fated expedition to the South Pole, "That when the end eventually came, it would have been quite painless really, just a nice warm feeling, a sort of drifting off to sleep."

And so it was for Joseph. First the cold, a painful cold, which was right and good, and cleansing; all that badness had to be washed away. And then the drifting, his naked body floating through the thin ice like Captain Scott's *Terra Nova.* And then, *thank you God and Jesus*… weightlessness… and… nothing.

CHAPTER FORTY

The Destruction of the Kingdom of Caleb

It was a huge face, pitch=black against the cavernous backdrop of flickering flame and giant shadows.

"Kit Mossman..."

He floated away again to the sound of horses' hooves and heartbeats for who knows how long, and when he awoke his nostrils were filled with herbs, forest smoke and roasted flesh; earthy scents of the deep dark woods. He was wrapped up tight in swaddling clothes, in the arms of a woodsman, that one who always saves *Little Red Riding Hood* and... all the others. The woodsman's breath was hot and meaty, like a wild beast. Lion breath.

There was that black dog again.

Hello girl, what's your name?

It cocked an ear as if Joseph had actually spoken, then rested its head again on the pillow of neatly folded pyjamas and dressing gown. A wooden mermaid stuck out of the dressing gown pocket, just within reach.

"Eat," said the woodsman.

It was a struggle to keep his eyes open. But it smelled so good. The woodsman ladled some broth from his cauldron into a tin cup and held it to Joseph's lips. One sip and ...

"Them's the boys," said Grandpa. "Sticks to your ribs that soup. See your Gran? See her soup? Ho ho. The old ham hough and lentil? My, yon's no a recipe, yon's a magic spell, eh mum?"

"Och you." But she was pleased as punch. She loved it when he complimented her on her cooking, complimented her on anything. A nice new hat or nice new shoes. *Ach it's just a hat. It's just shoes. A hat's a hat. Shoes are shoes.* If only she could have allowed herself to enjoy his adoration. "It's just soup," she said. "Soup is soup."

Grandpa was undiminished, "Roll up, roll!" It was time once more for Grandpa Kirkland's Medicine Show, "Git yo'selves a bowl of Old Ma Kirkland's Miraculous Soup – bad breath, bubonic plague or a broken heart – this soup is guaranteed to cure it all! Mind Andrew, mum? When him and Ishbel started winchin'?"

"Och, you know I don't like that word."

"Your Uncle Andrew, oh my word, I never knew he had it in him. Asked your Auntie Ishbel to marry him – I'd love to have been a fly on that wall – and she said she needed to *think about it*, well it was complicated you know, what with her family kicking with their left foot and all, and of course the days went by and there's no answer and your Uncle Andrew, who was... how old was Andrew, mum?"

"Twenty-odd," said Gran, rubbing her hands in her apron, wanting him to hurry on with the story, she liked this story, which had it all, conversion... and romance.

"That's right, twenty-odd going on forty, and she was sweet seventeen and running rings around him. There's no answer, so of course Andrew thinks he's been given the old heave-ho. What a state he was in, ho ho, face tripping him. Couldnae eat, couldnae sleep..."

"Couldn't... not couldnae."

"Perdon my dispeakable mennirs, Missus Kirklend... the only fare he could keep doon his threpple was your Grendmaithers lentil soup, eh mum?"

"Och, the poor boy was heartbroken, dad."

"Bowls of the stuff he consumed. An ocean of soup." He winked and jerked a thumb in the direction of Gran. "Oh aye, they keep you on tenterhooks the Kilhaugh gals. Got a reputation for it, so they have. Kilhaugh's where Cupid comes to sherpen his erras you know. I mind one lassie. I was just a lad, standing outside Agnew's, I'd just got a start there, and there she was, strolling down the main street and oh my, *what... a... looker*."

Gran rubbed at her apron hem, flushing, frowning,

tut-tut-tutting, pursing her lips to hide her grin. She heard this story almost every time they had lentil soup and never tired of it.

"Now what was her name?" said Grandpa, sucking his pipe like Sherlock Homes, "What *was* her name… Sandra? No, that's not it. Sheila? No…?"

Joseph took another sip of Caleb's rich broth.

"My Grandpa died."

"I know. A good man by all accounts. It's sad Joseph. And you have to let yourself be sad. There's no getting away from that. But as well as that, there's other things that need doing. You'll have some good stories about your Grandpa, eh?" Joseph nodded. "Well they have to be told. I'm serious Joseph. It's your duty you know, to tell these stories. *Let me tell you a tale about my Grandpa,* you'll say, *Samuel Kirkland was his name*, to anybody who'll listen; friend, family or stranger. That's the thing to do now. I mean that."

Joseph drained his cup.

"I need to see Archie."

Caleb said nothing but there was a challenge in his eyes, *So what is the Coward Joseph Kirkland going to do about it then? I dare you, Joseph Kirkland*

There was a long string of scripture texts, curled up at the edges, hanging all the way down from the roof like fallen bunting after Templeton Gala Day. How on earth? Caleb unpegged the nearest one, *The Cutty Sark*.

"Let the lying lips be put to silence," said Joseph Caleb turned it over to look at the words and raised an eyebrow: "No water damage to your brain then."

"Mister Agnew says the picture's just adornment."

"That right?"

"He says it's about the Scripture not the picture. He says…"

"Shush now." Caleb pressed the text against Joseph's lips.

His head felt heavy. He let its full weight sink onto Caleb's chest, and watched as he brought *The Cutty Sark* to life against a sea of fire and smoke, "The Captain and his crew had a right awful thirst, so they did. You see they'd no fresh water for days. So there they were looking out for land and they spot this rock in the middle of the ocean, like a wee island. And on this rock they see… what do *you* think they saw?" Joseph held up his mermaid. "Too right they saw a mermaid! Oh they were like most folk, like you if you'd been there. They thought it was their imaginations playing tricks on them, *It's that terrible thirst, it's driving us mad* they said, or *Oh maybe it's the devil* or *Maybe it's a demon*, and they were shaking with terror and trying to remember their prayers but it had been that long since they'd prayed, they couldn't get beyond *Our Father* or *Gentle Jesus…*"

"But she was there all right, that mermaid, and oh what a dreadful state she was in. Her tail in tatters, her hair all matted with broken bottles and beer cans, soup tins and sweetie wrappers and all other manner of man-made litter and leavings. But worst of all, in her arms was a wee baby boy, with a fish tail like herself, a *merbaby*, and the wee thing was that dry and floppy you wouldn't bet a ha'penny on it lasting till morning. A right pitiful sight so it was.

"Well the mermaid she holds up this wee merbaby and she says to the Captain, *Please good sir, will ye see tae it ma bairn finds a guid hame, for ah'm poorly and ah canna look after it onymair.* Now, you know it's terrible bad luck for a sailor to refuse a favour to a mermaid, so the Captain takes the wee merbaby onto the ship. Oh but the mother, she was so sad to see her baby go that her eyes wept freshwater tears, which is an awful thing, a painful thing, for a mermaid. Of course the sailors, never ones to miss an opportunity, collected her tears in bottles for drinking, which she let them do, and when she'd wept enough to give them fresh water for a week, down she goes back down below the waves, to who knows where.

"The Captain, he looks at this pathetic wee merbaby, more dead than alive now, and as he did so, what happens but the sea-skin falls away from its tail to reveal a wee pair of legs. Now, the Captain was a wise man, he knew the sea and its ways, and he takes the sea-skin and wraps it in seaweed to keep it safe, and to keep it soft and moist, because he knew that one day the merbaby would want its sea-skin back so it could rejoin its people."

"Of course a ship is no life for a baby and as soon as they found dry land, the Captain he takes the baby to the nearest church and leaves it on the steps, its sea-skin wrapped up in a bundle aside it. When the church folk found the baby they took it in, for they were good folk, well, good enough anyway. But good or bad, they were land folk, and had no knowledge of the ways of the sea and when they saw the sea-skin they were fearful, for they'd never seen the likes, and folk are scared of things they don't understand, and so what do they do, they hide the sea-skin away in a cave where the child will never find it.

"Well, the years creep by and the baby grows up never knowing where it comes from. It tries to live its life like a wee human boy, doing the things that wee human boys do and getting up to all the shenanigans that wee boys get up to, but it was never content. Oh the village folk did the best they could and were kind enough in their own way, but they couldn't change its nature, and every time the wee boy found itself near the saltwater sea, it felt this terrible longing..."

Caleb only paused for breath but Joseph had to ask, "Did its mother ever come back?"

Maybe Caleb answered, maybe he didn't. Anything he said was drowned out in this ugly din of pumped-up angry men and animals, all howling, squealing, gasping and grunting,

Filthy TINK.

Somebody get that FUCKIN' DOG.

Dirty BASTARD.

Get a fuckin' HAUD ae him.

Dirty TINKS!

It was cartoon-chaotic, like a Saturday Morning *Looney*

Tune, but with real sound effects; metal, glass, flesh, tooth and bone being slapped, snapped, crunched, and shattered, instead of swanee whistles and crashing cymbals.

WANT it EH? Ye fuckin' WANT it?

HERE, fuckin' HAVE it.

The men were ecstatic now, like evangelists, like Mirky driven to distraction by the promise of fresh bloody meat or Joseph by the promise of fire.

TORCH it for fuck sake.

Fuckin TORCH it.

Gie it tae me, AH'LL fuckin dae it.

The tent lit up. Joseph caught glimpses of familiar village faces drunk on hatred… And in the middle of them, Caleb's wood-carved face, illuminated, beautiful, and bloody, taking in everything all at once, especially Joseph.

You see me, Joseph?

Yes, I see you.

Joseph was hoisted from his makeshift bed into the air in a fireman's lift but not by Caleb. He kicked and wriggled and bit hard into an ear till his teeth almost met and he was dropped. He ran back to the tent, an inferno now, but a hand whacked him across the back of the head so hard his feet left the ground and the wind and the fight were taken clean out of him.

Caleb?

I see you. This story's not over son. Not by a long chalk.

CHAPTER FORTY-ONE

I Know I Am, I'm Sure I Am, I'm H.A.P.P.Y.

It was Friday morning, the day of the funeral. Gran was away up at the Hall to tend to Grandpa despite Auntie Abi's best efforts to reassure her.

"The Co-op are very good, Sarah."

"I just need to make sure."

"They know what they're doing, love. They'll make sure he looks nice."

"That's as maybe, but they don't know him like I know him."

Joseph drifted in and out of sleep. As usual folk were whispering, arguing, over him, *Should he be Baptised? Should he not? Should he be at the funeral? Should he not? Should he this, shouldn't he that, should he, shouldn't he…*

"Let's see what Doctor Baranski says," said Uncle Andrew.

"*Complete madness* is what she'll say," said Auntie Abi.

"I certainly don't think he should go to the funeral."

"Heaven forfend, we don't want a showing up do we?"

"And we've yet to find out what happened in that tent," said Uncle Mathew.

"What happened?" said Auntie Abi. "You and your pitchfork-wielding village idiots put two and two thegether and made five, that's what happened."

"Oh, so you think it's normal that…"

"*Normal*? And what would you know about that? We all know about *your* proclivities."

"What's that supposed…"

"He'll be there. With me. End of story."

When Doctor Baranski and PC Carmichael arrived Joseph

was sitting bolt upright, hands clasped on bed covers so drum-tight it might've been a hospital ward. His hair was stuck to his forehead with sweat, his spectacle lens was thick with condensation. She greeted him through the mist, "Hello Joseph," she said, all breezy reassurance, "I see you've woken up."

"Yes." But then again… He smiled, a beaming toothy smile, natural enough on someone else, but on Joseph Kirkland it just looked like a different flavour of odd.

She sat on the edge of the bed. Carmichael remained standing. He had on his professional police face, rather than his school bully, but it was clearly an effort to keep the bully at bay.

"Hello Mister Carmichael," said Joseph, the beaming smile intact.

Carmichael grunted something. It was not the Joseph they were expecting. Doctor Baranski put her hand on his forehead and winced, "How are you feeling?"

Joseph answered in that friendly sing-song voice school children reserve for special visitors, like a recitation, "Fine thank you, Doctor Baranski."

"Good. Now… I hope you're not dead set on having your baptism in the Sappie tomorrow."

" Auntie Abi said I've to do what you think is best," he said, in that same sing-song way.

"Good stuff," she took hold of his hand, "You'll be wanting to know about Archie…"

"Yes please."

"…and Maggie."

"Yes please. Thank you."

PC Carmichael shifted his weight, he was bored and wanting his turn now.

"Joseph…" she paused, perhaps formulating a child-friendly version of events, "The first thing you should know is it could have been worse. A lot worse. Archie's a very lucky boy. He lost a lot of blood."

"Oh dear," he said in a wee voice, and realising he was still grinning, reconfigured it into an almost melodramatic look of concern.

"But the bottom line is... he's going to survive."

"Oh good," he said, turning on the grin again.

"The thing is Joseph... they couldn't save Archie's legs."

Joseph gripped the sheets, "Oh dearie me," making himself nod, trying hard to immediately accept this new version of Archie, without looking at it too closely.

"He's going to be in hospital for a long time, Joseph."

"Yes," he nodded, "okay," and nodded some more. Nodding definitely helped, just doing all the actions, the normal gestures, that definitely helped.

"Joseph, you know, it's all right... if you feel..."

Joseph was concentrating so hard on saying and doing the right thing, he had no idea he looked so peculiar. He just knew that if he did not do these things, then he would completely unravel, "Have you seen wee Maggie as well?"

"No, not yet. I'll be seeing her today. But I spoke to the Robert Munday a wee while ago. They said she's doing fine. I get the impression she's a wee fighter that one; that they both are." She laughed, a nervous laugh, and Joseph echoed her. And when she stopped mid- laugh, with something like a hiccup, Joseph stopped too, with the same hiccup. If it was coming from anybody else it might be read as cheek.

"When will she go home?"

"These things take time. All sorts of decisions have to be made, about what's best and..."

"Right then," said Carmichael. He made a big show of taking out his notebook, not like a real policeman at all, but like someone pretending to be a policeman. "According to the Truman boy, you'd nothing to do with this railway carry-on... "

"Och Archie's just saying that because he doesn't want me to get into trouble." He shook his head and rolled his eyes – *Oh that Archie Truman* – a knowing look, a grown-up's look.

"Because I told him it was better if folk didn't know we were friends. But it's okay now. We built the railway thegether, so we did" Carmichael's pencil hovered above his notebook, "It's okay to write it down, Mister Carmichael. Archie's my best friend."

PC Carmichael did not write it down.

"And what about the tinker? What was he doing there?"

Joseph shrugged, "They were just there," then chuckled, "They're always there."

"And it's good they were," said Doctor Baranski. "Or things might have been…"

"Ok. Next thing," PC Carmichael looked down his list of *things to ask*, "When they found you in his tent, you were …"

"Just as much as you feel you want to say, Joseph," said Doctor Baranski, smiling. She was good at this. The smiling. The gentle touching. The comforting. The making it all seem all right, "Mister Carmichael says you didn't have any clothes on Joseph. Is that right?"

"Yes," he sang, That's right. No I didn't have any clothes on, Doctor Baranski."

"We just need to know, Joseph, to get a complete picture…"

"Mind ask him as well about those cuts and burns," said Carmichael, as if Joseph had suddenly left the room, "Mrs Kirkwood says she knows nothing about them."

"Duncan, would you mind if Joseph and I had a wee minute on our own?"

Joseph peered at PC Carmichael over the top of his spectacles, like Miss O'Donnell sometimes did when she was being asked some endearing but stupid question, "Caleb didn't hurt me, Mister Carmichael. He saved me. He's always saving me, so he is."

CHAPTER FORTY-TWO

Blessed Assurance

It was a good turnout. Sam was there after all, in his Royal Navy uniform. There were a handful of distant family members who Joseph had never met, folk from the Hall and quite a few old village worthies. Auntie Abi held Joseph's hand as they filed past the open coffin. Most folk just nodded or shook their heads. Some whispered a wee something, a prayer, a line of Scripture, something personal. More secular acquaintances such as Mister Jackson and Grandpa's other British Legion cronies muttered a simple *Bye bye Samuel, Cheerio Sam* or *See ye soon, mate*. Joseph wondered if he should to say something too, but when his turn came and he saw Grandpa lying in his satin-lined coffin, all he could think was, *Gran won't like this. She'll think it's too fancy* and *Grandpa should've made his own coffin like he said* and *He looks too serious with his false teeth in*. The nearest he came to a prayer was, *Please don't let them see Grandpa's hearing aids are missing.*

"Samuel Kirkland has gone back home, and we are here to celebrate!" drawled Mister Agnew, who didn't sound at all like he was celebrating. "That ..." He was pointing at the coffin "...is *not* Samuel Kirkland!" A few folk couldn't help but crane their heads to look. "That body is no more Sam Kirkland than his herringbone suit and brogues!"

Joseph could almost hear Archie whispering, *Oh no! Run like the clappers! Your Grandpa's been replaced by a Body Snatcher!*

Mister Agnew had stopped mid-flow. He was looking at Joseph. Everyone was looking at Joseph, and Auntie Abi nudged him, "Come on now!" she said, looking like it was a bad idea bringing him after all. Then he heard what everyone else was hearing, *giggling*; the sort of unrestrained giggling you got at the pictures when Laurel and Hardy's piano kept falling down the stairs. And it was himself who was doing the giggling.

As Mister Agnew waited for the gravitas to return, he cast a wary eye over Mrs Merryweather and Mrs Moretti, both of whom appeared to be immersed in their own private prayers, and mindful perhaps that they were Roman Catholics and therefore might be praying the wrong sort of prayer, he threw in a little something just for them, "We have no truck with *prayers for the dead* in this place. Because brothers and sisters, a prayer for the dead is a wasted prayer. The redeemed have no need of our prayer. The lost can no longer be reached by prayer. You want your prayers to do some good? Look in the eye of those around you. Have *they* been Saved? Have *you*? Pray for *these* folk, while there's time. Pray for yourselves." Satisfied, he returned to his original point, "No, Samuel Kirkland is not there and we will not mourn his passing. He has gone to a far better place. Samuel Kirkland has gone back home to the Lord. Of this we can be *absolutely certain*!"

Gran sat at the back with the other hatted women. She rocked back and forth, hands clasped, eyes shut tight, praying furiously. She didn't look like she was absolutely certain of anything any more, and she didn't look like she was celebrating either.

"This next hymn was a favourite of Samuel's. Indeed it's a favourite of many at Kilhaugh Gospel Hall."

Blessed assurance, Jesus is mine! Oh, what a foretaste of glory divine!

This wasn't a favourite at all. Grandpa liked the same cheery choruses as Joseph, and funny songs, his own daft wee made-up songs, music hall songs. And cowboy songs, *I'm back in the saddle again, out where a friend is a friend.*

"Joseph!" said Mister Agnew, clearly for the umpteenth time. Had he been giggling again? "Joseph's going to do the Books of the Bible. Sarah thought this is something Samuel would've liked."

All eyes were on Joseph. Hall folk nodded approvingly. Big nods for the benefit of outsiders. *See? See? See how a boy from the Hall pays his respects?*

"*Gen-e-sis, Ex-o-dus, Lev-it-icus and Num-bers* ..." But many of those eyes almost popped out of their sockets as Joseph, relaxed and confident, bent and twisted the tune to accommodate the new Books of the Bible he'd discovered, "*...Tobit ...Judith... Macabees and Macabees ... Wisdom... Sirach... Baruch...*" ... at Saint Rita of Impossible Things.

CHAPTER FORTY-THREE

A Kilhaugh Funeral One Foggy December

Uncle Andrew handed a coffin card to Uncle Hector, Uncle Mathew, Mister Chaddock, Mister Sangster and Sam. After some manoeuvring the six men took up their cords at the designated position around Grandpa's coffin which was resting on a couple of planks above the freshly dug grave. Mister Agnew read something final from the Scriptures as the men lowered the coffin. The grave didn't seem to be nearly as deep as Joseph had imagined it would be.

Joseph, Gran, Auntie Abi, Auntie Ishbel, Jenny and the other women and children stood well back. Funerals, like testimonies, were a man's business; Joseph's business one day. Right now though, viewing the whole thing through a spectacle lens from inside a thick cocoon of duffle coat, tweed and balaclava, he felt more removed, more like an observer than ever, like he was watching an obscure film – *A Kilhaugh Funeral One Foggy December* –muffled and undecipherable.

"Perfect weather for it," muttered Auntie Abi. "All we need now's a full moon and a howling wolf."

Gran took a couple of steps forward and began some *head shaking* and *tutting*,

"Nobody told me they were going to bury him next to a Roman Catholic."

Sure enough, to Grandpa's right was the pristine white gravestone of *Victor Lorenzo Moretti* with its telltale Romish "R.I.P." Auntie Abi couldn't resist and leaned over to Joseph: "Well at least he'll be all right for his Fry's Five Boys."

Grandpa would've liked that. That was more like it. Caleb was right. This is what should be happening: laughter, jokes, wee asides, nods and winks, cheeky taps of the nose, folk telling funny anecdotes and epic sagas. Things Grandpa had said and done. *Oh I mind the time… Mind that time…? Oh he was famous for his… Oh I'll never forget yon time he…*

The purvey was held in the lesser hall at the Munday Memorial and served in rugged coffee-morning crockery from big green enamel tea and coffee pots. Joseph drank his tea, ate his sandwich, his sausage roll and his custard cream. He graciously accepted hugs, sighs and condolences and he listened politely to elderly widows ages with Gran tell their own tales of widowhood with comical matter-of-factness and competition levels of eagerness, "It was a heart attack that took my Billy. His third so it was."

"Frank only had the one, but it was a big one."

"Brain haemorrhage. Jim never knew what hit him. One minute he was putting putty on the window in the lean-to and the next…"

Gran sat through it all, hanging onto her Bible, her anchor, her lifebelt, her who knows what else, nodding in all the right places, making all the right gestures, doing as she had to do. She'd been at enough funerals to know what was expected of her. But in between she was that scared and lost wee girl again. She caught Joseph's eye and shook her head, such a sad, disappointed wee shake of the head. Not just disappointment in him; it was everything. *You look scunnered mum*, is what Grandpa would've said. *You know I don't like that word*, she'd reply. He should go and talk to her, *Mind that time with the soup Gran… mind that time with his magic tricks… with the tea towel… Mind that time when you first saw him outside Agnew's? Mind all those funny daft wonderful happy times…*

He stood outside the Memorial Hall, turning the wooden mermaid in his hand, thinking how he'd like to put her in some water, a puddle even, but they were all frozen, and all the time trying hard not to think about what might have become of Archie, wee Maggie and Caleb, all of whom he'd brought destruction down upon.

"Not a word to anyone," said Auntie Abi, lighting up a cigarette. "How you doing?" Joseph shrugged. She put an arm around him. "Aye," she sniffed, took a long deep drag on her cigarette and exhaled her smoke into the fog, "Kilhaugh's a funny wee place." Joseph could feel her treading carefully, getting herself kitted out to enter this new and potentially dangerous uncharted territory.

"Full of wee gossips. Wee whisperers. Wee Chinese whisperers." She smiled at him, a complicit smile, "You don't need me to tell you that." She took another drag and tested the thickness of the ice on a puddle with the heel of her shoe.

"Your mum loved you. You know that, right? From the moment you were born. Oh my goodness, doted on you so she did. No regrets. Not about you. Not one ounce of regret. Her *wee man*, her *wee soldier*, that's what she called you; *My wee man*! *My wee soldier*! Mind? Och, of course you'll no mind." She made an odd noise, half-laugh, half-sob, and pulled Joseph closer then immediately let him go, and pulled him closer again, and she kept doing this, pulling and holding and letting him go, pulling, holding and letting go.

"Och, I'm sorry son, your daft auld Auntie's not very good at this. I barely understand it myself. Though in actual fact... in actual fact... there's nothing to understand. Grown-ups. Ha. What's to be done with us? Complicate things, that's what we do. Simple things. And the thing is... it is simple. Your mum loved a man son. That's it. In a nutshell. End of story. She fell in love with a man that folk said she shouldn't fall in love with. Happens every day, all around the world. And he loved her too, so he did. You should know that. Oh aye, he loved her too. There's no doubt about that. I never met him, mind. None of us did. But she said. And even if she hadn't, you could see. It was like she'd grown wings. She didn't just walk down the street like normal folk, she floated above it. Then... ach these things happen... it became obvious that you were on the way and then, her not being married compounded with him being… different…" She laughed. "Kilhaugh isn't Haight Ashbury, son. There was never any Summer of Love here, just endless grey winters of… I don't know… just endless grey winters." She laughed again and wiped away a tear, "It wasn't easy for her… for any of us. And then there was your Gran and the Hall, and Kilhaugh being Kilhaugh and ach… compromises had to be made son, and choices, hard choices. And he… this man… he could never settle here… a place like Kilhaugh would've killed a man like him." She sighed a huge sigh, "Aye. It was never going to end well. Never. And also, the truth of the matter is, Elspeth, your mum – it's funny saying her name out loud, especially to you – she wasn't well. She hadn't been well for an awful long time, son. Och not all the time, of course not. Said it was God's punishment. Can you believe that? As if He would punish an angel like your mum. But see when she *was* well, och she was such a laugh, so she was. A real comedian. Honestly. Exactly like your Grandpa in that respect. Two peas in a pod so they were. You should've seen the two of them thegether. Did these funny voices and… she was like Lucille Ball, so she was. Honest, I'd nearly wet myself. And what a beauty. Oh my. *You should be in the pictures*, I used to say. Out of earshot of your Gran. And so she should've, so she should've. But when she was in pain. Oh dear. Oh dear. And it wasn't the kind of pain you could make go away, no matter what you did, what anybody did."

The ice on the puddle shattered under her heel. There was no water beneath.

"Somebody had always been there for her, when it was bad. But you can't always be there for a person. Can you? Not all the time, son. No matter how much you love them. Not all the time. Not every second of every day. It's just not possible. Is it?" She looked around as though the words she was looking for might be inscribed on the fog. "After your mum was… we needed somewhere to scatter the ashes. Your Grandpa saw to all that. I don't know where he found the strength. Your Gran couldn't bring herself... well, you know what she's like. Thinks most things are a sin.

"There's these two dead trees, where your mum used to go, down by the Sappie. Och she loved it there so she did. You must have seen them on yer travels. They've both got these branches, hanging down, like arms, *the Gunslingers*. That's what your Grandpa used to call them, *the Gunslingers*. Did he never mention it? Well, he wouldn't. But that's... that's for another day. All you need to know right now is... It was awful hard, son. For all of us. Your Gran too. She loved yourmum despite her endless bible thumping. Anyway. Anyway. That's where they are. The ashes. Between those two trees. So. There. I've said it. Now you know, son. Now you know."

CHAPTER FORTY-FOUR

The Saving of Joseph Kirkland

The air was thick with it. Burnt wood, burnt herbs, burnt paper, burnt meat, burnt everything. And petrol. Joseph inhaled. On any other day he'd have been transported. Charred shreds of oily tarp and scripture texts hung from the bowed branches like the carcass of some butchered monster, a dragon maybe, wandered in from the dangerous uncharted territories. The ends of the guy ropes were still tied around the two trees. *The Gunslingers*. Of course. How could he not have seen that they were gunslingers? There was a fresh scorch mark down the front of the one of them, like a wound.

Joseph sat on a mossy rock beside the frozen burn that ran down past the remains of Caleb's camp. The fog was thinning out now and the burn had started to flow again, just a slow trickle, but enough to lift a few scab-thin slithers of ice downstream into the Sappie.

They were too big for his ears but with some twisting and turning he eventually managed to get the hearing aids to fit. He switched them both on together with a flourish like Grandpa used to. The sudden, deafening roar took him so completely by surprise, it almost knocked him backwards. Oh my goodness. Oh dearie me. Oh what a din. Is this what Grandpa heard day in day out? Now the trickling burn was a raging torrent. Now everything was raging, torrential. All manner of sounds that Joseph was not conscious of, but which had been there all the same as background hums and whines, were screaming now. The hitherto imperceptible rumble of traffic was thunderous. The soft rustling footfalls of hidden woodland creatures that only a dog could hear was a stampede. The cacophony of chirping, hissing, clicking, tweeting, buzzing, scratching, flapping and fluttering of hundreds, thousands of invisible birds and insects, was so shrill they might've been perched upon his head and shoulders. Even his own breath sounded like it was coming out of an iron lung. And the gentle breeze he could barely feel was a howling gale, blowing in fragments of conversation from far and wide, past and future, everyone, all of them, all babbling at once, all clamouring for his attention. Is it any wonder Grandpa was always switching them off? It was too much. All of this. All at once. All the time. Unbearable. A teardrop splashed on the rock. A breaking wave. And that was him. The floodgates were open now and there would be no way of closing them.

Later when he was done and drained and all shiny brand new, he set off for the Templeton road tunnel. He tried out loud some words of encouragement, the sort of thing that might lift Archie's spirits, give him hope, get the old Archie Truman imagination all fired up: "It doesn't matter if you've wooden legs. We can still be missionaries thegether. Folk'll maybe even remember you better. That'll be your special thing, like Blind Fanny Crosby's blindness. *Oh yes, I mind him, Archibald Truman, the Wooden-Legged Missionary*. It sounds like one of the Heroes of the Cross, so it does. And wee Maggie can come as well. The three of us. We don't even have to be missionaries, if we don't want to. We can just be explorers and write stories about our adventures, if we want."

He sniffed up some teary snot and laughed as he imagined Archie's reply:

They'll maybe give me robot legs. You can do that now, so you can. It'll be like having a superpower. We'll be able to jump over quicksand or that pit with the spikes and snakes or high up into the trees if we see a lion or a crocodile. "Joseph! Maggie! Get on my back!" or I'll kick a stone like a bullet and hit it between the eyes. They can do anything these days. We'll maybe end up in the comics or something, or maybe they'll make a film about us.

As he entered the mouth of the tunnel Joseph did an involuntary wee Archie Truman skip and a jump, shouting out just to hear the echo: "Hello!"

Hello!

"It's me!"

It's me.

"It's Joseph Kirkland!"

It's Joseph Kirkland!

"Ha ha!"

Ha ha!

"Ha ha ha!"

Ha ha ha!

He looked over his shoulder. Any moment now a dog will bark his name and a rusty old Bedford van will pull up beside him: *You'll be wanting a lift to Templeton Infirmary*, a voice will say.

That'll be it then. That'll be me.

The End

Hymn and Song Lyrics reproduced

Blessed Assurance – "Blind" Fanny Crosby (1820 – 1915)
Don't Turn the Dear Saviour Away – George Bennard (1873 – 1958)
Son of a Preacher Man – John Hurley & Ronnie Wilkins (recorded by Dusty Springfield, 1968)
Yellow Bird – Alan & Marilyn Bergman. (Recorded by the Mills Brothers, 1959)
He'll Have to Go – Joe & Audrey Allison. (Recorded by Jim Reeves, 1959)
This World Is Not My Home – Albert E. Brumley (Recorded by Jim Reeves, 1962)
Spirit in the Sky – Norman Greenbaum (Recorded by Norman Greenbaum, 1969)
That's Amore – Jack Brooks & Harry Warren (Recorded by Dean Martin, 1953)
Back in the Saddle Again – Gene Autrey & Ray Whitley (Recorded by Gene Autrey, 1939)

ACKNOWLEDGEMENTS

This book could not have been completed without the encouragement and hard work of a great number of people. These include:

Vagabond Voices' Allan Cameron for his expertise and creative counsel. Mark Mechan for the care given to the cover design. Janice Brent for her editing. Galina Miteva for letting folk know that this book exists. Peter Gilmour, Kate Hendry, Nalini Paul and the Open University for getting my writing ball rolling. Chris Dolan, Anne Marie di Mambro, Catriona Miller and Glasgow Caledonian University for support during an earlier incarnation of this story. Michael Duke and Jimmy McAleavey who, unknown to themselves, inspired me to continue with this story. My creative writing class at HMP Shotts for listening to some early pages and asking challenging questions. Tom Leonard, for his reading lists and encouragement. Benchtours Theatre (aka The Occasion) for years of collective storytelling. The University of Aberdeen & Curtin University, Perth, Australia for a much-appreciated boost of confidence on the last leg of this journey. Matthew Fitt for kind words of encouragement on writing in Scots. The National Health Service for helping to keep me alive long enough to finish the thing. The Scottish Book Trust for advice and Creative Scotland for financial assistance. Doctor Rebecca Robinson for reasons too personal and too numerous to mention.

The village of Kilhaugh and all its inhabitants are entirely imagined. This is a work of fiction.